BURNING WORDS

Ursula Loucks
Terry Loucks

I
InfoNovels
USA

Design by Mary Fisher Design
    Cover photograph by PhotoDisc, Inc., Copyright 1997
    Nag Hammadi photographs courtesy of The Institute for Antiquity and
        Christianity, Claremont Graduate University

Loucks, Ursula.
    Burning Words / by Ursula Loucks and Terry Loucks.
        p.   cm.

    ISBN 0-9656929-3-0

    1. Christianity—Origin—Fiction.
    2. Jesus Christ—Historicity—Fiction.
    3. Q hypothesis (Synoptic criticism)—Fiction.
    4. Nag Hammadi codices—Fiction. 5. Dead Sea scrolls—Fiction.
    6. Lost Books—Fiction. I. Title.
                          97-94293

This book is dedicated to Professor James M. Robinson

A man devoted to freedom of information
and to the fearless search for truth.
His many contributions to society and Christianity
are the inspiration for this book.

The authors would also like to thank
others who contributed to this book, including
Wilson Glass, Jim and Mary Rice,
David Miles, Charles Thompson, Linda Tawse and Mary Sasse.

Acknowledgments

The authors are grateful for all the people throughout history
who have burned books, destroyed cultures, suppressed knowledge,
or forced their beliefs on others. As you will see, they are part
of an important ancient tradition, and without them
this book could not have been written.

Note To The Reader

This is a work of fiction. All of the events and characters depicted in this novel are entirely fictitious or are used fictitiously. Some of the characters, especially those dedicated to academic integrity and scholarly research, have been strongly influenced by actual people whom we have had the pleasure of knowing. None of the characters, however, is a close portrait of a real person.

The reader will also recognize that we made a serious effort not to distort history in the telling of this story, especially with regard to manuscripts. In fact, we tried whenever possible to weave our fictional characters into a fabric of actual historical events. If you are interested in better defining that fine line between fact and fiction, between history and mythology, then the list of references at the end of the book could launch you on your own intellectual odyssey. The real lives are even more exciting than could possibly be portrayed in fiction.

The Nag Hammadi Codices

Sayings

He wasn't usually this tired after prayers, but he had taken less food than normal and sleep had come only with difficulty the night before. Even after all these years, the life of the ascetic had not grown routine for him.

Perhaps this tea will revive me, he hoped, wrapping his cold hands around the warm cup. He was alone, sitting at a wooden table in the middle of the library.

He turned over several of the pages to the place he had begun the day before and reviewed his earlier work. *Seems all right,* he thought, pleased that he had made no errors in his previous transcriptions.

He looked longingly across the room, and his eyes glassed over from boredom. He doubted if his work would ever see the light of day. It was the worse assignment he could imagine. All of the old translations were exactly the same. *Maybe I should add my own ideas to these ancient adages,* he half joked to himself.

Flipping through the remaining pages, he noticed that several of them stuck out a little further than the others. *What's this?* he wondered, opening the stack to these larger pages. He scanned quickly through them and saw still more adages. *Looks like more of the same,* he thought.

One saying drew his attention, however, and he spent a few minutes translating it carefully. *It sounds familiar,* he thought, *but it's not usually found with the others.* He read a little further and realized that these sayings were from the Great Teacher, and that they had somehow been filed with the others by mistake.

"This is incredible!" he exclaimed aloud. He quickly looked around the room to make sure he was still alone. *What have I found?*

Deep Dark Secrets
1971
Guatemala, near Lago de Izabal

Hunahpu and Xbalamque did not die in any of these tortures. They ground
their bones and cast them into the river, but the river did not carry them away.
Instead, the bones went down to the bottom where they were changed back
into two handsome youths.

—Popol Vuh (the Maya Bible)

Christina Sheridan glanced at her guide, smiling as she said his name in her
mind, repeating it over and over like a mantra. *Yax, Yax, Yax.* It was the
Mayan word for the center of the compass, and it was pronounced *Yawsh.*
Christina knew that Yax was proud to have the same name as the ancient
Maya rulers, Yax Pac and Yax Kuk Mo. Shorter than Christina, Yax had an
irresistible smile framed by the chiseled features of his wide bronze face…the
same features depicted in the stone carvings by his ancient ancestors.

Yax saw her studying him, and in his native Yucatec tongue asked,
"Christina, could you please pass me the backpack?" He wanted to please
her, and nothing did that more than providing her an opportunity to
practice his language. He was too polite to tell her just how much practice
she really needed.

When Christina was stymied in her attempt at finding a word for the wet
suits they had brought with them, Yax flashed one of his luminous smiles
and said gently, "We speak English, okay?"

"But I need more practice speaking Yucatec," Christina complained, as
she struggled into her wet suit.

"I know," he agreed.

Christina shot him a look, afraid he was making fun of her attempts to
speak Yucatec. Satisfied that his dark eyes revealed that he was not mocking
her, she chuckled, "I guess the ancients didn't do much scuba diving."

"They did not have a word for flashlight, either," grinned Yax.

"Yes, but—*torch*—is a good substitute."

Yax just nodded agreeably. He knew Christina to be a determined
person when she set her sights on achieving something, and eventually she
would master this language too. In fact, her love of his language was why
he had chosen to disclose his secret in the first place.

Christina had befriended Yax several years ago on one of her research
trips to the great Mayan ruins of Tikal, where he had been working on the
archaeological excavation crew. He had told her about this mysterious
cave deep in the Guatemalan jungle, with its many Mayan
hieroglyphs…glyphs that may provide an important missing piece of the

Maya puzzle. They had agreed to explore the cave on her upcoming sabbatical from her faculty position in the Anthropology Department at Harvard University.

They had started the expedition at daybreak, hiking several hours before reaching the cave. It had been a difficult task, jumping from boulder to boulder and occasionally scaling the canyon walls to get around difficult stretches of the river. At times they had to cling to overhanging vines to get onto the next ledge. They had even fallen once into the swift currents of the river, which although temporarily disconcerting, felt delightfully refreshing.

Having finally reached their destination, they were now resting on a boulder midstream of the swirling river which flowed from the gaping mouth of the cave. A seasoned swimmer and climber, Christina was nonetheless concerned about the proficiency level such an undertaking demanded.

"Yax, could you please pass the canteen?" Christina asked, pulling her blonde hair back from the glaze of sweat on her brow. She had an almost unquenchable thirst after the morning's vigorous trek up the river.

It was hellishly hot, with not a breeze in the canyon. And having only flown into Guatemala City yesterday, Christina was not yet acclimatized to the sweltering jungle humidity. They say there are two seasons in the jungles of Guatemala: the rainy season and the hot season. On her various trips she had experienced both and, except for a slight difference in rainfall, the temperatures were about the same. Hot—very hot. And muggy.

Even the birds and monkeys had stopped their chattering in the afternoon to rest from the equatorial heat. Earlier that morning on their journey up the river, Yax and Christina had been serenaded by Oropendola birds swinging in their hammock nests high in the jungle canopy gurgling their songs of exotica. All was quiet now except for the background static of the cicadas.

While sipping the water and feeling its coolness trickle down her throat, she stared up at the vegetation-choked sides of the limestone gorge carved out by the river. The steep incline disappeared into the fluffy clouds hanging over the rain forest. Climbing it was out of the question; it was at least 2500 feet to the top. "A half mile," she said softly, liking how much more dramatic it sounded when she put it that way.

Christina had always been captivated by the primordial jungle. She loved to be surrounded by the almost pulsating sense of life—and death and decay—that the ever-growing plants and trees provided. It seemed to her that nowhere else on earth could one find such a rich and complex fabric of living things...or thing. The rain forest was in many ways a single gigantic organism that grew upon itself, intertwining and interweaving a compound tapestry of life. It exuded color and flowers and fragrance directly from heaven.

It was a most sacred place with trees rising like gothic arches in this jungle cathedral. There was green on green—every possible hue of green—in the tangle of impenetrable vines and ferns. Here and there, orchids and giant ginger lilies perched proudly like Christmas ornaments.

Christina sighed. At moments like these, she felt at one with the world and in a state of grace. The rain forest had woven a magical spell over her which had temporarily distracted her from the task at hand.

"It is getting late," Yax said pointedly, breaking the interlude. Although he enjoyed the wonders of his native land, the extraordinary, when experienced regularly, often loses its ability to amaze and enthrall.

"You're right," agreed Christina, looking back at the way they had come and realizing that the most arduous part still lay ahead. She took one last swig of water then screwed the cap back on the canteen, marveling that she could be so calm when perhaps the greatest discovery of her life lay ahead in the cave.

The day's real goal was about to be realized: they planned to swim upstream into the cave as far as possible and then climb the rest of the way to a place where Yax had previously seen ancient Maya hieroglyphs carved into the cave walls.

Ever since Yax had told Christina about the secret cave, she had been planning for this day. Her hope was that these new hieroglyphs would help decipher the Maya Code, an almost impenetrable mystery for hundreds of years. If the glyphs in the cave proved to be as important a find as she was hoping, they would provide new insight into the ancient Mayan civilization.

Whatever their message, it would almost assuredly be quite different from those previously found on temples and tombs. The inscriptions on the temples seemed to be related to the monarchical succession. If luck was with her, the glyphs in the cave might not only be completely new glyphs, but also some of the same glyphs in a different context, perhaps dealing with Mayan mythology. Almost anything new would provide needed answers.

But first they had to get inside the cave.

"I'm ready," Christina told Yax.

"I hope so," he replied, zipping up his wet suit. "The hardest part will be the waterfall inside the cave. It will not be a piece of pastry."

"Piece of cake," corrected Christina, strapping her flashlight on her head.

"Yes, cake," agreed Yax. "Since the cave walls go straight up, we will have to dive under the waterfall and crawl up the rocks on the other side. This will be very dangerous because the waterfall is very powerful."

"Well, I'll try to be careful and follow right behind you," Christina said, knowing that Yax had been coming here since he was a little boy.

"Okay," replied Yax. "Follow me. The sooner we start, the sooner I can show you my ancestor's writings. Then perhaps you can tell me what they were trying to say."

"I'll sure try, Yax. I'll sure try".

With flashlights strapped to their heads and small packs on their backs, they slid off the boulder into the cool water and began the challenging swim upstream into the gaping mouth of the cave.

Christina somehow sensed, rather than actually felt, schools of tiny fish around them.

"Ah, these aren't piranhas, are they?" she called out playfully, trying to ease the tension of the challenge ahead.

"Not exactly."

"Not exactly? What does that mean?"

Christina saw the gleam of his Mayan smile in the near darkness of the cave opening. "They are toothless cousins."

"I hope you know your fish as well as you do your hieroglyphs."

"In this case, I do," he answered. "My friends and I have swum here many times over the years. This cave is one of the entrances to *Xibalba*, the Underworld. It is not the fish we fear."

With those last words echoing about them, they swam into the shadow of the cave mouth, feeling like intruders into the silent realm of the Underworld.

As they left the brilliant sunlight behind them, Christina marveled at the totality of the darkness: a darkness that almost swallowed the small beams of their flashlights; a darkness that seemed to pull even yesterday's light from their eyes.

"Whoa!"

"You feel it, then?" Yax asked. "You feel the strengthening of the current?"

"You bet," Christina replied, noticing that the current was much swifter as the river was channeled between the steep cave walls.

"I have been here many times, not to worry," Yax shouted over the roar of the approaching waterfall.

Both of them swam vigorously against the stream, stroking with all their might trying to make headway into the cave.

Finally Yax called out: "Here is a small gap in the boulders. We can hold on for a little rest against the current."

The respite was a welcome relief before plunging back into the current. The mist had thickened and the deafening roar had grown with every bend until they could barely hear one another.

As Yax had noted, the waterfall was no piece of pastry. He knew that the rocks leading to the next level were hidden behind the falls, and that they needed to dive deep to pass under the pounding fury of the river.

"Okay," Christina mouthed, nodding to indicate that she'd understood his gesture to dive.

When they both surfaced, Yax gasped and shook his head angrily. It took Christina a moment to understand: there was no flashlight on top his head. "Oh, no," she cried, staring into the inky depths, as they watched the lonely beam disappearing downstream in the current.

They exchanged sober glances in the dim glow of their one flashlight. They had no choice but to reluctantly proceed for the time being with just the one flashlight.

Their progress slowed by their misfortune, it took them a long time to reach the next section of the cave. Christina was surprised that the rocks were not slimy until she realized that nothing grew in the dark. *Nothing grows in the Underworld*, she thought to herself.

Here the river had gone underground for several hundred yards, and in the glow of the headlamp, they could see that the cave opened into a large cavern. They could feel the ground trembling slightly from the water rushing invisibly underneath, but they found that they could speak over the noise.

"I am very sorry for losing the headlamp, I should have been more careful," Yax gasped, still trying to catch his breath from the strenuous swim.

"You needn't apologize," Christina breathed. "It was just bad luck and it could've happened to me just as easily as you. I didn't realize the current would be so strong near the waterfalls."

"I think there is more water than usual, perhaps because of the heavy rains this week. Do you have another flashlight?"

"I thought to bring spare batteries, but it never occurred to me that we might lose a flashlight. How much further is it to the hieroglyphs?"

"Not far. We are almost there. There is just one more difficult part, but I think we will be all right, if we climb quickly."

"I'm with you then. We haven't come this far to turn around empty-handed."

With their one remaining flashlight they crawled quickly over the damp rocks. At one point a wide crevasse blocked their pathway. Yax, seeking out the narrowest point, assured Christina that he had done this before. He jumped across the void, albeit with little to spare, and showed her that it was possible. Realizing it was now her turn, and not about to let the gap interfere with her goal, she backed up a few paces, steeled her mind, then took a deep breath and sprang for her life.

She grasped Yax's shirt as she landed, her knees buckling as she slid to a stop.

"Now, wasn't that a piece of cake?" Yax teased her. "You actually jumped too far."

Christina grinned as she rose to her feet. They both knew that she had actually cleared the gap by a greater distance than Yax.

As they entered the large cavern, Yax smiled and pointed the flashlight at a small section of a nearly vertical wall.

It was what they'd come to see.

"Oh my God!" blurted Christina, as she gazed at the wall with a sense of wonder. "I've never seen so many glyphs in one place. It's absolutely incredible."

"I had hoped you like them," Yax beamed.

"I like them," Christina echoed, moving the beam of light back and forth across the many hieroglyphs. "This is better than I could've ever hoped for. Most of these glyphs are completely new, although I see variations of some we found at Tikal."

"Yes," agreed Yax, "I had thought so too."

"I could. . . I mean. . . " Christina stammered as she viewed their incredible find. "This could be one of the most important Maya discoveries ever made. There must be hundreds of hieroglyphs here and they're all in perfect condition."

"The cave," ventured Yax, glancing around the chamber.

"Huh? Oh, yes—the cave," said Christina, realizing what Yax meant. "It's protected them from the elements."

"There are more," grinned Yax mischievously.

"Even more?" asked Christina incredulously.

"Yes. Around the corner."

"Around the corner," Christina repeated slowly, feeling lightheaded. She had been hoping, expecting, but this—this was almost too much.

"Let's take a look," Christina said, her heart beginning to quicken in anticipation.

They rounded the bend in the cavern and the cylinder of light from the flashlight picked out hundreds, maybe thousands, of hieroglyphs. And that wasn't all. Interspersed with the hieroglyphs were stylized drawings.

"I'm must be dreaming," Christina whispered. "Either that or I've died and gone to heaven...er...I mean *Xibalba*."

"You like them, no?" Yax asked proudly.

"I like them, yes. Oh, yes."

The hieroglyphs appeared similar to glyphs from the Classic Maya period. Accented with black pigment in single and double columns on the walls, they were much longer than the inscriptions previously found on monuments and stelae.

"How far do they go?" Christina asked Yax.

"They go on for as far as you want to climb. Only a few of my people have gone all the way because the cave eventually opens straight into *Xibalba*.

"Oh please, I'd like to see them," Christina said excitedly.

"It is a very difficult climb," Yax warned her.

"I don't care, I just. . ." Christina stopped, realizing that she was overwhelmed with the enormity of the discovery. Composing herself, she said, "I think I have enough to study right here, at least for a little while."

Understanding, Yax nodded but said nothing. As many times as he had visited here, he was always awestruck by the hieroglyphs—shrouded in time, they were mute testimony to the greatness of his forebears. *Who had taken the time to painstakingly carve and paint these wondrous symbols over a thousand years ago?* he thought. *What were they trying to say?* He bowed his head in reverence.

Meanwhile, Christina had sat down on a flat-topped rock to view the hieroglyphs. She would have been pleased with far less—several dozen never-before-seen glyphs would have been a major find for almost anyone. But what she had seen here in the cavern was…well, nothing short of astounding. It wasn't just the size of the discovery, but also the quality.

She played the light over several images, pondering what they might be. *I hope those are examples of phonetic writing,* she thought. *God, oh, God, I can't believe this!* She picked out more images and spotted what looked to be a new way to write the month-sign, Pax. While the usual form was logographic, a symbol which represented the whole word, here the Maya seemed to have linked it with the phonetic form. If this was true, then it would be the first step to unraveling their written language.

Christina knew how important their writing system and calendar had been to the Maya. While Europe was still in the Dark Ages, the Maya invented a numerical system that allowed complex calculations. They then combined their complex math and an impressive collection of astronomical observations to develop a solar calendar more accurate that the one in use today.

She played the flashlight's beam on a figure playing ball. "Who's that?" she asked Yax.

"That person?" Yax put his hand to his chin and studied the carving. "Why I believe that is Hunahpu."

Christina nodded; she had just wanted Yax to confirm what she had already suspected. Hunahpu was the great Hero Twin of Mayan mythology; a religious figure not unlike a combination of Jesus and Odysseus. She smiled to herself as she thought how appropriate it was that the image of Hunahpu stood guard over the entry to the Underworld. After all, Hunahpu went down the road to *Xibalba*, survived the many tortures inflicted upon him by the Lords of Hell, and ultimately defeated them. At least that was the way the story went. Somehow, this cave with its craggy walls and its musty odors seemed just as likely a place as any to be the entrance to the dreaded Mayan Underworld.

She laughed out loud.

"What are you laughing at?" asked Yax, puzzled at her response.

Christina suppressed a sigh. "It's just that I'm so happy, Yax. I'm just so very, very happy. I can't wait to show this discovery to the other Mavericks."

"Mavericks?"

Christina chuckled. "That's just a phrase my colleagues and I use to describe ourselves because we're trying to prove the Old Boys' Club wrong. 'Old Boys' Club' is the name we've given to the domineering researchers in my field. They in turn call us the 'Young Mavericks'. This one cavern might very well increase the inventory of known glyphs by an untold number—by factors of ten or even hundreds."

"You will take pictures now?" Yax asked.

"Huh? Oh, Yax, you're right—the camera! I've got to take as many pictures of this as I can."

Yax handed her the waterproof camera case and she took out the small camera and began taking pictures of the most impressive glyphs. She then turned to drawing them on a small tablet in case the photos weren't clear.

Thus engaged, Christina didn't notice the passage of time nor the signals her body was sending until Yax tapped her shoulder and held out one of the chocolate bars they had brought along for nourishment.

"Thanks Yax, but I'm not—" hungry, Christina was going to say when she suddenly realized she was famished. "Thank you," she said, taking one of the bars, devouring it in three bites and continuing on with her work.

Even with the burst of energy the candy provided, they both were feeling the cold more and more. Christina began to shiver. Trying not to think about the cold, she decided to get the spare batteries.

"Please hand me the bag of batteries in my backpack, Yax. They're in the small waterproof pouch."

Bent over the bag, Yax found the pouch quickly, but looked up at Christina with a look of distress on his face.

"What is it, Yax?"

He held up the bag for her to see.

Christina's heart skipped a beat when she immediately saw that the bag was full of water. "Oh Yax. Oh no…" her voice died away as she tried to think back. *It must have happened when we dove under the waterfall. Maybe I hit my pack against a rock. This is horrible.*

The water around the batteries had turned a strange blue indicating that they were at least partially discharged. It seemed as if the Lords of Hell were rising up against the desecration of their sacred cave. *No, I have to take responsibility for this,* she thought, as she realized that she should have better prepared for their excursion into the cave.

Quickly making up her mind, Christina wiped off the wet batteries as best she could and put them into the flashlight. "Here goes nothing," she said, thumbing the switch. To their relief, the flashlight emitted a ray of light nearly as bright as might be provided by new batteries. "We have no way of knowing how long these will last," she told Yax. "They might be like new, or they could be almost discharged. I have no idea."

"We must head back right away. We can always return when we are better prepared," Yax cautioned.

Leaving so many of the glyphs unrecorded was just too much to bear. The last thing Christina wanted to do was to leave the cave without complete photographs of her discovery. There was the upcoming research meeting in Palenque, and her findings could be the sensation of the meeting. But if she left now, there would be no returning—at least not in the two days left before the meeting.

"The flashlight. . . " She stopped and began again. "I mean, could we possibly make it out of the cave in the dark?"

The idea held little appeal for Yax. "It is not a good idea, especially if one of us got hurt. Remember, we have to leap across the ledge and make it past the waterfall before getting to the river. How we jump across that ledge in the dark?"

Christina bowed to the inevitable. "You're right, of course." She glanced about the cavern. "Just a few more photos, please? I'll try to go as fast as I can," she pleaded, getting the camera ready.

Against his better judgment, Yax sat quietly in the punctuated darkness as she took photographs as fast as the camera's mechanism could operate. Try as he might, it was difficult for him to understand Christina's desperateness to get the photos in time for her conference. The notion of gaining the limelight at a meeting of her colleagues was difficult for the pure spirit of a Mayan to absorb.

"The batteries are starting to weaken," he finally spoke up, pointing at the firefly remnant of the flashlight. "We have only a few minutes, if that, to make it past the ledges."

"All right, we'll go," she shrugged reluctantly. She had hoped to photograph two more sections, but it would have to wait for another trip. "I think I have enough for the conference."

"Come," Yax urged her, as they scrambled from boulder to boulder with increasing haste in their race against the dying batteries.

No sooner were they across the ledges than the flashlight finally failed. But they had made it. The remainder of their underground journey would have to be made in total darkness.

"You must follow right behind me every step of the way if we are going to survive this," Yax shouted over the reverberating thunder of the waterfall. Using a type of "touch" language transmitted by squeezing arms, and placing each other's hands and feet firmly on solid climbing sites, Christina was able to follow Yax as they negotiated their way from rock to rock.

As they approached the waterfall, the light from the cave opening in the distance provided a faint but perceptible glow. Relieved at the prospect of getting out, Yax lost first concentration and then his footing. Too startled to cry out, he slipped into the river and was pinned by the pounding water between two large rocks.

"Oh my God!" screamed Christina, grabbing desperately for him in the dark.

The torrent of water drove him even more tightly between the boulders. He would have only seconds to live once his head disappeared beneath the water.

Manuscript

The two men seated at the booth had much in common, especially the way they were dressed. It was their differences which made them interesting. One had spent his life doing good, and the other was committed to evil of the most violent kind. It was this not so subtle difference which had brought them together.

"Well, I sure as hell don't take checks or credit cards," said the larger man, as he jammed his cigarette forcefully into the ashtray and blew smoke directly at the smaller man seated across the table. He waved for the waitress to bring more coffee.

"I didn't think so," said the gentler man. "It won't be difficult for me to arrange for payments in cash." His head reeled from the smoke. *He seems to wallow in his tobacco,* he thought repugnantly.

"Good, then who do you want eliminated?" said the larger man, without hesitation.

The kinder man looked around in a panic, fearful that they might be overheard.

"I don't want you to eliminate anyone. I just want you to find a manuscript," he whispered cautiously.

"That's not what I do best, and you'd be paying the full amount for my specialty," he said flashing a treacherous smile. "There are dozens of pros who could track something down for a much smaller fee." He reached for the salt shaker, twisted off the lid and poured the contents into a pile on the table next to the empty napkin dispenser.

"It was hard enough to find you," said the nicer man, "and I don't want to go through this again. Just get this manuscript, no matter what, and it'll be worth the fee."

"O.K., so let's get into the specifics," said the larger man, lighting up another cigarette, and spinning his Zippo cigarette lighter between his two fingers.

The dark red color of the large birthmark on his cheek seemed to glow from the excitement of a new assignment, even if it wasn't as challenging as usual. *If this idiot is willing to pay my ridiculous fee, then this will just be a nice vacation. And at least it's for a good cause.*

He slowly spread the tines of his fork apart with his large pocket knife.

Tulsey Town

As a man begins to live more seriously within, he begins to live more simply without.
—Ralph Waldo Emerson

Henry Beck never thought of himself as a Number Two Man, but that's what he was and he did it well. It had provided him with money, a stately home, prestige in the Tulsa community, and occasionally fascinating travel.

This morning was one of those times when he regretted never having done something on his own—something outside the large shadow cast by Colby Tiger. *When my friends and family remember me,* he thought ruefully, *it will be only for my loyalty and close friendship with the Chief. I've never really originated anything on my own.*

As an attorney, he handled the legal details of the oil business, but only after the deals had already been negotiated by Colby. Still, his loyalty had earned him a good living, and eventually he would enjoy a comfortable retirement. *Retirement, there was a sore spot. If the "Chief" had retired at sixty-five—like any normal person,* Henry brooded, *I would have been on my own by the time I was fifty.*

But Colby Tiger hadn't retired and, ten years later, needed his help more than ever. At age seventy-five, Colby had asked Henry to travel with him more often, and recently this also included his efforts to protect ancient manuscripts.

The traffic light finally turned green and he steered his black Mercedes onto Terwilliger Boulevard in the southern section of Tulsa among the impressive houses built during the oil boom. *There it is,* Henry said to himself as he spotted the house and turned in at one of the neighborhood's least pretentious homes.

As he parked his new car in the driveway next to an eight-year-old Ford pickup truck, Colby opened the front door and walked toward the car. Although he had slowed down a little with his advancing years, his large ramrod-straight frame, broad facial features, thick gray hair; and plain dealing ways, along with his backbone of character presented a man of inner strength. An old oak with deep roots.

"Mornin', Henry. Right on time as usual. Mind if we take the pickup today?" he asked with a half-smile, knowing full well that Henry would prefer driving his Mercedes.

"I'm not surprised," Henry replied thinking, *the Chief has been "taking the pickup" his whole life.* He knew it was Colby's way of clinging to his humble origins. By no means the only wealthy person in Tulsa to drive a pickup, Colby Tiger was the only one to do so on this particular stretch of Terwilliger Boulevard.

"Would you like to drive?" asked Colby, taking the keys out of his pocket.

"Not really. Why don't you drive? I know how much you enjoy it," replied Henry as if making a sacrifice. If truth be told, he wouldn't be caught dead driving this old pickup.

Photo Opportunity

"Yax where are you!" Christina shouted, failing in the dim light to find him. Desparate, she began to edge further down into the gushing water, hoping her body would divert the flow sufficiently for Yax to pull free of the river's grasp. But the current was too powerful and were she to lower herself any deeper, she might be swept to her own death.

Not able to hear herself think, Christina tried to still her racing heart and concentrate. *Think!* Her inner voice shouted at her. *Think!*

Finally, with only seconds left, an idea flashed in her head. *I know what to do!* Frantically, she pulled the camera from her pack and used the flash to illuminate the scene. The third flash revealed a small log which she jammed into the current, deflecting it just enough for Yax to raise his head from the raging water and gulp down air.

Inspired by her success, she hastily began piling rocks to divert even more of the water. After a few minutes, her back and arms aching, she was able to free him from the river's deadly embrace.

"I thought I'd lost you," she gasped.

Even more exhausted by the ordeal than she, Yax was unable to do more than lay against the rocks, his chest heaving. Finally, after he had caught his breath, he began to assess his own condition. He was gashed and bruised, but nothing seemed to be broken.

They eyed each other knowingly as their eyes adjusted to the faint brown light.

"Can you float down the river to the entrance with my help?" she yelled above the roar.

"I think so." His first words came out as a croak.

Then her faced suddenly clouded. "The camera!" she exclaimed. After the flash had provided the necessary light, she must have put the camera aside. She began groping frantically. "I can't lose that film," she moaned. "I just can't."

"It is not here," Yax said, indicating the rocks where she would have laid it.

"Where could it have gone?" Christina was beside herself, sickened at the thought of losing all her pictures.

"Maybe in the water," Yax said grimly as he began feeling in the pockets of water near her backpack while Christina continued to feel anxiously around the rocks. Suddenly, a thought struck her and she leaned back against the wall of the cave. *Yax almost drowned,* she told herself, *yet he didn't hesitate to help save my precious film…my success. Why did I insist on staying longer to take more pictures? Why do I always have to push the limit? After thirty-three years of never worrying about the consequences, you'd think I'd have learned by now.*

Christina was about to call out to Yax, to tell him that the film wasn't worth it, when he yelled triumphantly, "I've found it!"

He fished out the camera from its hiding place where the current had pushed it between two rocks and handed it to her.

"The film might still be okay?" he asked her, as she held the dripping camera.

"I hope so," she responded, trying to convince herself that the film wasn't damaged. "Now let's get out of here while we're still in one piece. What with losing the flashlight, getting the batteries wet, and almost losing you, I think the Lords of the Underworld are trying to tell us to stay out of *Xibalba.*"

Mayan Mavericks

Maya writing is not syllabic or alphabetic in part or in whole.

—Sir Eric Thompson

Twenty-eight thousand feet above the Aegean, Colby lifted up the window shade and saw the familiar sight of the Greek islands dotting the sparkling sea below. Only two more hours and they would be in Cairo.

He was tired and stiff-necked, having spent an uncomfortable night trying futilely to sleep in every position but a comfortable one. Over the years, Colby had journeyed to the oil-rich Middle East on business matters many times, and the Arabic banter of the bilingual flight crew seated near him was familiar. He spoke survival Arabic, but he could never really disguise the folksy twang of his Oklahoma accent, even when he spoke a foreign language.

Henry was seated beside him looking amazingly unrumpled from the overnight ordeal. But then, Henry always looked as if his well-cut clothes were freshly pressed. Small-framed, with deep-set eyes behind gold spectacles, his fine-boned face gave him the appearance of a bird. *A hawk,* Colby mused, *definitely a hawk.* Although Henry always smiled on cue, he never looked like he was enjoying himself. Even after all these years, Colby had never seen Henry break into a sure-enough, ear-to-ear grin. He inhabited a tight-lipped world of precision, efficiency and thoroughness, paying attention to the smallest of details. The perfect lawyer and aide whose dependability and loyalty had been a comfort to Colby, especially now with his Middle East projects requiring more time and energy.

The manuscript, worried Colby, thinking about its potential dangers and wondering how it would all turn out. *No use frettin' about something I can't control. Besides, it'll all ravel out in the next day or so.*

Waiting for breakfast to be served, perhaps to get his mind off his concerns, he turned to Henry and said: "Have I ever told you about Christina's research?"

"Just a little," smiled Henry, knowing that Colby always enjoyed talking about his favorite niece. "But if you don't mind, I'd like to know more before we meet her on our way back from Cairo. This will be a first for me. I've never had the opportunity to join an archaeological expedition before, and I can't tell you how exciting the prospect of this whole Palenque thing is." He then blinked several times before adding: "And I don't want to be an embarrassment at the gathering. All I really know is that the Maya built huge temples in the jungles of Central America."

"That's what most people have heard," agreed Colby, settling in to talk about a subject he loved. "It's true that around 800 A.D., the Maya quit building temples, abandoned their cities, and went back to their simpler life in the jungle. Although there are lots of theories, nobody really knows why. Many scholars, including Christina, think that the Mayan kings lost their control of the peasants who provided the labor for their massive tombs."

"These fantastic structures were tombs for the rulers?"

"That's right. In this sense, they have a lot in common with the Egyptian pyramids, although they were obviously used for ceremonies as well. What isn't well known is that the Maya weren't completely wiped out by the Spanish invasion of the New World and today still represent a large portion of the population of Central America. They speak over thirty different Mayan languages."

"Thirty languages?" mused Henry. "I bet most people don't even know there was one." He took off his spectacles and began cleaning them while Colby continued.

"It's amazing that we Americans know so little about America. In fact, the written history of the American continent didn't begin with Christopher Columbus or even Leif Ericson. It began with the Maya scribes in the jungles of Central America, who first wrote about the deeds of their kings some 2000 years ago."

Henry couldn't help looking somewhat skeptical. "I find it difficult to believe that their writing is that old."

"But it is," Colby said. "Only problem is that it disappeared over 500 years ago." He paused to let the fact sink in. Then he told Henry that soon after the Spanish conquest, a Catholic priest named Landa began the systematic destruction of all the Maya books, which he believed were graven images that cursed the Mayas and prevented their Christian salvation. In only a few years he had destroyed everything, except the temples which were hidden under the thick jungle growth."

"So this is why the Maya language hasn't been deciphered?" asked Henry.

"Partly," replied Colby. "But the story gets even more bizarre. When Landa realized the irreparable damage he had inflicted on the Maya civilization, destroying their written language in the process, he returned to Guatemala and spent the rest of his life documenting their written and spoken language in Spanish."

"So this is what they're using to decipher the Maya code?" asked Henry, intrigued by the complex story.

"Sad to say, that's not the case. It too suffered the same fate as the Maya language itself. The book disappeared."

"If I understand you correctly," Henry summarized in his lawyerlike fashion, putting his spectacles back on and looking intently through gleaming glass, "Landa not only destroyed the Maya written language, he also left behind the Rosetta Stone for breaking the code, and now that is also missing?"

"That's the story," confirmed Colby, "but for one final chapter. In the mid 1800's a French priest was ferreting through un-catalogued materials on the Americas in a Madrid library and to his amazement—and his credit—he found a 200-year-old badly transcribed copy of Landa's book."

Henry, shaking his head in wonderment, said: "What an amazing story. But there's one part that doesn't make sense to me. If Landa's book was the Rosetta Stone, why is the Maya code still a mystery?"

Colby's expression told him that it wasn't so simple. "For a long time, leading linguists were discouraged by the archaeologists from working on the Maya hieroglyphs. Until very recently, those who did get involved wasted a lot of time barking up the wrong tree. At first, they believed that the language Landa described was alphabetic, which turned out not to be the case."

"Alphabetic like English?"

"That's right. But an equally important factor was the domination of this field for the past fifty years by a pompous Englishman named Eric Thompson, who believes that the Mayan language is a primitive code with no more linguistic content than Rebus riddles or primitive cave drawings."

"What Victorian views!" exclaimed Henry.

"True, but Thompson didn't invent these *Victorian views* as you put them," Colby told him. "He followed a long line of Englishmen, scholars all, who believed that all cultures, and of course their written languages, must evolve in stages. Cultures must evolve, they believed, from savagery to barbarism and eventually to Englishmen."

Colby glanced at Henry to make sure he hadn't missed his sarcasm. He hadn't.

"It's disappointing to believe that prejudice could keep scientists from unraveling the Maya code," observed Henry.

Colby smiled sadly. "You must remember, they didn't believe that the Maya were real people, they were *pagans.*"

"Now I understand your interest," said Henry. "It's the same prejudice that destroyed the Indians of North America."

"Yes," agreed Colby, reflecting on his Native American ancestors who had suffered a similar fate when they were uprooted and relocated time and time again. The American colonists didn't respect their Indian ways, believing them to be inferior to their own *civilized* ways.

Realizing he'd let the conversation lapse, Colby continued: "So in 1945 when Thompson declared the Maya code unsolvable, only the fearless and the uninitiated dared to think otherwise. They say that the academic graveyard is filled with those who tried to question Thompson's authority."

"And that's where Christina enters the picture?" asked Henry.

"In a sense, yes," said Colby. "She's part of a research team, led by her colleague, David Kelley, that's trying a new approach, a new way to skin the cat, but they're facing stiff resistance from Thompson.

"David Kelley's group believes that the Maya hieroglyphs must be a written version of the Mayan spoken language. Instead of ideograms or pictograms, which merely present an idea graphically, like a cave man shooting an arrow, they believe the hieroglyphs are actually sentences, with subjects, objects, verbs and everything. Just like ours, only arranged somehow into a beautiful hieroglyph."

Henry's brow furrowed as he struggled to understand. "So, have Christina and her colleagues had any success with their new approach?"

"That's the rub. They're close, so damned close," Colby said. "All they need to do is find one sentence, just one, and the rest should fall into place quickly. Unfortunately they're stumped. That's the purpose of the meeting in Palenque—to see if the new hieroglyphs recently found at the Mayan ruins there might provide the missing clues. Then they might hit the nail on the head."

"And if the hieroglyphs don't offer anything new?"

"Spirits remain high, but Christina and her colleagues will be easy prey for that know-it-all, Thompson." He pounded his fist into the palm of his other hand. "Christina <u>has</u> to succeed if they're to give voice to the Mayas."

Just then, their food arrived. Since they were both ravenous, they devoted the next several minutes satiating their hunger before picking up the thread of their conversation.

"Christina's one of the leaders, isn't she?" Henry began.

"I tend to think so, but she insists that she's just an up and comer. She's a very bright kid, you know, and not just because she's my niece."

"If I remember correctly, she got her Ph.D. in anthropology from Yale," said Henry, knowing the answer full well.

"That's right. But what you might not know is that she also minored in languages and linguistics".

"Is there a difference?" asked Henry.

"I think linguistics has more to do with human speech and how it's structured in language. I'm really not sure. I know she gets into lots of details on the differences and similarities between languages like English and Chinese, for example."

Seeing Henry's nod, he continued, "Christina hit her stride as an undergrad after a couple of semesters when she became interested in the Maya Code. She had studied under Professor Michael Coe, who wrote the popular book on the Maya code. Because he is so well known, it gave her career a tremendous boost. After that, she published several papers as a post-doc at the University of Cambridge. The combination of Yale, Coe, Cambridge, and brilliance got her the position in anthropology at Harvard. She was very young to have come that far."

"She sounds like the kind of niece that would make any uncle proud," Henry said, straining a smile on cue. He realized that Christina held a special place in Colby's heart.

"Well, it was definitely brains and hard work, but there's more to it than that. She will tell you that it was her Catholic nuns."

"How so?" asked Henry.

"Christina will tell you at the slightest provocation that her dedicated high school teachers taught their subjects with love and inspiration. She credits those nuns with building her self confidence and motivating her to pursue an advanced degree."

"I've heard that about Catholic schools," said Henry, though his voice lacked any pretension to enthusiasm. The Catholic church was so outdated compared to his Protestant religion. "Her praise of the nuns almost compensates for the Church's other shortcomings."

Colby shot him a look, trying to gauge where Henry was coming from. He usually didn't show his true feelings, preferring to play his cards close to his chest.

Colby then advised Henry to be sensitive to Christina's Catholicism. Despite her faith, Christina was aware of the role that the Catholic church had played four hundred years ago in the destruction of the Maya language and culture. Christina considered her own work a form of restitution, perhaps even penance.

Soul of Guatemala

Christina could barely see Yax waving from the back of the bus as she was engulfed in its wake of billowing dust. They had barely arrived in time for Yax to catch his bus back north to Tikal. It was late afternoon by the time they had canoed back across the lake in the sluggish mahogany cayuco to this frontier town, aptly named Fronteras—the ragged edge of civilization.

Feeling exhausted but exhilarated, Christina boarded the first bus headed for Guatemala City. Called a "chicken bus", it was so named for its importance in getting Maya produce, including chickens, to market. Baskets full of produce and Mayan handicrafts were strapped to the rack on top of the bus. Live animals, mostly chickens and roosters, were rolled in colorful Mayan shawls and stashed in the overhead racks above the seats. Having spent its better years of service as an American school bus, the grammar-school-yellow paint was still faintly visible beneath the peeling layers of gaily painted colors.

The passengers, mostly meek indigenous Mayan families were crammed three to a seat with ten or fifteen in the aisles and a few hanging out of the doors. As the bus sputtered and coughed its way from village to village, they quietly endured the uncomfortable ride. This was the way of the Maya. Looking like their ancestors with wide faces, olive complexion, and varnished black hair, they sat straight in their seats—perfect posture from years of balancing baskets on their heads.

Like all chicken buses, it took forever to go long distances, since the bus rumbled along slowly on unpaved roads and stopped at every pueblo boasting a population in double digits, at every crossroads, and at every trail in the jungle. *How typical,* she thought, reminding herself that everything in Central America operated on *mañana* time. *This is going to be a long night*

It was a full-time challenge to breathe with the windows open to let in fresh dust, hot air and high-sulfur diesel fumes. And with old shock absorbers weaker than rubber bands, it was difficult to maintain her seat without bouncing into the laps of the two Maya women crammed on the bench next to her.

Christina smiled to herself as she thought that her family would have questioned her sanity. She also admitted to herself that she had always taken pride in being an intrepid traveler, preferring not to isolate herself from real-life experiences with the other foreign travelers. And this certainly qualified as a real-life experience.

The drivers, all seeming to know where everyone in Guatemala lived, appeared to be highly religious men, with the area at the front of the bus adorned better than most churches. St. Christopher statues and *Cristo es Senor* banners competed for limited space. It dawned on her that these statues were used universally, regardless of economic status or ethnicity. Her own mother, for one, had always kept a St. Christopher medal in the car. Christina had never taken them seriously and was today all-the-more convinced that these icons didn't work, since each bus encountered the usual minor disasters: overheating, flat tires, and once, a small robbery by an excessively nervous but polite bandit.

Christina had just begun to doze off, when she was abruptly awakened by the grinding of the wheels as the bus sputtered to a halt. She looked up to see an army unit blocking the road ahead.

While Christina knew that such stops were almost routine, she'd never become accustomed to them. The official government position was that these exercises were needed to search out guerrilla insurgents and their weapons. Christina knew, however, that the larger agenda was to intimidate the local Maya population, and keep the wealthy establishment in power. She was sickened that her American taxes, in the name of freedom, paid for these guns and childish games.

They're so young, Christina thought, staring at the Ladino soldiers standing akimbo, as their machismo role demanded. And indeed, the soldiers, young teenagers really, were not quite as big as their automatic weapons, which they brandished about carelessly like plastic toys. They herded the male passengers off the bus and forced them to stand spread-eagled against the side of the bus while they were frisked.

Meanwhile, looking out her window Christina could see other soldiers checking everything in the luggage compartment. They found the usual assortment of coconuts, baskets, potatoes, pineapples, and broken bus parts. *There are more old tires inside the bus than on the wheels,* she thought, *not that any of them has either air or treads.*

Inside the bus, the women retained their seats at gunpoint, and watched stoically while the young soldiers made their way down the aisle searching their possessions. The passengers seemed to have participated in this ritual all too many times and their bottomless dark eyes could not disguise their hatred for the Spanish military.

One of the older soldiers, an officer, stopped just in front Christina. He jammed his rifle butt into a multicolored sack in the overhead rack and provoked a rooster to screech out indignantly. Then he turned to her and, sizing her up for what seemed like an eternity, asked gruffly, "*Norteamericana?*"

"*Sí,*" Christina replied firmly, looking at him directly with her Kelly green eyes. This was no time to blink and seem weak.

"Your *passaporte, Señorita,*" he demanded in rough but understandable English.

Handing it over, she told the officer in flawless Spanish that she was an American archaeologist. While he scanned her credentials, her gaze never wavered as she did her best to maintain an outwardly calm demeanor, just like the Maya on the bus. *This is taking too long,* she thought. *Are they after a bribe? Or maybe…do they have their eyes on my camera?* She was chilled at the thought of losing her precious pictures.

Outside, she could hear the Spanish bus driver complaining to the soldiers that he had engine problems and needed to get into the next village before dark. And just as it appeared that these armed teenagers were about to wave the bus along, one of the soldiers who had been poking through the luggage compartment shouted triumphantly that he had found a weapon.

For a moment there was silence as Christina felt the wave of terror spread through the bus.

Oklahoma Gold

Every part of this earth is sacred to my people. We are part of the earth, and it is part of us. We love this earth as a newborn loves its mother's heartbeat.

—Chief Seattle

Colby was not a practicing veterinarian, and never had been. That was certainly his first love, but he really had no choice once his family found themselves in the oil business. He had often wondered how different his life might have been if he had stayed with veterinary medicine. Perhaps this was why he derived vicarious pleasure seeing Christina flourish in academic circles.

After his father's untimely death, he enjoyed running the business for several years. But later, once he had tired of the routine and no longer found it challenging, he was simply unable to find someone with the right talents whom he also trusted. So he reluctantly stayed on, but let Henry handle certain portions of the business which fit his legal training.

Colby was a full-blooded Creek-Seminole Indian and he was proud of his forefathers, Osceola and Red Eagle. One branch of his family, the Creeks, had fled south into the everglades of Florida from Georgia and Alabama after the disastrous defeat at the Battle of Horseshoe Bend in 1814. Here their diminished tribe of a few thousand people joined with the remnants of other tribes and even some runaway black slaves, forming what eventually became Florida's Seminole Tribe..."a people who never surrendered". Soon they were displaced again by the ever deceitful practices of the colonial government when all thirty-two million acres of their lands were confiscated. They were among the few who survived the "Trail of Tears" death march across the Southern states to Indian Territory in the winter of 1838.

Here they were dumped in a wilderness, adjoining what they called Tulsey Town, between the Arkansas and Canadian rivers. Eventually, his parents each received land grants after they were forcibly moved from more desirable lands.

Because his ancestors had lost their homelands, Colby's daddy longed for his own land. With money he earned at demeaning jobs, he bought up his neighbors' land grants, providing them with hard-to-come-by cash. Through working, scrimping, and buying when the price was right, he amassed more acres than he could walk in a day.

Then oil was discovered, and these vast lands, rich in prairie sod and buffalo grass, which had been least wanted by both the white pioneers and his fellow tribesmen, suddenly became valuable. The lands eventually became known as an oil basin, the Mid Continent oil field.

But even then, the lessons Colby's daddy learned from his frugal past kept him from selling out, as was common in those days. Instead, he watched for an opportunity to develop his hard earned resources with his own broad back and strong hands. He learned the oilfield game by working on drilling crews, first as a common laborer, then on the rig floor, and later as a derrickman. Although he only backed up the driller from time to time, he felt confident he could do the job full time in a pinch.

Senior Tiger had never borrowed a dime in his life, but being cash-poor, he realized that to develop his own land, he would have to take a gamble and post some of his land titles as collateral to buy a drilling rig. He debated with himself many sleepless nights until at last his resistance wore thin. And when he finally made the decision to try his luck, everything just fell into place.

In those days, some made it and some blew it, so equipment changed hands in strange ways. With a lot of searching and negotiating, he was able to buy an old reclaimed cable tool rig, just sufficient to drill a test well.

Tiger's ancestors had used a willow branch to witch for water, but he had learned that water to an oilman spelled a dry hole. About that time, he had heard of an old Doodle Bugger in town, who claimed that, for a small fee, he could find oil on any man's land. He couldn't afford the services of a geologist so there seemed to be no other choice. A deal was cut, and a date was set.

Colby could still remember—he was about ten years old at the time— when the Doodle Bug man came out to their place in a rickety surrey, drawn by a skinny blind horse, and asked, "Whare's the bounds of your property, Mizter?"

In a few hours the three of them had driven over most of the land, at least the part that Colby's daddy thought might be the most promising. Colby was intrigued and excited to be participating in this momentous decision.

At each stop along the way, the Doodle Bugger opened his little black box, jiggled a few wires, and scribbled in a pocket notebook, like he was recording secret information. Then they backtracked a few times, and finally he got down, carried the little black box to an old sycamore stump, thumped it as though he expected a genie to appear, turned slowly around a few times scrutinizing the ground and said, "Here's whare we sink the shaft Mizter Tiger, Sir. Thar's oil all 'round heah young man, and plenty of it. I gar'ntee you."

The work was hard and the dirt roads often deep in mud, but with a perseverance inherited from their ancestors, Colby and his determined daddy drilled in their first gusher. From then on the Tiger family—these so-called 'stinkin' Injuns'—were bathed in black gold and their hard-earned lands became the nucleus of their own bonanza, the Tiger Indian Territory Oil Company, Inc.

Yet, *Ole Man Tiger*, as he became affectionately named by the locals, was not one to live it up. Instead, he and Colby, worked side by side drilling more wells. They ran their own drilling rigs, laid the pipe from the wells to the storage tanks, and repaired all their own equipment, including the diesel engines and the pumping jacks. They rode the fences on horseback, and mended them to keep their cattle away from the oil, salt water, and heavy equipment.

And when their prairie and bottom lands were all drilled up, and the price of crude had risen to the fabulous amount of a dollar seventy-five a barrel, they followed the oil booms, wildcatting all over what now is Oklahoma and Texas, winning some and losing some, but over all Lady Luck and the Great Spirit were with them...and the Doodle Bugger.

Day in and day out, they sweated and burned from the heat in the summer, and they froze when the winter prairie winds blasted down from the north.

These were good times. The Oklahoma clay, their hearts, and their souls were all Creek-Seminole red.

Not a single thing was missing from their Oklahoma experience. The rainbow colors of oil on the slush pits vied with the fantastic colors of the prairie sunsets. The air was so full of rich aromas, that senior Tiger, said it was downright hard to breath. Colby loved the smells of muddy creeks, freshly mown hay, tornado rains, range cattle, sage, and to top it all off, the smell of sweet crude and partially-flared natural gas. The fantasies of the Plains had replaced their ancestors' love of the osprey and the gator with the red-tailed hawk, the jack rabbit, and the water moccasin.

Then the accident happened.

It wasn't a water moccasin nor a rattler, however, that struck ole man Tiger down, although a big one did strike his left leg one day while he was herding his fine Angus cows through a thicket. All oilmen had cattle in those days. It was just a sideline of the oil game, and a relaxing way to ease the tensions of their business.

Colby, by now a strapping young man of twenty-five, was taking a break from his veterinarian studies at Oklahoma State University, helping his daddy check the wells on horseback, just like in the good old days. He had brought a rifle and his father carried a shotgun—just in case they saw something tasty for dinner.

Colby was riding the pipelines and fences nearby looking for breaks, while Senior Tiger was balancing the weights on the giant pumping jacks. With one hand placed carefully at the base of the steel arm as the counter-weights cycled, his daddy could tell from the "feeling" of the bearings, whether or not the unit was balanced. As the arm lifted, the walking beam see-sawed, the sucker rods went up and down, and the diesel engine hummed relentlessly. Sometimes the sucker rods were too heavy, other times it was the counter-weights. Either way, they often had to be adjusted depending on how much oil was left in the well.

Colby's daddy had done this for years, and there was no reason for anything to go wrong, but it surely did.

That day, they must have been almost balanced, because Tiger, mesmerized by the motion, just stood there for a long time. Perhaps he was watching a coyote, or a rattle snake, or a hawk. Whatever it was, his hand suddenly slipped into a slot between the weights and the arms on the pumping jack. The rig closed on his arm like a giant vice, and he was instantly whipped off the ground like a prairie dog and crushed between the giant moving parts, all in a matter of seconds. It ripped his arms and legs off, threw them to the side like scraps, and then started to grind on his stomach.

Colby quickly spurred his horse and galloped to the oil rig, but the largest portion of his father's lifeless body had already been thrown into the air and had landed several yards from the pumping jack, crushed by one of the very forces that had made him a multimillionaire. The pumping jack continued to nod effortlessly and unemotionally...up and down, up and down, up and down...like a satiated predator.

Every time Colby played this scene in his mind, it was like a slow-motion movie except that he was in the picture. No color...just black and white and gray.

• • •

The evening traffic in Cairo was typically congested, and the fumes made their eyes water. There was a strong taste of their own petroleum in their mouths.

As they pulled up to the El Gezirah hotel, Colby was brooding over his disappointment that Christina was not joining them in Egypt. This project had become more complicated than he had anticipated, especially the possibility that he might acquire an extremely controversial early Christian document.

I ought to be involving her more in these Middle Eastern matters, thought Colby anxiously, *especially with the religious uproar that's bound to follow the announcement of this discovery. This is my most important project ever, and I must succeed at all costs.*

Low Intensity Conflict

Knowing, actually hoping, that they wouldn't dare execute an American anthropologist without orders from higher up, Christina impulsively stood up to her full height, and towering over the soldier for maximum effect, announced, "*La pistola es mía. Favor de devolverme mi arma; la tengo de protección contra los banditos.*"

The officer who had been holding her passport slammed his rifle butt into her sternum, knocking her back down into the seat. Relishing his role, he held the gun barrel to her throat and hissed, "*Cállate, puta gringa!*"

There was a tense pause. A few seconds later, Christina was horrified to hear several staccato bursts from an automatic weapon muffled only slightly by a nearby grove of trees.

She shook her head sadly, knowing that her actions had been for naught. One of the Mayan men on the bus had been martyred as a *Communist* in the name of *Democracy*, in the name of free enterprise, in the name of her own country. Sickened to the marrow of her soul, Christina said and did nothing. She had no choice. Once the soldiers had killed one person, it took very little for them to lose control and massacre the others. It would be of no use to report this to the American embassy. They always looked the other way, pretending that the military dictatorship was a democracy and that the Maya were trying to prevent their inalienable right to cheap coffee and bananas.

Later, as she unsuccessfully tried to sleep on the bucking bus, she thought to herself that she hardly ever saw American visitors in Guatemala who didn't have a hidden agenda. They were invariably either United Fruit Company executives, military advisors, archaeologists or missionaries. Yes, Guatemala was a complex country and being there brought forth conflicting emotions.

Christina marveled that the ancient Maya were so highly esteemed while the modern ones were despised. Since the Spanish Conquest, the Mayans had been systematically shoved off their land to make room for foreign coffee and banana plantations, and for the conspicuously wealthy Ladino Guatemalans who controlled the country. Still comprising over half the population in Guatemala, the Maya were scorned by the Westernized Ladinos for clinging tenaciously to their primitive ways...and their ancient lands.

Due to activism on the part of some Mayas to get back their land and to form labor unions for the coffee plantation workers, the military-backed regime had brutalized the Mayas, burned their villages, murdered them in the name of Communism and *disappeared them* by throwing their bodies into the volcanoes where they'd never be found. *Yes,* Christina thought scoffingly, *they had even turned the word 'disappeared' into a verb.*

Recently, the Guatemalan government had even begun killing activist priests and promoting the development of other religions—hence the country was crawling with missionaries of all sorts—Baptists, Adventists, Jehovah's Witnesses, Mormons, even Presbyterians—pawns in the government's attempt to weaken the Catholic Church's influence.

Back home in her comfortable university existence, it was difficult to comprehend that any of this was happening. *Low-intensity conflict* was the label given to the problems in Guatemala; American-sponsored terrorism was the reality.

Christina thought how depressing this all was because the problems were so big and there were no simple solutions. Before Guatemala, everything sort of fit into her pre-programmed definitions of reality; but today her reference frame had shifted and it was difficult to determine where the boundaries lay. It had been easy for her to theorize about it back home; but here she was living *in vivo*—not in a book.

The expressionless faces on the Maya women as they waited to see which of their men would not return to the bus would forever live with her.

The Maya were so different from Christina that the gap was almost impossible to bridge. Even as the driver shut the door and drove to the next village, the women managed to bottle up their grief, staring blankly ahead like stone monuments. Four hundred years of occupation had annealed their resolve.

Cardinal Sins

Christina had been wandering through a ghostly labyrinth, dreaming about being trapped in the cave, when she was abruptly awakened by the sound of automatic rifle fire. She was momentarily frozen in place until she heard the sound of people laughing. Then it slowly dawned on her that it wasn't gunfire she had heard, but firecrackers. Setting off strings of firecrackers was a common nighttime event in Guatemala City.

Nighttime? She groped for the clock on the nightstand to find that it was already five-thirty in the late afternoon. Temporarily disoriented, she gradually realized that she was in her room at the Santa Clara Hotel in Guatemala City. She must have fallen asleep again.

Her head felt dull from the long fatiguing night on the chicken bus. Even in her sleep, her subconscious continued to work overtime, churning the previous days events over and over again in her mind. Just as she was beginning to panic about her film, she remembered that she had taken it to be developed earlier that morning. Her film was supposed to be ready tomorrow—*mañana.* She raised her eyes heavenward. *With a little assistance from St. Anthony, that is,* praying—hoping really—that the film had survived the dunking.

She rubbed her eyelids, then stood up and stretched. Finally, she was able to manage a smile as she recalled her exhilarating trip into the cave with Yax. *It was the danger,* she reluctantly confessed to herself, experiencing a small pang of guilt. Danger always brought her more enjoyment than she might readily admit to others. *I could easily turn into an excitement junkie.*

She pulled aside the white gossamer drape and stepped onto the verandah into the long shadows of the afternoon. The jacaranda trees filled the courtyard with an explosion of lavender blossoms. Breathing deeply to savor their luxurious scent, she thought how the sights and smells in foreign lands seemed so much more intense than those back home. Somehow, the memories of her experiences in other countries always stood out in sharp relief against the routine of every day life.

Across the street, a Maya lady, clothed in her kaleidoscopically embroidered *huipile* garment, was selling individual cigarettes and penny-wrapper gum while nursing an infant. Two other children played quietly in an empty cardboard box under her makeshift stand. The woman's husband probably earned money by selling brightly colored belts to the all-too-few tourists; the same belts offered to the same tourists by dozens of other husbands on the same street. When the children had grown a couple more years, they in turn would help support the family by peddling hand-woven *friendship* bracelets to the tourists.

These are the Mayas, thought Christina bitterly, *once a great civilization. I must give them back their written language.*

• • •

As the shadows faded to purple dusk, she went inside and took a refreshing shower. And with her long blonde hair still wrapped up in a towel, she spread her sketches of the cave hieroglyphs out on the bed. She smiled self-satisfactorily when she saw how many of the new glyphs she had been able to capture with the last rays of her flashlight.

She knew that these represented a major discovery, perhaps even filling one of the gaps in the linguistic efforts to break the Maya code. She couldn't wait to see the wide-eyed expressions on the faces of her colleagues. *Pride goeth before a fall,* she reminded herself, unable to contain her joy but feeling slightly guilty with how much she appreciated receiving attention, especially from people she respected.

She was all the more glad she had invited Uncle Colby, although at the time she could not have known that the cave would be so prolific. She had originally invited him because everyone had such high hopes for this meeting. Not only had several new stelae covered with hieroglyphs been discovered in the jungle nearby Palenque, but more importantly, all the right talents were being assembled for the first time at this conference.

Uncle Colby had been funding her research for many years through his Tiger Foundation, and she had wanted him to be there on the outside chance the code was cracked. The glyphs from Yax's cave had greatly improved the odds of a breakthrough.

Christina appreciated her uncle's genuine interest in her life and loved him like a father despite her mother's discouragement to the contrary. "Christina," she would caution, concealing her disdain with motherly concern, "I don't think you should be spending so much time with Colby. He isn't a good influence on you."

Naturally, Christina ignored the unsolicited advice. She never wavered in her love for her uncle. If anything, she grew closer to him over the years and more distant to her somewhat parochial mother.

She could still recall the stories her family told of the scandal when Mary, her mother's only sister, married Colby. The marriage had broken all the rules, which to the family's dismay, had pleased Mary immensely. She had always been the rebellious daughter, while Christina's mother, Maureen, preferred to play by their mother's strict family codes.

The first rule Mary broke was marrying someone who was not a Catholic. This was cardinal sin number one. It was inconceivable to their mother that Mary would take this chance with her soul. How could she maintain the purity of purpose being married to a non-Christian?

The second rule she broke was marrying someone not from lace-curtain Irish Boston, but worse yet, someone from Oklahoma. Their mother would often say that she wasn't even sure what language they spoke in that "barbaric little place".

The last rule Mary broke was never put into words, but it ranked even higher than cardinal rule number one. She married, of all things, an American Indian.

Ignoring her mother's wishes, or perhaps just to prove a point, Mary viewed all three as virtues, not sins. Mary seemed to relish her newfound freedom, and disappeared from polite society to "somewhere probably west of the Mississippi River", as her family described her new situation.

Inevitably, these activities caused a stir back in Boston, especially with Christina's mother, Maureen, who had assumed the pious mantle of their mother. As a staunch Catholic with a priest for a son, Maureen had become increasingly concerned about her sister's waning interest in the Church and suspected that she was drifting into dangerous territory by letting her church attendance lapse.

But Mary didn't pay much attention to Maureen's warnings. Eventually giving up on her sister, Maureen turned the same unsolicited attention on Christina whenever she allowed her work to interfere with her obligation to the Church. Christina had always hoped that her brother Ryan's rapidly advancing church career would compensate for her own somewhat cavalier attendance. After all, there certainly was no doubt about the sincerity of her Catholic beliefs, only a little truancy.

All of this was compounded by Christina's growing attachment to her Uncle Colby. Since he and Mary were not able to have children of their own, and Christina's own father had died when she was barely a teenager, it was with the best of intentions that Colby took an interest in Christina and eventually helped pay for her college education.

A woman with little experience outside her home and family, Maureen was in no position to compete with Colby's resources and worldly knowledge. She had felt threatened by his participation, believing that he interfered with her influence upon her own daughter.

"Christina," he would say, "I respect each person's beliefs, especially if that person has examined them and holds them out of conviction, not just convenience." Like his Native American ancestors, he believed that humans are a harmonious component of the universe, in direct communion with the Great Spirit and all other life.

Not wanting to be cast in the mold of her mother, Christina kept quiet and made an extra effort to tolerate her uncle's unorthodox religion. Even so, it was inconceivable to her that he was not a Christian. As she had matured, however, their mutual commitment to uncovering and preserving the truth became more important than their philosophical differences.

Christina was aware that academics and collectors around the world knew that her uncle paid top dollar to purchase, preserve, and protect ancient documents and artifacts, choosing to make them available to the scholarly experts rather than keeping them for his own private enjoyment. Now that he was older and more or less retired, he had more time to spend pursuing this interest.

When she had last spoken to Uncle Colby, he had told her that he was flying to Cairo in hopes of acquiring an important early Christian document. To her surprise, he said he would like for her to join him, if at all possible, but she had already committed to the meeting at Palenque. This invitation was odd, because he had never included her in these matters before.

Something is definitely troubling him, she thought as she recalled the apprehension in his voice. He was not an easy man to scare.

• • •

There was a knock on the door. "Telegram for you, Miss."

Christina opened the envelope and quickly scanned to the bottom of the page wondering who would send her such an urgent message. It was from her mother.

As she read, her face clouded and her hand began to tremble.

Primera Mesa Redonda de Palenque
Mexico

Every action has an equal and opposite reaction. The reaction to the Primera Mesa Redonda de Palenque began even before it opened.

—Michael Coe
Breaking the Maya Code

Christina had tried not to let the others notice, but there were times when she had been noticeably distraught. Her colleagues at Palenque had been sympathetic, of course, but they couldn't let her personal problems interfere with that momentous event. They had work to do, and they had a chapter in world history to write.

They had gathered together with one of the three missing pieces of the Maya puzzle already in place. They already knew from the work of the brilliant Russian, Yuri Knorosov, that Landa's book, or what remained of it, was a Rosetta stone of sorts. Knorosov had realized that the symbols Landa had drawn were syllables rather than alphabetic characters. That might, in fact, have been the most important clue, but it was not enough to unravel the Maya code. The missing two pieces which they collectively uncovered at this *Mesa Redonda de Palenque* would be enough.

The second clue had come from the linguistic genius, Floyd Lounsbury, who had mastered so many languages while still a teenager that no one really knew how many languages he spoke. Christina knew that he at least mastered Greek, Norse, Sumerian Cuneiform, Chinese and even Iroquois. He had also taught himself Yucatec and Chorti Maya.

It was Floyd who had suggested that each glyph, although looking like a complete graphical image, probably had some internal structure similar to a sentence. He wasn't sure what the order was, but he had taken an educated guess, which in his case meant *very educated*, and he suggested the following internal order: time, followed by action, in turn followed by the subject.

Christina recalled the excitement which followed as they all broke up into smaller groups trying to find Floyd's *internal order*. Whoever found it would have been the first to read a Maya sentence and crack the Code.

After these many centuries, however, the riddle did not yield so easily, even with Christina's new hieroglyphs and the ones found recently in Palenque by their host, Merle Roberston. There was still one more clue to find.

Several disappointing nights later, when some of the less determined had already left the gathering, an odd group of three students, including Floyd Lounsbury, worked through the night. One was a student of David Kelley's, Peter Mathews, a long-haired and mustached hippie. He wore a unique T-shirt on which he had stenciled, of all things, one of the better known Maya codices, the Dresden Codex. A very detailed researcher, he had compiled an extraordinary notebook full of dates, glyphs and official catalog numbers.

The third member of this eclectic group was Linda Schele, Merle's artistic assistant in the field. She was a rough hewn but genuine Southern character, who would have been at home in a Faulkner story.

The three of them ran around at dawn the next morning yelling for everyone to wake up. "We did it! We did it! We did it!" They had broken the code! The meticulous hippie, the redneck artist, and the bashful genius had found the third clue.

They had discovered that the Maya had two ways of expressing the same word: one logographic and one phonetic. They even had some strange combinations of these two forms. The trio realized that it was really a matter of poetic license, or artistic taste, which of the forms each Maya author had chosen. They also found that certain glyphs, like the royal glyph and the city glyph, were frequently repeated at the beginning or ending of sentences.

Christina would never forget the commotion which followed. There was a certain magic in the air, created by the intellectual excitement and the cooperation between the participants. Everyone was ecstatically translating their own favorite hieroglyphs and showing them proudly to one another. It was an amazing moment indeed. In only minutes, the mysterious symbols came to life...mute no more.

For Christina that was a once in a lifetime creative experience.

It was also the saddest day of her life.

Roman Fires
391 A.D.
Alexandria, Egypt

All heresies are forbidden by both divine and imperial laws and shall forever cease.
—Gratian
Fourth century Roman Emperor

Ptah knew that the first time the Romans burned the library at Alexandria was hundreds of years ago in 48 B.C. Some still insisted that it was an accident and not the intent of Julius Caesar's troops.

There was little doubt this time. Alexandria had long harbored many different versions of Christianity, and the troops were in Alexandria specifically to destroy the branches which disagreed with the one in Rome.

Twenty-five years ago, in fact, Athanasius, the Orthodox Bishop of Alexandria, had publicly warned those who differed with him that their views and books were condemned. And even he had serious differences with the Roman Christians. Since then the lively debates at Alexandria between the Greeks, the Egyptians, the Palestinians, and the Romans over the teachings of Jesus had gone underground.

It had gotten even worse ten years ago when Emperor Theodosius declared Paul's version of Christianity the official State religion of the Roman Empire, and banned all other versions.

So Ptah knew that the invasion by the Romans was inevitable and that the Library would once again burn, and that was why he and his family were feverishly stacking books onto a wooden cart outside their home in Alexandria. Some of the books were his own, some had come from other wealthy individuals, and some were from the Alexandrian Library itself.

"How many men will you need once you get to the River?" he asked his brother, panic in his voice. Everyone in the family, including some close friends, were dragging the heavy baskets from the house to the cart.

"I think there will be enough men on the felucca to lift them onto the boat," replied his brother, Pachom, a Christian monk. "I will need some money to pay for their services."

"I think you should take one person with you, to bring back the cart," Ptah insisted. "He can also provide some protection for you."

"All right," agreed Pachom, reluctantly, "but I will attract less attention in this mayhem without too many others along. No one will bother a poor monk fleeing back up the Nile to his monastery."

"How far is it to Chenoboskeia?" Ptah inquired again.

Pachom smiled at his brother's concern for his safety. "It is three-hundred miles up the Nile, my loving and older brother," he replied, "but don't worry. I can assure you that the most dangerous part of the trip will be between your house and the pier. Once I am in the felucca and the books are loaded safely out of sight, it should be a very pleasant trip."

"It's just that I've never been that far up the River," apologized Ptah. "It seems like a long trip."

"The currents are weak this time of the year, and the steady winds on our stern are perfect for the trip south," his brother explained. "Once we are out of range of the Roman troops we will spend evenings on shore, but tonight we will not stop."

Even as they talked the fires could be seen burning throughout Alexandria not far away.

"It looks like your friend at the library got these books out just in time," Pachom said nervously, as he looked at the fires. "Are you sure you don't want your family to go with me to Chenoboskeia until this mess is over?"

"I think our family will be all right," replied Ptah confidently. "We have business ties to Rome and we've been assured that this part of the City will not be destroyed, unless someone is caught with condemned books, of course."

"Well if you all hurry a little faster," pleaded Pachom, "we will have a much better chance."

Everyone was obviously hurrying as fast as they could and the books were almost loaded into the cart.

"I still can't believe that Rome is going to such extremes to stamp out other versions of Christianity. The Church must be much stronger in Rome than it is here."

"And much more zealous," added Pachom, shaking his head in disbelief. "The teachings of Paul are in such radical disagreement with those of Jesus that I can't understand why they believe them in Rome."

"Because the addition of miracles and the Apocalypse obviously strengthens their control of the failing empire," opined Ptah.

"You would never know that the Empire is failing if you look at our city today," said his brother dejectedly. "Emperor Siricius seems all too strong to me."

"I certainly hope we are hiding copies of all of Jesus' teachings," Ptah said.

"Once I add my own books to the collection," answered Pachom, "we should have almost everything. We have the Gospel of Truth, the Gospel of Philip, our own Egyptian Gospel, and of course the Gospel of Thomas, which has most of Jesus' teachings."

"What about the Gospel of Mary?" asked Ptah, glancing at his wife.

"Oh yes," confirmed Pachom, "and the Gospel of Mary as well."

"Tell me again where you plan to conceal them," Ptah insisted, trying not to show concern for his brother's safety.

"I plan to seal them in large earthenware jars and bury them nearby in the desert until this danger passes. The arid climate, although difficult for us monks, is perfect for the documents. In case something happens to me, they should be safe for many years."

"Or to me," said Ptah reluctantly, dropping his eyes briefly.

"In case you need to find them without my assistance," his brother continued, "they will be at the foot of the cliffs of the burial caves."

"That sounds like a good landmark. Hide them well."

They realized that their good-byes would be brief, so they hugged and clung to one another as the last of the books and other supplies were tossed on the cart. Pachom prayed that this would not be the last time he saw his family.

"If we ever needed the strength of our Master, it is now," he said piously. "We must follow his teachings and find God in our purest thoughts. Remember, he taught us of our individual divinity and our communion with God, and that is all we have now that they have destroyed our churches and libraries.

• • •

Two days later fire destroyed the Library in Alexandria. Many religious treasures, which could not be removed in time, were burned. Also destroyed were many other important documents, including the writings of Democritus, the first scientific materialist, and the antipode of Plato. The disciples of the idealist Plato showed little remorse for the destruction of these controversial documents.

While the fire continued to rage, the felucca in which Pachom successfully loaded the teachings of Jesus was already a hundred miles up the Nile. He was grateful for the steady winds which filled the heavy triangular sail, jutting majestically above the wooden boat like the pyramids in the distance. He stood tall on the aft deck, tiller in hand, and the hot sun on his bronze face—a worthy descendant of King Ramses.

The Nile had always been the source of their physical survival, and that day it played an even deeper role, as he hurried his precious books toward the caves near Chenoboskeia.

Last Handshake

> But it's only the inspiration of those who die that make those who live realize what constitutes a useful life.
>
> —Will Rogers (Cherokee)

Christina marveled that her family did better at funerals than in ordinary life. The grief they shared over the loss of her uncle smoothed many long-simmering family disagreements. Everyone did their best to comfort her Aunt Mary, seeing her through this difficult time.

It had been three days since the memorial service, and the worst was behind everyone, although at times Christina and her aunt found solace in a good cry together. The service had been touching; the tears and mourning gave those closest to him an opportunity to show their appreciation and to rededicate their lives to some of his goals and values.

Christina had been curious how a Creek-Seminole funeral would differ from other funerals she had attended, especially since some members of Colby's tribe had become somewhat Christian, adding portions of the invader's religion to their own indigenous beliefs.

She knew that Uncle Colby believed in a personal relationship with God, the Great Spirit, and with the entire creation. Pointedly, however, he did not believe that God worked through clergy, or even the Lord Jesus. Colby had no creeds, except to be thankful for the Great Spirit, to be united with his people, and to love one another. He believed the words of his own Pied Riche, that people must help one another and the Great Spirit will accordingly help them all.

The night before Colby's body had been buried, his Indian family and friends conducted an all night vigil at Colby's cabin on his father's original allotment near the meeting place in Little Coweta. It was not a time of sadness, but a time to celebrate life, and Colby's life in particular.

As they had left the meeting place the next morning after the funeral services, a family member tolled the church bell once for each year of Colby's life. Later, at the burial ceremony Christina had noticed that there was a new blanket folded at the foot of the coffin, and that a small enclosure at the head of the grave contained some of his favorite personal possessions, presumably to make his journey to the Great Spirit more comfortable.

Then she and the other family members each tossed a handful of dirt into the grave, before everyone shoveled in the remaining dirt. She was standing next to her Aunt Mary during this *last handshake*, and the two them were unable to hold back their tears. Once they started crying, it spread to everyone.

Christina's emotions were more complicated than anyone had realized, because she had been harboring guilt for not having joined her uncle in Cairo. The mystery around his accidental death in Cairo had created a strange undercurrent throughout the gathering, and she was determined to learn more.

One Exception

The Indian child must early learn the beauty of generosity.

—Ohiyesa (Sioux)
The Soul of the Indian

Henry remembered the fatal trip to Cairo with Colby all too well. "That afternoon. Colby had insisted on going out on his own," recalled Henry remorsefully. "When I awoke from my nap, I gave him a call in his room, but there was no answer."

Everyone was captivated by Henry's account, although they were still numb from the funeral. They had all assembled at Mary's house to go over the will, and they were waiting for the estate attorney, Bill Kirchick, to get all his papers in order.

"About a half hour later the phone rang, and it was the hotel manager. He said that there had been an accident, and that Colby had been killed by a speeding automobile. They asked me to please come to the police station," said Henry with a wavering voice.

Father Ryan Sheridan, Christina's brother, noticed that it was difficult for Henry to tell this story, and he went to get him a glass of RC Cola from the kitchen. Henry waited quietly for him to return. The dining room was as quiet as an ocean calm before a *Norther.*

"I found more questions than answers at the police station," continued Henry, his voice back on an even keel. They couldn't give me a coherent account of the accident. All of his possessions, including his wallet and briefcase, were missing, except for the keys to his hotel room. Even stranger, they said there were no eyewitnesses, and yet it happened near a very busy street corner."

"Did Uncle Colby seem any different than usual that morning?" asked Christina, remembering his ominous comments to her about a Christian manuscript.

"He kept insisting on private meetings, which I assumed were related to his archaeological interests, but he was more adamant than usual." Henry paused to reflect. "No, Colby hadn't been himself in Cairo, and I became even more suspicious after talking to the police."

• • •

As Henry completed his comments, Mr. Kirchick showed from his posture that he was now prepared to begin the meeting.

"I think you all know that Mr. Tiger wanted Henry to handle this transition on his behalf, especially the activities at Tiger Oil, although he asked for my assistance with the legal details concerning his estate," began Mr. Kirchick. With his pinched face, his wire-rimmed glasses perched on his narrow nose, and his thinning white hair, combed from one side of his head across the crown of his skull, Mr. Kirchick was the very image of an estate lawyer.

Christina was a little surprised to find someone other than Henry involved in the legal details, but she realized that an estate as complicated as Uncle Colby's required specialized legal expertise.

Kirchick continued in a dry, nearly toneless voice. "The Tiger Foundation was established with a self-perpetuating Board of Directors several years ago, so the family need only involve themselves if they believe the funds are not meeting Mr. Tiger's objectives. As you already know, a large portion of his estate has been placed in this Foundation."

"I certainly do," Christina volunteered. "I've been one of the Foundation's main recipients for many years."

Mr. Kirchick peered owlishly at her over his glasses. "Indeed." He seemed to consider something, then said, "Perhaps you would like to read his instructions to the family. I can think of nothing that better captures his philosophy of life. I'm sure that he would have wanted you to read this to us all today." He handed a sheaf of papers to Christina.

Christina glanced at her uncle's words for a moment, composed herself, then began to read in a clear, strong voice:

Humans are infamous among the mammals, being the only ones
that kill each other in huge numbers. They have a second, perhaps

less noticeable foible: they destroy each other's ideas. Over the centuries, humans have succeeded in destroying words which threaten their established institutions and paradigms. We humans have been burning the words of others since our ancestors first thought to mark on hides and bark.

The most infamous torches are well known: the Hitlers, the Mussolinis, the Maos and Stalins, but the list unfortunately also includes our finest institutions. Most world religions, for example, have burnt books they deem heretical, and many of history's most famous academicians have suppressed opposing views, sometimes favoring an acerbic tongue over the torch.

Hitler burned the books in Germany. The Spaniards burned the Maya books in Central America. The Protestants and Catholics and Jews and Muslims burned each other's writings over the centuries. The philosophers and theologians burned not only the books of the scientists, but the scientists as well. The Roman Christians burned the books of other followers of Jesus.

The nomadic marauders from China burned everything. The American settlers annihilated the indigenous peoples of North America along with their rich cultures, and burned each other's books in the process. The universities and their books have always been the casualties of the people's revolutions.

Opposing words and ideas have always threatened those seeking or protecting power.

Somehow through the smoke, however, there is a persistent voice of truth which, with the bravest and most heroic of human deeds, manages to survive, in fact sometimes even to thrive. It thrives because a few individuals place freedom of ideas above all selfish interests, and because truth itself is indomitable, refusing over time to yield to human contortions. 'Truth alone triumphs,' according to the ancient Hindu saying.

The goal of the Tiger Foundation is to assist those who fight for the freedom of ideas, and those dedicated to seeking, liberating and protecting the human legacy of knowledge, wisdom and truth.

Christina's voice, strong throughout, broke at the end. After a lengthy pause she continued: "He has a note at the bottom in his handwriting. It says that his heroes are people like Michael Coe, David Kelley, and James

Robinson. It is the charter of the Tiger Foundation to seek out others of this merit."

I wonder who James Robinson is? thought Christina. *I know the other two.*

The room was quiet, except for several suppressed sobs. Somehow this lovable Creek-Seminole Indian had found his noble mission, in spite of the long and bloody trails his people had walked. Christina began to cry as she remembered that he never saw the fruits of his generosity; he never learned that the Maya code was broken at Palenque, just a few days after he died.

After a few seconds of silence, during which Aunt Mary fought her own emotions, Kirchick, trying to move the proceedings along, coughed discreetly and said, "There's more." After everyone regained their composure, he continued, "As you know, Colby Tiger provided for those closest to him by establishing handsome trusts which provide life-time income to the beneficiaries. These trusts are for Mary, Christina and, of course, for Henry's retirement.

This was no surprise to anyone until he added, "And for Maureen."

Christina was pleased that Uncle Colby had taken care of her mother. He had substituted for Christina's deceased father one last time. She glanced at her mom and saw a confounded look, as if she were simultaneously comforted and embarrassed.

She never understood the man until this moment, reflected Christina. *Not bad for an Indian from the boonies.*

"The antiquities in their home are for Mary's pleasure," continued Kirchick. "Most of his other valuable antiquities have already been donated to various museums, including The Huntington Library in California, The Shrine of the Book in Jerusalem, The Gilcrease and Phillips Museums in Tulsa, and The Five Civilized Tribes Museum in Muskogee. There is, however, one exception."

Joint Custody

Christina, who'd been looking down, raised her eyes and saw Kirchick come over to her with his hand outstretched.

"This is for you," he said, placing something small and metallic in her hand.

Christina looked at what lay in the palm of her hand. It was a key.

Aware of the buzz of excitement he'd created, Kirchick looked around the room and explained, "This is one of two keys sent to me by Mr. Tiger on the day of his death. I received them by a courier two days later."

Christina asked the obvious question: "What is the key for?"

"You have been given joint custody of a vault in Cairo at the Tiger Oil facility. The other key is being delivered, according to Mr. Tiger's wishes, to a Dr. Riggs Parker in Cairo. Neither of you can open the vault alone."

"Dr. Riggs Parker?" Christina asked dully. "Who is Dr. Riggs Parker?"

"I'm afraid I…"

"I know," spoke up Henry, causing everyone to turn toward him. "He's a recipient of one of the Foundation's research grants. Something to do with early Christianity and documents found in Upper Egypt near the Nile River. I'm not exactly certain. He teaches at Claremont College, but spends almost half of each year at the Coptic Museum in Cairo." He shrugged, "That's all I know."

"Do you know what's in the vault?" Christina asked him, wondering *who ever heard of Claremont College?*

"I have no idea," Henry replied. "Colby used it to store antiquities while he found them new homes. I've never been in it. He might have gone there alone while we were in Cairo…," his voice trailed off as he decided that this was not the time to bring up the events around Colby's death.

Mary, who had been listening intently to all that had gone on, found the strength to join the conversation. "I don't know, either. I can't understand why Colby didn't donate the contents to a museum along with his other antiquities. It doesn't make sense to me."

"You know what this means, don't you?" said Henry, giving Christina an odd look.

"No, I—" Christina couldn't think straight. Things were happening too quickly.

"You must go to Cairo and open the vault," Henry said as if it were the most obvious thing in the world.

"Yes, of course," said Christina, staring at the key in her hand. Henry was right. She had to go, especially with the mysterious events surrounding Uncle Colby's death. She recalled his advice about the high stakes antiquities business: the players were ruthless and there were no rules or referees. Who knew what adventures accepting the key might lead to? Still, she couldn't conceive of a worse time to abandon her Maya research.

Henry sensed her dilemma, and he offered to accompany her to Cairo. "I need to go to Cairo anyway on some unfinished business for Colby. I also know the people at Tiger Oil, which might make your first visit simpler. Having met Dr. Parker previously, I would be glad to make those introductions as well. It's completely up to you, but I would be pleased to go with you on this trip."

Christina considered his offer carefully. It was attractive, to be sure, but she'd been on her own for so long, fighting her own battles, that was difficult for her to admit she needed assistance. On the other hand, she would like an introduction to Dr. Parker. Accepting Henry's offer might also bring the other women, including her mother, peace of mind.

"That's a very generous offer, Henry," Christina finally said. "I accept. It would be very nice to have a friend on that trip. Maybe we can find out what happened to Uncle Colby."

Faith Tabernacle

Henry knew that Christina would not be interested in him romantically, but he had never entirely given up on the possibility. He thought she was extremely attractive, but then so were many other charming women in Tulsa, even a few at his own church, the Faith Tabernacle. Christina just seemed more powerful, with an academic appointment at Harvard and all her adventures in Central America.

He had not had a serious relationship for nearly ten years.

Henry often reminisced sadly about his late wife, Earlene, and their son, Jimmy. He and Earlene met twelve years earlier, and their love blossomed over a period of several months. Although a city boy, through and through, he had chosen Earlene, a country girl with homespun country values— honest, hardworking, and faithful.

Her family owned a modest ranch outside town, and the two of them had enjoyed hiking to the top of wooded hills and looking down at the cattle grazing in the valley. A small, clear river flowed over chert banks through the middle of the ranch, quite a refreshing contrast from the nearby Bird Creek, with its red clay banks.

Their courtship was bittersweet, however. He knew when they met that her remission from cancer might be temporary. Their marriage was much more complex than many, because Henry had wanted to make a loving home for her ten-year old son, Jimmy, who'd never known his biological father. He had hoped that this would bring healing to everyone, especially Earlene.

Her agonizing death fifteen months later had brought him much closer to his recently adopted son, and made them both grateful for the loving support of the church. Never having joined his church nor received Christ into her life, Henry worried often about Earlene's soul residing in eternal hell. But he hid this fear from Jimmy, assuring him that they would all be together again someday in heaven. Henry believed with all his soul that if he accepted Christ into his own life, then God might intervene on behalf of Earlene.

Henry's church took the Apocalyptic messages of the Bible literally— which to Henry's point of view was absolutely correct. He'd always found John's Revelations more interesting than John's Gospel. There was nothing mythical about the imminent Day of Judgment for him or his congregation.

Quelle

At breakfast the next morning, as the group sat around Aunt Mary's kitchen table, Christina knew that she had made the right decision, although dangerous travel was nothing new for her. Both Maureen and Mary were relieved that she wouldn't be going to Cairo alone, and even her brother Ryan thought it was a good idea.

"Do you think Christina will have any problems traveling in a Muslim country?" asked Maureen, still the protective mother.

"Not really," reassured Ryan. "I travel in that part of the world often, and there are so many tourists in Cairo, I don't think it would be dangerous." He paused for a minute. "Unless she gets out into the countryside, where the Coptic Christians are sometimes persecuted. They are a small minority there, you know."

"Well, what about Colby's…situation?" asked Maureen, glancing quickly at her sister and touching her on the arm. She didn't mean to stir up memories.

"You're right. That's something else. I still think she'll be all right if she doesn't wander far from Cairo. He looked to see if his remarks had been comforting to their mother, and added, "If Henry doesn't accompany you, I'd be happy to, but I can't get away immediately."

"Thanks anyway. Traveling with Henry will be no problem," Christina told him. She was biting her tongue, comparing his safe job at the Cathedral with her recent escapades in the Mayan cave. *Who's he to worry about me?* she thought. Trying to finally change the subject, she said: "Incidentally, I was pleased to hear about your progress in the Church. I wanted to tell you again this morning how proud I am of you." She smiled proudly at her mother. "Andy might be our first American Pope."

Aunt Mary had been deep in thought since Maureen's comment about Colby, and she spoke out suddenly as though just remembering something. "Christina, I almost forgot. I want to give you a folder I found on Colby's desk. I'll be back in a minute."

She returned moments later with the folder and handed it to Christina. "I think this is related to his trip to Cairo," Mary told her. "He was excited about finding some early Christian documents. He said it might be the most important discovery of his lifetime, if he were successful, but that it might also be just another blind alley."

Christina looked to see her name was inscribed on the folder, along with another word she didn't recognize: *Quelle*. Inside the folder Christina found two letters and a photograph. In the photograph Colby was standing in front of a mosque. One of letters appeared to be a lab report, but there was no company letterhead and no name or address. It bore the initials "M.S.', and described a small papyrus fragment, which the author had carbon-dated to the late first century A.D.

"That's not long after the death of Christ," said Ryan, looking over her shoulders. "It would be the oldest copy of the New Testament. That would be astonishing."

"How could that be the oldest?" asked Maureen, looking somewhat troubled. "Weren't the New Testament Gospels written by the disciples?"

"Of course they were, but most of the copies in existence date from the Middle Ages," explained Ryan. "There is a tiny fragment of St. John's Gospel believed to be as old as 125 A.D., and there are a few other fragments from the third century. A complete copy of a New Testament Gospel dating as early as the first century A.D. would be extremely exciting to the world of Christianity." He shook his head in wonderment to emphasize his feeling.

The other letter was hand-written in Italian. Christina didn't bother trying to struggle with the Italian, she simply gave it to Ryan.

"You can read Italian, can't you?" teased Christina, as she handed him the letter.

"I'll give it my best."

After reading it silently to himself, he coughed and said, "This letter was written by someone at the Vatican. I can tell by the paper it is written on." He held the paper to the kitchen light to show the watermark. "Is the envelope in the folder?"

Christina handed him the envelope, which she noticed bore a postmark from the Vatican.

"I thought so," said Ryan. "I look forward to these letters, although they come all too seldom. It's like getting a letter from the corporate office."

"What does it say?" implored Christina, impatiently.

"It says that the document they've been discussing is very important to the Catholic Church and that Colby should be extremely cautious." He paused. "It sounds to me like the Church wanted to purchase it from him, or perhaps have it donated to the Church. Which means he must have found whatever it is? Maybe it's in the vault? The earliest words of Christ might actually be in the vault!"

"This whole thing sounds complicated to me...and time consuming," Christina concluded, "but this is the least I could do for Uncle Colby. It's a good thing that I'm on a research sabbatical and don't have to be back at Harvard teaching classes, although my research has never been more demanding."

"You wouldn't reconsider my offer would you, little sister?" asked Ryan. "I might be able to take off a little time for this assignment."

Christina glanced at him oddly. He only called her little sister when he wanted something.

Gathering Firewood
1945
Upper Egypt, near the Nile River

And he said, "Whoever finds the interpretation of these sayings will not experience death."

—Gospel of Thomas
Nag Hammadi Library

Two peasants, their camels hobbled nearby, were shoveling a loose material into their saddlebags.

In the background, high above on the face of cliff Jabal al-Tarif, were hundreds of caves, some natural and some cut and painted as grave sites over 4000 years ago. Most of the burial tombs had been emptied by the ravages of time, including desert winds and grave robbers.

The place was called Nag Hammadi, and the two brothers were members of the al-Samman clan. They were there to collect a natural fertilizer for their fields near al-Qasr, a small hamlet on the ancient site of Chenoboskeia.

The site where they normally gathered fertilizer was depleted, so they were trying a new spot which looked more promising. It was near the edge of a large boulder which had fallen onto the talus from high above on the cliff. As they were diligently digging, one of them encountered something solid with his shovel.

"I think it might be too rocky here. Maybe we should move somewhere else," suggested Muhammed 'Ali.

"I'm doing fine, just move over a little toward me," replied his brother Khalifah.

"I've struck it again, whatever it is," complained Muhammed 'Ali. "It doesn't feel like a rock. It feels hollow. I'm going to see what it is."

"Maybe it's a buried treasure—a chest full of gold," joked Khalifah.

As his brother shoveled the talus to the side, he exposed a portion of a large earthen jar. He stooped to brush away the loose material. When they realized that they had discovered something quite extraordinary, perhaps an old burial urn or something, they began digging feverishly. Once enough of the jar was showing, they began pulling on it with all their might to free it from its talus tomb.

"What is it?" Muhammed 'Ali asked. "See how the top is sealed."

"It looks like a burial urn to me," warned Khalifah. "Leave it alone. If you break it, you might free the *jinns* and bring us all bad luck."

"Or it might be filled with coins, possibly gold coins, or jewelry from the pharaohs. This could be the answer to all our problems. Maybe we won't have to haul fertilizer to the fields anymore," argued his brother. "Remember the story our grandfather told us about a neighbor finding buried treasure?"

"He said he found some useless things that the people in Luxor were willing to buy, but they didn't get very much money and that was a long way from here," qualified Khalifah.

"Well, this might be different. It might be gold or silver," his brother persisted. "I'm going to open it."

"And I'm going to stand behind this boulder just in case. I think you're crazy."

Muhammed 'Ali raised his mattock above the red earthenware jar, nearly a half meter tall including the neck, and struck the edge against the jar. A 1600-year-old plume of dust sparkled like gold dust in the sunlight, looking very much like an evil spirit. Khalifah had no doubt that his position behind the boulder was the safest place to be.

Muhammed 'Ali eagerly pulled the broken pieces of ceramic away looking for the gold.

Instead, he found thirteen very old books made of papyrus and bound in leather skins. "Books!" His dreams of gold were dashed. His brother was elated that no evil *jinns* appeared to have escaped.

Muhammed 'Ali wrapped the books up in his tunic, hoping someday to make the long trip to Luxor or perhaps to find some other use for their dubious discovery.

• • •

On the way home, as they were skirting the rival village of Hamrah Dum, with whom they had feuded for years, they encountered their blood enemy Ahmad.

He was alone, passing the other way, and they fell upon him with a vengeance.

"Villains, dogs, assassins!" shouted Ahmad, as they knocked him to the ground. Khalifah held his struggling body as his brother stabbed Ahmad repeatedly in the face and chest with his sharp mattock, until he was nearly dead.

"An eye for an eye!" yelled Muhammed 'Ali with a vengeance.

Just before Ahmad's body stopped quivering, Muhammed 'Ali cut open the man's shirt, shoved his knife below the ribs and ripped his stomach open from one side to the other. He then pulled out the entrails, as his brother freed them with his knife, and strewed them on the ground. Next, he thrust his knife up into the rib cage, and after several attempts, cut out the still throbbing heart.

He held it into the air defiantly and yelled out the name of his father, Ali, whom this man had ruthlessly murdered only six months earlier.

They further mutilated the body, chopping off the limbs, and then tossed the heart into a sack to devour later with their family as the ultimate blood revenge.

When they arrived home there was far more excitement over the heart and the slaying of the despised Ahmad than over the useless books, which were thrown into the kindling pile, next to the mud brick oven outside where the animals were kept.

No one could have known, or probably cared, that these were the oldest and most authentic teachings of Jesus of Nazareth, and that the last fires which they escaped were set by the Romans 1600 years ago.

Their mother rose early the next morning to prepare the morning meal and bake the daily bread. She noticed the old and decrepit books, bound in animal hides, and ripped out a few sections for kindling. Soaked in a little oil, they burned easily and she soon had a small flame, to which she added a few more wadded pages. She enjoyed the unusual color of the flames, leaping high and bright inside the blackened oven.

She turned her gnarled and experienced fingers to the task of grinding the meal and making dough for the bread. She was grateful to Allah for the food to feed her family, and for the fuel for the fire; they were both difficult to find in her barren world. The demands in her life allowed only a brief flicker of happiness in her dark eyes.

During the ensuing police investigation of Ahmad's murder, Muhammed 'Ali gave some of the books to a Coptic priest at the nearby Christian Orthodox Church for safe keeping. The remainder he kept for himself and for his mother's mud brick oven.

This innocent deed launched an complicated odyssey of greed and deception which would not cease for many years.

• • •

The Coptic priest showed one of the codices to his brother-in-law, a local history teacher. In due time, the teacher sent it to a friend in Cairo for assessment. The friend exploited the situation by selling the codex to the Coptic Museum in Cairo.

One day in 1947, two years after the codex's discovery, the museum's director Togo Mina showed it to the French Egyptologist, Jean Doresse. Doresse was overwhelmed by what he saw and told Mina that this discovery would mark a new beginning for the study of the origins of Christianity.

The world nevertheless waited twenty-five years for this epoch to begin.

Mina later learned of a second manuscript held by Albert Eid, a Belgian antiquities dealer, in Cairo. Once Doresse had authenticated this second codex, Mina tried to convince Eid into donating it to the museum. Instead Eid smuggled it to the US, where he tried repeatedly but futilely to sell it at an inflated price.

In 1949, frustrated by events, Eid hid his codex in a safe deposit box in Belgium. Meanwhile various institutions, especially the Orthodox churches, were attempting to gain control of the documents. Eid was sued by the Egyptian government for smuggling, but died before the case could be resolved. In 1952 his widow, at the urging of a professor named Gilles Quispel, secretly sold the codex to the Jung Institute in Zurich for $8,000.

Quispel then published the codex, known as the Gospel of Thomas, in 1959, an act which was met with indifference by the religious establishment. The experts had safely, and mistakenly, dated it much later than the canonical New Testament. This gospel also made no mention of the Christian kerygma or the life of Jesus, and was therefore considered only marginally valuable to New Testament historians.

Nothing could have been more misguided.

Meanwhile, most of the remaining codices discovered by Muhammed 'Ali fell into the hands of a one-eyed outlaw, who sold them to an antiquities dealer named Phocion Tano, who often represented the Italian collector, Maria Dattari, in Cairo.

In 1948, just before Eid smuggled his codex to the US, Tano tried to sell his codices to the Cairo Museum, but the Egyptian government threatened to nationalize them if the price was too high. Four years later, in 1952, the government acquired all of the codices for a very low price.

Dattari was angry at the low price and brought a lawsuit against the Egyptian government, which she eventually lost three years later. In the interim, the documents were unavailable to the research community.

With all the known codices safely secured inside the Coptic Museum, and all the scoundrels and antiquities dealers on the outside, the drama surrounding the documents should have been ending.

It was in fact just beginning, with the appointment in 1952 of Dr. Pahor Labib as the Director of the Coptic Museum. Unbelievably, for the next twenty years only a few scholars would be permitted research access to the oldest teachings of Jesus, the Nag Hammadi codices.

Breakfast at Heathrow

Both of them had traveled enough that they knew flight delays were inevitable, but they were nevertheless upset with the news.

"The red-eye flight to Heathrow is always tiring, but I got less sleep than usual," complained Henry, who hadn't yet shaved.

"Me too," agreed an exhausted Christina. "I never really got to sleep last night after that horrible movie."

"Too much on our minds," commiserated Henry, as they sat down at the café in the area for international passengers in transit. Christina had tea and a scone, and Henry had hot chocolate and a couple of croissants. They both eyed the many small jars of different jams and jellies with great anticipation.

"After this I might eat a real English breakfast," announced Christina, looking at the next table. The person had two soft-boiled eggs, potatoes, bacon, toast and a grilled tomato.

"Me too," agreed Henry, looking enviously at the same food.

Christina opened one of the small jars and spread marmalade on one piece of her scone. *I've got to know more about this Dr. Parker,* she thought, *but I've already asked Henry several times. He must think I'm fascinated with the man. Oh well, I'm not relenting until I know what happened to Uncle Colby, and Dr. Parker is my only link.*

"Please tell me again what you know about Dr. Parker," she asked.

"I think he is <u>still</u> involved with research into early Christianity and some documents found in Upper Egypt near the Nile River, and he spends a great deal of time at the Coptic Museum in Cairo," said Henry, amused by her persistence.

"What do you know about the Coptic Museum?"

"On our last trip, Colby and I visited the museum, but we didn't see Dr. Parker. It's full of artifacts and old documents. Seems a dreary place to spend six months, if you ask me. It's hotter than an Oklahoma prairie."

I've spent many months in dusty and dreary museums, thought Christina, *and enjoyed every minute.*

"What kind of documents do you think are in Uncle Colby's vault?" she asked. "The kind Dr. Parker is studying?"

"I doubt it. It would more likely be a very old copy of a New Testament Gospel."

"Why would someone kill him over that?"

"It would definitely be a conversation piece," smiled Henry, failing at jet lag humor, "and one that an antiquities collector or even one of the churches would be proud to own."

"You don't think a church would kill someone over an old copy of a New Testament Gospel?" said Christina doubtfully.

"It doesn't seem possible in modern times," said Henry, poorly disguising the innuendo.

I wonder if he's implying that my Church might go to such extremes? thought Christina.

"If you want my opinion," volunteered Henry, "and it's nothing more than that, I think Colby got involved with some shady antiquities dealers. He dealt with some desperate characters in his attempts to salvage important documents. And it's somehow related to the vault in Cairo. Whatever is in that vault must be very valuable on the black market. I'm very curious to see what's inside."

"So am I," agreed Christina, wondering again if Dr. Parker was somehow involved in her uncle's demise. If nothing else, his proximity put him high on the list.

"Have you seen the folder Uncle Colby left on his desk?" asked Christina, changing the subject. She pulled it out of her briefcase.

"I doubt if I can be of much help. He didn't include me in many of his private projects."

"Would you mind taking a look anyway?" asked Christina. "Maybe the two of us will come up with some ideas."

She opened the folder and showed Henry the two letters and the photograph.

"I have no idea what these letters are. They have no meaning at all to me," he said, handing them back to Christina. "The same is true of this photo, but I could make an untutored guess about the building."

"What do you think," said Christina. "I'm open to any suggestions."

"Well it looks like a Muslim mosque to me," suggested Henry. "The kind seen in Turkey, and for that matter Cairo."

"Do you think I should show this folder to Dr. Parker?" asked Christina, putting it back in her briefcase. "He might have seen that mosque in Cairo."

"Not as long as he's a suspect," said Henry.

Christina agreed and looked at her watch.

"Let's check the departure monitors and see if there's any good news," she suggested, wiping her mouth with a paper napkin and tossing it on the table.

"Hope springs eternal," responded Henry sarcastically.

• • •

A handsome man was seated across from Christina on the airplane, and she glanced at his wedding band, reflecting on her own choice of career over marriage. She had no regrets—well, not many—but it was a fact that fewer men were available at her age. The ones she found attractive were usually married and busy raising families. She'd met several interesting divorced men, but their lives were too complicated, with children and strained relations from their previous marriages.

An attractive woman, Christina had not been without suitors, including some who wanted to stray from their marriages. A combination of her morality and her early Catholic training made most of these relationships unacceptable. She had decided as a young woman that sex with men that she wouldn't consider marrying was not even a possibility. There had been precious few of these, and she did not remember them fondly.

At age thirty-three, she had long since over-specified her ideal man. She wasn't a fanatic about looks, but she did want him to be attractive: not a Paul Newman, but at least an Alan Alda. She was uncompromising, however, regarding intellect and a passion for life. Her ideal mate would hopefully be a Catholic, at least as serious as herself. More than a theology, the Church had been inextricably woven into the fabric of her family and community. When she was younger, her social activities had revolved around the Church, and it had long since become a reassuring presence. Despite the occasional boredom and redundancy, she'd grown ever more comfortable with the rites and the rituals; at times, she even enjoyed the mindless repetition, perhaps the same way a grandmother enjoys knitting sweaters for loved ones.

Garden City House
Cairo

Jesus said, Let him who seeks continue seeking until he finds.

—Gospel of Thomas
Nag Hammadi Library

They pulled up to the Garden City House, and Dr. Parker welcomed them warmly as they stepped out of the taxi. "Unless I've been terribly misinformed, you're Christina Sheridan," said Dr. Parker, after quickly looking her over. He volunteered a pleasant smile.

"Guilty as charged," Christina said, as the two men exchanged greetings. "My goodness," she continued, trying to disguise her suspicions, "we certainly didn't expect you to be waiting at the entrance for us."

Dr. Parker shrugged. "It's no problem. I thought you might need some help with your bags since our modest boarding house doesn't have the luxury of bellboys. Also, the elevator is one of those old self-service, and I thought I might give you a brief lesson on its eccentricities so that you'll be able to come and go as you please." Then he turned, picked up her bags and led them into the dusty foyer, but her cold manner had not escaped him.

"Thank you," said Christina, surprised at his graciousness. She glanced at the old Arabic inscriptions on the ceilings, which must have been made of gold at one time, but had long since lost their glory.

After an endless ride in the small, antiquated brass elevator, he ushered them out into a modest reception area on the third floor, and he handed them their keys which were already sitting on the counter. "My advice to you is that you try to keep going, because if you nap, you won't sleep a wink tonight because of the time difference."

They nodded agreement, letting him think they were novice travelers.

"Good, because I've asked Mrs. Scarzella to set two extra plates for her delicious spaghetti dinner. You'll need a good meal in your stomach before collapsing for the night."

"That's great," agreed Christina. *He's very considerate,* she thought. *Perhaps a little too much so?*

They left their bags by the counter and followed him into the dining room, where they seated themselves at one of the smaller tables.

Now that's a good looking man, thought Christina, appraising Parker's appearance. *Not bad for an academic.* His tall trim build, maple sugar eyes, dark hair, and strong angular face were definitely appealing, more so than she'd expected. In fact, his pleasant and earnest demeanor was utterly disarming, but she wasn't going to let down her guard until she knew more about her uncle's death.

"As I told you, Henry," Parker was saying, "this boarding house is more modest than you're probably accustomed to, but it's popular among us lowly paid academics because it's reasonably priced, clean, and—to use the old cliché—a home away from home. And Mrs. Scarzella's food is excellent, when she has time to cook." He looked at Christina, uncertain exactly where she fit on the luxury scale, now that she had money...and plenty of it...after Colby's death.

Trying to overcome his fatigue, Henry nodded and replied woodenly, "Thank you for arranging our accommodations. We appreciate it very much." Privately he thought, *It's not exactly the Taj Mahal, but I guess it'll have to do for now, although it could definitely stand a new coat of paint...if they can get off all the old ones.*

"I think it's time for some slightly more formal introductions," said Dr. Parker, stroking his beard. "As you probably know, your uncle was my friend and mentor for many years, and played a very important role in my life. I was shocked when I heard of his death. Please accept my condolences. I too feel his loss deeply and can only imagine what you must be going through."

Sounds too good to be true, thought Christina suspiciously.

"That's very kind," Christina said, with an empathetic nod from Henry. "We were very close; he was like a father to me." She smiled sadly. "I miss him very much."

"I've rarely seen a man so committed to preserving cultural and religious heritages."

"That was Uncle Colby, all right."

"Would you mind telling me about your Mayan research?" asked Parker in an effort to lighten the conversation. "Your uncle told me that you and your colleagues were trying to break a bulldog Englishman's domination of the field."

"Well actually, there was a breakthrough at a recent meeting in Palenque, just prior to my uncle's death" responded Christina, wondering how much to tell him. "Can I assume that you're a linguist too?"

"Yes, but primarily in Biblical languages such as Greek, Aramaic and Hebrew. My specialty is the Coptic language, which I learned from James Robinson. I spend a great deal of time each year translating documents here at the Coptic Museum."

That must be the James Robinson that Uncle Colby mentioned in his Will, remembered Christina.

"Then you'll understand our recent discoveries at Palenque. We confirmed predictions that the hieroglyphs are actually the written Mayan language, and that it's a mixture of logographic and phonetic symbols. They weren't merely mystical ideograms as Thompson had insisted for so many years."

"Amazing. I love to hear about intellectual monopolies being broken. You must all be really proud of your accomplishments."

"Enough about me," Christina said, coloring slightly. She raised her hand as if to silence an objection and added, "No, really." After Riggs laughed appreciatively, she said, "Tell us about your own research. I understand there's at least one monopoly in your field also, Dr. Parker." *If nothing else, he's good with words,* she thought.

"Please call me Riggs," he told her, flashing his ready smile again. "Well, ever since I met Professor Robinson at the Claremont Institute for Antiquity and Christianity, I've shared his passion for breaking the monopoly on the Nag Hammadi codices, Christian manuscripts which were discovered thirty years ago in Upper Egypt.

I'd love to ask him more about Claremont College, thought Christina, *but he's probably sensitive about Harvard. Everyone else is. For all I know, Claremont College is world famous in his field anyway.*

"With the exception of a few inferior translations," Riggs was saying, "these documents have still not been made available to the academic community. They're written in Coptic, my specialty, so you can imagine my eagerness to read them."

"Thirty years?" asked Henry.

"Thirty long years." said Riggs with no trace of humor. "Professor Robinson and I, and Biblical scholars everywhere, are becoming concerned for their safety. You'll see later, if we have time, that they've not been properly protected and are deteriorating badly."

"How could this be?" asked Christina, slowly realizing that whatever else this man might be, he took his academics quite seriously.

"That's a story of its own. It's even more difficult to believe, when you learn that Jean Doresse, the French coptologist, predicted their discovery would mark a new epoch in the study of the origins of Christianity. A new epoch, indeed! We haven't even been able to get our hands on them."

"What's being done to break this monopoly?" asked Christina, fascinated as much by Riggs as his story. His slight southern drawl and the way he peered directly into her eyes mesmerized her like a swinging amulet. *It's a shame he's involved in this mess with Colby,* she thought.

"Professor Robinson's tried everything," Riggs continued. "Nothing has worked, including his many personal audiences with the museum's director, Pahor Labib. Now Professor Robinson's resorting to international politics. He's brought the problem to the attention of UNESCO and is prodding them to set up an oversight committee on the Nag Hammadi codices. We have no idea what this committee will decide, once it meets, but our long term dream would be to prepare a complete edition of photographs of all the Nag Hammadi manuscripts. This would place the discovery at the disposal of scholars worldwide."

"Is the problem with Pahor Labib?" asked Christina, seeing the parallels with Eric Thompson in her own field.

"Not entirely, but Pahor Labib has capitalized on the politics, and he loves to masquerade as a scholar. Those who know him think of him as somewhat vain and pompous. But the Nag Hammadi codices have also been the victims of religious, academic, and even international rivalries for nearly twenty years, involving the French, the Germans, the Protestants, the Muslims, and various orthodox Christian churches."

"Now I understand why Uncle Colby was funding this project," Christina said.

"I have a feeling you two could talk all day about your common interests," interrupted Henry somewhat curtly. He was clearly bored with the conversation, and wanted to get on with the business at hand. "But don't you think we should discuss Colby's vault before it gets much later?"

"Good idea," agreed Riggs, recalling how rude Henry could be at times.

"Did you receive your key?" Henry asked, getting right down to business.

"I did," Riggs replied, "but I have no idea what to do with it. I hope you two know what's going on."

"We know it takes two keys to open the vault, once Henry gets us into the Tiger Oil facility, but we have no idea what might be in the vault."

"Neither do I," said Riggs, "but I think your uncle used it for documents and artifacts in transition...properties he hadn't yet found homes for." He paused for a moment, stroked his beard, and then volunteered, "I have a guess what's in there, but it's only a guess."

"Guess away," said Christina, hoping Riggs might reveal something about his involvement in her uncle's death.

"I think whatever it is, it's somehow related to the Nag Hammadi codices. There are several possibilities. For example, it might be one of the missing codices. Muhammed 'Ali, one of the Bedouin who discovered them, insists there were more codices than are currently at the Coptic Museum."

"And Uncle Colby might have purchased one of these recently?"

"Exactly, but there's also a second possibility. Someone might have found other codices. Not a single cave nor a single shovel of dirt has gone unexamined by the locust of local and foreign hopefuls. They seem oblivious to the ongoing feuds between the nearby villagers."

Riggs continued, his voice betraying a mounting excitement. "We might even find fragments from previously discovered codices. They've been finding fragments in this area since the middle of the 18th century, and some of them might be from Christian manuscripts."

"I'm amazed they're still finding them, but I guess I shouldn't be. The same thing happened with the discovery of new Maya codices."

Riggs offered still another possibility. "Our *treasure* might also be photos of the Nag Hammadi codices."

"That doesn't make sense," said Henry. "Colby would have given them to you and Professor Robinson."

"If he could," responded Riggs. "He might have been legally constrained, at least during his lifetime. I know of other situations, where institutions accepted unofficial funds in exchange for copying privileges. The idea is to have a spare in case the original deteriorates or is somehow destroyed.

"Such copies," he continued, "are usually restricted by contracts. It's possible that Colby had this ace up his sleeve, but was hoping that Professor Robinson would eventually succeed by more direct means."

Henry could stand the anticipation no longer. "Why don't we just go to the vault? I can persuade the security officer to let us in. Otherwise we have to wait until tomorrow morning."

"Let's go," said Riggs, pleased with Henry's enthusiasm.

"Who could sleep now?" agreed Christina, suspicious of Riggs' detailed understanding of Colby's contracts.

Diamond Cutters
1956
England

He stopped to wipe the steam from his glasses and to adjust the light once again. His colleague took the opportunity to breath deeply and sip some lukewarm tea from a nearly empty cup. The cup made a loud noise as it slid from his fingers and hit the saucer.

"Damn," he said, "the more I try not to worry, the more nervous I get. I could never have been a diamond cutter."

"I'm nervous too," answered John Allegro, checking the equipment one more time. "This is worse than diamond cutting. This is the only scroll of its kind, and two thousand years in the desert have made this copper more fragile than a spider web. There's more green oxide than there is copper."

"Let me check the alignment of this blade again," suggested Professor Wright-Baker. "I wish we had the funds to do this right."

John could see that his friend was concerned about the apparatus he had jury rigged for this operation.

"Don't worry," he said, "there's no budget for this, and I take full responsibility. I really appreciate your help on this project. Let's hope the contents of the scroll are worth all this trouble."

They both looked once again at the ancient copper roll, which had become so brittle over the millennia its contents might remain a mystery forever. They planned to cut it with a small circular saw, supported in a sliding carriage, which would hopefully run perfectly true and not shatter the paper thin material. Hints of writing could barely be seen on the outside of the fragile scroll.

"What do you hope to find inside?" asked Professor Wright-Baker.

"I have no idea," answered John Allegro, "but it must be important. It was found with the Dead Sea Scrolls at Qumran, and it's the only one that was written on metal instead of parchment or papyrus."

"That's ironic," observed the Professor, "the one made of copper ended up just as fragile as the ones on parchment."

John smiled. "It is ironic. They must have thought that copper would last forever." He paused in thought. "If they went to all the trouble to put the message on a copper scroll, it must have been something very valuable to them."

"That's what I was thinking," responded his friend.

"Let's just go ahead and cut the damn thing," suggested John. "It's never going to be any easier."

Professor Wright-Baker nodded his head in agreement.

As he placed his hand on the sliding carriage and switched on the small circular saw, he looked at John for reassurance. He wiped sweat from his forehead with his left shoulder as he pushed the spinning blade into the deteriorated scroll. A cloud of ancient green dust spewed into the air.

He stopped, pulled the blade back for a short reprieve, and began once again.

"Damn," he mumbled, as the piece of the scroll dropped onto the table.

"That's O.K.", John quickly assured him. "There's a crack in this part of the roll. You're doing just fine."

"I'm going to need a scotch after this," joked the Professor.

John Allegro picked up the small piece and turned it over carefully. On the inside, hidden all these centuries, was some Hebrew writing.

"Can you make it out yet?" asked his friend, bursting with curiosity.

"Keep cutting," answered John. "It's a list of treasures buried somewhere in Judea."

A smile spread across the face of Professor Wright-Baker. "Maybe that will bolster the research budget at Manchester College," he laughed. "It certainly needs it."

Captive Codices

The combination of the Dead Sea Scrolls and the Nag Hammadi codices will put the New Testament more clearly into context so that the sharp contours of its profile emerge.

—James Robinson
Nag Hammadi Library

A very large man with a magenta birthmark on his left cheek watched them enter the taxi and then followed as they headed toward the business district of downtown Cairo, on the eastern bank of the Nile, where all the oil companies had their offices.

"That will be twenty pounds," said the driver, which brought peals of laughter from Riggs. "You know better," he countered. "I'll pay five, or you can let us out right now." After a short pause, the driver smiled, accepted the offer, and sped off toward the Tiger Oil facility.

Christina wanted to know more about the Nag Hammadi codices. "Why are the Codices so important?" she asked Riggs. "I've heard of the Dead Sea Scrolls, but not these Codices. I know they're different discoveries, but it gets sort of confusing, since one is much more famous than the other."

Before Riggs could reply, Henry scratched his head and asked, "What's the difference between codices and scrolls?"

"Two at once? I'll answer the shortest first. The codex came into existence in the first century as an alternative to the traditional scroll. The codex, or book, was more economical because there could be writing on both sides of each page. It was also easier to access the middle or the end. The scroll, however, remained popular among some cultures, for example the Jews, and for official documents."

"People just got tired of unrolling the scrolls?" asked Henry.

"That's right, especially if the best part was at the end," smiled Riggs. Now for Christina's question. You're right that most people have heard of the Dead Sea Scrolls, but few have heard of the Nag Hammadi codices. I think the proximity of the Dead Sea Scrolls to Jerusalem and the dating to the time of Jesus raised great expectations, among both advocates and opponents of all three Western religions: Christianity, Islam and Judaism."

"What were the dates?"

"The Dead Sea Scrolls were apparently buried around 70 A.D., about thirty-five years after Jesus' crucifixion.   Christians hoped these Scrolls would validate the New Testament, with perhaps some new information about Jesus, and a great deal of publicity exploited this possibility."

"Why would the other religions be interested?"

"Muslims also revere Jesus," continued Riggs, "but they don't accept him as incarnate God; so they would have been pleased if the Dead Sea Scrolls revealed Jesus as just another prophet. As would the Jews, of course, but they also hoped the Scrolls would fill the intertestament gap in Jewish history, the 250-year-period between the Old and the New Testaments, including the destruction of Jerusalem by the Romans and the early development of Rabbinical Judaism."

"Why would agnostics be interested in these Scrolls?" Christina asked.

"Skeptics hope the Scrolls will contain historical facts that would deflate Christian claims for the Christ. Among the most popular is a hope that the resurrection will be shown to be without a historical basis."

"That's not likely," Christina said, reassuring herself.

"In contrast, the Nag Hammadi codices were not buried until late in the fourth century, and they were all written in Egyptian Coptic, instead of Hebrew or Aramaic."

"Coptic..." Christina mused. "Could you tell us a little more about that language, please?" Henry nodded, indicating an interest, but he was quite intent watching the slow progress of the taxi through the crowded streets of Cairo.

"Okay," Riggs said, drawing the word out. He sensed that he was moving too quickly for newcomers. Speaking more carefully, he said, "Coptic is the Egyptian language written with Greek symbols and phonetics. It was introduced in about the second century, and it's now used primarily in the services of the Egyptian Christian Church, also called the Coptic Orthodox Church."

"The other reason the Nag Hammadi codices got less attention than the Dead Sea Scrolls," Riggs continued, "is that they were found in the Upper Nile Valley of Egypt, and were generally believed to be too young...and too Egyptian...to have revealed much about early Christian history."

"Makes sense to me," agreed Christina.

"Except for one thing," added Riggs, about to reveal the basis of his own important mission. Professor Robinson and other New Testament scholars have raised the possibility that the Nag Hammadi codices are in fact Coptic translations of gospels that have never been seen before. He also believes that they may be translations of Greek originals which were about the same age as our New Testament gospels, perhaps even older."

Christina was shocked.

"But that's not possible," Christina argued. "All the gospels are in the New Testament, and they were written by the disciples."

"We don't have time to get into that right now, but the quick answer is that our New Testament only contains some of the gospels, and many others were either omitted or destroyed. The gospels we hope to find in the Nag Hammadi codices could be new ones."

"I'm confused," Henry complained, with an emphatic nod from Christina.

"Let me summarize," Riggs responded. "If Professor Robinson's correct, and there are new gospels in the Nag Hammadi codices, then it could have far more implications for Christianity than the Dead Sea Scrolls. That's why I'm so determined to break the monopoly and get hold of these Codices."

Determined? I should think so, thought Christina, convinced that Parker would have done anything to get his hands on these controversial codices...anything. *This is the boost his drab little career has needed for a long time. A fifth Gospel would certainly put him on the map.*

Henry seemed once again to become interested in the conversation. "Just think, Christina, you might be the co-owner of a new gospel, or at least a very old version of a New Testament Gospel. That's pretty exciting."

"I think I've had more excitement in one month than any human being should be allowed," Christina responded, concealing her suspicions. "First, the breaking of the Maya code, and now the chance that I might be one of the first Christians to read gospels that have been buried for nearly 2000 years!"

Christina was beginning to understand why her uncle gave her the second key. *He must have smelled a rat at the last minute, and wanted me to keep Riggs from getting these new gospels. Perhaps I'm not the only one beguiled by this snake charmer.*

As they drove on in silence, each with their own thoughts on the treasure in Colby's vault, Christina was suddenly shivered with fear: *If I'm right, then Henry and I are next on his list.*

Tiger's Tempest

Recognize what is in your sight, and that which is hidden from you will become plain to you.

—Gospel of Thomas
Nag Hammadi Library

Once the security guard at Tiger Oil recognized Henry, he immediately permitted them entry. He expressed his sympathies for Colby's death and escorted them to the private antiquities vault. Christina thought that the guard seemed uneasy, but attributed this behavior to the unusual hour. She had seen both Henry's and Colby's names on the access log several times, so she knew this was routine. She wondered if the guard was suspicious of Riggs.

The vault, to Christina's surprise, looked more like a walk-in refrigerator than a bank vault. There were gauges showing temperatures and humidity, which the guard explained far beyond their interest...and their patience...as Riggs and Christina inserted their two keys into the locks and pushed open the heavy door.

Once inside the room, which was about the size of a garage, they saw empty shelves on three walls of the room, apparently used by Colby in the past for the storage of artifacts or scrolls. The only exception was a set of special shoe-box size containers, the type used for storing microfiche, which was sitting on the far shelf Beneath the shelves, on one wall, were several lateral file drawers.

Riggs looked at the other two, as if for approval, then opened one of the file drawers. It was full of letter-size photographs. His face was taught with anticipation as he carefully removed one and held it to the light.

Watching Riggs' reaction, Christina assumed that they were photos of the Nag Hammadi codices. "Are they—?"

"No," he mumbled softly. "Whatever these are, they're not written in Coptic. They are definitely not my Nag Hammadi codices...they look like they're written in Hebrew and Aramaic," he said, frantically thumbing through the file. "Now I'm really confused."

Christina saw a bleak look on his face and realized that Riggs was nearly devastated. She wasn't sure exactly what all this meant. On the one hand, it was clear that he had let his hopes for the Nag Hammadi codices soar too high. On the other, his motive for killing Colby had instantly disappeared.

"Well, whatever this proves to be, it must be something valuable, or Colby wouldn't have put us to all this trouble," he theorized as he began to open one drawer after another. Henry and Christina joined the search, and soon it became clear that the files were full of similar photographs.

In desperation, Riggs opened one of the smaller boxes on the back shelf and verified that it contained microfiche. So did the other two boxes. He then put on a white cotton glove, laying nearby, and pulled several from the boxes. Henry and Christina waited anxiously as he slid the first one into the fiche reader.

"It looks like the same documents as the photographs; they're also written in Hebrew and Aramaic. I don't know what these are. It'll take me a little while to translate one of them," he said, turning to the task.

Henry, obviously frustrated by the delays, opened the last file drawer, the one nearest the door. It was empty except for a single folder. "Maybe this is important," he exclaimed, pulling the folder from the drawer. "It must be some sort of master file."

Inside was a letter from Colby to a man named John Allegro, explaining the contents of the vault. Colby had drawn a line, apparently hastily, through Allegro's name and under it had written *Riggs and Christina.* The first paragraph of the letter was brief but devastatingly to the point. The files, Henry read, contained a complete photographic set of the Dead Sea Scrolls.

"Well, I'll be...!" gasped Riggs, normally in control of his words. "Colby somehow got photos of the Dead Sea Scrolls, including the ones under close wrap at the Museum in East Jerusalem. We're looking at photographs of the most controversial documents west of the Indus River. Unbelievable, simply unbelievable!"

Christina wasn't sure of the importance of this discovery, at least not from an academic standpoint, but she did know that she had been completely wrong about Riggs. It was clear that he actually had no idea what was in the vault, and it was also clear that Uncle Colby had completely trusted Riggs. Why else would he have substituted both their names for this Allegro fellow? It was now evident to her that Allegro was the culprit, not Riggs, since Colby had removed Allegro's name at the last minute and changed the keys.

"How in the world did Uncle Colby get the Dead Sea Scrolls?" asked Christina rhetorically, trying to regain her equilibrium.

Riggs shook his head. "I don't know." Then he stared intently at the photos in his hand. "Apparently no one knows of the existence of these photos. No one except Allegro, of course. Somehow your uncle managed to have the original Scrolls photographed and kept it a secret all this time."

"What does this mean?" asked Christina, troubled by her new responsibility.

"It means that we just sailed into the biggest storm currently raging in biblical scholarship. Every Bible scholar I know would kill to see these photos."

Christina looked at him warily, thinking of Colby's recent fate.

Seeing in Christina's expression that he had chosen the wrong phrase, he decided to try once again: "Well, they would do almost anything...uh...I mean...the debate around them is extremely heated, and we just inherited nothing but trouble.

The three of them sat quietly, reflecting on the situation.

Finally, Christina broke the silence: "In other words, these Scrolls could well have been the reason for Uncle Colby's death."

"I'm afraid so," said Riggs, as they turned to Henry who continued reading the rest of the Allegro letter.

The letter explained that soon after portions of the Scrolls were assembled in the Palestinian sector of Jerusalem, a group including Tiger and a member of the Bechtel family were allowed to make photographs in return for a timely and generous donation. The French Catholics at the nearby Ecole Biblique, who were part of the International Team translating the documents, had been concerned that these Scrolls might further deteriorate or that they might be damaged in some military action. Colby later made the same agreement with the Israelis for the portion of the Scrolls controlled by them. In both cases he promised secrecy unless something happened to the originals.

Colby had honored this promise since 1961, but the prolonged delays in publication by the International Team had caused him to reconsider. If necessary, and only as a last resort, he would reverse his promise in order to break the monopoly, convinced that the Dead Sea Scrolls belonged to the world, not to one religious or academic group.

"I'm confused," Christina said. "Uncle Colby's letter to Allegro raises more questions than it answers."

"Like what?" asked Riggs. He had his own thoughts on the matter, but wanted to know Christina's views.

"Okay," she began. "Why do the Israelis have some Scrolls and an International Team the others? How did the Palestinians get involved? What is the role of the French Catholics, and why have there been delays in publication? Was there concern that Uncle Colby might publish his photos of the Scrolls? Who is John Allegro, and why did Uncle Colby change Allegro's involvement before his own death? Does Allegro know anything about Uncle Colby's death? Worse yet, is he somehow involved?"

"Is that your only question?" laughed Riggs.

Christina smiled weakly in response, still tangled in her thoughts. She knew that her Church would not delay publication. *Quite the contrary*, she thought, *they'd be anxious to share the good news with Christians around the world.*

Sensing her quandary, Riggs continued, "I could probably answer many of your questions, but it'll take some time."

"Many...?" Christina said. "Not all, then?"

"Not all," Riggs confirmed. I don't know that much about Allegro. I've met him, but..."

"But what?"

Riggs sighed. "Ease off, mate. I'll do my best to answer your questions, but I don't respond well to the Harvard offense."

"You're right," she apologized, "my curiosity got the best of me, and it's been a long day. Maybe we should call it a night."

"I'm heavily reefed too," said Riggs, "and we lost Henry a long time ago."

She turned to see Henry aimlessly opening one file drawer after another, as if hoping to find one more surprise.

"So what do we do now?" asked Christina.

"Well, I hate to say it, since you just got here, but we really ought to go see Allegro in Jerusalem."

"I think you're right," she agreed, knowing that Allegro was now the link to Colby's death. "What do you know about Allegro?" she probed as nicely as possible.

"I know that he was the only agnostic on the otherwise Christian International Team assigned to the Dead Sea Scrolls, the ones dominated by the French Catholics at the Ecole Biblique. When the publications were delayed, Allegro precipitated an immense feud by going to the press with his side of the story."

"Would that have caused Uncle Colby to change Allegro's role at the last minute?"

"It's certainly possible," responded Riggs. "Even though your uncle enjoyed breaking monopolies, Allegro's effectiveness must have been damaged by all that notoriety."

Christina sat quietly for a minute. The only sounds were those of Henry futilely opening and closing file drawers and fluorescent lights buzzing overhead.

"I think we should all three go to Jerusalem," she finally volunteered, "and maybe then we can figure out what to do with these Scrolls."

● ● ●

Later, as they walked down the hall of the Garden City House toward their rooms, Henry said, "If you two can get along without me, I'm going to head back to Tulsa tomorrow. There isn't really that much more for me to do here."

"I had hoped you would go with us to Jerusalem," said Christina, showing her disappointment. *I really don't want to travel alone with Parker,* she thought. *Why is Henry abandoning me so quickly?*

"As you know, there's still a great deal of work remaining on Colby's estate, and you're in good hands now."

Good hands? she thought. *What's so good about Parker and Allegro? At least one of them is a problem.*

She decided to conceal her concerns, for the moment, and responded bravely. "You've been very helpful," she said giving him a hug as they stopped at his door. "I'm sure Uncle Colby would have been grateful for all the assistance you've given me."

"Thanks," he said reddening a little, "and keep me posted on what you learn about Allegro and that International Team. Meanwhile, I'll try to see if Colby put anything in writing with de Vaux...especially with regard to a secrecy agreement."

As Christina walked down the hall toward her room, Henry pulled Riggs toward him discreetly and whispered: "I'll be investigating Colby's death and would appreciate any suggestions you might have. Based on your remarks tonight, I'm convinced that the French Catholics are not beyond suspicion: they certainly had a motive to get control of Colby's Dead Sea photos."

Riggs took a half-step back, surprised to learn that Colby's death might not have been an accident.

• • •

Once inside his room, Riggs stood thoughtfully, checked his watch, did a quick calculation, and dialed the overseas operator.

"Thank goodness you're in the office," he said, with a sigh of relief, when Professor Robinson answered his phone despite the time difference.

"Riggs, is that you?"

"You won't believe what happened to me today, James," he began, eager to share the contents of Colby's vault.

"It would have to be really good to beat my day," said James Robinson, holding the phone with his shoulder so he could continue arranging papyri fragments on his desk.

"All right," said Riggs, knowing he'd win in the end. "Tell me what happened to you."

"We finally made some progress on the Nag Hammadi codices. Today I received a call from Bammate at UNESCO, and they've not only agreed with the Egyptian government to form an Oversight Committee, they've asked me to be the chairman."

"That's wonderful, James," Riggs said, sharing his favorite professor's good fortune. As chair, Robinson would finally have chaperoned access to the Codices, whether the Museum Director, Pahor Labib, liked it or not.

"Do you plan to accept the position?" he asked in mock seriousness.

"I'm giving it some thought," Robinson bantered back. He'd fully expected some kidding from Riggs on the subject. "Now what were you going to tell me?"

"I first have a question," replied Riggs. "Does that mean that you can make copies available to everyone?"

"Not unless I can convince the committee, and that might take some time," he answered reluctantly, knowing how desperately Riggs would like to get his hands on the Codices.

Riggs was silent, wondering if Robinson's appointment as Chairman would lead to anything more than his own personal access to the Codices...which was at least a step in the right direction, but certainly not enough for Riggs.

"So, what's your good news?" said Professor Robinson, breaking the uncomfortable silence and getting back to their conversation.

"Not that much, really, except I own a complete photographic set of the Dead Sea Scrolls, both the Israeli Scrolls and the ones controlled by the International Team," Riggs said flatly. He waited for the fish to pick up the lure and carry it a few feet. Then he planned to set the hook.

"The Dead Sea Scrolls?" repeated Professor Robinson, incredulously. "You wouldn't kid a friend about something that serious, would you?" He turned away from his desk, leaned back in his chair, and moved his heavy glasses to the top of his head.

"No, it's true," laughed Riggs. "I'll bet you're sorry now that you bothered me with the trivial news about UNESCO."

The lively long-distance conversation that followed put a major dent in Riggs' meager research budget. They reveled in their simultaneous successes, and Robinson agreed that the pledge of secrecy on the Dead Sea Scroll photos must be honored, at least for now, and that he should immediately visit Allegro to see why he was dropped at the last minute. Robinson warned Riggs that Allegro had created so much controversy that his credibility was now seriously in question. He suggested a cautious and guarded approach to Allegro.

"Allegro should have stuck with scholastics instead of politics," said Robinson. "I have a very high regard for both Father de Vaux and Frank Cross, and I see no basis for Allegro's theory about a Catholic conspiracy." He regretted the Insider's monopoly, however, and was pleased that they now held the trump card, if it was needed later."

"One more thing," said Riggs.

"Should I sit down this time?" he joked.

"It's almost that good," he said, baiting him with a long pause. "It takes two keys to open the vault. The other one's owned by Tiger's niece, an attractive young woman and an accomplished Mayan scholar."

"I can't wait to meet her," said Professor Robinson. "In fact, I'll be there in three days." He chuckled and added mischievously, "Remember the saying about all work and no play?"

"Hey, I saw her first," protested Riggs. "And <u>now</u> the bad news."

"How could a good-looking American woman in the Egyptian desert be bad news?"

"She's a *Haah-vaadh* type."

"What's wrong with that? Some of our best friends are at Harvard."

"Well this one gives new meaning to the stodgy Harvard stereotype...she's colder than a Boston winter."

"I can't believe she could resist your southern charm for long" said Robinson.

• • •

Christina lay awake in her room...unable to sleep...thinking about Uncle Colby's death and the Dead Sea Scrolls. She had more questions than answers.

She missed her uncle more than usual at times like these. In the past, she would have picked up the phone and shared her activities with him, but now she faced the harsh finality of his death. This aching emptiness, she feared, would never be filled.

Her thoughts turned to the folder he left on his desk. *What was he trying to tell me?* She strained to find a connection between its contents and the surprising events of the day. Instead of finding answers in the vault, she had found even more questions, and worse yet, she had learned nothing about his death.

Searching her mind, she tried to find possible links between the folder and the photos of the Dead Sea Scrolls. Could the fragment which was carbon-dated in the laboratory report simply be from one of the actual Dead Sea Scrolls? The first century date seemed about right. Could the letter from the Vatican priest have been referring to the Dead Sea Scrolls? If so, how did that tie in with the French Catholics on Allegro's International Team? They had their own Scrolls, so they had no obvious motive to get their hands on Uncle Colby's photos...unless, of course, they feared that he would publish them. She could think of no link at all between the Dead Sea Scrolls and the photograph of Colby in front of a mosque, although she had seen several mosques during the ride from the airport.

If I could find that mosque in Cairo, she thought, *it might give me a lead on his death. Might give me a lead...everything is a might.*

But the biggest question of all was how any of this tied to Colby's high level of excitement about the trip to Cairo. He had never asked her to join him before, and he had definitely sounded nervous. He had even described some manuscript as "the biggest discovery of his lifetime," which would hardly describe some old photos in his vault...even photos of the Dead Sea Scrolls. There was something very important still missing.

Perhaps John Allegro is that something? she puzzled. There certainly was no doubt about his motive. According to Riggs, Allegro wanted to get his hands on the Dead Sea Scrolls…one way or another.

Riggs, she thought, as she began to fall asleep. *I don't think I disguised my suspicions of him very well. No wonder he got so irritable.*

Questor

In spite of his striking good looks, Riggs Parker had never been married. There had been close calls, of course, the closest being Frances Snow, an attractive, outgoing young woman. But his academic interests had always come first. She eventually tired of the pursuit and married a policeman who shared her enthusiasm for a large family. Riggs had made his choice, but her decision nevertheless hurt him quite deeply. Since then, he had been more honest with himself, and acknowledged that at this stage of life, his career was the top priority.

Intensely serious about his research, Riggs unwittingly intimidated others with his intellectual rigor and his boundless energy. Like many academics, he sometimes immersed himself in his research for days on end. He had earned two Doctor of Theology degrees, from the University of Basel and from Princeton. His minor was in biblical languages, where he proved to have a natural talent.

Dr. Parker's presentations at the Society of Biblical Literature were always well attended. His talks consisted of brilliant scholarship presented in an entertaining style. Although he was relatively young, his peers were already according him second place, behind only Professor Robinson, in the unofficial pecking order. Robinson's extraordinary capabilities and unmatched courage eclipsed everyone in modern biblical scholarship.

Riggs was not nearly as pious as Dr. Robinson, whose Presbyterian parents had subjected him to a disciplined Calvinist upbringing. Riggs was respectful of the Christian church, but brutally impartial in his assessment of the historical foundations of the New Testament. He believed in letting the facts speak for themselves. Many of his colleagues suspected that his objectivity regarding the historical Jesus sometimes put him well outside even the most liberal Christian scholars

Religious in his own way, however, Riggs considered blind faith to be worse than no faith at all. He had tried to position his own Christian beliefs so that they could withstand future scholarly revelations. He had come to believe that faith in traditional Christian creeds and doctrines was less important than following Jesus' teachings, at least for his own destiny.

He believed that the true teachings of Jesus had been lost or distorted by the Christian churches over the centuries, and his mission in life was to find the most authentic versions of these teachings. His search for the unabridged words of Jesus had brought him to Cairo, to the Nag Hammadi codices, which were hidden in the desert sands since the days of the New Testament.

Fishawi's Tea House

"You can stuff that right up your ass," said the very large man angrily, as he slammed his Zippo lighter down on the small table between them. The other man winced and glanced around the room at all the other people. As he feared, most of them were staring disapprovingly at the two of them, but there was nothing he could do. The situation was completely out of his control.

The room was full of smoke, and smokers, and tables full of small coffee cups, which were being constantly refilled with a strong brew of Turkish coffee. Each person was drawing smoke through the long colorful hoses which protruded from their ornate brass water pipes; the bubbles were rising through the colored liquids, cradled in elaborately decorated glass containers. It looked very much like a small symphony orchestra of hubble bubble pipes, except that all the players were as old as desert sands, and the only sound made by the instruments was the gurgling of smoke bubbles.

A man with no future, and even less change in his pocket, passed among the pipes with a bucket of hot embers, prepared just minutes before, which he heaped on top of the smoldering tobacco in each pipe: tobacco zealously chosen by each smoker from a lifetime of experience. The gnarly old ember man, with desert dried skin, was fortunate to receive anything more than a puff of smoke in his face, as he groveled among the tables hoping for a few coins. His hands were blackened and twisted, probably forever, from his charcoal trade and from polishing the shoes of the customers, while they puffed away on the proprietor's pipes and downed almost pure caffeine.

I don't know how I let him talk me into meeting here, thought the quieter man, as he looked around the room in dismay. *How was I to know that a tea house would be full of old men smoking these awful water pipes, and that it would be impossible to breath.*

At that very moment the larger man drew his lungs full of the foul, smoky concoction, causing his pipe to shake from the boiling bubbles, and defiantly blew dark billows of smoke into the smaller man's face. The quieter man's coughing and wheezing which followed, brought him a great deal of pleasure, as he laughed and tended to his own embers.

"You might not like what happened," bellowed the larger man defiantly, as he leaned over and pushed his face threateningly across the table, "and neither do I, but it was an accident, and there's no going back. You're in this as deep as I am, unless you want to run to the police with your half of the story."

The smaller man shrank back in his chair and shook his head slowly from side to side. He knew that he would be implicated in Colby's death, whether it was an accident or not, and that this lunatic could take him down with him if the authorities got involved. *I hate to admit it, but I'm in this as deep as he is now,* he thought.

At that moment the angry man swung his half empty coffee cup down on the table, startling everyone around, and captured a large cockroach scampering across the surface. A sinister smile broke the lines on his face like shattered glass as he grabbed one of the embers with his tongs and began to roast the squirming bug in the palm of his hand. The quieter man became ill from the stench of burning flesh...he was certain most of it was human.

The larger man never even flinched as he pushed his burning palm, bug and all, into the face of the other, causing him to reel back in terror and disgust. He then picked up a fresh ember and held it close to the smaller man's eyes, forcing him back against the yellowed wall, as the other men looked away in fright.

"You and I are partners now," he growled in a low voice. "Isn't that right?"

The trembling man nodded his agreement, and pulled back to the table as the ember was dropped back on top of the tobacco in the chillum bowl.

"You've got to get the manuscript, or this whole thing is for nothing," he whispered cautiously, hoping his new *partner* had regained his composure. "And there's really only one chance for that."

"What's that?"

"Don't lose site of his niece, Christina," said the nervous man. "She'll hopefully lead us to the manuscript."

The wine-colored pigment on the side of the larger man's face seemed brighter, as the old men in the tea house began, once again, to enjoy their tobacco and coffee.

Lost Gospels

Peter said to Mary, Sister, we know that the Savior loved you more than the rest of women. Tell us the words of the Savior which you remember—which you know (but) we do not, nor have we heard them.

—Gospel of Mary
Nag Hammadi Library

"Would you like to see the Nag Hammadi codices at the Coptic Museum in Old Cairo?" Riggs asked, trying to melt the Boston ice, and knowing that any serious Mayanist would find it great fun.

"I'd love it," beamed Christina, with a smile Riggs couldn't miss. "Assuming your tour also takes in the pyramids.".

"Why not, if we have time? "Incidentally," explained Riggs, always the organizer, "I've made an appointment for us with John Allegro in Jerusalem tomorrow, and Pahor Labib is expecting us this morning at the Coptic Museum. I also have an early lunch planned at a favorite place, if you can survive for now on a Danish from Mrs. Scarzella."

"I can, but I really could use some exercise after all that time in the plane."

Riggs gave her a curious look, realizing from her feline figure that she must normally get plenty of exercise. "It's a nice brisk walk from here to the bus stop. Or we could walk the three miles to Old Cairo," he joked. You can decide later," he said, holding back the brass folding gate on the old elevator. He led the way out the front door, turned right toward Tahrir Square, and began weaving his way through traffic like a nimble soccer player. They had joined the not-so-holy civil war between the taxis and the pedestrians.

Christina thought how much different the people looked than she had expected. Many of the men wore flowing galabias, afghans really, in dark muted colors. All of the women, rather than being dressed in black, wore modest Western clothes, and honored their Muslim traditions by framing their Egyptian faces with colorful scarves. To her, they looked very much like stylish nuns.

They were lucky to find seats near the back of the crowded bus, which made its way laboriously south along Kasr Al Eini toward Old Cairo.

"Isn't this more fun than a taxi?" asked Riggs.

"Much better," she agreed, "I always try to ride the buses in other countries to get a feel for the culture."

"Me too," agreed Riggs, thinking there might be hope for this haughty millionaire after all.

They seemed to be at a loss for words.

"Wasn't that something last night, finding photos of the Dead Sea Scrolls? It must have been a real shock to you," volunteered Christina, trying to make conversation. "I had no idea what we would find, and yet it was a shock to me too."

"Shock is the right word. I can't say that I'm disappointed, because the Scrolls are a real treasure, but I would have been much happier if we had found photos of the Nag Hammadi codices."

"Which reminds me," continued Christina, "I wanted to ask you some questions about your Codices..."

"Sure," he interrupted.

"...after I give you some important details about myself."

He looked at her oddly and nodded for her to begin.

"I think it's important for you to know that I'm a Catholic...Irish Catholic...from a very Catholic family...with a priest for a brother. Although I don't go to church very often anymore, I still consider myself a believer."

Riggs hid his disappointment. *That's a shame*, he thought. *She was just starting to dismount from her Harvard high horse, and now I have to guard every word I say. This woman is a real challenge.*

She saved Riggs the task of finding a response. "I was bothered last night," she continued, "by some of the things you said about Christian history and your Codices. Could you please explain it again."

"Are you certain you want to pursue it this early in the day?" he said with hesitation.

"I'll try to listen with a scholar's ear," she insisted.

That's nothing but good intentions, he thought. *If it's the first time she's heard this stuff, it'll be threatening to her beliefs no matter how hard she tries. Talk about bad luck. I'm absolutely the worst person for this job...I even scare my liberal friends at times, let alone a staunch Catholic.*

"First you need to know," he began cautiously, "that many New Testament scholars have lost confidence in the Gospels as historical documents. I'm afraid there's little historical basis for many of the claims by the orthodox churches."

"What do you mean by *orthodox* churches?"

"I mean the Catholic and Greek Orthodox churches and most of the Protestant churches that broke away after Martin Luther...those that believe in some version of the Apostles' Creed."

"The Catholics were the first, of course," confirmed Christina proudly.

"You won't get an argument out of me on that, but you might with the Greeks and the Egyptians."

"I know about the Greek Orthodox Church, but is there also an Egyptian Orthodox Church?"

"That's where we're headed," smiled Riggs. "It's right next door to the Coptic Museum. The Christian church here, called either Egyptian

Orthodox or Coptic, represents a small but venerable minority in predominantly Muslim Egypt…a precarious minority, I might add."

"Is it aligned with larger Christian churches?" asked Christina naïvely.

"Oh no, the Coptic Church has been fiercely independent of both the Roman and the Greek churches since its schism over theological and political differences in the fifth century, about a hundred years after the Nag Hammadi codices were buried."

"Okay, now here's my real question: How could the Codices threaten the orthodox churches?"

"Are you really ready for this?" he asked again.

"Of course I am…I think."

"Most scholars agree that the Gospels were not written by the disciples," he explained cautiously, "and the Gospels in our New Testament were only a few of many gospels in circulation at the time. Other gospels were either destroyed or banned by the Church fathers because they didn't agree with the early creeds."

"Meaning the Apostles' Creed?" confirmed Christina.

"Basically." He looked at her face to see her reaction. "Is this subject too sensitive for you?" he asked.

"Well, I don't believe a word of what you're saying, but you might as well continue. You've definitely raised my curiosity."

"It gets much more controversial," he continued. "Most of the New Testament can be traced to Paul, not to Jesus, and the four Gospels aren't independent accounts, but largely modifications of Mark's Gospel and earlier oral history. The claims by church officials of historical accuracy are impossible to defend."

"That certainly doesn't prove that the events in the New Testament never happened," challenged Christina.

"Not at all. It simply means that they have less historical basis than is usually claimed, and this comes at a time when the Christian churches are also facing the scientific challenges of evolution, DNA, and the Big Bang theory. They are facing two threats simultaneously, one outside and one inside."

"Why one inside?" asked Christina, as they passed yet another Muslim mosque.

"Most New Testament scholars are affiliated with orthodox churches and their research has become embarrassing, if not downright confronting to their sponsors."

"You mean they hold academic positions sponsored by the churches?"

"That's the conflict in many cases."

Christina then asked, "Where do the Nag Hammadi codices enter into this debate?"

Although he knew she wouldn't relish the answer, Riggs replied: "Professor Robinson and I believe that some of the Codices are actually

72

gospels that were politically unfavorable to the Church and thought to have been destroyed by the Roman armies."

"I don't believe the Church would ever destroy gospels," said Christina defensively, "but I'm nevertheless curious about gospels that have escaped editing almost 2000 years...by hiding in the ground. I'd like to see those myself."

"Well, we're almost there, and you'll be able to do just that, assuming Pahor Labib will give you more than five minutes with the Codices, which is unlikely...and that you can read Coptic," he joked.

"It all sounds unlikely to me," concluded Christina. "The odds are against your Codices actually being lost gospels. Haven't you been able to read parts of them, after all the time you've spent at the Coptic Museum?"

"They're locked in cabinets in the Old Library, which is hard to get into, but I've managed to spend some sleepless nights reading ones I've found on Pahor's desk. I know there are several gospels we've never seen before, but I haven't had enough time to read them carefully."

"What kind of gospels?" asked Christina skeptically.

"Well, there's the Gospel of Mary," baited Riggs, knowing he would get her attention.

Christina reacted strongly, but more favorably than he had anticipated. "You might have a gospel written by a woman? That would be interesting, after the men have controlled everything for two millennia."

"It's been longer than that," corrected Riggs, "and I'm afraid none of the gospels, even this one, were actually written by the people for whom they are named. They were just attributed to them many years later, probably to enhance their credibility."

"We'll agree to disagree on that point," Christina declared, feeling quite confident that the Gospels were written by St. Matthew and the other disciples. "However, I would love to read what Mary Magdalene had to say about Jesus, even though she wasn't a disciple."

"We probably wouldn't agree on that either, but I've read parts of her gospel, and it's very interesting," he said. "We call her Mary of Magdala, incidentally."

"So you believe Mary Magdalene, excuse me, Mary of Magdala, was a disciple?" she asked.

"Maybe his favorite," he smiled mischievously, as they stepped off the bus near the Church of the Holy Virgin, and headed for the Coptic Museum next door.

Ancient Tinder

The morning light filtered through the wooden filigreed windows of the high-beamed Old Library where the Codices were stored. Christina cradled a fragile codex in both hands, with the temerity of a father holding his first newborn baby. She couldn't believe that this ancient manuscript had survived all those centuries entombed in the desert sands. Miraculously, it was in even better condition than the Maya codices half its age. She shivered at the thought that she might be holding the word of God...or the anti-Christ. Either way, this was no ordinary book. Her hands trembled at the thought. *No wonder Riggs wants so desperately to read these Codices.*

She was tempted to compare the events surrounding her own Maya codices. The Maya had been silenced when their written language was destroyed by the Spaniards. The Maya codices, however, were available to anyone interested once they had been rediscovered in Europe. Everyone had copies, but no one could read them; the code to the hieroglyphs had been lost over time. She marveled that the Nag Hammadi codices were quite the opposite, and yet the same. The early Christians had also been silenced when their codices were destroyed by the Romans, but Riggs could have read these Coptic words, if he could just get his hands on the Codices...for more than a few minutes. These ancient authors were being silenced by modern politics, not by a missing code, since a handful of Egyptian Christians had kept the Coptic language alive all those centuries in their liturgy.

"They're amazing, aren't they?" said Riggs, breaking the silence. He could see that she was spellbound.

"Truly amazing," she agreed, as Pahor Labib reached over to open the ornate leather cover.

A strip of leather was turned over each edge of the lined covers. A flap was formed by a cow's tail, and this was augmented by a thong which circled the book.

"Now that's real leather," she laughed, as the cow's tail dangled across her wrist.

They all three laughed together, but Riggs was finding Pahor's exhibition far less entertaining. Although Riggs had seen him charm the visitors many times, he knew it would not get him or his scholarly colleagues any closer to the Codices.

"You can see how they folded several papyrus sheets and sewed them down the middle to form the quire," Pahor explained, pressing back one of the old pages so she could see. The edges of the papyrus leaves had frayed and some pages had what looked like moth holes through them.

"That's very interesting," marveled Christina. "What's this rough material inside the back cover?"

"We call that *cartonnage*," elaborated Labib proudly, in his charming Egyptian accent. "It is a papyrus composite the ancient binder used to strengthen the leather cover. It is made from old letters, and we were able to date these Codices from the dates on the letters."

"You mean you didn't have to carbon-date these manuscripts to determine their age?" Christina asked, remembering the laboratory report in Uncle Colby's folder.

"Not yet," said Labib, carefully closing the Codex and placing it back in the cupboard with the others.

• • •

"Can you imagine thirty new gospels?" said Riggs excitedly as they left the museum.

"How could there be thirty?" she wondered out loud.

"Well all together, there are about fifty tractates, or monographs, in the thirteen Codices. Based on titles alone, six of these fifty tractates are believed to be duplicates, and some tractates are probably too fragmented to translate. That leaves about thirty fairly complete new texts...more than exist even for the New Testament Gospels."

"That's surprising," puzzled Christina. "Still, surely not all the new Nag Hammadi tractates will turn out to be gospels."

"Probably not, but hope springs eternal. You can see why I want so desperately to translate them. I'm sure there'll be several new gospels, and many new teachings from Jesus."

"You've certainly got my interest," answered Christina. "Incidentally, Mr. Labib seemed nice enough to me. It's difficult to believe that he won't let you translate them."

"Don't be fooled by his charm," warned Riggs. "He's quite a showman for the pretty ladies. I've been coming here for years to translate other Coptic documents. I can assure you that he isn't going to give up the notoriety that goes with those Codices, nor his misguided hope for eventual fame. He has no incentive to change a thing."

"So there's no hope?" asked Christina.

"Actually there is," beamed Riggs. "I got some really good news last night when I phoned Professor Robinson. He got the green light from UNESCO, and they've asked him to be the chairman of the Oversight Committee."

"That's wonderful," said Christina enthusiastically. "So you'll have access to the Codices soon?"

"At least Professor Robinson will have access...as Chairman," Riggs said with a hint of jealousy.

"He must be as good at international politics as he is at New Testament scholarship."

"Almost," said Riggs proudly, realizing that for some reason winter in Boston was beginning to thaw. "You'll find out for yourself soon enough. He'll be here when we get back from Jerusalem."

Shrine of the Book

Riggs tried to get the attention of the waiter as they seated themselves at a little table by the window. Groppi's was a popular rendezvous for locals, known for its good food and even tastier sweets, and Riggs hoped it would be a good setting for their discussion about the potentially explosive meeting with John Allegro.

"Now that I'm a co-owner of a complete set of Dead Sea Scroll photos," Christina was saying, "don't you think I should know something about them?"

"How much do you want to know?" joked Riggs. "There's enough to fill several books. In fact, the saga of the Dead Sea Scrolls is one of the sadder commentaries on human decency, involving every type of deception and greed."

"And let me guess," anticipated Christina, "some involving my own Church?"

"I'm afraid there's never much distance between newly discovered New Testament documents and the Catholic Church. In this case, however, I believe those who monopolized the Scrolls were protecting their academic reputations more than their religion."

"Sounds familiar," said Christina, remembering her own experience with Eric Thompson. "Academic ambition has smothered many ideas over the years."

Riggs tried again unsuccessfully to get the attention of the waiter.

"There are really two stories," he began, "both involving significant portions of the Scrolls. It's easier if I call one group the Jewish or Israeli Scrolls and the other group the Catholic or Christian Scrolls, although this obviously refers to the control of the Scrolls and not the contents. Is this all right with you?"

""Sure," responded Christina. "You can play hardball. There's a certain symmetry to your choices."

"Most of the drama surrounding the Jewish Scrolls is in the way they were acquired. The drama around the Christian Scrolls, in contrast, begins after they were acquired. I'll start with the Scrolls that ended up in the hands of the Israelis."

"That's very cautious," bantered Christina.

"The first Dead Sea Scrolls were found in 1947 in red earthenware jars in a cave near the ancient ruins of Qumran by a Bedouin shepherd boy who was pursuing a lost goat."

"Isn't that two years after your Nag Hammadi codices were discovered in Egypt?" asked Christina, displaying her new knowledge.

"That's very good," said Riggs.

Christina smiled proudly, and Riggs finally caught the eye of the waiter and ordered two cups of Turkish coffee. "Finally," he muttered impatiently, as the waiter walked slowly toward the kitchen. "It's easier to get a pyramid built here than to order a cup of coffee."

"We call it mañana time in Guatemala," commiserated Christina.

"Where was I?" he asked himself, rubbing his beard. "Oh yeah...the Scrolls...it's amazing that any of these Scrolls survived the first few months," he continued. "While in the hands of the Bedouin some were stolen, some were lost, and some were actually used as kindling."

"The Dead Sea Scrolls lay safely buried in jars for nearly two thousand years and then someone used them as <u>kindling</u>?" repeated Christina loudly. "That's incredible."

"Someone very poor," defended Riggs, "and not very well informed."

"That's still horrible," said Christina.

"It is," agreed Riggs, "but I know of a worse case where they should have known better."

"Tell me," begged Christina.

"The monks at St. Catherine's Monastery on the Sinai peninsula, where the oldest complete Greek translation of the new Testament was discovered in 1844, actually burned manuscripts for heat. Now, <u>they</u> should have known better."

"I can't believe that monks would burn the words of their own Savior," said Christina with disgust.

"It's true," confirmed Riggs.

As the waiter finally placed the steaming cups of coffee in front of them, Riggs made a suggestion. "Why don't we go point to the sweets we like in the counter. It will be much faster, believe me." As they each pointed to the pastry of their dreams, Riggs continued the saga of the Dead Sea Scrolls.

"The seven or eight Scrolls which survived the Bedouin ordeal made their way through a local sheik, to a Christian antiquities dealer, and eventually to a man in Jerusalem named Athanasius Samuel, the Archbishop of the Syrian Jacobite Church."

"Is that another Christian Church?" she asked.

"It's another independent orthodox Christian Church which broke away from Rome."

"Sounds like Wall Street," joked Christina.

"If not worse. By the way, the Jacobites call their Archbishop the *Metropolitan*," explained Riggs before continuing. "Along the way, a feud led to at least one Scroll being sold to the Muslim Sheik of Bethlehem. It's not known for certain if this Scroll was ever seen again."

"Incidentally, what was the name of the antiquities dealer?"

"Why do you ask?" said Riggs, helping Christina with her chair, as they returned to their table.

"I thought he might be involved in my uncle's death."

"His nickname was Kando, but I doubt if he's even still alive."

"I have another question. Who did these Scrolls belong to officially?"

"At the time of the discovery, the western bank of the Dead Sea belonged to the Palestinians...who were Muslims, of course. Officially, all antiquities were to be given to the Department of Antiquities, then housed in the Palestine Archaeological Museum in East Jerusalem, known as the *Rockefeller*."

"So what you're calling the Jewish half of the Scrolls were discovered by Muslims, who sold them to the Christian Metropolitan Samuel instead of donating them to their own museum?" recited a skeptical Christina.

"You got the picture, all right. Now let me anticipate your next question. The Palestinian Museum was named for Rockefeller because of its early funding."

Christina smiled. "I didn't think Rockefeller was a common Muslim name." She took the last bite of pastry and began sipping on her coffee. "So Metropolitan Samuel ended up with the Jewish Scrolls?"

"At this stage, but there's more. It's rumored that Metropolitan Samuel went to Damascus, to show his superior in the Syrian Jacobite Church the Scrolls he'd purchased. While he was there, if you can believe this coincidence, a CIA operative named Copeland was approached by an Egyptian merchant who had one of the Scrolls in a sack."

"That is quite a coincidence," smiled Christina derogatorily. "You don't suppose the Metropolitan was trying to raise a little cash...for his congregation of course."

"Stranger things have happened. Anyway, to continue, Copeland immediately arranged to take photographs of the Scroll on the roof top outside his hotel room. And in a scene reminiscent of the Keystone Kops, the wind blew portions of the Scroll all over Damascus, apparently losing it forever."

"What about the photographs?"

"Copeland claimed to have left the few photos he took in a desk drawer, never to be seen again. He wasn't certain of their fate. Had they been stolen or innocently discarded, or was his story a cover-up for other events?"

"What other events?"

"Other events involving the exchange of money," smiled Riggs mischievously.

"Oh yes, of course."

"Some very famous people enter the Israeli story now," he continued, "including an even larger cast of sleazy merchants. An Armenian antiques dealer representing an Arab dealer from Bethlehem approached Professor Eleazar Sukenik, head of Archaeology at Hebrew University."

"Here we go again," smiled Christina. "An Israeli, an Armenian and an Arab."

"You're catching on quickly...At great personal danger, Professor Sukenik later traveled clandestinely to Bethlehem to examine the Scrolls on the very night that the UN created Israel in 1947."

"These Scrolls must have seemed like a good omen to the Israelis."

"Sukenik believed the appearance of the Scrolls at this momentous time in history was symbolic. So Sukenik raised funds and bought the three Scrolls."

"And that's the end of the tale of the Jewish half of the Scrolls?" presumed Christina, since Riggs was preparing to leave the table. She thanked him for the delicious snack, as he placed an Egyptian pound on the table, which seemed to include the tip.

I'm going to have to figure out this new currency myself, she thought. *I haven't had to purchase anything yet.*

"Not quite" Riggs was saying. "Professor Sukenik then pursued the Scrolls held by Metropolitan Samuel at St. Marks Monastery in the Jordanian sector."

Christina was confused. "I thought those were the ones he bought in Bethlehem?"

"Apparently not, or at least not all of them. So he met with the Metropolitan in the British YMCA near the Jordanian side of the Mandelbaum Gate and negotiated for the remaining Scrolls. Then he had some very bad luck."

They stopped in the doorway of Groppi's, and they both enjoyed the warm sun on their faces. "I know a nice place to bask in this sun," said Riggs, heading down the busy street. It was difficult to stay together in the crush of pedestrians, so he offered his hand to Christina.

"What happened to Sukenik? Was he captured?"

"No, his funding dried up, and the Metropolitan opened the bidding to the Americans. Metropolitan Samuel had contacted the American School of Oriental Research in Jerusalem, which sent some of the prints to Professor William F. Albright at Johns Hopkins University. He quickly confirmed their authenticity with the earliest dates of about 100 B.C., and proclaimed them the greatest manuscript discovery of modern times."

"So we have American Jews bidding against Israeli Jews, who are receiving donations from American Jews?"

"Probably, but in the meantime, the Metropolitan smuggled his Scrolls into a safe deposit box in Beirut, where they remained until the end of the first Arab war against Israel in early 1949...then they were moved to New York City."

"So the Americans stayed in the bidding," confirmed Christina.

"Until 1954, when Yigael Yadin, the Israeli war hero and son of Eleazar Sukenik, covertly purchased the remaining four Scrolls for the Israeli government, and returned them to Israel where they joined the three his father had acquired."

"Do you know how much they paid?"

"I've heard it was $250,000."

"And what happened to all these Scrolls once they were in the hands of the Israelis?"

"The Scrolls are currently housed in Jerusalem in a special facility called 'The Shrine of the Book,' and most of them have already been translated. Access to the Scrolls is permitted to both academics and the public under appropriate circumstances. The Israelis definitely set a good example of 'freedom of information' with the portion of the Scrolls under their control. They were proud of them and shared them with the world."

"I guess I can assume that was not quite the case with the Christian half of the Scrolls," anticipated Christina.

Riggs smiled, thinking, *Be careful what you ask, Christina. You might not enjoy the answer.*

Insider Information

As they walked into the sunny park, a few blocks from the Groppi café, they wouldn't have noticed that a very large man with a birthmark was following them, like a cat stalking a lizard. He was good at his profession, and they were definitely not experienced at this game.

Riggs was preoccupied. He knew that he had to expose Christina to a hundred years of New Testament research, none of which was good news to the faithful. He was reminded of the metaphor of his friend, M. Schweitzer-Mordicai, who lamented that Bible scholars are like children who are sent away for an education...only to be told not to share any of their new-found knowledge which might disturb the family.

"I'm ready for the second story," said Christina, enjoying the tranquillity of the sunny park. "The one about the evil Catholics."

"But before I get to that, let me first tell you what the scholars found when they translated the Jewish portion of the Scrolls," he suggested, postponing the other as long as possible.

"Did they discover any new gospels?"

"Not in the Scrolls at the Shrine of the Book. In fact, their absence caused some concerns. Some scholars felt that there should have been some mention of the resurrection of Jesus, since these Scrolls were buried thirty-five years after the crucifixion, and an event of that magnitude would surely have been recorded."

"What did they find?" asked Christina, not at all disturbed.

"Instead they found several copies of Old Testament books, which proved to be similar to existing Hebrew manuscripts. This was reassuring to Jewish historians, because the Dead Sea Scrolls were much older than existing copies."

"That doesn't sound real interesting to most Christians," said Christina, shaking her head. "At least not for me."

"Not as much as something new about Jesus would have been," agreed Riggs. "It included a second copy of Isaiah, a commentary on Habakkuk, a copy of Psalms, and some new psalms. They also found some new documents that had been written by people living in the area, including Qumran itself and nearby Jerusalem."

"Who were these people? Jews or Christians?"

"Good question. Much of the debate today is over who these people were. Some were believed to be Essenes, one of three main Jewish groups at the time. One Scroll, called the *Rule of the Community*, describes a covenant of eternal love binding its members to God. It also describes two spirits in man's nature: the spirit of light and truth, and the spirit of error and darkness."

"Nothing more exciting than that?" smiled Christina.

"Well, the most exciting material was the *Commentary on Habakkuk*. It told of the persecution of a messiah called the Teacher of Righteousness, whose teachings were not unlike those of Jesus, but who apparently lived at least a hundred years before Jesus."

"Was he crucified also?" asked Christina, knowing that query would protect the uniqueness of her Jesus.

"Some think so," Riggs answered reluctantly, "but there is no agreement. He was definitely persecuted by his enemies, but we are not certain exactly how. There is little doubt, however, that he was considered the Messiah by his followers."

Christina was not pleased with that answer. She had always thought that Jesus was the only messianic teacher martyred at that time in history.

Oh well, she rationalized, *the New Testament has many accounts of Jesus' crucifixion and resurrection, and this is only one Scroll.*

"Now do you want to hear about the Christian half of the Dead Sea Scrolls?" asked Riggs, bringing her back from her own thoughts. He noticed how Christina's elegant posture accentuated her long-stemmed beauty, as they sat down on a small bench near the Champollion entrance of the park.

"I'm ready, but I want to come back to the Teacher of Righteousness sometime later," she said, wondering why she had never heard of this religious figure before.

"The half of the Scrolls," Riggs continued, "that eventually came under the control of the International Team were discovered a few years later in nearby caves. They had nothing to do with the Metropolitan Samuel and his many adventures."

"And yet they're also called the Dead Sea Scrolls?" asked Christina.

"Yes, because they were found in the same area. What makes these Scrolls controversial is that they have never been published. In fact, they were never even released to scholars, except for a small group called the *Insiders Team*."

"The Insiders Team?"

"That's what many of us sarcastically call the so-called International Team which has jurisdiction over these Scrolls. They've had an academic monopoly for over twenty-five years."

"Why does my Church get the blame for this?"

"Because many of the Insiders happen to be Catholics, and this has made them vulnerable to charges of conspiracy."

Christina assumed there was some explanation, but offered no rebuttal.

"It is also unfortunate for your Church that the head of the Insiders, Father Roland de Vaux, is a member of the Pontifical Biblical Commission, under Cardinal Joseph Ratzinger. This commission is responsible for ensuring that scriptural interpretations are consistent with Catholic doctrine, and some detractors link this commission with the Holy Inquisition."

"What nonsense!" exploded Christina, her sensibilities offended. "What an outrageous charge! There is no modern day Inquisition!"

Riggs ignored her outburst, saying mildly, "Well, the publication delays have opened the Insiders to criticism from everyone, even from those of us with no particular bias. I warned you this wouldn't be easy Do you want me to continue with the story or is it too disturbing?"

"Of course," answered Christina, but she had at least drawn the line.

"Soon after the first Scrolls were discovered by the Bedouin shepherd in 1947, a member of the UN Truce Organization enlisted Father Roland de Vaux, at the Ecole Biblique in East Jerusalem, to work with the Director of the Department of Antiquities for Jordan and Arab Palestine in excavating the remaining caves."

"It seems to me the Scrolls you call the Christian Scrolls could equally well be called the Muslim Scrolls," observed Christina.

"You're right," admitted Riggs. "But the story's not that simple."

"I have a feeling these Scrolls also changed hands a few times."

"Right again.   In 1949 the Qumran caves, the Rockefeller Museum, and the Ecole Biblique all passed into Jordanian control, and de Vaux's team paid handsome fees for any new Scrolls discovered by the Bedouin. Rumors spread that the money came from the Vatican, but in fact, most of it came from the Rockefeller Museum."

"I'm not surprised about the rumors," said Christina, tiring of the innuendoes, but holding her tongue.

"One reason these two stories get confusing is that the antiquities dealer, Kando, was involved with all of the Scrolls."

"He really got around, didn't he?"

"He had a monopoly on the Scrolls discovered by the Bedouin," explained Riggs,   "and the Bedouin had a monopoly on cave hunting. Kando then sold Scrolls to de Vaux, whose team had a monopoly on academic publications.   In this way they accumulated over a thousand fragments, and since they weren't kept in a controlled environment, they began to deteriorate at the Rockefeller Museum."

"It sounds to me like the monopolies were working," joked Christina.   "A thousand fragments sounds good to me."

"And then there was one political catastrophe after another," continued Riggs, ignoring her rationalization of the monopolies.   "The Scrolls were stored in a damp vault in Amman for over a year during the 1956 Suez Crisis, and this accelerated their deterioration.   Ten years later, the Rockefeller Museum was nationalized by the Jordanian government, in nefarious hopes of pilfering the museum's endowment from a British bank. A year later, the Rockefeller was seized by Yigael Yadin himself as a spoil of the Six Day War."

"What a mess.   When would the Insiders, as you call them, have had time to translate these Scrolls?"

"Well, de Vaux and his team were at the Rockefeller and the nearby Ecole Biblique the entire time.   I'm not sure they got much work done, because they were also excavating the ruins at Qumran."

"They were probably more interested in the archaeological dig than in the translations," surmised Christina, recalling her own experience with the archaeologist, Eric Thompson.

"Possibly.   The story then ends with two big surprises."

"Let me guess.   Father de Vaux converted to Judaism?"

Riggs laughed.   "You're joking, but you're not far off.   First, Yigael Yadin discovered an intact Scroll hidden under the floor of Kando's house.   It was the famous "Temple Scroll" and I'm sure we'll talk about it tomorrow with John Allegro.   Second, Yadin left Father de Vaux in charge of the Scrolls at the Rockefeller, despite rumors of de Vaux's anti-Semitism."

"Let me see if I understand. The second half of the Scrolls are now in a Palestinian museum, named for the American Rockefellers, in the Jordanian sector of Jerusalem, under the control of the French Catholics, who now report to the Jews in Israel," ventured an incredulous Christina.

"You got it."

"And no one can understand why there are delays?"

Building Seas

Later that night, as they were washing up their dishes from the food Mrs. Scarzella left in the fridge, Christina asked Riggs why Yigael Yadin didn't remove Father de Vaux from his position as head of the International Team.

"I think it's a combination of things," Riggs replied. "The Israelis didn't want to offend either the recently defeated Jordanians or the Vatican. Remember, this was only four years after Pope John XXIII had exculpated the Jews for the crucifixion of Jesus."

"That's possible," mulled Christina, "especially since Israel was such a young country. It's an intriguing question. By the way, what's the plan tomorrow?"

"Well you better wear your hard hat for the meeting with John Allegro, because he won't be nearly as diplomatic as I've been. He won't be subtle about a Catholic conspiracy."

"If I could avoid this meeting, I would," grumbled Christina, "but that's the only way we can learn what Uncle Colby had in mind for his photos of the Dead Sea Scrolls."

"You're right. We might also learn more about their scheme for breaking the academic monopoly."

"And why Uncle Colby removed Allegro as custodian of the Cairo vault," added Christina. "It should be an interesting day." *And I'll maybe figure out if he was involved in Uncle Colby's death,* thought Christina.

As she finished drying the last dish, Christina asked him where he got the nickname, "Riggs."

"As a kid, I loved racing sailboats, especially the Laser. When I had a bigger budget, I moved up to Solings, and today I race J-Boats whenever I can."

"So...sailboats...rigging?"

He shrugged. "Simple, huh?"

"Well, it's definitely unique."

"Last year I got together with a couple of friends and we chartered a fifty-foot Beneteau out of Grenada and sailed south to Venezuela."

"That sounds exciting. Maybe you could take me sailing sometime?"

"Sure," he readily agreed. "I could take you in a felucca right here on the Nile River," and giving her a curious look, he added, "if not to the Greek Islands a short hop north of here."

"That sounds like fun."

He raised an eyebrow. She had become downright tolerable after all.

• • •

As she closed the door to her room, she realized that despite her efforts to the contrary, she was beginning to let down her guard against the handsome Dr. Parker. It was more than his charming demeanor and his diplomatic handling of their sensitive religious discussions. He seemed to have an inner strength and a serenity that were obviously based on more than creeds and doctrines. He seemed to be overflowing with both intellect and kindness at the same time, qualities rarely seen together.. except, of course, in Uncle Colby. And also like Uncle Colby, he seemed to see through her at times. She found this unsettling yet at the same time comforting. In his own quiet way, and without the benefit of Uncle Colby's resources, he was waging his own battle against academic monopolies. In this sense, they were kindred spirits.

She thought again about Uncle Colby's folder. Nothing she'd learned today explained the contents, but she now understood why her uncle was involved with the Dead Sea Scrolls and the Nag Hammadi codices.

As disturbing as it was to her, she found herself fighting hard not to suspect her own Church for his demise. The French Catholics certainly had a motive to protect their monopoly from the photos in Uncle Colby's vault. But such extreme behavior was difficult for her to rationalize, unless some small group of fanatics were involved.

Allegro, she thought. *He must be the key.* He had certainly become her primary suspect, especially with Uncle Colby's last minute switch at the vault.

The Crucifixion

There is no strong performance without a little fanaticism in the performer.

—Ralph Waldo Emerson

Journals

All these aisles are starting to look the same, Riggs thought to himself, as he and Christina wove their way through the dusty stacks of books in the main library of Hebrew University, overlooking Jerusalem on Mount Scopus.

"Is John Allegro in Jerusalem most of the time?" asked Christina, following behind.

"Not any more," answered Riggs, stopping to get his bearings. He knew they were close to the Archaeology section, but he hadn't been able to find it yet. "Allegro told me that he hasn't been here for several months...not since he left in the middle of the controversy."

"Why is he here right now?" continued Christina, as she picked a book off the shelf and blew the dust playfully at Riggs.

As he dodged the dust artfully, he answered: "He told me that he was attending a conference on the Dead Sea Scrolls, where he's giving a talk on the now infamous Copper Scroll."

"Did you tell me about the Copper Scroll?" asked Christina.

"No," said Riggs, with a sparkle in his eye, "That's very advanced material."

"Well after withstanding your lengthy introduction yesterday," teased Christina, "don't you think I'm ready for very advanced material?"

"Sure you are," he said, pretending to ignore her oblique compliment. "If I can just find John Allegro. Wouldn't you think I'd know my way around this library by now?" Just as Riggs was giving up, they rounded a stack and found Allegro seated at a small table and immersed in his own papers. Riggs quickly made the introductions, as the two of them pulled up a couple of hard wooden chairs.

John expressed his condolences for Colby's death. and his willingness to assist them in any way possible.

"John Allegro," began Riggs, hoping to boost Allegro's sagging ego, "was the only member of the International Team who published all of his assigned translations. He was also the only one who dared to differ with their consensus views."

"The only one foolish enough," added John, glancing nervously at Christina. "I greatly underestimated their power."

Christina tried to ease the tension by shifting the conversation to a more comfortable subject. "What are you working on now?" she asked, pointing at the papers in front of him.

"I've returned to my original love," he said, "which is the study of religions and the origins of myth, although I continue my interest in philology and the history of languages."

"That sounds very interesting. How did you prepare for that field?" asked Christina, egging him on. She realized that his was the most ordinary face she had ever seen, with the pasty skin of a post office employee and glasses much too small for his face. She wondered how he could breath with them sitting half-way down his nose.

"Both my BA and MA," he added proudly in perfect Queen's English, "were in Oriental Studies from Manchester University, and my Ph.D. was in Semitic Studies at Oxford, under Professor Driver." "Several years ago I published a translation of many of the Scrolls and fragments from Cave 4 at Qumran, and it did a lot for my scholarly reputation."

"He also published a popular book on the Dead Sea Scrolls," added Riggs, "which launched him into the public limelight almost overnight."

John was once again silent, glancing down at the pad of paper in front of him and tapping his pen. He then said with great emotion, "And two short years later I resigned my faculty position at Manchester under extreme pressure. I went from the top to the bottom almost overnight...and now none of the better universities will come near me."

"How could this happen so quickly?" Christina asked, wondering, *Could my own career be so vulnerable?*

Before John could respond, he was momentarily distracted by a man in the next aisle who was slowly paging through a book he had removed from one of the shelves. Since this section of the library was usually empty, John hadn't expected them to be disturbed. As the man turned to walk to a neighboring table, John noticed a large grape-colored birthmark on his face.

"How many days do I have to tell this story?" said John sarcastically. He had decided that their conversation wouldn't bother the other man, who was now sitting at the next table some distance behind Riggs and Christina.

"You have my attention," assured Christina. *Now that I'm in the Dead Sea Scrolls business, I might run into some of the same problems at Harvard,* she brooded to herself.

Riggs nodded agreement. The man at the next table went back to the shelf near them and began sorting through the books once again.

"First, I must admit that politics isn't my strong suit," began John, "and I was foolish enough to become the only non-Catholic on the Insiders Team."

Riggs glanced at Christina as if to prepare her for the attack. Her face showed resolve.

"That's all they are...*Insiders*...and they hide behind the deceptive label of the International Team. Everyone except me is a Catholic, and they're using their monopoly on the Scrolls to protect both their Church doctrines and their academic careers," said John, with little restraint on his anger.

"I actually want to learn what happened," said Christina, "but I probably should warn you that I'm a Catholic. I wouldn't feel right if I weren't completely candid about this."

"Well you're in for a rough ride, if you want to learn anything from me," warned John, somewhat rudely. "Father de Vaux and his Catholic cronies destroyed my academic career, so my feelings on this subject are not ambivalent."

"Who are the other members of the International Team?" she asked, bringing him back to the subject.

"The <u>Insiders</u> Team," corrected John angrily, "consists of Monsignor Skehan from the States, Father Jean Starcky from France, and Father Joseph

Milik, originally from Poland and now from France. Initially a German named Hunzinger was on the team, but when he resigned, he was replaced by a French Priest, Father Maurice Baillet."

"Seems that everyone has the title 'Father' and ties with France," said Christina reluctantly, unable to draw any other conclusion.

"Don't forget the French Father de Vaux, who heads the team," added John.

"I can see why you might want to call it the French Catholic International Team," joked Christina, putting on one of her winning smiles.

"What about Frank Cross?" challenged Riggs. "He's not a Catholic. Neither is John Strugnell."

"You're right," conceded John reluctantly, "but Strugnell has spoken of converting, and they both apparently made some accommodation with de Vaux. I think they agreed to stay out of his politics, in return for a US monopoly on the Scrolls. In hind sight, I probably could have done the same thing in England. "

"But you didn't," reminded Riggs.

"No, I did just the opposite," said John, with an introspective look on his deeply lined face. "It all began with the Copper Scroll."

Christina glanced again at Riggs, knowing that she was finally going to learn about this mysterious Scroll.

"This was the only Scroll made of metal," he continued, "and I convinced de Vaux to have it sliced very carefully into small pieces. It simply couldn't be unrolled without shattering, because it was so old and fragile. I took it to Manchester College of Technology where a friend carefully sliced it into several pieces. He had improvised a special rig just for that purpose."

The bitterness had left John's voice, at least momentarily, as he seemed to enjoy the memories of those exciting times. "It wasn't my assignment to translate the Copper Scroll, but once the pieces were exposed it became far too great a temptation."

"What did it say?" asked a very curious Christina.

"It described an immense treasure, which had been hidden in locations throughout Palestine. Only the Temple of Jerusalem could have amassed such a large treasure, and from the dating of the Copper Scroll, we knew that it had been hidden in the Qumran cave about the time the Romans destroyed the Temple in 70 A.D. Can you imagine my excitement at the time?"

"You thought you might find the treasure?" guessed Christina.

"Not really. I was excited because the Copper Scroll proved that some of the Scrolls were from Jerusalem, and therefore indicative of mainline thinking at the time of Jesus."

"This was an important time in the formation of both Christianity and modern Judaism," added Riggs, for Christina's benefit.

"I decided to include this discovery in the book I was about to publish on the Dead Sea Scrolls," continued John, "believing the excitement generated by the Copper Scroll would be good for scholarly inquiry...and, of course...book sales."

"What happened?" probed Christina.

"De Vaux said he wanted to withhold publication, at least for a few months, in order to avoid attracting crowds of treasure seekers. I conceded reluctantly and removed the Copper Scroll section from my book as it headed for the printer."

"The book was a success anyway, wasn't it?" recalled Riggs. His back was turned to the man who had by then returned to the nearby table with several books.

"It is still a very popular book, but there was more," continued John. "I soon learned that de Vaux had other motives. He was trying to protect a pet theory, hatched by himself and his Insiders, that all the Dead Sea Scrolls were the exclusive work of an isolated Essene cult which lived at nearby Qumran."

"I can understand academics protecting their pet theories at all cost," conceded Christina. "I've seen the same behavior in my own field, but I don't understand how this could also protect the Catholic Church. Am I missing the point here?"

Riggs decided to answer this question for Christina's benefit. "It's really very simple. If there were any materials adversarial to Christianity in the Dead Sea Scrolls, it would be much easier to discount them if they had been written by an isolated enclave of Jewish fanatics."

"Weren't the manuscripts more likely to confirm Christianity, with eye witness accounts of the crucifixion or the resurrection?" asked Christina. "If you ask me, it sounds like Father de Vaux was merely protecting his pet theory. My Church had nothing to lose."

"Perhaps," responded John, letting the chips fall where they may. "The Catholic Church claims that their Christianity was initially uncontested. They will admit, somewhat reluctantly, that schisms developed several hundred years later, but they maintain that in the years immediately following the crucifixion, there was agreement among the followers of Jesus."

"I certainly believe that," agreed Christina.

"We now know that there were several versions of Christianity, especially among the followers in Palestine, and that Paul's version, which was popular with the Greeks and the Romans to the north, later prevailed only because the other versions were destroyed as heresies by the powerful Roman armies."

Christina glanced at Riggs, who gave her a reassuring look. He knew this would not be easy for her, because he had confronted these same tormenting facts in graduate school.

"The Christian churches fear that documents describing these extinct versions of Christianity might suddenly reappear in discoveries like the Dead Sea Scrolls," concluded John.

"Or the Nag Hammadi codices," added Riggs, quite pleased that John was running interference for him by covering so many of the controversial issues with Christina.

"I find the idea of competing versions of early Christianity quite upsetting," protested Christina. "Do you mean 'competing' in the same sense that the Baptists and the Catholics compete with each other?"

"More in the sense that Christianity and Buddhism are different," answered John, "because the versions of early Christianity which were proclaimed heretical were radically different from Paul's religion for the gentiles. Some versions, for example, did not claim that Jesus physically rose from the dead or that he was born of a virgin. Other versions considered Jesus to be a prophet like Moses or Isaiah, rather than God incarnate. Still others believed his teachings provided a path to inner spiritual knowledge, and they rejected his death as a means to eternal life.

I'm not going to argue with him, concluded Christina, *because he clearly has an anti-Catholic agenda. It's simply not a matter for debate whether God made a miraculous appearance in this world, in the body of Jesus, for the purpose of forgiving our sins; it's a historical fact, and thank goodness for that.*

"Were the contents of the Copper Scroll ever published?" asked Christina, trying to change the subject.

"When I realized that de Vaux intended to delay publication of the Copper Scroll indefinitely, I decided to publish it independently," responded John. "That was the final straw."

"Had there been other incidents?" asked Riggs, leading John along.

"Oh yes," smiled John, warming to the subject. "A few years earlier I had taped three short talks on the Dead Sea Scrolls for British radio in which I explained that hints of Christianity could be found in the Scrolls."

"What hints?" inquired Christina, preparing herself for more upsetting news.

"We found other examples of the Last Supper, the Lord's Prayer, the crucifixion, and even teachings later attributed to Jesus," answered John, not mincing his words.

"These events weren't unique to Jesus?" pleaded a deflated Christina. This was all coming at her too quickly.

"No, they apparently happened to other Jewish messiah's, including one named the Teacher of Righteousness, who is described in the Dead Sea Scrolls."

There he is again, thought Christina, *that Teacher of Righteousness.*

"You should tell her what happened after your radio programs aired," insisted Riggs, trying to bring the conversation back to John's own experiences. Riggs' leg was becoming numb, and he stood up in order to get some circulation back in his legs. The man with the birthmark quickly turned in the other direction, nervously twirling his Zippo lighter between his thumb and forefinger.

"They were picked up by the New York Times and the Time Magazine, which ran headlines like 'Crucifixion Before Christ'," remembered John despondently. "I can tell you who was crucified. It was me. And the executioners were de Vaux and his Insiders. That was the beginning of the end for me, but I was too naïve to see it coming."

Following Riggs' lead, John stood up to stretch and looked around the library. The strange researcher at the next table had already left, leaving his books stacked high on the table.

Christina joined them and stretched her arms above her head to relieve the tension in her back. She was uncomfortable from the hard wooden chairs and John Allegro's disturbing information. *I just can't believe,* she thought, *that there were several versions of Christianity in the beginning, and that all but one was destroyed by the Romans. I also can't believe that the Church was founded outside of Palestine by Paul primarily for the Greeks and the Romans. This is all very disturbing, and I need some answers. I hope Riggs can explain everything later.*

"Can I interest you two in lunch at the student cafeteria?" suggested John, reeling from his all too vivid memories of this ordeal. "The food's tolerable, and the prices are great. Perhaps then we can talk about the vault in Cairo."

You bet we need to talk about the vault, thought Christina. *There's no doubt in my mind that Allegro would like to see the Scroll photos published...and maybe Uncle Colby got in his way.*

Cross Fire

For once in her life, Christina was glad not to be included in the conversation. She had fallen behind Riggs and John as they talked about the Scrolls from Cave 4.

I know I should be upset with Father de Vaux for monopolizing his portion of the Dead Sea Scrolls, she thought to herself, *because I've seen in my own research how damaging monopolies can be. If the archaeologists had been more receptive to the contributions of the linguists, the Maya Code might have been broken many years earlier.*

However, the situation with the Dead Sea Scrolls was more complicated, at least for her, because her own Church was implicated in the monopoly.

This was a little too close to home for her liking. Although not convinced that the French Catholics were guilty of anything more than academic ambition, she felt uncomfortable defending their actions. She had the same problem rationalizing her affiliation with the same Church which destroyed the Mayan culture in Central America, but those events had at least taken place several centuries ago. The Dead Sea Scrolls controversy was happening right now, and she was right in the middle of it, whether she liked it or not.

The Catholic religion, she rationalized, *has been good for me and my family. It's helped us get through the difficult times and has been a uniting force in our family.*

But Christina also had to admit to herself that she was continually embarrassed by the behavior of the Church hierarchy. There had always been an incongruity between the religion of her own parish and the officials in Rome.

She was appalled by what Allegro had said about other versions of Christianity. This wasn't something to be taken lightly. Her entire faith was anchored on the belief that God had appeared on earth, through the miraculous birth of Jesus, for the purpose of redeeming sins and preparing the way for eternal life. For Christina, His death on the cross and His Resurrection three days later were simply not matters open for scholarly debate.

My head spins even to think about it.

Riggs and John stopped and turned to Christina. "I've talked John into eating lunch at Feferberg's on Jaffa Road," said Riggs jovially. "That's my favorite Jewish deli in Jerusalem, and you're buying. How does that sound?"

"Great," mumbled Christina absently, still thinking more about the nourishment of her soul than her body.

• • •

"I recommend the chopped chicken liver, unless you have a taste for gefilte fish or boiled tongue," said Riggs, feigning a straight face.

Christina wrinkled her nose.

"Actually, everything is great here," smiled Riggs.

"I think I'll stick with pastrami on rye, with one of those great koshered dills," replied Christina, pointing at the food on the next table. "I'm much more adventuresome in the jungle than I am in Jewish restaurants." She could almost taste the vinegar as the man at the adjoining table took his first bite of a giant pickle.

They were sitting in the spacious dining room in the rear, where the subdued light and wood-paneling created a comfortable setting. The room was buzzing with lively conversations, and the waiters were rushing from table to table, carrying plates amply heaped with food.

"Can we talk about Colby?" asked Riggs in his attempt to steer the conversation back to their problem in Cairo.

"Sure," responded John. "As I said on the phone, I wasn't surprised that Colby had removed me as custodian of the vault. He was well aware of the turmoil in my life and of the potential conflict those photos would create for me. My role as custodian made less and less sense every week as the drama unfolded. I told Colby that it would be very difficult for me to honor his agreement with de Vaux because of my personal situation.

"Frankly, I think the photos should be made public anyway, independent of my problems. It has been almost thirty years since they were discovered, and the Scrolls controlled by the Israelis have been available for years. It's time, don't you agree, for the world to see the half of the Scrolls controlled by the Catholics."

They were saved a response as the busy waiter dropped plates of food in front of each of them. He all but tossed their silverware at them before rushing off to another table.

"Must be an immigrant from Manhattan," joked Riggs.

They all enjoyed a good laugh as they began tasting their food and looking for lighter conversation. Christina flagged down a passing waiter and ordered another round of beer.

"Thanks," quipped Riggs to Christina. "I'll have to let you buy more often."

"If I don't get another faculty position soon," joked Allegro derogatorily, "I'll be wanting you to buy more than lunch."

Christina and Riggs laughed out loud from all the tension that had been building during the morning. They sensed that there was more than humor to his remark.

"Could you tell me more about Colby's plans for the Dead Sea photos?" asked Christina, bringing the subject back to her uncle.

"Colby wanted to break the Insider's monopoly on the Scrolls," responded John, "and the two of us worked unsuccessfully on that goal for years. I was anxious to have them published, but he was resolved to play by the rules of his agreement. He always thought of his photos as a last resort."

"That's understandable," empathized Riggs.

"He knew about my problems with the Insiders, and he wanted very much to come to my rescue. I think it provided him with a real dilemma...not being able to help a friend. The two of us had been through a lot together over the years. You see," he said glancing at Christina and then lowering his eyes, "he gave me a lot more than financial support for my research: he believed in me when everything else was falling apart. I had a deep respect and affection for the man from Oklahoma." He tried to conceal the tears welling in his eyes.

Christina reached across the table and touched his hand. She knew now that he was not involved in her uncle's death.

"I think Colby made the right decision by giving the two of you the responsibility for the Scrolls," John said, after he had recovered his composure, "and frankly I don't envy you in the slightest. You make a perfect team: Riggs knows a lot about the Scrolls, Christina is a close relative, and you are both respected scholars. I'm sure that you'll figure out what is best, but I believe that someday you're going to have to make those photos available to everyone. The Insiders will never do it on their own."

Christian Roots

There is only one religion, though there are a hundred versions of it.
—George Bernard Shaw
Arms and the Man

"Was John Allegro accurate in his assessment of Father de Vaux and the Insiders?" she asked Riggs, as they walked along the cobbled streets of the Via Dolorosa—the Way of the Cross—in the Old City of Jerusalem. Christina was relieved that the two of them were finally alone and she could ask him all her questions.

"I think he might be a little paranoid about a Catholic conspiracy," he answered, "but after what he's been through, I can sympathize with him to some extent. There seems to be no doubt about the International Team being predominantly French and Catholic, don't you agree?"

"That's true, but how could one ever judge Father de Vaux's motive? Is he protecting his pet theory to save face academically, or is he trying to protect the foundations of Christianity? Or is he just basking in his fortuitous monopoly? How could we ever know?" asked Christina. "His theory might even be correct, you know."

"That's basically the debate which is raging in the press and among Bible scholars. I for one, think the Insiders should make their Scrolls available to all the scholars," suggested Riggs. "That way everyone would have the same information."

"You and I face the same decision, only ours is complicated by Uncle Colby's agreement with Father de Vaux. I don't really know what to do with our photos."

"Neither do I," agreed Riggs. "Fortunately, we're under no pressure to make a decision immediately."

"Can I ask you a more sensitive question?" asked Christina, as they passed the Monastery of the Flagellation, Station II, the place where Jesus

was scourged and took up the cross, at least according to 12th-century
Crusader traditions.

"Sure. Why not?"

"Was John right about alternative versions of early Christianity?"

Riggs sat silently for a long time, choosing his words carefully. He
sensed that Christina was skating on the thin ice of her religious creeds.
"The easy answer is 'Yes,' but there is much more to it than that. There
were many later schisms in the Church, which you probably know about,
but John was talking about the first hundred years or so. You do know
about the later schisms, don't you?"

"I know about Martin Luther in the Renaissance," answered Christina.

"Yes, that was the start of the many Protestant branches of Christianity
about 400 years ago. Prior to that, in about 1000 A.D., there was the major
schism between the Eastern Orthodox churches and the Roman Catholics,
which had been festering for several hundred years. That included the
Greek Orthodox and the Russian Orthodox churches. Even earlier than that
the Syrian Orthodox and the Egyptian Orthodox had separated from the
Roman church."

"It's a good thing we Catholics discovered the Americas," joked Christina wryly.

"Well, all those converts sure didn't hurt the membership rolls any,"
grinned Riggs. "There was actually one other major schism, but no one
calls it that. The Islamic movement was initially an attempt to return to the
original teachings of Jesus, and in the process the Muslims demoted him to
the status of a prophet."

They walked up the stepped street to a brown metal door, Station VII,
the place where Jesus fell the second time from the weight of the cross. "I
thought Muhammad was their Jesus?" queried Christina.

"Over time Muhammad's role was elevated by some of his more
ambitious followers, but for most Muslims he is not considered a god."

The street had become almost impossibly crowded as they entered the
Arab market. Shopkeepers on both sides of the narrow street hawked their
wares from small cubbyholes set into the ancient stone.

"We're getting off the track here," chuckled Christina. "Is it because
we're in the Muslim Quarter? What I really want to know is what happened
at the very early stages of Christianity?"

"You think you do, but you might not like what you hear."

"At least I know that you're not as paranoid about Catholics as John
Allegro," asserted Christina. "Let's give it a try."

I'm making some progress, thought Riggs, *at least when she compares me
with Allegro.*

"After Jesus was killed by the Romans," he continued, "word of his teachings and deeds spread first throughout Galilee, Judea and Palestine where he had lived and taught. They took root in the Jewish soil in which they were first planted. Energized by his family and disciples these teachings spread to the north into the Arabian and Greek cultures, and they spread to the south into the Egyptian culture. They eventually spread to Rome itself, to the muscle of the empire."

"And Paul spread the word to the Greeks and the Romans?" confirmed Christina.

"Yes, but it's more complicated than that," continued Riggs. "The acknowledged leader of the emerging Christian community in Jerusalem was James, called the brother of Jesus, and he and the other disciples became the custodians of the original body of Jesus' teachings. James was the proponent of Jewish doctrinal purity and rigorous adherence to the Law, including the Ten Commandments, of course."

"There's nothing upsetting about that," said Christina, hopefully, "except we are taught that Peter founded our Church."

"There's very little scholarly information available on Peter," responded Riggs, preferring to talk about Paul. "The first schism in early Christianity was precipitated by Paul, who later became the chief adversary of James. He apparently had never even met Jesus. From the perspective of the Judean Christians, Paul became the first Christian heretic. From the perspective of the New Testament, however, Paul became the first Christian, because his version was later transplanted to the capital of the Roman Empire where it eventually vanquished over all the others."

"It's simply not possible that Paul was a heretic," insisted Christina. "How did his version differ from that of James and the other disciples?"

"At first very little, especially when Paul was preaching to Jews of the Diaspora in Syria, Turkey and Greece. As his mission expanded northward, however, and began to include more Greeks and Romans, he and others incorporated mythology from these cultures. The Greek mystery religions, for example, appear to have been an important source."

"You must realize that what you're saying sounds like mythology to me," insisted Christina. "Can you be more specific about how Paul's message changed?"

"Sure," said Riggs, once again back on familiar ground. "This is my field of research, you know."

"We'll see," warned Christina, with a pert smile.

"In the Letter to the Thessalonians, about 50 A.D, Paul promised that Jesus would arrive soon from the sky. When, to his embarrassment, this didn't happen, he solved the problem about seven years later, in the Letter to the Corinthians, by adding the resurrection. With this version of the story, Jesus had already come back from the dead, so there was no longer a need to wait. Paul also added the Eucharist and credited Jesus with the founding of Paul's church, which empowered his mission to the gentile world of Greece and Rome."

"Do you mean that there was no Eucharist and no Resurrection in James' Christianity?" asked a baffled Christina. It was slowly dawning on her that Riggs was dead serious about these ridiculous claims, and he had obviously studied the subject seriously for many years.

Riggs could tell from the fragile tone of her voice that he had struck a nerve. "Well," he continued reluctantly, "communal meals with wine and prayers were common in Judaism, and therefore in all early versions of Christianity. Resurrection of the dead on the Day of Atonement was also a common Jewish belief at the time of Jesus."

Above them loomed the great medieval bulge of the Church of the Holy Sepulcher, revered by most Christendom as the location of the crucifixion and burial of Jesus, the last five Stations of the Cross.

"I still don't understand the differences between the two Christianities," complained Christina, as they turned right on the Suq El-Lahhamin heading for the Jewish Quarter of the Old City.

Riggs tried again, wanting this subject to end soon. This just wasn't any fun. "In the Christianity of James, Jesus was a prophet, and the relationship between each person and God remained central. In the Christianity of Paul, which is the Christianity of the New Testament, Jesus became a full-fledged man-God, whose legends, miracle for miracle, came to match those of the rival Greek deities with whom he was competing. The New Testament is not about the Jesus of history, it is about the Jesus of Paul's invention, which includes more mythology than we all care to believe."

Christina stopped walking, found a stone bench and sat down in dazed silence, pondering his words. From where she sat, they could see the Wailing Wall in the distance, with the faithful from many countries issuing their prayers through this revered remnant of ancient Judaism. Her first attempt at speech faltering: "And once Paul's version was empowered by the Roman armies, the other versions fell to the sword and the flame?"

"Except," he smiled victoriously, "for the Dead Sea Scrolls and the Nag Hammadi codices, which remained safely buried for nearly two millennia. The Scrolls apparently were buried before James' Christianity was widely documented, but it does tell us about Judaism at the time of Jesus, including communal meals and resurrection of the dead on the Day of Atonement. The Nag Hammadi codices were buried three-hundred and fifty years after the death of Jesus and promise to reveal James' Christianity and perhaps more about Paul's." He paused for emphasis: "They may even reveal other versions of Christianity."

For the first time, Christina truly understood how high the stakes were for the Scrolls and the Codices. *No wonder there is so much intrigue and deception,* she thought, *and no wonder monopolies were so quick to form. I can understand now why Uncle Colby got involved.* She shuddered at the prospects of more than one legitimate Christianity. *Aren't there already enough religious wars in the world?,* she wondered, as a group of elderly women, dressed in black veils and robes, passed by on their way to prayer at the Dome of the Rock. Islamic devotees had been passing this way for centuries, in response to the beguiling chants of the muezzin calling the faithful to prayer.

"I'm more embarrassed than shocked," said Christina, defensively. "I'm embarrassed that I'm not qualified to debate this topic with you. I've no reason to doubt that you believe what you've told me, and that you've devoted a great deal of study to the subject. My problem is that I need to do the same, now that I realize there are conflicting views on this important matter. I really never approached the subject from a scholarly perspective, having learned most of what I believe to be true at Church as a young woman."

"You'll find the debate very interesting," promised Riggs, hoping they could now move on to a more neutral topic.

"The next time we discuss this subject I'm going to know more than the Apostle's Creed and the Lord's Prayer. You can be sure of that," resolved Christina.

"Incidentally," said Riggs, changing the subject, "I got directions to the caves at Qumran from John Allegro. Do you have everything we need for the climb?"

Questions Questions Questions

Christina looked in the mirror as she placed her toothbrush next to the sink and wiped her mouth with one of the small towels provided by the hotel. She turned her head from side to side, causing her blond hair to brush her bare shoulders. *I've seen worse,* she thought, as she viewed her lithe figure. Her sinewy muscles were well-toned from recent climbs in the New Hampshire mountains.

She was looking forward to their expedition to the Qumran caves in the morning. Not only would they see the origin of the Scrolls they inherited, but they would finally be doing something fun and invigorating...something she was good at...climbing. Her ego definitely needed a boost. She missed the heady days of Palenque, where she was a star among her peers, and where she was always well prepared. Ever since she met Riggs, they all too often dwelled on the New

Testament...which clearly was not her strong suit, although perhaps her most sensitive.

He might know all about the first hundred years of Christianity, but tomorrow we'll be on my turf. We'll see how he does dangling at the end of the first hundred yards of my rope.

She glanced briefly in the mirror before turning out the light, and walked over to the desk. She picked up some research notes and placed them on the table by her bed and drew back the cool sheets. She smiled at the flowers, still fresh and beautiful, which had been delivered anonymously to her room earlier in the day. As she slid into bed, she thought about how tactfully Riggs had explained these complex subjects. She appreciated his sensitivity and could see why her uncle had selected him as her co-custodian of the vault.

The vault, she thought, *what are Riggs and I going to do with those photos?*

She realized that although they weren't any closer to a resolution on the Dead Sea Scroll photos, they now at least understood what her uncle was trying to accomplish with them. She also wasn't any closer to the resolution of Colby's death, since her suspicions about Riggs and Allegro hadn't materialized. And finally, she still hadn't learned anything new about the mysterious folder, except that it didn't seem to involve the Cairo vault.

One thing is certain, she concluded. *The document Uncle Colby had been chasing was even more interesting than either the Dead Sea Scrolls or the Nag Hammadi codices, because he was already involved in both of those when he asked me to help with what he believed to be his most important discovery.*

There was no doubt now, thanks to her painful discussions with Riggs and Allegro, that Colby's discovery had something to do with the heretical branches of early Christianity. *Hopefully,* she thought, *it will confirm the authenticity of the New Testament.* The timing of Ryan's visit next week was opportune, and she resolved to ask him about this and the many other vexing issues raised by Riggs and Allegro.

As she reached over and turned off the light, her last thoughts were on John Allegro. *The most important thing I learned today was how not to handle our copy of the Dead Sea Scrolls, or any other controversial documents...especially if I find the one Uncle Colby was pursuing. I'll have to tell Riggs about that folder someday...and I need to call Henry with all this news. He'll be amazed. I also need to ask him if he found a written secrecy agreement between Colby and de Vaux regarding the photos.*

Figure-Eight Descenders

"Look...There's the first hint of the sunrise," observed Riggs, pointing at the faint silhouette etching itself across the tops of the Judean hills.

"It's eerie, in a way;" said Christina, when you think about all the history in this part of the world. We're sure not the first to make this journey."

Christina was at the wheel as they sped along Highway 1, heading east on the road to the Dead Sea. In the light of the emerging dawn, they began to make out the Bedouin camps in the nearby hills. Patchwork tents, curling smoke from cooking fires, and herds of sheep penned nearby...with no hint that thousands of years had passed them by.

"They look peaceful enough to me," observed Christina, recalling Allegro's earlier concerns about their plan to scale the cliffs of Qumran. He had told them that the dangerous part, assuming they were good climbers, was not the steep marl cliffs, but the Bedouin, zealously protecting their turf. Father de Vaux had given the Ta'amireh Bedouin a monopoly on any scrolls or artifacts they discovered in the Qumran caves, and they were known to kill any other Bedouin scavengers who got near their caves.

"Maybe they're like bees, and we shouldn't disturb their hive," said Riggs, looking to see if Christina had second thoughts about the climb.

"I guess we'll just have to smoke them," laughed Christina, warming to the idea and defiantly speeding up the car. *At least these caves won't have waterfalls*, she thought, remembering Yax's ordeal.

Riggs chose not to express his own concerns, which went far beyond the Bedouin. Caught up in her enthusiasm for the climb, he had been less than candid in his description of his limited climbing experience. *I hope I can keep up*, he thought.

"Speaking of smoke," Christina continued, as she turned the car south on Highway 90 toward Masada, "I talked to David Kelley before we left this morning, and he said that Eric Thompson was madder than a hornet about our breakthroughs at Palenque."

"I thought you said he turned down his invitation to that meeting," recalled Riggs.

"He did, but we've embarrassed him by proving that his paradigm was wrong all those years, and David recommended that I get back to Harvard and protect my flanks."

"You mean he's working behind the scenes?" asked Riggs, recalling Allegro's plight.

"It's possible," worried Christina. "I've never had to play the political game before, and he might have friends at higher levels."

"Well, you better get used to it," counseled Riggs, "because we have the same problem with Colby's photos of the Dead Sea Scrolls."

"Not to mention your Nag Hammadi codices," added Christina.

"You're right," agreed Riggs. "I've decided not to let the same thing happen to me, at least not if I can avoid it. If I ever get my hands on the Nag Hammadi codices, I'm not going to take on the establishment single handed."

They drove along in silence. The one thing they had both learned from John Allegro was the dangerous politics behind biblical manuscripts.

"Well, hopefully," said Riggs, breaking the silence, "Thompson will be going after Professor Coe and not the younger players like yourself."

"Possibly," agreed Christina, "but I have no idea what Thompson might be doing, and if he's on the warpath, this is not a good time to be away on my uncle's business. I think I'll head back as soon as possible."

"So soon? Just as I was beginning to warm up to the idea of having a *scroll mate*, even if she is a little set in her ways."

Christina took her eyes off the road and glanced at him. She could tell from his wink that he was just joking about her ways. "Scroll mates? I guess so…it's a lot easier to say than co-custodian of the vault."

Riggs smiled. "Then scroll mates we will be."

If not soul mates, thought Christina, realizing how deeply their lives had become entangled in these few days.

Before them stretched the narrow ribbon of flat land between the barren cliffs to the west and the Dead Sea to the east. The morning light painted bright ochre streaks across the weathered sedimentary slopes, and the sparkling sea lay languid before the first breeze of the day.

"I thought the Dead Sea would look…well, dead," observed Christina, surprised at the intense Mediterranean blue color of the sea.

Riggs rolled down the window and breathed in the fresh air. "I think the air is denser," he commented, "or is that my imagination?"

"Denser?" she asked, breathing in the invigorating air.

"This is the lowest point on the earth, you know, and that does something to the air."

She smiled. He wasn't kidding after all.

"The dead part of the sea, incidentally," he explained, "is that nothing lives in it because of the salt…and that's also why everything floats so high on the water."

"So everything's dense around here," she joked, "the water and the air."

"And maybe me," laughed Riggs, as he suddenly remembered the climb ahead. "What kind of equipment did you bring for the climb?"

"I always bring a few pieces of gear with me on trips…key pieces…things that are lightweight and hard to find in other countries. I never bring rope, of course, because it's heavy and easy to find.. You know I purchased three lengths, and they're in the trunk with the other stuff. It isn't exactly Kernmantel rope, of course."

"I wouldn't know the difference, to tell the truth," smiled Riggs, "unless it was lines on a boat."

"Kernmantel's the best for climbing, but it won't make any difference on such a short climb," she explained. "I think tennis shoes will be fine too. I seldom bring my rock boots or harness with me on trips, because they're just too bulky. I'm planning instead to carry the things I brought on my bandolier," she explained.

"Like what?" asked Riggs, confirming his fears that she was a serious mountain climber and that he might be in over his head.

"I always carry a few quickdraws, a couple belay plates, and several sizes of my favorite chocks," she blurted. Last night in my room, I cut some pieces of rope and strung the chocks. We should have everything we need."

"What are chocks?" asked Riggs, showing once again his unfamiliarity with the sport. *It's absolutely amazing that she improvised all this in her hotel room,* thought Riggs. *She's something else.*

"They're little hexagonal-shaped pieces of metal, with holes in the center, and they attach to almost any little crack or hole in the rock. They replaced pitons several years ago," explained Christina, enjoying the attention she was getting from Riggs. "In the old days, they used little round riverbed stones for the same purpose. Then someone discovered that big hexagonal nuts worked even better. In fact, some climbers call them *nuts* instead of chocks."

"Will they be hard for me to use my first time?" asked Riggs, trying to conceal his nervousness.

"I'll have to see the slope before I can say. We might be able to free climb…it all depends," advised Christina. "Incidentally, I also brought a few carabiners and, of course, a couple figure-eight descenders. None of this stuff takes up much room in my luggage, and it lets me climb anywhere."

"Well, they always say it's easier to go up than to come down," joked Riggs, not completely convinced. "Personally, if all else fails, I think I could still rappel the old fashioned way, with the rope under one thigh and over the other shoulder."

"It's not something you would forget," encouraged Christina.

"There they are," exclaimed Riggs with great excitement. "We'll never have a better view than this."

Christina quickly pulled the Jeep off the highway, over several mounds of sandy rubble and onto the dry river bed of the Wadi Qumran. *I had no idea the cliffs would be so high in the middle of a desert,* she thought quietly. *They look like Mayan temples piercing the sky.*

"That's Allegro's Cave 4, I think," said Riggs, pointing at one of the black openings near the top. He moved his hand slightly to the left and pointed to the next one. "That's Cave 5 next to it, and that looks like Cave 3 further back. That's where they found the Copper Scroll, I think."

"Let's go," bubbled Christina, her adrenaline starting to flow. "We can hide the car over there behind the second slope."

"Don't forget," reminded Riggs, recalling Allegro's advice, "this wadi floods in the rainy season, and if that happens this Jeep would be washed right out of here."

"Is it the rainy season?" asked Christina looking up at a lonely cloud.

"I thought that might get your attention," winked Riggs. "It hasn't started yet this year."

"Yet?"

"Yes…yet."

"Oh well," quipped Christina, as the car bounced over the rough terrain, "It's only a rental car."

"Then why are you turning the Jeep around?" teased Riggs.

"For a fast getaway from the Bedouin Mafia," she said with a twinkle in her eye.

They donned their packs and climbing gear and hiked deeper into the wadi, which dwarfed both them and the car. Unknown to them a second car had turned into the wadi, being driven by a man with a noticeable magenta birthmark on the side of his face.

He calmly placed a pair of binoculars on the hood, flicked his Zippo lighter until it finally lit, took a long drag of the cigarette and leaned back against his car for the long wait. In the practiced manner of the professional, his eyes scanned the wadi to confirm that they were alone. All was quiet, except for a small ibex scampering away from the intruders. He was tempted to pull out his .45 magnum and shoot it…just for sport.

The Ascension

"I don't think we'll need anything but determination for most of this climb," suggested Christina, as she surveyed the situation with a practiced eye. "The talus goes more than half way up the cliff, and although the top part is much steeper, it looks quite weathered with lots of places for us to jam our feet and hands."

Riggs was not convinced, as he strained his neck back to look up at the towering bluff.

"If the going gets tough, I'll place some chocks along the way.

"Is that what the ropes are for?" asked Riggs.

"One of them. I'll secure this long one at the top for our descent from the cave," she said, indicating one of the two coils of rope she had tied over her shoulder.

As she reached up behind her head to fasten her hair down at the base of her neck, Riggs noticed how beautiful she was, dressed in Khaki shorts, a white shirt, and a bright- colored bandolier slung across her feminine chest. In spite of her wholesome appearance, he thought, she looked very much the part of a gun slinging Mexican bandito...except for a few missing cartridges.

She's a pretty sight, he repeated to himself, as she began striding up the talus. He could see her well-formed calves as he followed quickly in her steps.

As she had predicted, the climb was not technically demanding at first, requiring nothing but strength and stamina, as the loose sand gave way under each step. Progress was slow but sure, as they crawled up the steep slope: one step for height and two for the sliding talus.

She stopped for a rest at the top of the talus, where the steep cliffs began, and watched as Riggs slowly completed this segment of the climb. The two of them sat quietly admiring the transparent blue sea, framed by the Jordanian mountains in the distance, while they both caught their breath. The panoramic view from this height was magnificent. Christina then removed several chocks from her bandolier and slid the loops over her arm for convenience. She was ready to attack the most difficult part of the climb.

"That's not too good," she said, as she grabbed one of the rocks in the marl slope, and it came right off in her hand.

"It's awfully loose, isn't it?" observed Riggs, as he shifted the weight of his backpack.

"I probably should have brought my pitons for this face," shrugged Christina, "even though they're old-fashioned. It's going to be difficult placing chocks in this stuff."

Right then a rock came hurtling down from above and glanced off of Riggs' back, as they both pressed their bodies as tightly as barnacles against the face of the bluff.

"We don't need that problem," winced Riggs, as he peered up the slope.

Christina then found a good place to jam her hands and lifted herself up a few feet. She then managed to place one of the chocks in a strong crack between two large rocks in the marl. "Give this a try," she counseled Riggs, as the two of them began inching their way up the cliff.

"Watch this trick," she called down to Riggs, as she executed a series of pressure holds and layaway moves, which brought her well up the face of the crumbling marl.

Not willing to be outdone, and dodging the debris, Riggs duplicated the moves somewhat clumsily, but nevertheless successfully.

"You're a natural," shouted Christina, encouragingly. "We're almost to the cave." She paused for a moment to develop her strategy for the final approach. "I think I'm going to run some belays for this final ascent, even though the marl is a little too crumbly for the chocks. We really don't have a choice...now," she said pointing straight down.

Riggs was clinging to the sheer wall with all his strength and looking over the Dead Sea, some thousand feet below. *Maybe now I understand the name*, he thought to himself. *What I won't do to keep up with this woman.* Suddenly, the marl gave way under his hands and he began to slide backwards down the cliff. In desperation, he quickly jammed two fingers into a small crevice and winced as they held the full weight of his body. He knew that he couldn't stay in this position for long, with only his wedged fingers for support, so he tried to get his dangling feet onto a nearby narrow ledge. He fought back a wave of fear when he realized it was just out of reach.

"I'm coming," screamed Christina, as she pulled a 'Rock 9' chock off her bandolier and scrambled quickly to his side. She deftly jammed it into a small crevice between two stones, held onto the loop with one hand, and lifted some of his weight to free his strained fingers. The loose rocks showered past his head and shoulders, but that was the least of his troubles.

"Grab this loop," she shouted, but he was well ahead of her, responding instinctively.

The two of them hugged the face of the cliff and rested while he regained his strength.

"Thanks," he said, examining his fingers to see how badly they were damaged. "Finger jams are great in emergencies, but I couldn't have held that one much longer."

"You did great," comforted Christina. "We really don't have much further to go. You stay here, and I'll go the rest of the way alone. When I get to the cave, I'll secure this rope with a chock or two and drop it down to you. That should give you a little extra help while your fingers get stronger."

"What about you?" asked Riggs, concerned that she would not be protected during her ascent.

"It looks all right from here," assured Christina, and I have mantelled bigger shelves than the one at the cave entrance. I should have no problem."

Mantelled bigger shelves? thought Riggs. *I wonder what that means?*

He was soon to learn as Christina scaled the remaining distance without a single chock and managed to pull her body over the shelf and into the mouth of the cave.

"Wow," he whispered, as she turned around in the cave entrance, untied the rope around her shoulder and dropped it down to him.

He had no difficulty climbing the last few yards, and he soon climbed through the cave entrance and sat down next to her, with a huge smile on his sweaty face. She too sported a victorious smile.

"We did it," exclaimed Christina, "We completed the perfect crime. We're in one of the Qumran caves."

'Thanks to you," said Riggs, as he wrapped his arm around her shoulder gratefully, and they examined his skinned knuckles. "I think I'll live," he said, thoroughly enjoying the touch of her hands.

"I'm glad you didn't fall. That would've been a rough ride down: free-fall the first half and sandpaper the second," kidded Christina. She held his hand a little longer than necessary.

"As much as I hate to admit it, your idea wasn't so crazy after all."

"In hindsight, that is?" she joked.

"Yeah, I like the hindsight part," he replied, standing up to check the rappelling line one more time, and displaying his renewed confidence now that the worst was behind him.

"We have a great view for lunch," said Christina softly, as she stood closely beside him.

Qumran Camaraderie

The striated walls of the cave were pocked from wind erosion, and the cavern was about the same size as their Cairo vault.

"I expected it to be larger and darker...and perhaps cooler," observed Christina, as she looked around the sun-brightened walls. "These large openings sure let in a lot of light, at least compared to the caves I've been in before."

"It also lets in the hot desert wind," noticed Riggs, as a warm breeze swirled around his bare legs. "I think we'll want to leave before the sun shines directly into that opening."

"Not until we have our lunch," pleaded Christina, reminding Riggs that they only had a couple of rolls for breakfast.

"With a glass of wine," exclaimed Riggs, proudly pulling a bottle of Israeli Carmel wine from his backpack, and displaying it with panache.

"Wine?" she gulped. "In a Qumran cave? Now that's great planning."

He smiled devilishly, with a sparkle in the corner of his eye, as he carefully opened the bottle and poured some wine into each of their drinking cups.

"It's a good thing you didn't drop that bottle," she joked, as she began to unwrap the sandwiches.

He raised an eyebrow in mock seriousness. "That's why I hung on for dear life."

"If I had known, I'd have never let you slip in the first place."

They laughed and raised their cups for a triumphant toast.

"To the Dead Sea Scrolls," proclaimed Christina, "...our Dead Sea Scrolls."

"And to my new scroll-mate," added Riggs, his bronze eyes boldly taking in her beauty.

"What cave do you think we're in?" asked Christina somewhat flustered, but nevertheless flattered by his attention. His steady gaze roused deep emotions she had not experienced for a long time.

"I think this is Cave 3, where they found the Copper Scroll," Riggs replied, reluctantly breaking the spell to look around the cave. "I've seen photos of these caves, and this large rock is unique." He pointed to a single boulder near the center of the cave, surrounded by an uneven floor covered with granular limestone.

Christina looked around the cave, reflecting on its historical significance. "Can you imagine the scene in this cave 2000 years ago when the people buried their sacred scrolls?" she fantasized.

"Do you want to know who these people were?" he said, reverting to his scholarly ways.

"Sure," she said, taking another sip of wine. The boulder made a good backrest as they sat on the cave floor enjoying their lunch together.

"Well, they were strange bedfellows...brought together by the invading Roman armies. There were monks from the nearby village of Qumran, some Temple priests, and probably some wealthy people from Jerusalem. They had one thing in common: they wanted to hide their precious writings before General Vespasian destroyed the area around Jerusalem."

"Were the monks the ones the Insiders called an isolated Jewish sect?" confirmed Christina.

"You learn quickly," beamed Riggs, rubbing his sore fingers. "But there are two big problems with the Insiders theory. The archaeologists on Father de Vaux's team found a forge in the nearby ruins: the kind used to make weapons."

"Hardly the sort of thing needed by ascetics," said Christina dryly, handing her cup to Riggs for some more wine.

"Hardly. And worse yet, there are over two-hundred different hand writing styles on the fragments—far too many for a small countryside monastery. There probably weren't that many scribes in all of Judea, maybe even Palestine. It proves to me that the Scrolls came from a larger community than just the nearby Essenes."

"So what is your theory about the forge?"

"That's easy. The Essenes at Qumran, like all the other Jews, joined the fight against the Romans and even their own Jewish priests, some of whom had become no more than Roman puppets. When the Jewish revolt began, the Qumranians participated with the other Jews, until their ultimate defeat at the hands of Vespasian's son, Titus, in 70 A.D."

While he talked, Christina noticed his glances lengthening, almost tempting their eyes to stay fixed. Was it the wine, or was it her overactive imagination? She could feel her heartbeat quicken, and only when he looked away did she start breathing almost normally again. Time stood still, and she lost track of what Riggs was saying.

"Christina?" Riggs interrupted her silence.

"Oh yes," she mumbled, trying futilely to remember the subject. "I agree...I think."

Riggs laughed, "It's not the most exciting subject in the world." He then reached across to pick up another sandwich and allowed his arm to brush her knee ever so gently. A current of excitement raced up her leg and into her chest. She chose not to move away as he touched her, as if to signal her acceptance. She became almost motionless, as her head began to spin again. He was so close she could smell his musky scent.

He looked again at her for much longer than either of them could endure, and then was the first to look away. He started to say something about their lunch, but could not find the words. He too was losing the thread of the conversation.

After an uncomfortably long silence, Christina found the words she was seeking. "How are your fingers doing?" she said quietly, giving an excuse for the two of them to touch.

He held out his hand for her to see, and she cradled it softly in her two hands, looking at the scrapes. He moved his fingers a little to increase the contact, stroking her fingers with his, and a wave of excitement spread over her entire body. Sensing these feelings, and wanting more, he quickly raised his other hand and grasped the two of hers. She immediately noticed how much warmer his hands were, and she felt faint from a flush of heat under her eyes and on her cheeks. She wanted this first moment to last forever.

His arms began without him, as a lump of anticipation began to grow in his throat. He slowly traced one hand up the length of her arm while continuing to hold her hands with the other one. She closed her eyes to enjoy the feeling in private, giving him the complete control he wanted. A hint of a smile formed on her full lips as his hand caressed her shoulder, then her arched neck and gently lifted up her chin.

He traced the outline of her receptive red lips with his finger, and kissed her gently, bringing his other hand to the side of her face. She raised her hand to his, in a gesture of compliance. He slowly moved his hand, touched by hers, from her cheek to her forehead and back across her golden hair to the back of her neck. She opened her green eyes only for a moment, for them to scream acceptance, and then shut them again for the journey back, as he kissed her more deeply the second time.

Nothing existed but his gentle touch, as his hand moved back to her cheek and flowing hair. She signaled her delight by accepting the fullness of his mouth. Their lips did not part, but sought more and more contact, never satisfying the desire, but enjoying the pursuit.

This cave was their universe. Their bodies were both noticeably alive. He stood and lifted them together with the kiss. Her breasts were tingling, and signals were flashing into her loins.. She wouldn't have minded if he had accidentally brushed against her firm breast as his hand dropped away from her face. But he didn't. Instead, he wrapped his arms tightly around her body, and drew her swollen breasts close to him. His body was asking for more, but his mind had found enough pleasure in their first kiss.

Christina, in her wildest dreams, could not have imagined a more romantic setting for falling in love. They were high in the sky, in a secret cave, breaking all the rules, and surrounded by the ghosts of ancient manuscripts. She felt herself flying out of the cave and soaring across the sky like Pegasus...too close to the sun.

Desert Danger

I against my brother
I and my brother against our cousin
I, my brother and our cousin against the neighbors
All of us against the foreigner.

—Bedouin Proverb

Riggs noticed sand falling past the cave opening from above, and wondered what sort of animal would be crawling on these cliffs. *Probably an ibex*, he thought, *nothing else could hold on to these steep slopes.*

They were putting the barely eaten lunch and empty wine bottle into their backpacks, when the cork fell into a crevice under the edge of the boulder. As Christina kneeled down and reached for it, the marl crumbled away, and the cork fell into a small pocket which had been partially covered.

"What's this?" she said, peering curiously at the small opening. As she felt into the crevice her hand passed through into a larger space, perhaps a pocket of erosion or an opening into a yet undiscovered part of the cave.

"What have you found?" inquired Riggs eagerly. His expression was expectant, as her hand went into the hole beyond her wrist. Their archaeological instincts were both on high alert.

"Let's dig it out a little," he said, reaching for a knife in his backpack.

Christina carefully exposed the larger part of the hole from above and reached in under the large boulder, with her arm up to the elbow.

"What do you feel?" asked Riggs, hoping it was more than powdered limestone.

A broad smile appeared on Christina's face, and he knew that she had found something.

"Be careful," cautioned Riggs.

"I don't think it's necessary," responded Christina as she pulled out a small menorah, covered with the remnants of an old leather bag.

They looked at each other in total amazement.

"Can you imagine how many archaeologists have passed by this treasure since the Scrolls were discovered twenty five years ago?" said an astonished Riggs.

"Not to mention Bedouin looters," added Christina with a pleased smile.

"This is a good omen," smiled Riggs, referring to their budding romance.

As they were examining the tarnished silver menorah, Christina noticed a small cloud of sand blowing past the opening. She grabbed Riggs by the arm and pointed at the falling sand. They instantly realized, without a word spoken between them, that someone was coming down from above. Their pulses raced, and they looked at each other trying to figure out what to do next. Riggs put his fingers to her lips to caution silence, then he quickly stuffed the menorah into his back pack under the lunch, and slid his knife into his pocket.

Riggs whispered one word: "Bedouin."

But it was too late. A scruffy looking man, with a soiled white tunic and headdress, swung boldly into the cave on a rope from the plateau above...with a small curved dagger clenched between his teeth.

He yelled something in Arabic to his cohorts above as he grabbed the handle of the dagger, and moved menacingly toward Riggs and Christina in a crouched position. More sand began to fall past the opening, as the other Bedouin made their way down the face of the cliff.

Riggs' first thought was about the menorah. It would be hard for him to feign innocence, especially if the Bedouin searched his backpack.

My backpack! thought Riggs. *There's more than a menorah in there.* Acting instinctively, he pulled the wine bottle out and broke off the bottom on the boulder. As he handed the jagged edged bottle to Christina, he felt in his pocket for his rigging knife.

I hope we look terrifying, he thought, merely doing what he had seen in the movies. The jagged glass edges on the bottle and the open rigging knife actually looked quite lethal in their hands, but neither one of them had any confidence in their chosen weapons. Something must have been right, however, because as they inched their way toward the cave opening, the Bedouin man backed deeper into the cave, his sadistic smile revealing his broken yellow teeth.

As the legs of the second Bedouin appeared in the opening, Riggs realized that they were trapped and soon to be outnumbered, and that these guys were playing by different rules. With no time to waste, and with the most primal of reactions, Riggs suddenly thrust his knife up into the crotch of the dangling Bedouin.

He shrieked with pain and was barely able to pull himself back up the cliff, even with help from the others. The first man moved further into the back of the cave with his dagger still poised threateningly; he seemed less certain of himself, now that the odds were more even, and these tourists had shown such unexpected behavior.

"This is our only chance," yelled Riggs at Christina, who leaped immediately onto the rappelling line and began the long descent.

"See you at the bottom," shouted Christina, as her voice faded into the abyss.

"I'm right behind you," called down Riggs, hoping that they could escape before the Bedouin thought to cut the rope. Wavering for a moment, he looked nervously over the ledge at the gaping void, then back at the angry Bedouin, and chose the lesser of the two evils. The rope screamed through his hands as he plummeted toward the bottom, not having had time to secure it properly around his body. At times, but not often enough, he was able to push away from the cliff face with his feet, protecting himself during the perilous descent.

Meanwhile, having landed safely on the talus, Christina squinted into the sun to see how Riggs was doing. To her horror, she saw that his descent was out of control, and even worse, that the man in the cave was sawing the rope.

Suddenly the rope parted, and Riggs dropped the last twenty feet into a rolling ball onto the sloped talus. Christina, fearing the worst, ran after him, slipping through the crumbled talus, and was relieved when she saw him stand and begin shaking the sand out his hair.

"That's not a bad place to land," he said happily, as she came to a sliding stop at his feet.

As they jumped quickly into the Jeep, Riggs threw the car into gear and raced out of the Wadi Qumran leaving no stones unturned. Christina noticed fresh tire tracks from another vehicle on the river bed, but it was hardly the time for new theories.

"We left our rappelling line," joked Riggs with a sardonic grin, as they looked back at their sanctum from a safe distance.

"Do you want to go back and get it?" bantered Christina.

"Maybe later," he replied with the smile of a man who had escaped death. He put his arm around her shoulder for the first time, and it felt damn good to be alive.

Turning the Corner

In the New Testament there is internal evidence that parts of it have proceeded from
an extraordinary man, and that other parts are of the fabric of very inferior minds. It
is as easy to separate those parts as to pick diamonds from dunghills.

—Thomas Jefferson

"Do you think that happens to all the tourists?" Riggs asked sarcastically, as they sped through the Judean wilderness on the way back to Jerusalem. The boiling highway, if they were to believe the mirage before their eyes, had been rippled by the desert sun...a washboard they never seemed to encounter. A strong hot wind blew through the Jeep, barely protecting them from the scalding heat.

"Only the ones foolish enough to drink wine in their caves," laughed Christina, still exhilarated from their close encounter with the Bedouin.

"Who do you think made those tire tracks we saw on the way out?" pondered Riggs.

"I have no idea," mulled Christina, "unless it was the same person who sent the Bedouin into our cave." She turned around to see if they were being followed, but the road was empty.

"Who might that be?" asked Riggs innocently.

"Well," hesitated Christina, wondering if it was a good time for this subject. "Well...I guess you need to know that I thought Allegro might have been responsible for my uncle's murder."

Riggs jerked the wheel in surprise and the tires screamed on the steaming asphalt.

"What makes you think he was murdered by John Allegro? He wouldn't hurt a fly."

"It's a long story," answered Christina slowly, hoping to avoid some of the details.

"Might as well get started," encouraged Riggs in a toneless voice, "it's a long drive back to Jerusalem. The next thing I'm going to hear is that I too was a suspect."

Christina couldn't hide her embarrassment, and a blush could be seen rising through her sun-drenched cheeks. "I had to suspect everyone until I got here...especially those close to him."

Riggs drove quietly, wondering if this explained the cool reception he had received from Christina when she first arrived. "Why do you think Colby was murdered?"

For reasons Christina did not understand, she was not yet ready to reveal everything to this man, and yet just minutes before she had been dizzy in his arms. She just needed more time to sort out the confusion. She was especially nervous about the contents of Colby's folder, because she did not yet know what manuscript he had been pursuing. She had every intention of telling Riggs everything…eventually.

"Henry said that Uncle Colby's briefcase was missing and that the police were acting strange about the whole situation. And it took place on one of the busiest corners in Cairo, yet there were no witnesses. And…"

"And of course Colby changed the names on the vault at the last minute," interrupted Riggs, finishing her train of thought.

"That's right," agreed Christina, hoping the questions would end there.

"I really don't think it was John Allegro," repeated Riggs, looking for a nod of agreement from Christina. "And those Bedouin back there were probably just defending their turf."

"Probably," agreed Christina with little enthusiasm, not completely ruling out the possibility in her own mind.

Riggs put his hand gently on her knee and a serious look spread across his face. "Can I share a concern of mine with you?"

"Sure," she replied, pleased that he wanted to confide in her.

"The more I think about Allegro's predicament, the more nervous I get about the situation with the Nag Hammadi codices. We really need to get our hands on them before they too become a political football. Once the word gets out that they might contain controversial new gospels, the powers that be will get involved, and Robinson might get caught in the same storm that capsized John."

"Robinson and you," she pointed out.

"Yes, Robinson and me, except I might never get my hands on them, and Professor Robinson got tenure a long time ago," he said, as his voice faded to a deep whisper.

So that's the real problem, she thought to herself. "You don't have tenure yet?" she asked, trying not to sound haughty. He knew that she was already tenured at Harvard.

"My tenure's dangling by the thread of these damn Codices. I've bet it all on the Nag Hammadis by spending the past years perfecting my skills in Coptic. I had planned to hit the ground running, and now I can't get my hands on the manuscripts."

She knew how strongly he must feel about tenure: nothing meant more to junior professors. It not only meant financial stability and the freedom to speak out on controversial issues, but more importantly, it was a rite of passage to academic respectability. She also knew that if it didn't happen early in one's career, then it probably would never happen, and Riggs' career would be in academic purgatory forever.

"If I can ever help…"

"I'll let you know," he interrupted with a wink, "especially if it involves rope climbing."

"Well, if you ever do get your hands on the Codices," reasoned Christina, "it would be best not to take on the power structure single-handed. We learned from Allegro that the politics get complicated unless everyone has copies of the manuscripts. It becomes your word against that of the establishment."

"You're right," added Riggs, "and the same thing could be true for our photos of the Dead Sea Scrolls...except we could just mail out copies, and there would be no one to stop us."

"Unless Henry finds a written secrecy agreement, of course," reminded Christina.

"Or unless the person who killed Colby has his eye on us," warned Riggs.

Unless, of course, thought Christina, *Colby was killed over the other manuscript.*

They drove along in silence as they left the desert behind and began the ascent up the long grade to Jerusalem. The temperature was a little cooler as they reached the higher elevation, but the afternoon sun was still overhead.

"Meanwhile," said Christina, putting her hand on his shoulder, "now that we're friends, can I ask you a personal question?"

"Friends?" kidded Riggs, enjoying her touch and remembering their embraces.

"Please tell me," implored Christina, pretending to ignore his comment, "that Allegro's views of Christianity were distorted." She doubted that his answer would change, but she knew now that she could trust his answer.

"I must admit that I have doubts about Allegro's Catholic conspiracy theories," said Riggs, "but the part about alternatives to Paul's imaginative version of Christianity is, unfortunately, quite true. This was one of the first disappointments I faced as a young New Testament scholar; the other was when I learned that the Synoptic Gospels (Matthew, Mark and Luke) seemed to be independent validations of the same events only because they all shared common sources."

"What do you mean by that?"

"First you have to know that the Gospels were written at least thirty-five years after the crucifixion and not by eyewitnesses. Before they were written, various Christian communities developed their own oral traditions. What we call the Gospel of Mark was written first, and then Matthew and Luke combined portions of Mark with other common sources and their own oral traditions."

"You mean the authors of Matthew and Luke just copied Mark?" asked a shocked Christina. She had always derived comfort from the agreement between the three independent eyewitness accounts. Since they were all essentially the same, she had thought, they must be true."

"They didn't consider it plagiarism in those days. There were no copyright laws," he joked. "In fact, it was common practice for writers and storytellers to incorporate good stories they heard."

"That's not the part that bothered me," grimaced Christina, knitting her brows.

"I know," he said compassionately, patting her hand.

"No wonder they are *synoptic*," said Christina derogatorily. "If two different people rewrote the book <u>Black Beauty</u>, adding some new materials, the stories would definitely seem synoptic. That's no way to write history."

"Well, you have to understand that these traditions were written down by evangelists and not by historians. Even if it had been written by historians, their concept of history in those days was very different from the way we think of it today."

"What else do I need to know?" she asked, wondering what else she had been taught was misleading.

"Well, there's the age of the New Testament manuscripts and the ways they got their names."

"Let's hear it," she responded, wanting to get it all over at once.

"The oldest extant manuscripts date back only to the early third century, and they are written in Greek," Riggs told her reluctantly, "not Hebrew or Aramaic, which the disciples would have used."

"Then how do they know who wrote them?"

"They don't. These stories circulated anonymously until Church authorities gave them names sometime in the third century."

"No one knows who wrote the four Gospels?" gasped Christina, shaking her head in disbelief. "The Church just made up the names?"

"I'm afraid so."

"Let me get this straight. No documents go back to the time of Christ?" asked Christina once again.

"That's right. The soonest the first manuscripts could have been written was at least thirty-five years after the crucifixion, and the oldest copy we have of this dates from the early third century. Can you imagine if thirty-five years of oral tradition was allowed to pass before the first book was written on the assassination of President Kennedy?

Thoughts swirled through Christina's mind as she recalled all the conspiracy theories surrounding the Kennedy assassination, and that event was not only photographed but covered by many independent news organizations. She was even more struck by the sudden realization that the laboratory report in Colby's folder had a first century date.

Could he have found the oldest copy—the original perhaps—of a New Testament Gospel? she wondered. *Perhaps even the Gospel of Mark?*

A Man of Action

They looked at each other in anticipation as they sat down on the side of the bed in Riggs' hotel room, still sweaty and dusty from the drive back from Qumran. He was nervously folding a message from the front desk marked "Urgent." They expected the phone to ring any moment.

Thinking back, Riggs realized that Robinson must have arrived in Cairo yesterday and spent the day at the Coptic museum. What could have happened in just one day for James to call him in Jerusalem with an urgent message? Whatever it was, Riggs wanted Christina to overhear the conversation, just in case it was good news.

"Hello?" Riggs answered on the first ring. He nodded to Christina to confirm that Robinson was on the line.

"I've spent some time looking at the Codices," Robinson began.

Christina moved closer to Riggs so she could hear Robinson speaking.

"They are incredible...absolutely incredible...even better than we imagined."

A smile spread over Riggs face as he put his arm around Christina and gave her a squeeze. The two of them were hanging on Robinson's next words.

"But...," he began dejectedly. Christina squeezed Riggs leg in nervous anticipation.

"But?" Riggs said with a wedge of anxiety lodged in his throat.

"But, Labib isn't going to let anyone but the Committee look at the Codices."

Christina could feel Riggs slump with the bad news. She knew how high the stakes were in this game, and it looked like they were dealing Riggs out of this hand.

"But..." Robinson continued, not letting Riggs dangle any longer than necessary, "I've been doing some thinking."

"Go on," urged Riggs, wondering what he had come up with. He knew from experience that when Professor Robinson was *doing some thinking*, big things usually happened.

"Well, ever since you told me about your photos of the Dead Sea Scrolls, I've been thinking that the Nag Hammadi codices deserve at least as much attention, maybe even more. What if, for example, we took some photos of our own...late tomorrow night?"

Riggs' was speechless as he turned his face toward Christina. They looked at each other to confirm that they were hearing the same thing. Robinson was planning to covertly photograph the Codices, without Labib's permission, and send copies to scholars around the world. It was a bold plan.

"And mail them out?" anticipated Riggs, with Christina nodding yes.

"And mail them out," confirmed Robinson. "We've played by the rules long enough. It's time for the world to see those manuscripts, and it's fallen on my shoulders to get the job done."

Christina poked Riggs in the ribs with excitement, encouraging him to volunteer their services.

"Need some help from two linguists?" joked Riggs.

"Two? Don't tell me the spring thaw came in Boston?"

"Sort of," said Riggs sheepishly, as Christina wrinkled her nose at what sounded like man talk.

As Riggs and Robinson began to talk more about their favorite subject, Christina absently thumbed through a stack of papers on the bed and came across a newspaper clipping of Robinson receiving an award for his Biblical scholarship. She held it up and Riggs nodded that she should read it.

The article praised Robinson as one of the most important voices in New Testament research, not only for his individual contributions, but also for his steadying view during these turbulent times for Christianity. As she already knew, he was Professor of Religion at Claremont Graduate School, and also Director of the Institute for Antiquity and Christianity. His degrees, publications and academic achievements were enough to fill a book. He had studied or taught at Princeton, Harvard, Basel, Zurich, Heidelberg, Marburg, Strasbourg and Paris. His language, she noted, included German and Coptic, in addition to Greek, Latin, Aramaic and Hebrew.

My goodness, she thought, *he's a polyglot like Floyd Lounsbury back in my Palenque days.* She read on. Robinson had been president of every prominent international theological organization and he had founded three important communiqués: *The New Testament Colloquium, Hermeneia, and The Journal for Theology and the Church.*

"Impressive isn't he?" said Riggs, as he put down the phone.

Christina looked up and nodded. "From the way you talked about him, I knew that you respected him, but I had no idea how important a person he is. Why would he risk it all to break in and take the photos?"

"You'll know when you meet him. He's a person with incredible moral courage and, like yourself, he's an intrepid explorer. He's put himself in danger for the sake of knowledge many times."

"I can't wait to meet him," she said reddening from the oblique compliment.

"When you do, you'll be even more impressed with his humility and decency. He's a true Christian and a wonderful humanitarian. You'll sense it the moment you're around him."

"How could he be a Christian," asked Christina, "if he knows everything you've told me about the New Testament?"

"I'll let him speak for himself," answered Riggs respectfully, "but I know that he has a deep understanding of God and that he believes that the teachings of Jesus are more important than the stories and legends which developed after the crucifixion, even though these stories convey important messages. He believes that the gateway to salvation is not only through the church door, but also in the heart and in following the teachings of Jesus. He believes our Christian behavior is as important as our Christian creeds. He's a refreshing voice, and as you can tell, I think he's the most wonderful person in the world, and I'm not alone in this sentiment."

"I have many of the same feelings toward Michael Coe, my own Major Professor," responded Christina, reminiscing fondly.

"Isn't it coincidental how our lives have been brought together?" asked Riggs. "We're both linguists, we've both fought academic monopolies, and we both believe in giving voice to ancient writings."

"Maybe it's not a coincidence at all. Maybe Uncle Colby had this in mind all along."

"Well, Old Colby always did have a great sense of humor," said Riggs playfully.

The way he looked at her did not seem humorous to Christina. In fact it was a look of naked desire. She suddenly realized that they were sitting on his bed alone, and that he was no longer just an innocent scroll mate. She had hardly even noticed the bed in his room before, but suddenly it seemed to fill the entire space. The thought brought blood to her face, causing a warm blush under her eyes.

His eyes clouded for a second, he swallowed, and then he said quietly, "Can I walk you to your room?"

Could he have known my thoughts, she wondered?

At her door, he gave her a sweet goodnight kiss, and ever the organizer, reminded her of the return flight to Cairo early in the morning.

Once inside her room and leaning against her door, she whispered to herself: *I should have just pinned him down on his bed and gotten it all over with. I was sure in the mood. It was nice of him not to try though...I think.* Was he showing respect, or did she mistake his intentions? Either way, it would not have been an easy decision for her to make. Her own life had been complicated by her Catholic upbringing, even though he would not have been the first.

118

Although he would be the first Protestant, she smiled to herself, *...or whatever he is.*

She doubted that this would have changed the advice from her mother, the nuns who taught her catechism, and her brother the priest. She laid back on the bed, exhausted from the climb, titillated by their budding romance, and exhilarated by the clandestine plan to photograph the Codices right under Labib's large nose.

Through the window she could see that the full moon had risen over the ancient walls of Old Jerusalem and was reflecting brightly off the golden dome of the Dome of the Rock.

It's the danger, she thought.

Sayings Gospels

And the companion of the Savior is Mary Magdalene. But Christ loved her more than all the disciples and used to kiss her often on her mouth.

—Gospel of Philip
Nag Hammadi Library

"Tonight's the night," said Professor Robinson, as the three of them sat down for a quick supper of Mrs. Scarzella's lasagna. They were noticeably tense.

"What's the plan?" asked Riggs anxiously, wondering how he planned to get into the museum at night.

"I got the key from the cleaning lady," smiled Robinson, displaying the key triumphantly. He passed it around to each of them, as though it were a sacred object.

"How did you get that, James?" asked Christina.

Professor Robinson, or James, as she now dared to address him, had just changed from his business suit and tie to his more comfortable attire, which included a Danish ski sweater he wore against the evening chill. When the sun went down in this desert clime, it was much cooler than visitors expected, but he was well prepared as usual. His heavy horn-rimmed glasses sat squarely on his erudite face and the temples pushed through his long bushy sideburns. He had already won Christina's affection, with his slightly impish smile and unbridled enthusiasm.

"Rather than waiting for me to leave tonight," he answered, "she asked me to lock the door when I left later. I think we can assume that there'll be no one at the museum tonight, and if we work quickly, we should have the photographs completed an hour or so before Pahor arrives in the morning. He never gets there before nine."

"That makes our mission a little less impossible," grinned Christina, obviously relishing the intrigue. She could understand why the cleaning lady would immediately trust his innocent eyes and air of integrity. Riggs had been correct that this man was far more humble than his credentials.

"But nevertheless, a great deal of work," reminded Professor Robinson, with just a hint of his refined Southern drawl. "We have less than twelve hours to photograph fifty tractates. I estimate that there are well over one-thousand pages, which means each of us must take a photograph at least every three minutes, to be safely out of there before Labib arrives."

"That sounds feasible," calculated Riggs, impressed that Professor Robinson had planned to this level of detail. *As usual,* he thought.

"Don't forget that we also want to back-light each page with UV looking for hidden markings," reminded Professor Robinson.

Riggs nodded his head: "Twelve hours might not be enough time."

"You're right, we'll need every minute," he said, eating a little faster. "Today, for instance, after the cleaning lady left, I found still another new Gospel, bringing the total to four Gospels that are not in the New Testament. This one describes a Christianity quite different from Paul's."

"Four more?" asked Christina.

"I'm certain there are more," said Robinson, looking kindly at Christina. "I can't wait to get my hands on these documents for more than a few minutes at a time."

"I can't believe that tonight, after all these years, I'm actually going to have in my hands words of Jesus which have escaped the vagaries of editing for almost two-thousand years!" said Riggs, hoping that nothing would go wrong at the last minute.

"Indeed we will," resolved James.

Christina could sense the electricity of discovery in the air. This feeling wasn't new to her, having just experienced it herself on the night her group broke the Maya Code at Palenque. She actually shared their enthusiasm, at least vicariously, if for no other reason that this fulfilled one of Uncle Colby's dreams. Not to mention Riggs' career...hanging in the balance.

"I hope that we'll also find at least one Sayings Gospel," continued Professor Robinson, "just to prove their existence."

Christina looked quizzically at her new friend. "What's a *sayings gospel?*"

James, who had obviously taken a liking to her, turned his full attention to his favorite subject. "The Gospels in the New Testament are called narrative gospels, because they include stories about the life and deeds of Jesus, in addition to his teachings. Biblical scholars now believe that these were preceded by Sayings Gospels, which only include his teachings."

"Like Proverbs or Psalms?" confirmed Christina.

"That's the idea," agreed Professor Robinson. "Probably more like Proverbs, but the point is that the first Gospels included only his teachings. The stories about his miraculous life were added later to the Gospels in our New Testament."

"Are you saying," asked Christina, "that the sayings gospels would be more authentic than the narrative gospels?"

Professor Robinson nodded. "I'm saying that they would be older and presumably recorded closer to the actual historical events."

"How can scholars tell that the sayings gospels preceded the narrative gospels?" asked Christina.

"We don't have time for that complicated subject tonight, unless we want to postpone the photo session," said James, half joking with a twinkle in his eye, "but it involves linguistic techniques you would readily understand. We call them 'rules of written evidence', and they include the analysis of clusters, of context, of revisions and comments. We also study what we call 'Christianization', which is the assimilation of older legends into Christianity from other sources. It is often accomplished by attributing these older words to Jesus himself."

"If I understand you correctly," said Christina, confirming the new information, "if we can find a sayings gospel among the Codices, it would be very important, because it would prove that the stories about His life in our New Testament were added later to the stories of His teachings."

"It's that simple," agreed Riggs. "Furthermore, if we can prove the existence of a sayings gospel, then theories about other Gospels of this genre would gain credibility. I can tell you more about that after the photo session."

"Well, guys, good luck on your sayings gospels" said Christina, not totally convinced, "but personally, I'm going to be looking for the Gospel of Mary...I mean the Gospel attributed to Mary," she quickly corrected.

James glanced at Riggs, who smiled as he said proudly: "She's a quick study."

"Well professors," said Robinson, taking a look at his watch and drinking the last of his coffee. "It's time for the break-in. Do you all have your masks to wear?

They all laughed nervously.

"I feel like a triple agent," giggled Christina

"Or a jewelry thief," countered Riggs.

"Or a linguist," joked James. "I can remember when the study of ancient texts was a library sport. The only risk was inhaling too much dust. My graduate students will never believe this story."

• • •

Pahor Labib set his alarm that night for five-thirty in the morning, because he was meeting Victor Girgis very early at the museum. He was not pleased that he would have to rise so early, but it was the only time Victor could meet due to other travel commitments. Pahor propped his cane against the night stand, laid his thick glasses on the table, rubbed his eyes and ample nose, and stretched out for a little sleep.

Photogate

Five men said to have been carrying cameras, electronic surveillance equipment and burglary tools, were arrested shortly after 2 am today after a floor by floor search that led to the executive quarters for the National Democratic Committee.

—New York Times, June 18, 1972

"Are we almost done?" asked James, pushing his two underpaid assistants to the limit. "It is nearly seven, and we want to be out of here long before Pahor arrives."

Codices were stacked all over the long conference table, which they had commandeered for their photographic equipment. A 35mm camera with a close-up lens had been set up on a tripod next to the table, and Professor Robinson manned the camera while Christina positioned each page of the tractates. Riggs moved about the room, collecting and organizing the materials for the camera crew. Each flash of the camera's strobe punctuated their movements like an old silent movie. They were glassy-eyed from working all night, using just flashlights and a small lamp borrowed from a nearby desk

"We thought we were done until we found this codex in Pahor's office," said Riggs. "It looks like Codex XII. Why is it so thin?"

"That must be the one Muhammad 'Ali's mother burnt for firewood in her oven," agonized James, shaking his head from side to side in disbelief. "I don't even like to think about it. There sure isn't much left."

Suddenly, a loud knock on the front door of the museum echoed through the tomb-like galleries. Christina quickly flipped off the lamp as the three of them stood motionless, their eyes adjusting to the dark.

"Who could that be?" gasped Riggs, as he ran to the window and looked cautiously across the courtyard. In the grainy light of the dawn, he could not make out the caller's identity.

"If that's Pahor, we're in trouble," James whispered. He silently motioned for them to quickly clean everything up, as he reluctantly handed Codex XII to Riggs, who placed them all in the cupboard. They all hoped that Pahor wouldn't notice the codex missing from his office.

Victor Girgis knocked on the door a second time.

"Does he see us in here?" asked Riggs.

"I don't think so," answered Christina, who was keeping an eye on him through the courtyard window. "Where will we hide if he comes in here?"

"Triple agents always hide in the broom closet," breathed Riggs, feeling giddy from a combination of fatigue and now adrenaline.

"They always get discovered in the broom closet," warned James, having no trouble at all being serious. It was his reputation that was at stake.

"How about next to one of the mummies?" whispered Christina with a muffled giggle.

"That's another museum," blurted Professor Robinson loudly before he could mute his voice. This inane repartee between the young lovers was trying his patience. "You two get under my desk, and I'll pretend I've been doing research all night."

"Here's my chance," said Riggs, trying his best to sound lecherous as the two of them squeezed under James' desk, arms and legs tangled in a knot.

The two of them listened to their heartbeats throbbing in their ears as Robinson sat at the desk shuffling papers, trying his best to look innocent.

Footsteps resounded across the courtyard. James pushed his chair back and tip-toed to the corner of the window. Through the wrought iron grille, he saw Pahor Labib walk up to Victor Girgis and talk to him for a few terrifying seconds. They then walked away together.

"Breakfast," said Professor Robinson, as he headed for his desk to chastise the two worthless assistants under his desk. "They must be having a breakfast meeting somewhere."

"You mean they're not coming in?"

"I don't think so," James replied. "Get me Codex XII...and hand me that camera."

Wavicles
1927
Bell Scientific Research Laboratories

> It does not exist, it does not not-exist, it does not both exist and not exist, nor does it neither exist nor not exist.
>
> —Ala Nagarjuna
> First century Buddhist

"I'm working on the most important physics experiment of the century, and yet I've been delayed for two weeks by this damn electronics problem," moaned a postdoctoral student named Stewart Keeton. "I can't take many more of these sleepless nights."

"I thought you were going to meet with Dr. Davisson today, asked Jette, his sultry girlfriend of three weeks. "Doesn't he know what to do?"

"Everyone's stumped. I've got one more idea, and that's it for tonight. I'm dead tired," he said rubbing his red eyes. "I'm hoping this new voltmeter will be sensitive enough to find the problem." He began placing the probes carefully onto key locations in the circuit.

She rubbed his head and shoulders as though he were Adonis, and with a glance toward the closed door put her hand on the inside of his leg. "Maybe a short break would get your systems working again," she tempted him, eyeing his empty office. "Don't you think we need some private time?"

"If I have any more *private time* with you tonight, I'll fall asleep for sure. Do you know how many breaks we've already taken?"

"I just can't get enough of you," she purred.

"I feel the same way, but I've got to find the problem with this circuit, or Dr. Davisson can say goodbye to his Nobel Prize," implored Stewart. Fortunately for him, and physics, Stewart's excess intellectual capabilities had managed to suppress his male hormones for the better part of his thirty years; but since he met Jette everything had become dramatically out of balance, especially his hormones.

"Why does Dr. Davisson think he might get the Nobel Prize?" asked Jette, once again rubbing her hand on the inside of his thigh.

She's a vixen, thought Stewart, trying not to lose his concentration as her fluffy auburn hair tickled the back of his neck. *Definitely a vixen.* "Because he's testing the hypothesis of wave-particle duality."

"What does that mean?" she asked. Her spotty accomplishments as a part-time art student had not prepared her for these conversations.

"It would mean that matter can't decide whether to be a wave or a particle, so it runs around capable of being both. But once it's forced to make a decision, it becomes one or the other."

"You mean it's got a split personality? It's schizophrenic?" joked Jette, giving it her own interpretation. "Or is it androgynous?"

"If you insist, you can call it schizophrenic, but the name 'wave-particle duality' is more acceptable around the lab here."

"Could you explain it to me again?" she pleaded.

"I'll try, but it isn't easy you know…this is leading edge physics. If you had just a little math or science background, it would be helpful."

"Try me," she said, blowing in his ear just enough to distract him once again. She was determined to show an interest in her new lover's work.

"First you need to know the difference between waves and particles," began Stewart.

"We've already been through this." she recited. "Particles are little things that bounce around like billiard balls."

124

"That's right," he said, as he continued to test his electronic circuits.

"Waves are like the ones on the beach," she continued, proud that she had remembered.

"Radio signals and light are also waves," he added, "although the radio waves are invisible. We physicists think of waves when we see light dispersed by lenses and prisms."

"Like in a rainbow," she smiled. "It's really not difficult to see the difference between billiard balls and rainbows, or between particles and waves. It's the next part that's difficult for me."

"You're right. The story would be quite simple except for two surprises," warned Stewart. "Einstein came up with one, and the French scientist, de Broglie, came up with the other one."

"This is where you usually lose me, but I promise to get it tonight," purred Jette, while stroking her finger on the back of his neck.

Stewart twisted one of the dials on his voltmeter to change the sensitivity. "Einstein made what at the time was a radical proposal. He said that light waves might also behave like billiard balls...very tiny billiard balls, of course."

"Einstein thought that light could be both a wave and a particle?" confirmed Jette.

"It sounds strange, but it turns out he was right, and they gave the very small billiard balls of light the great name *quanta*. And they later came up with the name *wavicles* for things that can be either waves or particles."

"Wavicles are schizophrenic," remembered Jette, who was making sure his mind was not completely on physics. "They can be either or both."

"You seem to understand it better every time," praised Stewart. "Wavicles are things, like light, which behave either as waves or as particles, depending on what situation they encounter. If we put the light wavicle through a prism, it knows to behave like a wave and spread out into a rainbow. If we shine the light wavicle onto a photodetector, it knows to smack it like a tiny billiard ball and cause an electrical pulse to flow. The wavicle is smart enough to figure out which of its split personalities to exhibit in any particular situation, and it always has the capacity to be either one."

"Makes sense to me," she said, "except for one thing. "What difference does it make? Why are all the physicists so excited?"

"Well they got even more excited later, as you know, when De Broglie entered the game, but the initial excitement came from the realization that the light had to have two different pasts, one for each of its personalities. The wave personality had a completely different past or history from the particle personality."

"So which past was true?" she asked innocently.

"Both," he answered, with a twinkle. "Now do you understand why the idea generated so much excitement. Wavicles don't have a unique past. They can choose from different ones just to please us. Once we decide which personality we want to observe, they accommodate us with the appropriate past."

He looked up from his voltmeter with a beaming, but tired smile.

"And guess what?" he exclaimed, with a hint of Eureka in his voice. "I just found the timing problem with this apparatus. One of the vacuum tubes must have a bad grid plate. Help me hold this nickel crystal so it doesn't break. I have to remove these tubes."

"This one?" she said, gingerly reaching toward the instrument.

"Careful. Protect it with your life," he said, handing it to her carefully. The nickel crystal is the heart of the experiment. If you break it, Dr. Davisson will kill me."

He glanced at his watch and realized that it was only two o'clock in the morning. He knew that if he could get the apparatus running, it might be possible to complete the first phase of the experiment that night, before Dr. Davisson arrived at the lab the following morning. In spite of his fatigue, he began to work with renewed enthusiasm.

"Now we're up to the part in the story which I never understand," said Jette with a hint of trepidation in her voice. She didn't like to look stupid, but the next step was definitely not easy for her.

Showing his ability to do three things at once, Stewart continued to repair the apparatus, talk to her, and have his back and legs massaged, all at the same time. "The next surprise came from Prince de Broglie."

Jette kidded him that the next surprise might come from her, as her hands became more adventuresome. "You're not the only experimentalist here," she laughed.

"Let me give you some dates as references. Einstein got his only Nobel Prize for schizophrenic light quanta six years ago in 1921, some fifteen years after he published his revolutionary ideas. These ideas met tremendous resistance from the physics community, because he was essentially unknown at the time. He was very young, and his name didn't command the respect it does today."

"I thought he also got a Nobel Prize for relativity?" interjected Jette. "*E equals em see squared* and all that."

"Not really. He never got the Nobel Prize for relativity."

"That's amazing?"

"And then three years ago, in 1924," he continued, "Louis de Broglie, had a very tantalizing idea."

"Is this the one about everything in the world being wavicles?" anticipated Jette.

"That's it," responded Stewart. This was his favorite part. "De Broglie said that if light waves can be very tiny billiard balls, why can't billiard balls, or elementary particles, be waves? If so, then all matter, not just light, would be schizophrenic, being both particle and wave, and the understandable and predictable world we inherited from Newton would be gone forever."

"Gone forever?"

Stewart smiled at his sweetheart, as if to assure her that she was not immediately threatened. "These things take time, but eventually the whole world will have a different sense of reality. We've been adapting to Newton's paradigm now for nearly two hundred years.

"I never realized that Newton had influenced my sense of reality," kidded Jette. "I never met the man, and I certainly don't understand his physics."

"You're right," agreed Stewart, trying not to discourage her attentiveness. "But our society nevertheless accepts his premise that the world is predictable...like a giant machine or clockworks."

"And now it's not?" asked Jette.

"It won't be if our experiment confirms de Broglie's wave-particle duality, because that will mean we can no longer know for certain where particles are and where they're going. Worse yet, we won't even know for certain what they are. Some of my professor's say it will be even more mysterious than that."

"What did they say?" said Jette, giving his inner thigh a little more attention.

"They said that wave-particle duality could also mean that the human consciousness is somehow involved in our physical measurements, and that reality might be internal, rather than external nor objective. They think that the very act of observation could influence physical reality. They see the observer and the observed as a single entity."

"So if they're right, we humans are playing a much more important role in the material universe than just that of idle observers?" recited Jette dutifully. "It sounds like an Eastern philosophy, if you ask me."

"It actually does," agreed Stewart. "Today in one of my classes the professor wrote down a quote from the philosopher, Alan Watts, concerning the creative power of the present tense:

The moment of the world's creation is seen to lie, not in some unthinkably remote past, but in the eternal now.'

"I can't believe that a simple experiment could have such deep philosophical implications," said Jette, beginning to understand why Stewart worked so relentlessly.

"Well, it's not exactly simple, but you're right. This experiment could have very deep implications on the nature of reality. It would introduce a disturbing uncertainty to the physical universe as well as some puzzling paradoxes," said Stewart, feeling exhilarated about his role in history. "We would never again know for certain where particles are and where they are headed. They might even be at more than one place at the same time."

Jette just shook her head in amazement and returned to their youthful games.

The two of them eventually fell asleep on a blanket next to the apparatus, dreaming of wavicles, wave-particle duality, Nobel Prizes, observer-dependent reality, and best of all young love.

Robinhood Robinson

Nothing great was ever achieved without enthusiasm.

—Ralph Waldo Emerson
Essays

Christina could see the chaos behind him, as Riggs opened the door to his room and the musky smell of a gymnasium struck her nose. "This place is starting to look like an archaeological dig," she said with a look of disgust on her face. "Or a bombed out city during World War II." She waved her hand at the stacks of research papers and half eaten meals from the kitchen, meals she had brought him because she worried that he was not getting enough to eat.

He looked sheepishly at his own mess and motioned her in.

"Not on your life," she said, as though refusing a leper. "Have you looked in a mirror lately?"

"Not really," he said pathetically, rubbing his bloodshot eyes and the new growth of his beard. His marathon effort to translate the Nag Hammadi codices had begun to take its toll, and he knew he looked freshly keel-hauled.

"You look like a drug addict," she said. "Worse yet, you look like a translation addict. If you don't get a better lamp, you're going to be a blind addict."

He just stood there, thinking about the Coptic words he had just translated. "I'm about to finish a rough translation of an important tractate," he mumbled, showing no signs of remorse. Then trying to shift attention away from his own appearance, and that of his room, he said: "I just talked to Professor Robinson, or Robinhood, as they're calling him back home now."

"How is...Robinhood?" she asked coolly, having difficulty not blaming her new friend, James, for the mess which stood before her. Riggs was, after all, his student.

"He's fine, and he said to say hello," answered Riggs. "He just finished mailing out the copies of the Nag Hammadi codices to everyone."

"That didn't take very long," observed Christina, counting the days on one hand.

"No, it didn't, and that's the problem. Now the race is on to translate them, and I'll have to work all the harder to be the first."

"How could you work any harder?" asked a skeptical Christina. She had hardly set eyes on him since he had begun his research binge a few days ago.

"Well, I'm going to have to...somehow. I'm not going to get this close to success and throw it all away."

She knew exactly what he meant, but this time it fell on deaf ears. She had played second fiddle to his career enough the last few days to know that she didn't enjoy it in the slightest. "Well you might be throwing away more than your success, if you don't get some balance back in your life," she warned.

He looked at her like a puppy that had just wet the carpet. He was sorry for his neglect of their budding romance, but he didn't really have control of the situation. "I don't know what else to do," he said with a sigh.

"Then I guess there's no point in asking you again to go with me to the police station?" she asked, knowing all too well what his answer would be. "I really need a translator who could help me with the Arabic. I really don't understand all the nuances when they answer my questions."

He looked down away from her eyes, and she could see his thoughts drifting back to his research. "I really need to stay with it," he said apologetically, pointing back at the table in the middle of the room, as though it were a port in a storm. "I know you need me, and I really would like to help, but if I don't stay with this, I'm going to lose the race."

She was furious with him, and didn't even try to conceal her anger as she spun around and stomped down the hall.

"I'm sorry," he said meekly, but she was already out of range. He shut the door quietly and walked sadly, but with determination, back to his makeshift desk. He knew what needed to be done, and nothing was going to stop him. Nothing. *Women,* he thought. *I just can't worry about this now. I'll have to straighten it all out later.*

Christina understood Rigg's problem, at least in principle, but it did little to soothe her anger. Nothing mattered more to academics than peer group respect, especially in fields like linguistics. Professors like her and Riggs certainly weren't in this field for the financial rewards, and Riggs was right when he joked that not many Nobel prizes had been given for finding a Sayings Gospel...or breaking the Maya code.

Yet the principle was little comfort. Here was a man to whom she had almost given her deepest love, and now he had shown that nothing was more important than his own research. *How could he just turn off his feelings?* she wondered. *I could never do that.*

As she walked into the reception area at a full gait, she was all the more resolved to accomplish two things in Cairo and get back to Boston. She had her own career to worry about, especially with Thompson on the warpath. But first, she wanted to try once again to find the police station which handled Colby's death. The one she was planning to visit today was her last hope, because the others had no records on the case and were far from helpful.

She also wanted to pursue some new leads on the mosque in Colby's folder. Having shown the photo to dozens of policemen and enterprising taxi drivers, her prospects were looking dim. As she had learned the hard way, there were thousands of mosques in Cairo. Nevertheless, she was not leaving until she had exhausted every possibility; it was the least she could do for her Uncle Colby.

To make matters more complicated, her brother Ryan had telephoned last night with the surprising news that he planned to visit her in three days on his way back from the Vatican. He said he had some news that couldn't wait, and of course she had some questions of her own.

She nodded politely at Mrs. Scarzella, pulled the gate to the elevator closed and pushed the down button. *It's hard to be nice to anyone*, she thought, *when you're furious at someone you really like.*

Bizarre Bazaar

Christina stopped at one of the many stalls and pushcarts in the crowded *Khan el Khalili* bazaar to look at some Egyptian cotton cloth. *How would I ever carry these on the plane?* she thought, being all too practical. She had already filled her room with earlier purchases, including exquisitely worked leather and metal handicrafts. As the vendors converged from all directions, haranguing her to purchase their wares, she was drawn by the sweet scent of perfume extracts in the next store, and she moved further down the narrow street.

A man with an unusual magenta birthmark on his left cheek followed close behind, hidden by the crowds of people in the marketplace.

I've got to keep moving, she thought, *or I might confuse Mrs. Scarzella's directions to the police station.* Noticing that the next vendor, an old woman selling spices, was blind in one eye, she turned right and headed down an alley hardly wide enough for two people. *I couldn't miss that instruction*, she thought. *How many of these shopkeepers have only one good eye and are selling spices on a corner? It was a lot simpler than I expected.*

In the distance she could hear the sweet mournful tones of the muezzin calling the Islamic faithful to midday prayer. She had been in so many mosques recently that she was tempted to join in, but she didn't want to remove her shoes and cover her arms and head one more time. *I know I visited most of the mosques around this part of town, but I can't remember if that is Ibn Qalawun or El-Barquq,* she thought, admiring the spindly minarets reaching up to Allah.

Following Mrs. Scarzella's instructions, she turned left at the large dried fruit stand operated by an old man who was missing several front teeth. *There couldn't be more than one fruit stand like that,* she thought, happy to be on course. She walked past a man selling charcoal grilled yams—skin and all. He looked like a soot covered chimney sweep, and she was intrigued by how many locals were waiting to be served.

As she walked along, stopping at almost every shop in the dazzling bazaar and fending off the ubiquitous shopkeepers, her thoughts drifted back to her uncle's death. She always ended going up the same blind alley. John Allegro certainly had the motive: he wanted the Scrolls released to the public and he had been removed as custodian of the vault. However, he didn't seem like that type of person. Father de Vaux and the Insiders certainly didn't need the photos, because they already had the originals.

And it was impossible to suspect Riggs anymore. He was obsessed with the Nag Hammadi codices...and little else. *That exhausts the list,* she concluded. *It must be someone I don't know. Someone involved in the new manuscript Uncle Colby was trying to acquire.*

The only clues she had to go on now were in the Quelle folder. She thought about each of the three items, but as usual she couldn't find any obvious connections. What could be the link between a Muslim mosque, a letter from the Vatican and an unsigned laboratory report dating something to the first century? If that something was an old Christian manuscript, she could imagine a common theme...except for the mosque.

She knew from the conversations with Riggs and Professor Robinson that Colby might well have discovered a radical new gospel, perhaps even a sayings gospel. Whatever it was, it probably wasn't just a very old manuscript of a New Testament Gospel. That wouldn't have been worth killing over.

Or would it? she thought. Maybe he had found a very old version of the Gospel of Mark, one actually written by a disciple or an eyewitness. That would certainly have been unprecedented. It also would have explained the interest shown in the letter by the Vatican priest.

Maybe Ryan can help me with that part of the mystery. He certainly knew people at the Vatican. Of course, that was somewhat like saying you knew someone in St. Louis or New Orleans. There were thousands of people in the Vatican. *I'll ask him anyway.*

Then she had a second thought. What if there was a connection between Ryan and Father de Vaux through the Church? She didn't want to make things even more complicated by putting Ryan in a compromising position. *Maybe I'll wait until I hear from Henry about the secrecy agreement before I tell Ryan about the contents of the vault.*

The obvious person too help her was Riggs, and more than once she had thought of telling him about Colby's Quelle folder. His recent behavior made that highly unlikely. *There's no way I'm going to tell Riggs until he comes out of his catacomb.*

Such had been her thoughts the last few days. Theories swirled through her head but led to nothing. *I'm a lousy detective,* she thought. *How much more time can I spend in this city chasing phantoms? The clues are drying up, whether I want to admit it or not.*

Realizing that she must be lost, she stopped and looked around. If she had followed the directions properly, the police station should have appeared by now. All the shops were beginning to look the same, with determined shoppers crowding into the streets. The sounds and sights were overwhelming, aggravated by the fumes from fish and open gutters. She saw one street sign which she laboriously translated into *Muizz Lidin,* but that was no help whatsoever. *Arabic is tough,* she thought. *I've been more confused than this in Guatemala, but at least there I can speak the language and get directions.*

Her heart sank when she saw the same one-eyed lady selling spices. She must have somehow doubled back on herself while she was deep in thought. *I should have kept my mind on Mrs. Scarzella's instructions,* she thought, chastising herself.

She was fighting claustrophobia as the crowd swept around her, flowing in one direction like a swollen river, capturing everyone and everything in its path. A sleazy man dressed in a gray galabia , edged close to Christina. She tried to ignore him, but he pressed closer using the crowd to his advantage. Speaking in heavily accented English, he offered to sell her an ancient Egyptian codex, which he claimed had been recently discovered near Nag Hammadi.

What a fake, she thought, shaking her head to indicate her lack of interest and waving her arm to motion him away. Instead, he grabbed her arm, much too forcefully, and began pushing her through the crowd toward a small door in one of the shops. He continued to pretend that he was only trying to sell her something, but his grip on her arm was actually quite painful. As she resisted, she felt a sharp stab in her side and realized that he was pressing a short knife beneath her ribs. She now had no choice but to go with him.

Could this man be Uncle Colby's assailant? She was sickened at the thought. *Or am I being robbed? My brief case might have been too inviting,* she thought, her pulse quickening as she remembered that Uncle Colby had also carried a briefcase the day he was killed. She looked around for help in the crowd, but everyone except her was dressed like the assailant. *Where are all the tourists?* she thought desperately. She was surrounded by men in dark galabias.

Without any warning, the assailant's grip on her arm suddenly went limp, and he stumbled headlong into the doorway, grabbing futilely at a small bloody spot on his back. Standing in his place was a large man, of obelisk proportions, wearing a tan business suit.

Where did he come from? she wondered.

"Tourists often get lost in this area," he said politely, with in a raspy French accent. "Can I help you find your way?"

"Thank you," said a greatly relieved Christina. She was still shaking. "What happened to that man...the one trying to rob me?"

"I don't think he'll bother you again today. He has his own problems now," he smiled balefully, his steel blue eyes showing less emotion than a fish. "Where were you headed?"

"To the police station," responded Christina gratefully, realizing how humorous that must sound. "On other business," she quickly added.

"We're only a few blocks from there, and I'll be happy to walk with you."

She nodded. Having her own bodyguard seemed like a great idea, especially in that part of town. In two short turns they were out of the bazaar, and the streets began to look familiar once again, as a familiar mosque loomed in the distance.

"I'd be amazed if the police are of any assistance, especially if you don't speak Arabic," the stranger volunteered. "The way their system works, the less you know the better for them."

"I've already been through that," agreed Christina, angered at the reminder that Riggs had refused to help her today. She would lay this drama, in all its glory, at the foot of his cross someday...soon. "I think I've been to every police station in Cairo, and I don't speak any Arabic."

"Most of the tourists visit the pyramids and the mosques," he said, trying to force a smile on a face which had seen few. A permanent frown was etched across his wide forehead.

"Well that's a long story," she responded, not wanting to share her problems with this stranger. She couldn't reconcile his helpfulness with his stern, almost stoic, appearance. Was she only imagining a deeply concealed hostility in this man...like a ticking bomb about to explode...or was he just on edge?

To her great relief, they arrived without further incident at the police station, and in parting he told her how to find the main street without backtracking through the alleyways of the bazaar. She thanked him generously for his assistance, noticing as he turned to leave that he had been hiding an unsightly birthmark on the left side of his face.

That's a shame, she thought, trying not to stare. *But he was sure a good Samaritan to me.*

Cairo Cops

The only woman in Fishawi's Tea House coughed loudly from the smoke she had tried hard not to inhale. The gnarly old ember man, with desert dried skin, tried to heap more coals on top of the tobacco in the chillum bowl, as she desperately waved him away with one arm. There was a twinkle of amusement in the dark eyes of every man, as they drew the smoke through their hubble bubble pipes and watched. She would have been noticeable by her gender alone in this male bastion, but her Western dress and insistence on smoking brought even more attention from the Muslim men who surrounded her.

Tears from the smoke ran down her face as she laughed at herself for finally giving in to her curiosity. *I've always wondered what these bubble pipes would taste like, and now I know. That's enough for me,* she thought, as she motioned the waiter for more Turkish coffee and some bottled water. The other smokers were now left with only their pipes for entertainment.

I picked a strange place for a little solitude, Christina thought, but she didn't want to be around Riggs today, and this is as good a place as any to think things through. *At least I won't be bothered by the street vendors in here.*

A smile crossed her face at how hypocritical she had been. Here she was trying to smoke a bubble pipe, while only an hour before she had been revolted by the column of smoke rising between the nicotine stained teeth of the officer at the police station. His desk had been covered with cigarette ashes, and he wheezed the whole time she was there.

Oh well, she thought, *it really is the only sin allowed by the strict Muslim code. Maybe I'm being unfair. Almost every man in Cairo is a chain smoker.*

She didn't feel she had been completely unfair, however, in her contempt of the police officer, who was so fat that his thighs hung several inches over the side of the chair...or where the chair would have been. Even with the only fan in the police station, his shirt was dripping wet, like a man suffering from malaria. His flaccid skin showed through pink where it pressed against the wet shirt.

Even after that ordeal, the smoke and the sweat, she had learned nothing about Colby's death. The official position remained, in spite of her many queries, that he had been killed in an automobile accident, nothing unusual in the crazy Cairo traffic. They weren't about to spend any more time on the matter.

She sat quietly, sipping her coffee and wishing the taste of the smoke would go away. Her thoughts drifted to all the disturbing information she had learned from Riggs, Allegro and now Robinson, about the New Testament and the origins of Christianity. Subconsciously, she was far more upset with this news than she had let on, perhaps even to herself.

What would it mean if I've been misled about the miracles performed by Jesus? She shuddered at the possibility.

Her religious training had been very straightforward, both at home and at church. God had created man perfect, in his own image and likeness, and He had created the world for man's enjoyment. But man yielded to temptation in the Garden of Eden, a mistake which damned him to eternal suffering. Out of compassion, God sent Jesus, his beloved Son, to earth two thousand years ago to redeem man by sacrificing His own life on the cross. To show His power over the forces on earth, even death itself, Jesus rose from the dead and later ascended into Heaven, where He waits on the right hand of God until the appointed hour.

It was a comforting story, because she knew from it that God cared for her, and that no matter how terrible life might be on earth, there was always a perfect life hereafter...at least for those who believed in Jesus and dedicated their lives to His ways. She was also comforted by the fact that she would someday be reunited with loved ones who had died before her, unless they had strayed.

This was the dogma that had become the fabric of her being and more importantly the fabric of her family and their community. It was not to be questioned.

She was, however, not an easy woman to fool; her academic degrees and her Maya research at Harvard were proof of that. She was certainly aware of the miracles in the story, and if hard pressed she would have admitted that miracles like that never happened in modern times...especially the resurrection of three day old corpses.

She could rationalize, however, that it must have happened once—a long time ago—and the proof was in the New Testament and the teachings of her Church. As unbelievable as it sounded today, God apparently did come to earth in the body of Jesus and rose from the dead. And before returning to Heaven, he established the Catholic Church and passed on his earthly powers to Saint Peter and successive popes...the same powers utilized by Ryan in the performance of his priestly duties.

What scared her now was the possibility that Paul and the authors of the New Testament Gospels were apparently not eyewitnesses; and worse yet, these weren't independent accounts of historical events. Even if they had been, there was no way of knowing if what they wrote was true or not. They had no more, or less, credibility than other authors at the time...the authors, for example, of the Dead Sea Scrolls or the Nag Hammadi codices or numerous other documents.

The authority of the Catholic Church, with its otherwise unbelievable miracles, hung on the thin thread of papal succession back to Jesus, or God. Yet the manuscripts Riggs and Professor Robinson were translating seemed to be just as authentic as the ones behind the New Testament.

If Jesus wasn't God, then what's the deal? What will happen to me after death, if Jesus didn't prepare the way? And how can I explain all the suffering here on earth? Certainly God wouldn't have made a world like this.

Her fears went even deeper. If the creeds of the Church were not true, or at least were not based on historical events, then what was the meaning of life? Did it mean that her life was no more important than a hermit crab? Was life on this planet just a random event? A fluke? Was she just part of the green slime of organic life which covers this planet?

Her head shook without moving, and despite the afternoon Cairo heat, a chill flowed through her body. Unfortunately, she was still angry at the one person she would most like to ask.

• • •

Later that afternoon, having futilely explored two more mosques, she was passing through the lobby of the Garden City House, when she noticed a picture of Pope Paul VI on the front page of the London Times. She walked over to the coffee table and picked up the well-used newspaper. The article, which she didn't have the energy to read completely, described the annual showing of the Turin Shroud, the cloth in which Jesus was wrapped during his three days in the tomb.

It would be nice to see that some day, she thought.

She grabbed a soft drink out of the fridge, signed the sheet, and headed down the hall to her room. As she passed Riggs' door, she was tempted to knock, but she walked right on past.

I wonder if he knows how much nicer it would be to sleep with me than those precious Codices of his. I'm afraid he'll never know.

Encryption
(Sometime in the Past)

Three men labored to push away the large stone and sat down to rest from an overly demanding task. Sweat poured down their light brown skins onto their almost perfectly white tunics. They suddenly leaped to their feet, bowed deeply out of respect, and moved aside for a man they obviously regarded quite highly.

He didn't bother to thank them.

Instead, he lit an oil lamp and lowered it by hand into the dark hole below. He couldn't see anything from that angle, so he laid down and positioned his head carefully inside the dank opening. The flickering light revealed very old damp walls, rectangular in shape; in the middle was a smaller stone vault, about the size of a coffin. The top of the smaller vault was covered with several inches of wax drippings, apparently the accumulation of many centuries of spent candles.

He stood, with some difficulty, and patted each of his pockets to find the right one. He then removed a knife from this pocket and, to the horror of the servile onlookers, lowered himself completely into the burial chamber. As cramped as he was, from his contorted position he still had enough room, barely enough room, to scrape away the thick layers of wax.

As he worked, the onlookers dared to creep closer...eyes widened with fear...and peered into the dark hole. He was a strange site indeed, squeezed between the wall and the crypt, with one arm making short stabs at the wax. His progress was very slow. They looked at each other in disbelief. What kind of man would lower himself into a tomb?

He stopped to rest and commanded one of the workers above to reach down and wipe his brow, a task performed quickly and deferentially. The minutes passed, with little to show for all the effort, but he seemed determined. He often stopped and laid quietly in his cramped quarters just to regain strength in his arms.

Finally, a pattern began to emerge on the stone under the wax.

I knew it, he thought, *there's always some sort of imprint carved into the ends of these crypts.*

Seeing the vague pattern gave him renewed strength, and he quickly scraped most of the remaining wax to the side. He moved the oil lamp to give better light, and studied the pattern intently.

It looks like the outline of two feet, he thought, wondering what message that might convey. *Two feet with some small marks.*

He took the sharp point of his knife blade and dug deeper into the small marks.

This is too good to be true, he smiled, *but it's exactly what I suspected.*

Words of Our Master

If your teachers say to you, "Look, the kingdom is in heaven," then the birds will get there before you. If they say to you, "it is in the sea," then the fish will precede you. Rather the kingdom is inside of you, and it is outside of you. When you come to know yourselves, then you will be known; and you will realize that it is you who are the sons of the living Father.

—Gospel of Thomas
Nag Hammadi Library

Riggs burst into Christina's room without even knocking. "I've completed the rough translations!" he announced, a smile spreading across his unshaven face.

She was sitting at her desk, surrounded by her own research papers, but her thoughts had been mostly on her brother's forthcoming visit. She was disappointed that Riggs seemed unaware of her two day old boycott. "Does that mean that you're rejoining the living?" she said, not trying very hard to conceal her sarcasm. "I can't believe you've finished that quickly."

"I really haven't," he responded, qualifying his exuberance. "My results are much too rough to publish, but I've translated enough to know what's in them. He paused to get her attention, hoping her natural curiosity would win the day.

"So what did you find in your Nag Hammadi codices?" she asked coolly, deflecting his boyish enthusiasm.

"I'll tell you over dinner," he offered. "I know you'll be convinced that it was worth it all. I have a table for two at Al Rubayyat. How does Indian food sound for a change?"

"You actually thought ahead and made a reservation?" asked Christina in disbelief. "Maybe there's hope."

He smiled, with hopes of his own.

• • •

"Did you find a sayings gospel?" begged Christina, after their second glass of champagne. She had decided to give him another chance, especially since there were no more manuscripts on the horizon.

Riggs knew he had done the right thing to hold back the information until his fences were mended with Christina, and the candlelight and champagne had improved her attitude. "Yes," he said so loudly that the people at the next table overheard. He tempered his voice. "I also found several completely new narrative gospels, many of which were written by Christians who disagreed with Paul and the Romans. There's a Gospel of Thomas, a Gospel of Philip, a Gospel of Truth, a Gospel of the Egyptians, and even a Gospel of <u>Mary</u>. It's obvious why the Romans wanted to destroy all of these competitive Gospels. They prove that early Christianity was ripe with diversity, as well as disagreements."

"Tell me about the sayings gospel," entreated Christina.

"I will in a minute," baited Riggs, "but first let me serve you a few Nag Hammadi hors d'oeuvres." He paused for impact. "In one of the new Gospels, Jesus and Thomas were twins." He looked to see if she was surprised. "In another Mother Mary was not a virgin." He paused again for impact. "In still another, Mary Magdalene was a disciple!"

"Mary Magdalene was a <u>disciple</u>?" gasped Christina, shaking her head in disbelief. "That's incredible."

"It sure is. According to her gospel, she was not just a disciple; she was a prominent disciple, perhaps Jesus' favorite, a visionary and a spiritual teacher. She may have been the most enlightened of them all."

"That's not difficult to believe. Women are often more spiritually inclined than men. But why would the Romans want to omit the Gospel of Mary from the New Testament?"

"Don't you think it might have interfered with the male domination of the Christian Church over the past 1600 years?" asked Riggs, with a little smirk in his smile.

"Just a little," agreed Christina. "I really want to read the Gospel of Mary once you've finished translating it. I'm intrigued by its feminist tone."

"And there's more," continued Riggs, leaning over the table excitedly. "One gospel argues against the Original Sin. Another speaks of the feminine element in the Divine, celebrating God as both Father and Mother. Others, even more controversial, suggest that Jesus' resurrection was only symbolic, not an actual historical event. And I haven't even gotten to the sayings gospel yet."

Christina sat quietly, her head spinning from the champagne of new ideas. In the passage of only a few minutes, the foundations of her religious beliefs were being shaken by the shocking contents of gospels, banned gospels, which had lain silent since the origins of Christianity. She had suspected as much, based on conversations with Riggs and Professor Robinson, but now her worst fears had been confirmed. "The Nag Hammadi gospels were more than a time capsule, weren't they?" implored Christina. "They were a time bomb."

"Unfortunately, that's a good description," agreed Riggs, "and I hope we don't get hit by any of the shrapnel. I don't know how the churches are going to cope with these new gospels, but they can't ignore them forever."

"It's going to be harder to burn them this time. Too many people have copies now, thanks to you and Professor Robinson."

"You were there too," reminded Riggs, making sure she got her fair share of the credit...or the blame.

"You might as well tell me about the sayings gospel," said Christina with appropriate resignation. "I haven't yet given up on my Christianity, but it's getting harder to argue for its uniqueness. I might as well get all the bad news at once."

"The sayings gospel is really good news, if you're interested in the teachings of Jesus. It's called the Gospel of Thomas, and it has over one hundred sayings, many of which we've never seen before. You're right, however, about a potential controversy. As expected, this sayings gospel contains no narrative accounts of the life and miracles of Jesus; it contains only his teachings. If there's no mention of the Passion, the Crucifixion and the Ascension in the oldest of the Gospels, then these stories must have been added later."

"Which doesn't prove that the stories are false," rebutted Christina. "It just proves that the miracles were not the first thing people were compelled to record."

"They must have been very good sermons," joked Riggs, with tongue in cheek. "It just proves that at least one branch of Christians was more impressed with his teachings than with his resurrection from the dead." He turned his attention briefly to the task of ordering his meal. While Christina tried to absorb all she had heard, he motioned for the waiter to fill her glass once again with the last of their champagne.

She couldn't remember a better bottle of champagne nor a more disturbing conversation. "I'm sure you happen to have an example of these teachings," prodded Christina, as she pointed to his stuffed shirt pocket.

"Oh yes," he smiled, pretending that the notes were just a coincidence. He put on his horn-rimmed glasses, sorted through them, and stopped on one he liked very much. "By way of introduction," he continued with a glance over his glasses, "the Gospel of Thomas describes quite a different Jesus from the one in the New Testament. The Jesus of Thomas acknowledges each person, not just Jesus, as a potential Christ, receiving their true being from God. Rather than having come to save us from our sins, the Jesus of Thomas came as a guide to show mankind the path to spiritual understanding."

Christina looked perplexed at such an unusual description of Jesus.

"Here's a sample of his teaching in the Gospel of Thomas," said Riggs, beginning to read from his notes:

"I am not your master. Because you have drunk, you have become intoxicated from the bubbling stream which I have measured out (Thom 13). He who will drink from my mouth will become like me:

I myself shall become he, and the things that are hidden will be revealed to him (Thom 108)."

"It's not completely different from my Jesus in the New Testament, but I must agree that the Jesus in Thomas sounds more like a teacher than the one in the Apostles' Creed." She knew that her face revealed her anguish.

Riggs reached over and put his hand on hers. "Would you like me to stop?"

"Of course, I'd like you to stop." After a long pause, she continued: "But now that I've started down this path, I've got to take it all the way."

"Good for you," he said squeezing her hand again. "This 'alternative Jesus', which we find in the buried Gospels, teaches that when the disciple attains enlightenment, Jesus no longer serves as his spiritual master. The master and disciple have become equal, even identical."

"If you'll excuse my skepticism," warned Christina, "but that sounds Eastern or Buddhist to me?"

"Actually, I found an Eastern perspective in many of the Nag Hammadi gospels," continued Riggs. "They often describe a 'Living Jesus' very similar to the 'Living Buddha.' Personally, I don't find this too surprising because trade prospered between the Greco-Roman world and the Far East during the second century. Both religious ideas and missionaries had migrated west from India long before that. Buddhism and other religious ideas spread east from India to China and Japan at the time of Jesus, so it seems reasonable that they also spread to the west."

"Well if Buddhism was spreading in both directions from India," observed Christina wryly, "it didn't get very far into the West."

"That's true," reflected Riggs, searching for an explanation. "The Jesus we find in the Gospel of Thomas would have appealed to Christians who believed that answers were to be found in personal prayer...and in the search for the divine essential self within."

"Doesn't that describe all Christians?"

"To an extent. However, I've noticed that for many Jews and Christians a chasm separates humanity from its creator; their God seems Wholly Other, at least to me. The Eastern Jesus, the one in the Gospel of Thomas, encourages individual salvation, or knowing oneself and hence knowing human nature and human destiny. He teaches that to know oneself, at the deepest level, is to know God. In this Gospel the self and the divine are identical...every person is a Christ. In other words, the individual can commune directly with God and enjoy the Kingdom of God now, not only after death or the Second Coming."

"I guess that *is* different," toiled Christina, thinking how upset Ryan would be if he knew she was even toying with these heretical ideas. After all, the reasoning went, we humans, flawed by Original Sin, were supposed to rest all faith in the absolute authority of the Church and its teachings. "Christina," Ryan would often say, "salvation is through the Church."

Trying to salvage her tattered beliefs, she made one last valiant proposal: "Maybe the Buddhist religion migrated into Palestine at the time of Jesus, and the authors of the Nag Hammadi gospels simply confused the two theologies. Maybe they mistakenly attributed Eastern philosophies to Jesus."

"It's more likely," he countered, "that Jesus' teachings actually had an Eastern orientation, because we see the same thing even in the New Testament."

"You must be kidding...or you desperately need some sleep."

"I actually could use some sleep, but I'm quite serious. To see my point, however, you must focus primarily on his sayings, not on the deeds attributed to him. The Sermon on the Mount, for example, has an Eastern orientation, and that might explain why it was considered so revolutionary at the time."

"Maybe," said Christina. Her face mirrored her skepticism.

"And then Paul and the Romans combined Jesus' Eastern teachings with Jewish and Greek theologies to create their own version of Christianity. This included elements of the Greek mystery religions, and the resurrection from Judaism...resurrection of the dead on Judgment Day."

"You believe that they added the Resurrection to the Eastern teachings of Jesus?"

"Well, as my good friend, Elaine Pagels, says: 'It is the winners who write history—their way.' They certainly were the winners, at least until we found the Gospel of Thomas."

"I have one last question," said Christina., as the waiter approached their table, laden with steaming dishes of Tandoori chicken, several curries, and a basket of puffy poori breads. "Which side of this debate was Mary Magdalene on?"

"His favorite disciple," smiled Riggs mischievously, "interpreted the teachings of Jesus as a path to inner spiritual knowledge and rejected his suffering and death as the means to eternal life. The Gospel of Mary and the Gospel of Thomas are in agreement on their depiction of Jesus."

"Is the Gospel of Mary also a sayings gospel?" asked a disturbed Christina.

"No, it's a narrative gospel."

"I give up," pleaded Christina. "But not for long. My brother, Ryan, is coming tomorrow, and I'm going to get answers to all of these questions from him. My problem is that I don't even know where to begin. You were right about one thing: the Nag Hammadi gospels are going to cause quite a controversy. They already have."

Riggs had forgotten about her brother's visit. "What do you want me to do while he's here? I could disappear into my room, because there's five years of work facing me on these translations."

"That's a deal. I don't want to explain my pagan boyfriend to him anyway. I hope he doesn't guess that we've become good friends. As far as he's concerned, you're 'just the other key' to the vault."

"Ouch," whined Riggs. "Now I'm just the other key? What ever happened to scroll mates?"

Tea Cozy

"I'll make us a cup of tea," offered Christina, "and we can take it to my room."

"Great. I won't be able to sleep anyway. I'm much too excited about everything, and strung out from the long hours of research. I'd invite you to my room, but it's strewn with photographs and papers."

"Thanks, but no thanks. I don't think I ever want to go into your room again."

Once inside her room, they pulled the extra chair up to the night stand and used it as a table for their tea…and the pastry they had found in Mrs. Scarzella's fridge. Christina turned on a cassette tape of The Supremes, but kept the volume low, trying not to disturb the other guests. It wasn't much, this room at the Garden City House, but it had become her home away from home.

"My task is almost done here," said Christina, bringing up a subject they had both avoided. "I haven't learned anything useful from the police about my uncle's death, and I'll be heading back to the States soon. I want to spend more time on my research, and I need to take more photos of the hieroglyphs in my Guatemalan cave. Do you think we need to make a decision regarding the photos in the vault before I leave?"

"Personally, I don't think we should do anything right now. I don't think we need to rush either way. According to Henry, there's no written secrecy agreement, so we can do whatever we think is right, both for the Scrolls and regarding our obligation to Colby."

"I agree. We should monitor the progress of the Insiders Team and decide what to do when we both get back to the States. Maybe they will surprise us and actually publish the Scrolls."

"I wouldn't hold my breath. It's already been twenty-five years," said Riggs shaking his head dubiously.

"What are your plans?" asked Christina, changing the subject slightly and hoping he too would be coming back to the States soon.

"I could also come back now," he responded, "since I've finished the rough translations. Everything from this point on could equally well be done at Claremont. In fact, I could work more closely with Professor Robinson and his students if I were there. He's invited me to co-author some of the translations with him, and so now I don't have to proceed independently."

They sat silently, sipping their tea.

"I haven't really thought through all the details," began Riggs, "but I think of us as staying in touch somehow."

"I feel the same way," said Christina, getting lost in his maple eyes, "unless you go on another research binge. In your hands, Coptic documents are a form of substance abuse. I thought we might have to send you to some Rehab Center."

They both laughed, and he touched her softly on the cheek as if to brush away tears with the back of his hand. She loved his touch. It sent shivers through her entire body.

"So, does that mean that I'm forgiven?"

"I didn't think you noticed that I was upset."

"I'm not blind, only a translation junkie. Of course I noticed, and I'm really sorry. It won't happen again...unless we discover more codices."

"Heaven forbid," she said as she knelt in front of him.

Leaning over in his chair, he pulled her tight against his knees, cupped her face in his hands and brought their warm moist lips together. Time stopped. They were both in that private place reserved for the thoughts and feelings of lovers. It was theirs.

She slowly pulled his seated legs open so that she could hug him more tightly and their embrace would be more fulfilling. She felt his excitement, and knew that her body was keeping pace. At times like this their relationship seemed barely more than lust. They stood so that they could feel each other everywhere, and their probing kisses had grown wet and desperate, striving for more and more of that delicious feeling. Their mouths never separated as their heads whirled to the dance of love.

His arm brushed lightly on the side of her breast, as if by accident, sending an exploding sensation through her entire body. The breast he touched, just on the side, screamed for more. The nipple was so hard that it actually began to hurt. She fantasized putting it in his warm mouth and letting him suck away the pain. She fought her own thoughts of ripping off her blouse and showing her breasts to him.

As he dropped his hand from her face, to once again encircle her waist, he brushed not the side of her breast but the front, right across the erect nipple. Very slowly his hand went across the throbbing nipple...very slowly, but much too fast for both of them.

She reeled, inside and out. Her brain literally whirled.

He felt a galvanic taste in his mouth from the excitement Riggs was fighting his own battle against fantasies. He was imagining the two of them completely naked and rubbing their inflamed bodies together, because he knew that was the only way they could ultimately gain some relief. His groin was aching for gratification and release. It seemed to him that it was always aching, even when they just touched during the day. His body was so sensitive to Christina, that even her scent excited him physically.

They both had difficulty standing and their bodies melted slowly onto the bed. Their legs were intertwined, and she encouraged him, with her own motion, to move his legs around so she could feel occasional pressure on the inside of her thighs. It was blinding when he did it just right.

He could now cup his hand more directly on the side of her breast, and she did not discourage him as his thumb massaged her nipple. In fact she nearly bit his tongue in their wet embrace when his finger actually pushed against the hardest part. Each time he touched her nipple directly, she pushed her crotch more tightly against his pressing leg.

There they laid, entangled, kissing, rubbing and fantasizing of so much more nakedness. So much more everything. So much more relief from this fire that burned within them.

Then it happened. Christina surprised them both, as she stood up quietly and walked to the door, still holding tightly onto his hand. She stood there for a moment, her eyes pleading for another time, as he slowly opened the door to her room.

Riggs knew that, at least in Christina's mind, her brother's visit had started a day early.

Quest for Quelle

Truth is a pathless land.

—Krishnamurti

"How's this for a sensational headline? Does it grab your attention?" said Christina, preparing to read from the newspaper. "Tomb of Jesus Discovered by Archaeologists in India."

"That's ridiculous," responded Riggs with a smirk. "These journalists know no shame."

"Or is it the archaeologists?" smiled Christina.

The two of them were having a leisurely breakfast in the garden before Riggs disappeared into his codices and Christina went to meet her brother at the Cairo airport. Fortunately his flight arrived well after the morning traffic.

Purely out of curiosity, Christina thumbed through the newspaper pages back to the main article. "Here's a photograph of the archaeologist standing in front of a mosque and..." Her voice stopped abruptly. "My God, its the same mosque as the one in Uncle Colby's photograph," she exclaimed, her eyes bright with excitement and a smile spreading across her face.

Riggs gave her a quizzical look, wondering what could possibly be so interesting in the newspaper. Here was a woman who explored Maya caves in the jungles of Guatemala and scaled mountains for recreation, and yet she seemed unable to speak. He was ready for some answers.

After almost recovering her composure, she explained: "This is the first hint I've had on the things I found in Uncle Colby's folder."

Riggs was perplexed. "What hint? What folder? What mosque? What's all of this about?

But Christina was already up and running toward her room. "Come with me," she yelled over her shoulder. "No...wait," she said changing her mind. "I'll bring it here in a minute. In the meantime see what the article says."

He had never seen her so excited, even in the caves at Qumran.

She ran so fast that the other guests, mostly academics, thought something was seriously wrong. They looked away nervously, feigning indifference, but kept the scene in their peripheral view...out of sheer curiosity. Even Mrs. Scarzella was perplexed.

By the time Christina returned, waving the folder high in the air, Riggs had quickly read the rest of the article. "The tomb, or what they call the tomb of Jesus, is in Srinagar, India. The archaeologist is a Professor Gupta at the University of Kashmir."

"Look at this photo," she gasped breathlessly, comparing the features with the one in the newspaper as she leaned over his shoulder. "Isn't that the same mosque?"

"It sure looks like it to me. Colby is definitely standing in front of the mosque in this newspaper article."

"You mean the tomb of Jesus," corrected Christina, with a smirk. "My uncle is standing in front of the tomb of Jesus in India," she repeated in disbelief. "This is unbelievable!"

They looked at each other skeptically, their minds racing for an explanation.

"Where did you get this photograph?" Riggs asked. This was the first time anything other than his Codices commanded his attention.

"It was with some things my aunt gave me after his death," she explained, feeling guilty that she had not told him about the folder earlier. "She found a folder on his desk, and he had told her that he was on the trail of the most important discovery of his lifetime."

Riggs raised an eyebrow, realizing there was a lot more to this story. "And?"

"I've been meaning to tell you about the folder, but we were busy with the Scrolls and Allegro, and then with the Codices. Until now, nothing in the folder made sense anyway. Frankly, until we opened the vault, I believed the answers would be found in there." *I'm not going to tell him about my survey of the Islamic mosques in Cairo, unless he asks,* she decided.

"Instead you found more questions?" taunted Riggs, hurt by reminders of her earlier suspicions of him.

"But now at least I understand the photograph. Only one thing doesn't fit. Aunt Mary said he was searching for an early Christian document, not a phony tomb of Jesus. Surely Uncle Colby wouldn't have been that easily deceived?"

"Do you mind if I look at the other things he left you," inquired Riggs, forfeiting the opportunity to scold her for not including him sooner, "unless they're of a private nature?"

"Here," she said, quickly moving the folder over to him. "I've treated his project with some discretion, at least until I could get an idea of what it was all about. But, there's nothing in here you shouldn't see. In fact, you might even know what these other things are."

Riggs opened the folder and carefully looked at the letter from the Vatican and the confidential laboratory report.

Christina wondered if he was paying her back for her secrecy by remaining silent a painfully long time.

"Unbelievable!" Riggs blurted out , looking at the folder itself. "Was this on the folder when you got it?" he asked, pointing at the word 'Quelle' on the tab.

"Yes," said a baffled Christina. "What does it mean?"

"Why in the hell didn't you tell me sooner?" groused Riggs, unable to conceal his anger any longer. "Do you have any idea what this is?"

"No," said Christina defensively. "Obviously not. I'd decided not to tell anyone, even you, about this folder, until I found out more about Uncle Colby's death."

"We'll get back to Colby's death later," he said, with a sour look she found foreign to his face and actually quite terrifying. "You should have shown me this folder a long time ago. It explains everything."

Her eyes asked for more information, but her face was penitent. *Maybe I should have told him sooner.*

"Quelle," he began pontificating angrily, "is the name scholars have given to a document which they believe pre-dated the Synoptic Gospels, and was copied extensively by the authors of Matthew and Luke."

"Why that strange name?" asked Christina. "It meant nothing to me."

"Quelle is the German word for 'Source', which is exactly what this document would be. It would be the source for the Synoptic Gospels. It is considered the Gospel of Gospels by scholars," he glared.

"Quelle is the historically accurate story of the life of Jesus?" recited Christina, expectantly.

"Not really the story of his life, but rather his teachings. Quelle is believed to be a sayings gospel, not a narrative gospel like those in the New Testament. As such, it would confirm the view of scholars that the life of Jesus was added to his teachings much later by the Romans, presumably to make them more convincing." He couldn't believe she had withheld information this important from him all this time.

"But how does that differ from the Gospel of Thomas you and Professor Robinson are translating?" asked Christina, trying to piece the puzzle together. "Isn't Thomas the first known sayings gospel, and that's why you two were so excited?"

"That's right," responded Riggs, slowly getting over his initial anger. "The Gospel of Thomas proves the existence of sayings gospels, and it was probably written about the same time as Quelle. On the other hand, Quelle is expected to be older and much larger than Thomas and to contain more of the teachings in the New Testament."

"Let me see if I understand. Quelle was written before the New Testament and contains the original teachings of Jesus?"

"That's correct, and this folder tells me that your uncle was on the trail of an extant manuscript of Quelle!" whispered an overwhelmed Riggs. "Let's see what else we have here," he mumbled, looking at the two letters again.

"How could there be Christian documents in the tomb in India...in the tomb of Jesus?" Christina asked with great difficulty, since the concept was absolutely implausible.

"The newspaper article says that documents found at the Buddhist monastery in nearby Hemis convinced Professor Gupta that it was the tomb of Jesus. That must be where your uncle found Quelle, or at least someone who had seen Quelle."

"A Christian document in a Buddhist monastery in northern India?" said Christina with unconcealed skepticism. "Highly unlikely, don't you think?"

Eastward Bound

> Once upon a time, before there were gospels of the kind familiar to readers of the New Testament, the first followers of Jesus wrote another kind of book. Instead of telling a dramatic story about Jesus' life, their book contained only his teachings...Then the book was lost.
>
> —Burton Mack
> The Lost Gospel: The Book of Q

"This one's obviously a laboratory report; and for some reason it has no letterhead and only the initials 'M.S.', presumably for confidentiality," said Riggs as he reviewed the two letters in Colby's folder. "It shows a date for some fragment as the late first century A.D., which is close to the date Quelle would have been written. That cinches it. Colby apparently brought a fragment of Quelle from Srinagar..."

"Or Hemis..." interrupted Christina.

"...or Hemis," continued Riggs, "and had it analyzed by this unknown laboratory. It all fits. Either Quelle, or someone who knows the whereabouts of Quelle, is in India, and there's a very good chance that someone is Professor Gupta, based on the photograph of Colby in front of the same tomb."

"The other letter is in Italian," explained Christina, "but it's been translated. My brother said that it's written on special Vatican paper, and I believe it was written by a priest there."

Riggs read Ryan's translation aloud:

> *"With regard to the ancient document we discussed, you are correct in calling it the most significant discovery in recorded history. It will have unprecedented impact on the reshaping of Christian history and mythology, and as such would be extremely valuable to the Church. Hopefully you are aware of the dangers presented by this situation, but I will meet you as previously arranged in the hope that a suitable home can be found for this extraordinary document."*

Riggs was silent for a moment, and then shared his conclusions with Christina: "The Vatican must have learned that Colby was tracking Quelle, and this letter indicates that they want to secure it from him."

"That doesn't sound like Uncle Colby to me," puzzled Christina.

"Nor to me."

"I'm not sure even I would give something like this to any one church. The Codices and the Scrolls have taught us the perils of religious monopolies."

"If the Vatican knew Quelle had been discovered, however, they'd be compelled to pursue it, whether or not the mission was hopeless. I believe they had arranged to meet with him," surmised Riggs.

"Perhaps in Cairo?"

"We'll probably never know, but I can assure you that nothing would attract more trouble than the rumor that Colby had located Quelle. Antiquities dealers and religious extremists of all persuasions would flock to the scene like proverbial moths, and an 'accidental' death would be penny ante in this game."

"I don't think Uncle Colby would have told anyone, do you?"

Riggs shook his head. "That doesn't rule out someone like Professor Gupta or the mysterious 'M.S.' who did the laboratory analysis. Once M.S. determined the age of the fragment, he could have guessed that the document was important to Christianity—or for that matter, Judaism—whether or not he knew it was Quelle. In fact, Colby might have taken M.S. into his confidence."

"Well, at least now we know that there was a motive for his death. It certainly couldn't have been an accident." Christina wanted to know more about Quelle. "Did you think you had discovered Quelle when you found the Gospel of Thomas in the Nag Hammadi codices?"

"Sure. Finding Quelle is never far from the mind of a New Testament scholar," confessed Riggs. "Some scholars had even hoped it would be found among the Dead Sea Scrolls."

"The ones controlled by Father de Vaux?"

"Yes, and rumors are still rampant on this subject," said Riggs, shaking his head. "If the Insiders had found Quelle, which is highly unlikely, very few believe that they would have shared it with the public. It would simply have been too controversial."

"So Quelle wouldn't be in the vault?" joked Christina.

"Highly unlikely. But we might take a look someday," he teased with a wry smile.

"Why wasn't Quelle included in our New Testament?" asked Christina naïvely. She obviously didn't anticipate the answer.

"It would have been excluded, and in fact banned, by those who followed Paul's Christianity. For the Roman Christians the teachings of Jesus were far less important than his miraculous life, as the incarnate Son of God, who brought salvation to the world by his death and resurrection. The teachings of Jesus became mere ornaments on the kerygma proclaimed by Paul."

Christina reluctantly recited what she had learned. "So you think that the Quelle Christians were branded heretics and their Gospel, Quelle itself, was destroyed by the Roman Christians about the same time the Nag Hammadi codices were hidden?"

"Either that or it just fell into disuse," affirmed Riggs.

"But why would anyone lose interest in the teachings of Jesus?"

"Because the teachings which the Romans preferred were already incorporated into their favorite Gospels along with the narratives of the Resurrection, which supported their creeds," explained Riggs, "and because the Quelle Christians probably refused to accept Jesus as their God. They worshipped his teachings, but not the man, and continued to have only one God. Rome demanded allegiance to Paul's man-God, Jesus, and to their religious hierarchy."

Christina was silent. She had never thought of the man Jesus as becoming God; rather she thought of Jesus as being God, on an important mission to earth to save souls. This was all very confusing. The notion of Jesus as merely an enlightened man, like Mahatma Ghandi or Buddha, was just plain unacceptable to her. How could a guru, even an outstanding guru, make arrangements for her soul in Heaven? And the most important question of all: if Jesus wasn't God, how could she possibly achieve eternal life? She decided to save all these personal questions for later.

"You really believe there were Quelle Christians who followed only His teachings?" repeated Christina, with complete skepticism.

"Why sure. And they were not much different from Thomas Christians. Their Jesus was probably the Eastern Jesus we talked about yesterday. The one who taught that every person is a Christ and that the Father, Mother, God can be found within each of us."

Ridiculous, she thought, *I'm going to get the answers to these questions from my brother.* She was suddenly reminded to check her watch, and jumped to her feet. "I'm late picking up Ryan at the airport. I'll be back later. Can we see you for breakfast tomorrow before he leaves, and I'll make the introductions?"

"If you insist," he joked. "...Of course," he corrected.

It suddenly occurred to him that he had more to do than translate the Gospel of Mary. "Don't you think I better get flight reservations for Srinagar?" he asked.

She paused briefly in thought. She had flown to the Middle East for Uncle Colby, so why not go half way around the world? Besides, she was dying of curiosity about the Quelle manuscript, and would even like to see the so-called Tomb of Jesus in Srinagar. "Does that mean I'm forgiven for not telling you about Uncle Colby's folder?"

"It's hard to stay mad at someone who's just pulled Quelle out of her hat."

"I guess I just got lucky on that one." The smug smile which crossed her face made her all the more attractive. "Do you think we should contact

Professor Gupta?" She was pointing at her watch and motioning desperately toward the door.

"I'll give it a try, but it won't be easy given the time difference between here and India. On the other hand, I doubt if he'll be overwhelmed with responses to the newspaper article," called out Riggs, as Christina disappeared around the corner.

He sat there, finishing his coffee and reviewing the excitement of the past few minutes. He smiled when he realized that Christina, in her haste to meet Ryan at the airport, had left the contents of the Quelle folder laying all over the breakfast table. He picked them up carefully, glancing cautiously around the garden. *From now on,* he thought, *we'll have to be more careful, unless we want to share Colby's fate.*

Jacob's Ladder

The one mediator, Christ, established and ever sustains here on earth his holy Church, the community of faith, hope, and charity, as a visible organization through which he communicates truth and grace to all men.
—Catechism of the Catholic Church

"How's Aunt Mary dealing with Uncle Colby's death?" asked Christina, postponing her more sensitive questions about the origins of their religion.

They were walking briskly on Kubri el Tahrir, the bridge across the Nile to Giza, where they planned to spend some time in El Tahrir park on El Gezira island. It was an ambitious walk from Mrs. Scarzella's house, but they both wanted the exercise. Their strides, youthful in the bright sun, were reminiscent of many happy childhood hikes together. It was as if the burdens of their maturity and the differences which had grown between them over the years were swept away by the steady Nile winds.

"She is doing as well as could be expected," answered Ryan. He had short, small hands for his size, but very nice character lines in his face. Physically he was perfect for the priesthood, with a thick head of hair, a ready smile, and almost no hesitation before a big embrace. "She and Colby were very close, you know, and his death has been a real shock to her system. Fortunately, it has brought her and mother closer together." He spoke evenly, separating each word like beads on a rosary.

"They're both without men, at least for the moment," observed Christina.

"I was hoping this tragedy would bring Aunt Mary back to the Church," said Ryan. "It is not too late yet, but she is definitely placing herself at risk."

"I doubt if she'll ever come back. She's become quite independent over the years."

"I hope you're wrong, Christina. Mother is working on her, I'm sure, at least in a subtle way."

Subtle? she thought. *Nothing subtle about mom and her religion.* She decided to procrastinate a little longer about her own questions.

"What did you learn about Colby's death?" said Ryan, interrupting her thoughts.

"The Cairo police department was a disaster for me. I learned nothing, which I frankly think is all they knew. They certainly aren't as dedicated to paperwork as we are." Her wink let him know that this was not complimentary.

"They didn't even know whether or not it was an accident?" he asked, sharing her disappointment.

"Not really, but I'm more than ever convinced that it wasn't an accident," she confided. "I have no specific information on his death, but he was apparently involved in several dangerous pursuits, all involving ancient manuscripts." She was purposely vague about Quelle and the contents of the Cairo vault, not wanting to put Ryan in a conflict with his Church.

"What about the man who has the other key?" continued Ryan's line of questioning.

They stopped in the middle of the El Tahrir bridge and looked up the Nile to the south. The wooden feluccas of yore, sailing quietly in the river, contrasted sublimely against the towering glass hotels in the background.

"His name is Riggs Parker...Dr. Riggs Parker...and he's been quite easy to work with," said Christina, concealing her true feelings for him. She didn't want Ryan to know that she was enamored with *the other key.* "I've asked him to join us for an early breakfast in the morning before your flight, if that's all right?"

"That will be fine," he responded perfunctorily. "What is his background?"

"He's a New Testament scholar from the Claremont Graduate School," she answered, hoping this would mean nothing to him.

"I've never met a New Testament scholar outside of the Church that wasn't a heretic," he said, with his usual authoritative air. "He would be a good one to avoid."

She tried not to sound defensive, but replied, "I think you'll find he has a deep belief in God."

"His own god, maybe," ridiculed Ryan, "but not Christ our Lord. Does he have anything to do with Professor Robinson at Claremont?"

"Professor Robinson was his major professor," related Christina, partially disguising her pride. It was now clear to her that Ryan was well-informed on these matters.

"Then there's hope. Professor Robinson is an outstanding scholar, even though he sometimes gets too involved in the search for historical accuracy. Our favorite professors at the better divinity schools think highly of him."

Christina was relieved. As long as Ryan thought of Riggs as Robinson's student, everything might be all right.

"What did the two of you find in Colby's vault?" continued Ryan's probing.

She thought for a moment. *I know I can trust him, but Uncle Colby did promise to maintain confidentiality about the Scrolls, and there is a remote link between Ryan and the Ecole Biblique.* Then she answered guardedly, "Just photographs of some early Jewish documents. We need to find a home for them eventually."

"There might be an interest in Jerusalem?" he joked. His jokes never seemed to amuse anyone other than himself.

He's sure full of questions today, thought Christina, ignoring his flawed humor. *I've never seen him so inquisitive. I'd better get him talking about himself or he might stumble onto Quelle and our trip to India.*

"What brings you to the Vatican this trip? Did they make you Pope and we just didn't hear yet? Shouldn't your *little sister* be the first to know?"

"It's almost that good," he grinned, and she believed him just for a second.

She could see that he was bursting with pride unfitting his priestly attire. They strolled through the ornate wrought iron gate into the park, stopping to admire a statue of a woman holding fruits in her apron.

"They're going to promote me to Auxiliary Bishop, with right of succession to the See," he exclaimed. "They like the work I've done in the Boston diocese." He looked at her expectantly, waiting for her to congratulate him.

"You're very happy, as you should be. You've earned it," said Christina, genuinely pleased that his dedication and tireless service had been rewarded by the Church. "I'm ecstatic too," she laughed, and the other people in the park were amused to see a priest and a young lady laughing and swinging in circles of joy. Even the sight of a collared priest would have been novelty enough in this Islamic city.

Looking at his smiling face, she recalled the times when they were growing up together. He was five years older than her, and very much the big brother. As a young man, he had unswerving faith in the Church, much more so than her. He never questioned, he just believed. His was a genetically pure confidence in the creeds and doctrines of the Church. She pursued his promotion further: "What does 'Right of Succession to the See' mean?"

"I will automatically replace the aging Bishop upon his death."

"Is he ill?" she joked.

"No...fortunately," he replied, deflecting her humor, "but I did say *aging Bishop.*" The accompanying smile managed to reveal simultaneously a deep love for both the Bishop...and his position.

There aren't very many people he can share his ambitions with, she thought to herself, proud that he confided in her this way. "I really believe that you could become Cardinal someday, or even higher. You've got that special combination, both a gentle spiritual presence and a strength in your dealings with people."

"Maybe," he replied with calculated modesty as they resumed their walk in the park. "I do have an excellent knowledge of our catechetical traditions, and the congregation seems to find my sermons inspirational. You should see the line of people expressing gratitude after Mass."

"I have," she smiled, "it looks like a Rock Concert."

"No, I'm being serious. I love ministering to the poor and the needy. I look forward to bringing comfort to the sick and the dying at the hospitals, especially the little children. I love it all: confessions, counseling, and all the ceremonies and the sacraments."

She gave him another hug, showing him that she was proud in many ways. *For him,* she thought, *the priesthood remains a work of love, in spite of his brief lapses into ambition. He is truly God's finger touching the sick and needy.*

It hadn't been easy for him, she reflected, giving up the prospects of his own family. With his athletic build, he certainly cut a fine figure in his cassock, enough so that women were unable to completely conceal their interest in him. Celibacy was certainly a bigger sacrifice than most were willing to make. Instead of his own family, he shared the burdens of his congregation.

Yet his celibacy had always distanced him from genuine participation in human affairs. He seemed a little too theoretical, a little too distant. Since their father died, Ryan had imagined himself the head of the family. Christina tolerated this fantasy, which was shared by both him and their mother, but she also knew that it was her income, not his masculinity, which would stand between her mother and any serious financial difficulties. She had never doubted that the Church came before his family, certainly before her, if he ever had to choose.

There seemed little doubt, however, that he had chosen the right career. He had some wonderful leadership qualities, which clearly had not gone unnoticed by the Church. He always thought before he spoke, and his delivery was deliberate and persuasive. He was politic, but not political, in the sense that he was always in the right place at the right time with the right answers, but he appeared to be a man without ambition. His humility was much deeper than a veneer, and yet he had always been the one chosen for the next higher responsibility. His progress in the Church had been spectacular, if such a thing were possible.

Hail Mary, Mother of God

Every day people are straying from the church and going back to God.

—Lenny Bruce

"Ryan, who wrote the New Testament?" Christina asked, with all the appearances of meekness. She glanced at him to see if the subject was too sensitive and knew from his confident smile that he was all right..

He looked at her suspiciously, knowing she would not normally ask such an obvious question without something on her mind. "The Evangelists," he answered without hesitation.

"Who were the Evangelists?" she continued the line of questioning.

"In most cases the Apostles, the disciples of Jesus, of course. They were written by Saint John, Saint Matthew, and the other Saints, including Saint Paul."

"And Saint Peter?" she asked.

"As you know, Saint Peter founded our Church, following the command of our Lord in Matthew 16, but apparently Saint Peter didn't write his own Gospel...either that or it was lost. The other Gospels, and the writings of Saint Paul, all tell essentially the same story, so there's really no need for one more," he answered authoritatively.

"Were the disciples men of letters?" she asked respectfully.

"Not in all cases. Some might have had scribes which wrote down their first hand observations of Jesus a few years later."

"Did Saint Paul have first hand observations of Jesus?"

"Of course he did," he said somewhat indignantly. "Jesus reappeared to Saint Paul after He had risen from the dead."

"No, I mean prior to His Resurrection."

He looked at her with extreme disappointment. "You've been spending too much time with the scholars," he said in a scolding, almost condescending voice.

"The reason I ask," she said defensively, "is that the oldest fragments we have of the New Testament Gospels were written in Greek a few hundred years after the Crucifixion, and even the most liberal estimates place their origins well after the disciples would have died. They appear to be later recordings of oral history, not first hand accounts." *I can't believe I had the courage to say that,* she thought. She was concerned how he would react and found her words sticking in her throat.

He started to give an answer, but she interrupted bravely: "And they all tell essentially the same story only because they are based on St. Mark and some common earlier sources. They really aren't independent eye-witness accounts...are they?"

He looked at her in dismay.

I don't think I can press this any further, she thought. *Maybe I should just change the subject before he gets too upset.*

It was too late. Ryan had already warmed to the discussion. "The Holy Catholic Church, Christina, as you know was founded by Jesus, who was succeeded by the first Pope, his disciple St. Peter. That Apostolic Office has been unbroken down to the present Pope Paul VI. The Pope, as a result of this Apostolic Succession, has certain spiritual powers and is infallible on issues of faith and morals. The Bishops inherit their authority, and their spiritual powers, directly from the Pope and the Apostles. The New Testament," he said with finality, "was written by the Evangelists, based on the first hand experience of the Apostles, including Saint Paul." His straight torso seemed to support his confidence in this matter.

"I think I was just trying to better understand who the Evangelists were and when they wrote the Gospels," she said apologetically. "They apparently weren't the disciples themselves, which raises the question of who they were and on what authority they wrote. That's really my question. What gives the New Testament any more authority than other ancient stories?"

He stopped and turned to her, with the same look he had given her over the years when he was seriously disappointed. The same look she got the few times she brought home grades lower than *A's.*

"Can I change the subject slightly?"

"You can change it dramatically if you like," he retorted.

"Were there any Gospels written about Jesus which were not included in the New Testament?"

He remained silent for longer than she had expected, but when he responded it was with complete confidence and with no sign of emotion. "This isn't really my field of study, Christina. I'm a practitioner, not a scholar. But it's my understanding that there were some accounts of the life of Jesus which were omitted from the New Testament. Some of these were merely repetitive of the Synoptic Gospels and St. John, and some were outright heretical, full of lies about Jesus."

"Do you mind if I ask who made those decisions?" she asked, as diplomatically as possible.

"Again, I really don't know, but it was very early in the formation of the Church, when there was complete agreement between all the disciples. It was long before there were any schisms or disagreements."

"Before Martin Luther and the Protestants?" she asked.

"Definitely," he answered, knowing himself to be correct. "Even before the schism with the Eastern Orthodox Church, which still uses essentially the same New Testament...incidentally. There's no doubt in my mind that everyone was in agreement on which heretical documents should be omitted from the New Testament."

"Well, you see, it's not so simple for me anymore, because I've recently heard about some very early schisms in Christianity, and I'm not talking about when Muhammad led the Islamic schism in the seventh century."

"We don't really consider that a schism in the Christian Church, Christina," he said, reproachfully. "Are you talking about the schism between the Chalcedonians and the Monophysites in the fifth century?"

She shook her head.

"Are you talking about the differences between Arius and Origen in the fourth century?"

Again she shook her head. "I was talking about earlier than that," she explained. "Even before Constantine, the first Christian Roman Emperor, was baptized on his deathbed by a heretical Arian Bishop."

He was shocked with her new knowledge of the subject.

"I was talking about the first schism, if you will, between Paul in Antioch and the disciples led by James in Jerusalem."

Ryan was silent for awhile. "My training," he began, lacking his normal confidence, "on early Christianity isn't really that detailed. These were not things I needed to know in caring for the sick and dying and administering the Sacraments. I only know some basic truths about the Church, not everything of an academic nature. Christina, I can't answer all your questions. I just think you're heading down a road which will bring you, and ultimately our family, nothing but grief and unhappiness. I hate to see this happening to my little sister. It isn't possible to intellectualize beliefs; there are some things we must simply accept on faith."

"I'm prepared to have faith in matters related to God, but I must confide in you that if the New Testament isn't grounded on historical facts, as I was taught, then it's much more difficult to believe these stories. In modern times, for example, I wouldn't believe that someone came back from the dead after three days, unless they were in a coma of some sort. It's even harder to believe that it happened two thousand years ago, unless we have irrefutable eyewitness accounts. Otherwise, how could we possibly know all the details surrounding the Crucifixion?"

Ryan saw that she was extremely confused, and just shook his head from side to side.

"My questions really aren't all that academic. I'm not asking you the difference between coinhere, and consubstantial and hermeneutical and uniate and Homoousian and Arian," her list went on. "These I would call too academic. I'm not even asking you the difference between God, Jesus Christ and the Holy Ghost. My question is much simpler than that. I want to know if there were Christians, or Jesus people, or whatever we want to call them, who differed with the Roman Church and whose Gospels were burned. I also want to know if some of those Gospels taught that the Christ is in all of us, and that the path to God is through our spiritual thoughts rather than only through the Church."

Ryan could see that she was going through a major collapse in her faith, and he knew that he was not strong enough academically to bring her back to safety. He was afraid for her, and more importantly for her soul. All he could do was to somehow bring her back to the basics of their religion.

"Christina," he lectured, "at some point you have to believe some fairly simple things. You have to believe that God loved us enough to send his only begotten Son to this miserable earth to die for our sins, and that this single act of love brought us eternal salvation. It's really no more complicated than that."

She sat down on a nearby bench in a state of shock, not only from his lack of answers, but also from the fact that she'd had the courage to tell him her deepest concerns. He sat down next to her and he put his arm around her like in the old days.

"Can we say a prayer together?" he asked gently.

She nodded, yes.

"Hail Mary, full of grace, the Lord is with thee," he began a familiar recitation. "Blessed art thou among women, and blessed is the fruit of thy womb, Jesus. Holy Mary Mother of God, pray for us sinners, now and at the hour of our death. Amen." He was genuinely concerned for her well being, both emotionally and spiritually.

He closed his eyes and continued in his comforting voice. "I believe in God, the Father Almighty, Creator of Heaven and earth; and in Jesus Christ, His only Son, our Lord; who was conceived by the Holy Ghost; born of the Virgin Mary; suffered under Pontius Pilate, was crucified, died and was buried; He descended into Hell; the third day He arose again from the dead; He ascended in Heaven; sitteth at the right hand of God, the Father Almighty; from thence He shall come to judge the living and the dead; I believe in the Holy Ghost; the Holy Catholic Church, the Communion of Saints; the forgiveness of sins; the resurrection of the body; and life everlasting. Amen."

As he prayed, she wondered if there was a special place in Purgatory for people like her, because she was giving audience to the possibility...just the slightest possibility...that her entire religion was built on nothing more than Paul's embellishment of Jesus' teachings.

Just before she could voice her concerns, Ryan advised her to leave the Middle East and return to her Maya research. She was being *tempted in the desert* and not doing particularly well.

Neither of them knew that Maya was the name of the Virgin Mother of the man-God Buddha. Neither of them knew that there were many similarities between the legends of Jesus and Buddha. In this bizarre way, then, she would be returning to Maya research, in India of all places.

She wondered why there were so many different branches of Christianity, with new ones forming every year, if the trunk of the tree, the Catholic Church itself, might have weak roots. *What are all the disagreements over,* she puzzled, *if it's not historically true in the first place?*

She remembered one of Uncle Colby's favorite quotations by the American Indian As-Go-Ye-Wat-Ha, speaking to the European missionaries: *Brother, you say there is one way to worship and serve the Great Spirit. If there is but one Religion, why do you differ so much about it?*

It occurred to her that Ryan really needed to learn more about his own religion and the origins of Christianity, but decided that as an Auxiliary Bishop it was probably not a realistic expectation. His career, she feared, had probably become more important at this stage than his beliefs. She realized that he didn't have answers for her, and that he was probably a captive of his own dogma. He just knew how to say certain things at the right times, but his understanding was limited and his answers seemed convoluted, almost regressive, as if he were backing up from the answers to the questions.

But it was not too late for her. She resolved to explore the subject with more courage, even though she felt abandoned and faced a profound sense of emptiness. *I don't know where I'm going,* she lamented, *but I know that this time I must get there on my own.*

What's the Matter?
1964
Stanford University

Without being aware of it and without being rigorously systematic about it, we exclude the Subject of Cognizance from the domain of nature that we endeavor to understand.
—Erwin Schrodinger
Winner, Nobel Prize in Physics, 1933

As Dr. John Stuart Bell walked with British confidence to the podium in the small lecture hall in the physics building, his mouth was galvanic with anticipation.

I'm always nervous before a colloquium, he reflected, *no matter how well I know the subject.*

He steeled himself with reassuring thoughts. *This is my subject, I completely understand it, and no one in the audience is better prepared than I am. So there is nothing to be nervous about.* But these thoughts provided little comfort when he saw the luminaries of physics assembling in the first row where they could impinge, in fact attack, his every idea.

There is nothing more unmerciful, even barbarous, than the way physicists probe into each other's theories, he thought, preparing the overhead projector for his transparencies. *Especially if you challenge their holy creeds.*

Which is just what he planned to do, as the faculty positioned themselves for the battle. The front row was where the venerable old bulls would sit, while the brilliant youths, with their acerbic academic lances, would be scattered throughout the audience.

As was the tradition, his host, Dr. Cohen, began the seminar by summarizing John's credential. A speaker must have a Ph.D., of course, and ideally have studied under well-known professors at a leading universities. Additionally, John Bell's vita was enhanced by his status at CERN, the Center for European Nuclear Research located in Geneva.

Dr. Bell began, as was the tradition, by paying his respects to Dr. Cohen, to Stanford University, and of course to each and every one of the venerable old bulls.

This might weaken their attacks, he hoped…*if only slightly.*

"I am disturbed," he began, "by the fact that our two most widely accepted theories in modern physics, namely relativity and quantum theory, are in disagreement."

He saw the old bulls shift their weight in their chairs. He had drawn the line in the sand, and they were preparing for battle.

"I am even more disturbed that we choose not to discuss it. Are we any different from the Christian Clergy, who pretend that the historical Jesus is invulnerable to modern scholarship? Are we not also in a state of denial?"

He did not want them to answer these rhetorical questions, of course, so he moved quickly along. He knew that their questions would come soon enough when he attacked each of the sacred cows.

"My research over the past year has been devoted to finding a simple equation which will embody the conflict between relativity and quantum theory. Such an equation will allow the experimentalists to resolve this issue once and for all."

"Have you found such an equation?" asked one of the old bulls, trying to force him into a corner early in the first round.

"Yes, in fact I derived it while I was here at Stanford on sabbatical from CERN. I will present it later in the colloquium."

I fended that question well, he complimented himself. He certainly had their attention at this point, if not their undying affection.

"My introduction to the subject will be elementary, so that everyone can understand, even the undergraduates," he joked. Everyone loved benign sarcasm directed at the undergraduates.

"We know from Einstein's relativity theory that no signal can travel faster than the speed of light. This is not a great imposition on most of our lives, because light travels very fast, at least compared to San Francisco traffic."

There was a little laughter from the junior faculty members, but the old bulls remained stoic behind their spectacles.

"The speed of light," he continued, "seems sluggish only compared to intergalactic distances. Since the universe is 15 billion light years across, the speed of light on that scale seems like a snail's pace. But as you all know, Einstein's speed limit is very important. It makes our world intelligible. Without it, time would not only run forward, it could also run backwards, and sequences of events would not make sense to us. The speed limit Einstein discovered gives everyone a sense of time and order, and it gives us physicists what we call 'causality'. We can be certain that 'causes' will always precede 'effects', and not the other way around. We really couldn't cope with the world if it were not for this causality.

"At this stage in the history of physics, relativity theory has been tested and proven not only in the galaxies, but also inside atoms and our particle accelerators, where speeds approach that of light. There is absolutely no doubt about its accuracy, not to mention its mathematical beauty. Any new *Theory of Everything,* which some of you are seeking, must incorporate relativity theory in order to be compatible with nature."

He paused. The audience seemed pleased. They were always happy when someone read from the Gospel according to St. Einstein.

"Our other widely accepted theory, quantum theory, has been tested even further. It too has never failed us. Since the turn of the century, not one experiment on atoms and elementary particles has defied this theory, and each year it is proven even more accurate. It is a credit to its founders, some of which are in this lecture hall, that it is the most beautiful, most accurate, and most robust physics theory of all times.

"If a single electron jumps from one quantum level to another in an atom, the quantum theory predicts the frequency of the emitted light with unbelievable accuracy. If a billion billion billion electrons swarm like bees in a copper wire, the quantum theory accurately explains the electrical and magnetic properties of the wire, including even superconductors and semiconductors. If there is any theory we would all defend with our lives, it is the quantum theory."

He looked again at the audience for corroboration. The old bulls loved hearing how smart they were in discovering the quantum theory.

"Then you can understand my disappointment when we spend most of our time praising relativity theory and quantum theory instead of dwelling on the fact that they have one annoying paradox."

The mood of his audience soured immediately, especially in the front row. They were beginning to see red.

I can't hope to change the minds of the old bulls, he thought, *but maybe some brilliant young physicists in the audience will accept my challenge and push beyond the prevailing orthodox views.* He summoned the inner courage to continue even though he knew it would infuriate most of the old bulls.

"I'm not talking about the fact that quantum theory is saddled with uncertainties and probabilities, which many of us find troubling. Einstein, for example, complained that *God would not play dice,* implying that there must be a way around the statistical nature of the quantum theory." *I could keep them arguing among themselves on this subject,* he thought, *but I want to move on to even better ground.*

"What I am talking about today, is the disturbing fact that quantum theory tells us that elementary particles are communicating instantly with each other across the entire universe. *Instantly,* of course, is obviously much faster than the speed of light. In this sense the elementary particles themselves are exempt from Einstein's own speed limit. It is not that they travel faster than the speed of light. They don't, because this would violate what we call causality. But they do communicate among themselves instantly, with what Einstein referred to as a *ghostly action at a distance.* We give this troublesome phenomenon the innocuous name *non-local field,* perhaps so that it will not receive too much attention from outsiders." He stood erectly, with hands on each side of the podium, knowing that his audience did not want to hear this again. He also knew that they would not, in fact could not, argue with what he had said. He had his facts straight.

"What nature seems to be telling us is that humans cannot send signals faster than the speed of light, but that elementary particles do it all the time. The quantumstuff out of which we and our universe are constructed, appears to ignore Einstein's speed limit. It is somehow communicating instantly across the entire known universe.

"This has bothered us all to a certain extent, but it has bothered me to the point that I have tried to find a way around the dilemma. Is it possible, I have asked myself repeatedly, to develop a new quantum theory which does not have this idiosyncrasy? Does a different, and yet to be discovered, version of quantum theory exist which does not require elementary particles to communicate instantly? If we knew it was impossible, we wouldn't waste time looking for a new version. We could, perhaps, learn to live with the implications of this unnatural action-at-a-distance. On the other hand, if we knew it was possible, we could strive harder to find a more palatable version of quantum theory.

"So my research has been directed toward finding a simple equation which will let experimentalists someday answer the following question:

'Is it possible to devise a quantum theory that rules out instant communication between elementary particles?'

"Before I show you the mathematical proof of my equation, however, I want to address some of its philosophical implications. He eyed the bulls in the front row. "I know that most of you don't like to discuss philosophy, and would rather focus on the physics and the mathematics. I assure those of you that I will return quickly to the mathematical proof itself.

"I dare to broach the philosophical aspects of my subject, however, because I think our community should become more actively involved in this debate. Our undergraduates should know that this subject is not without notice among theologians and philosophers. Are we going to relegate the meaning of our physics to those outside the discipline?

"I am also previewing my personal opinion, which I readily admit has no experimental corroboration: namely, that we will ultimately find that all versions of quantum theory are cursed, or blessed, with instant communications. I believe we will find that elementary particles are allowed to play by different rules than humans, and this will fuel philosophical debates, both inside and outside of physics."

One of the old bulls, by far the most famous one, leaned forward as if to command the floor before speaking. Everyone was silent in anticipation. Dr. Bell's heart raced, and his mouth once again became metallic, although he knew that he would be safe once he got to the mathematics.

"Isn't this just the age old debate between Niels Bohr and Albert Einstein?" asked the old bull, peering over his glasses.

John Bell was greatly relieved that the remark was not critical of his own work. *But how could it be?* he thought. *I haven't even showed them my equation. The sooner I can get to the mathematics, the safer it will be for me.*

As promised, however, he continued to discuss the philosophical implications. "Yes," he responded, "the best minds have been debating this issue for years. It's not new. The maturation of quantum theory has simply brought it to everyone's attention. Niels Bohr and Albert Einstein debated the subject, followed by great thinkers like John von Neumann, Eugene Wigner, and David Bohm...and the people in this room."

He had been wise enough, once again, to feed the egos on the front row.

"Einstein believed that there was a piece missing in quantum theory, which if it could be found would explain both the probabilities he found distasteful and the conflicts with relativity. He hoped that this missing link would once again make physics the study of an objective external reality...one independent of ourselves. He devoted a substantial portion of his life to this proposition without success. Others have since continued the quest.

"He would not be at all pleased with my equation, because in principle it allows elementary particles to communicate instantly with each other over the entire universe. Nor do I believe that he would want to hear philosophers describe elementary particles with terms like 'omniscient', which are normally reserved for metaphysics. But what other choices do they have? They certainly look omniscient compared to us humans.

"Most physicists," he continued, "do not agree with Einstein that a piece of the theory is missing. The consensus view, held widely by many, is that the world of the quantum is simply not comprehensible; it cannot be explained in the language of everyday life. Our orthodox creed, if you will, is that the world inside the atom is merely mathematical, no more and no less. To someone outside our field, this might sound remotely akin to denial, although I use that term circumspectly."

He saw one of the bulls pulling his favorite pipe out of the clammy pocket of his Harris tweed coat, which showed some wear on the leather elbows.

"There is an escape from this dilemma," he continued quickly, hoping the old bull would not speak, "but it is not without its own hazards. Reality can be reinstated in the world of the quantum by attributing it to the observer. Many physicists, including the recently departed Niels Bohr, believe that physical reality is observer-dependent. Reality is meaningful only in the context of an observation. They believe that it is impossible to separate the attributes of an elementary particle from its measuring device.

"These physicists cannot understand why Einstein was able to accept observer-dependent yardsticks and clocks in his relativity theory, and yet could not accept observer-dependent elementary particles in quantum theory. They believe that our role as observers might be essential to the existence of the physical universe."

One of the old bulls interrupted. "I talked to Einstein many times on this subject, and he simply would not relinquish his belief in an objective external reality, and I happen to share that view. If we accept the proposition that reality is observer-dependent, then we would find ourselves only a short step away from what I consider science fiction, namely attempts to link physical reality with the human consciousness."

The room was noticeably quiet as people mentally chose sides on the developing debate.

"Would someone please tell me what is meant by an objective external reality?" pleaded an undergraduate.

"I'd be glad to," said one of the bulls, turning around to address the audience. "It means a material reality which would exist objectively and externally whether we observed it or not. It also means a reality we can agree on by repeated independent observations made at different times and places. *Objective external reality* remains the dream of most physicists, but I happen to agree with Niels Bohr that the new quantum theory has eliminated this possibility."

John Bell was thinking. *Well, at least I have the old bulls fighting amongst themselves, which takes some of the pressure off of me. I have to be careful not to let the colloquium get out of control, or I'll never have time to derive my new equation for them.* Which is just what happened when the most revered old bull entered the fray.

"With all due respect, gentlemen, is it possible that some of us still hope for the days when physics could be explained without reference to the human consciousness? Yet each of us knows that something out of the ordinary is required to explain what happens when matter appears miraculously out of the vacuum. We also know that something out of the ordinary is required to break Von Neumann's infamous chain. That something, in my opinion, can be nothing other than the human consciousness."

"I agree completely with Eugene Wigner," the old bull continued, "whom we all respect, when he says that something metaphysical is happening when we observe matter. Frankly, I think it is wonderful that we seem to be participating in the creation of physical reality. What could be better? And it is also wonderful, at least for me, that a higher intelligence appears to be involved."

Just as this speaker's life-long adversary began to stand, and everyone wondered if the colloquium would lose its equanimity…and its focus…the speaker made movements as though taking his seat. He then surprised everyone, especially his antagonist by sneaking in one last comment: "I don't know why we find this so disturbing, when we have already accepted contracting yardsticks and dilating time in order to rationalize a world in which light always travels toward us at the same speed, regardless of the speed of its source. We do not seem to mind being the center of that drama."

John Bell realized that the old bulls had made his point for him. Namely, that just below the surface of every physics discussion lurked this controversy on the deeper meaning of the new quantum theory. He decided to regain control of the colloquium, knowing that this debate could last for hours.

"I think all of you know," he began, "that highly respected physicists line up on all sides of this endless debate. I think that this is good, and it is the primary reason why I developed the equation which is the subject of this seminar. If I'm to complete the detailed mathematics before the hour ends, you must now give me your full attention.

"Unless you can find an error in my mathematics, this equation will at least place the dilemma in the hands of the experimentalists. Once they have built fast enough instruments, we will know whether or not 'instant communications' between elementary particles are unavoidable in our favorite theories. We will know if elementary particles are partially exempt from Einstein's speed limit and live in a world that disregards causality…one of our holy grails."

John Stuart Bell then began covering the blackboard with equations, and the audience became quieter and noticeably more comfortable. They preferred logical mathematical derivations over the ephemeral world of philosophy, and finding mathematical errors was something on which even the old bulls could readily agree. There were no errors, however, in the derivation which followed. Dr. Bell had done his homework.

Venice of India

"Have you ever seen a more beautiful place?" asked Riggs. They were standing together, with their arms around each other, looking around the lake at the floating gardens.

"The flowers are lovely on the surface of the lake," agreed Christina. "I know now why Westerners refer to Srinagar as the Venice of the East, with all these lakes and canals. It seems that almost everyone lives on the water. I just love those little gondolas running people from place to place, like in a fairy tale. This is exactly what I hoped it would be like."

"Me too," agreed Riggs. "Incidentally, did you know that Srinagar is the capital only in the summer?"

"How did you know that?" said Christina, wrinkling her nose at this extraneous information.

"I read it in the magazine on Air India," said Riggs smugly. "I'm an instant expert on these matters. In the winter the capital is moved to Jammu, a warmer city to the south and somewhat out of the mountains. I'll tell you something else I learned."

"What?" said Christina, looking fondly at her new talking encyclopedia.

"This State is called Jammu and Kashmir, not just Kashmir. Why haven't I heard that name before? It is also interesting to me that it borders on both Pakistan and China…Tibet of course. These borders have been in dispute for many years. Even today, parts of Jammu and Kashmir are claimed by all three countries."

"So we're in the middle of a war?" exclaimed Christina. "It doesn't look like it from the verandah of this houseboat."

"I don't think they fight all the time, but there may well be some skirmishes in the countryside," explained Riggs.

"Incidentally," said Christina, changing the subject. "How do you think we should handle Professor Gupta?"

"Well, I think we should tolerate his stories about the Tomb of Jesus just long enough to find out what he knows about Colby's search for Quelle."

"You don't think the tomb is real either?" asked Christina.

"I have no doubt that Jesus was buried somewhere, along with the many others who were put to death by the Romans, but it's a long way from the empty tomb in Jerusalem to northern India. I find the idea completely unbelievable."

"I agree, but for entirely different reasons. If you hadn't already done so much damage to my childhood religious beliefs, I would have argued against a tomb anywhere. But today I'm a little ambivalent even on that. Not ambivalent enough, however, to believe that He was buried in northern India. Why would He have gone so far from his home?"

"Which reminds me," said Riggs, changing the subject. "Did I tell you that Professor Gupta said on the phone that he had worked with your uncle on <u>several</u> projects?"

"Yes, but I wasn't sure whether or not he mentioned Quelle."

"No he didn't, and I didn't want to mention it unless he brought up the subject first. Unfortunately, he didn't volunteer a thing. I hope we'll learn more once we meet him."

"Agreed."

"By the way," smiled Riggs, giving her another hug, "if Gupta invites us to dinner, let's decline tonight. We can blame it on jet lag." He pulled her very close and kissed her on the neck.

She immediately turned and brought their lips together for a warm and lingering kiss. She felt his immediate response. "Did you have something else in mind?"

"The setting is much too romantic for three," proposed Riggs. "We could get a quick meal on the way home and then spend the evening right here looking out on the gardens and the other floating homes. Can you imagine this view at sunset?"

"Or after dark with all the lights reflecting on the water?" she countered. "You've got a date...that is, if you'll promise to finally give me back my Quelle folder." She looked at him with a perky smile. He had been playfully blackmailing her with Colby's folder ever since she left it on the table the day her brother visited Cairo.

"I'll give it back if you promise not to leave it on the breakfast table again."

The water taxi approached and the driver confirmed that he was to pick them up and transport them to Dr. Gupta at the University. They stepped into the brightly decorated boat and snuggled close together in the middle seat, as the pilot proudly pushed his craft away from their floating verandah. They smiled at each other as the boat moved a little faster and began to glide past other floating homes and gardens.

"I think we've found paradise," said Christina, looking deep into Riggs' eyes, "and I'm not just talking about finding Quelle."

"I'm looking forward to our first evening together in a real home," said Riggs, "with separate rooms of course."

A Star in the East

> Good scholars, honest scholars, will continue to differ about the interpretation of archaeological remains simply because archaeology is not a science. It is an art. And sometimes it is not even a very good art.
>
> —William Dever
> Near-East Archaeologist

"I am very very sorry about your uncle," offered Professor Gupta, in his lilting Indian accent. "We were very very good friends and worked on several projects together. He contributed to our museum in many many ways—not just financially."

Christina accepted his condolences graciously.

They were seated in his spacious office at the Ministry of Culture. As Christina looked around his office, which was filled with grand maps, large bookcases and many antiquities, she thought, *I could spend at least a year just touring his office. It's a museum in its own right...incredibly interesting.* She also saw several hints of his academic degrees and awards in frames on his walls. She noticed a Ph.D. in Archaeology from the University of Calcutta, and a second one from Oxford, in England. They had also learned that he held two impressive titles: Director of the Kashmir Research Center for Buddhist Studies and also Director of the Museums, Collections and Archives in Kashmir,

Noticing Christina's interest, he stood, walked to the wall nearest his desk and pointed to another embossed document. "This is my favorite," he said, without a hint of obsequiousness. It indicated his current membership in the International Conference for Anthropological Research in Chicago.

Enough for my hopes that he would be a charlatan, thought Christina, with some resignation. She knew from the look on Riggs' face that he shared her feeling. Whether they liked it or not, they were sitting in the office of a high ranking Indian official and a respected member of the international research community.

"What kind of projects did you work on together?" she asked, as they all sat down on the tall straight backed chairs.

"He helped us procure antiquities for our museum. I'll be more than pleased to show them to you tomorrow, when we have more time. We first met in 1950, when we were both involved in rescuing documents from the intellectual and religious purges of the Chinese Communists. It was a very very exciting time. A few documents miraculously survived the destruction of the Buddhist monasteries in Tibet, and funds were needed to get them to safety," he explained. "This is when I first saw your uncle in action."

"I had no idea his travels brought him this far east, but I'm not surprised that he was trying to protect precious manuscripts. That was his life's mission, of course," reminisced Christina. She was trying to think how to get the conversation pointing at Quelle, without giving away any information. "We are trying to complete some of the projects he was working on. He was in the middle of several interesting ones."

"On his last visit, about a year ago," volunteered Professor Gupta, "Mr. Tiger was following a lead on a controversial document written only a few years after the crucifixion of Jesus. He went to Hemis, high in the Himalayas, where he saw the document in the monastery. He returned with only a tiny fragment, which the monks gave him quite reluctantly, and he said he would have it carbon dated."

Christina and Riggs glanced at each other as discretely as possible, realizing that they had stumbled onto the trail of Quelle. This was indeed a stroke of good luck, having found the link to the unsigned laboratory report in Colby's folder. They knew that he must be talking about the same carbon dating.

Hardly able to contain herself, Christina followed up immediately: "Would a trip to Hemis be possible? We always enjoy a good climb, and while we're there we can follow up on this document."

Another climb? thought Riggs.

"Your timing is fortunate," responded Sunil optimistically, "because the trip into the Himalayas is almost impossible in the winter. But since it's June, you should have no difficulty with the weather, although it is still a very difficult trip. You might even be there during the festival in Leh, which makes the trip worthwhile anyway."

"Oh, I'm sure it will be rewarding," said Riggs, sending Christina a secret message regarding Quelle. He was so excited his heart was actually fluttering.

Sunil continued: "First you must get a letter of introduction from the exiled Dalai Lama in Dharamsala."

"Where is Dharamsala from here?" asked Christina, trying not to show her disappointment in this additional delay.

"It's about 150 miles, but in essentially the opposite direction from Hemis. This process, however, usually takes a week...at least a week."

The prospect of touring Gupta's "Tomb of Jesus" for one week while waiting for the letter of introduction was depressing to Christina, until she remembered their romantic floating paradise.

"Is there any way to speed this up?" probed Riggs.

"Well, there are no guarantees, but what I have done for others is to attach copies of your applications to the Dalai Lama with my own personal letter of introduction to take with you on the way up. Depending on the extent of your requests, this might get you started early while you wait for your letter to arrive later in Leh."

"And if that doesn't work?"

"The punishment is delightful: imprisonment in the lovely village of Leh for a week or two. Nothing could be more wonderful. Each year a handful of brave mountain climbers pays handsomely for the same privilege. You will love every minute of your delays," promised Sunil, who seemed to realize that they were in love. "Especially if you enjoy your time together."

I thought we disguised our feelings better than that, thought Christina. Riggs looked at her and smiled roguishly.

"Leh is in the Ladakh region," he continued, "and the bus trip takes you over the outlying ranges of the Great Himalayas. Depending on the weather and the condition of the bus, this can take between two days and two weeks. It is very hard to predict.

"Do we then hike to the monastery from Leh, Dr. Gupta?" asked Christina.

"Please call me Sunil. *Dr. Gupta* sounds too formal for Mr. Tiger's niece. It's a challenging hike of about thirty-five kilometers," he continued, "unless you are fortunate enough to connect with a mule train returning to the monastery."

They looked at each other. Riggs knew he had no choice, because Christina would say yes and he would have to accompany her. At least she was making it look as though a mutual decision was being made.

"Let's do it," smiled an eager Christina. The enticement of climbing the Himalayas and finding Quelle was almost too good to be true. Riggs undoubtedly had these priorities somewhat reversed.

Another Empty Tomb?

And they entered in, and found not the body of the Lord Jesus.

—Luke 24:3

Christina was looking from side to side at the ornate buildings, as they walked a little further up a very steep hill in the Old Town of Srinagar.

"We call this area Anzimar, and this is the Khanjar Quarter," said Gupta. "You'd be surprised how few visitors we have these days, thanks to the dispute with Pakistan over Jammu and Kashmir. It has scared everyone away."

Riggs looked to see if this might include Christina, but it obviously did not. Her thoughts were elsewhere. Instead of feeling foolish, as she had anticipated, she was actually looking forward to seeing Professor Gupta's Tomb of Jesus...and not only to confirm that it was the mosque in Uncle Colby's photograph. Gupta's lofty position in the government and his professional demeanor had convinced her that he believed what he claimed, in spite of her own skepticism. At the very least, she thought, the visit to this old tomb would be interesting, regardless of who was buried there.

As they turned right onto a cross street, she suddenly recognized the building in Colby's photograph...the one she had also seen in Gupta's press release. It was made of white plaster, with multiple high arches and ornate wooden doors and windows. There were three roofs, stacked on top of one another with the smallest at the top, giving it the appearance of a pagoda.

The Tomb of Jesus would have rated more than corrugated iron for a roof in Jerusalem, thought Christina, not sharing her amusement with the others.

"This building is called a Rozabal, a title reserved for someone noble, wealthy or saintly. It was constructed many years later around the tomb itself," he said leading them through the impressive front doors which towered above them.

Inside, the building was dimly lit, with sparse light filtering through the windows. It had the appearance of a very small cathedral or chapel, except for a wooden shrine in the middle, covered with square details. The shrine made it look more like a mausoleum. There was no one else in the building, and it was so quiet that they could hear their own breathing.

A man tending the garden outside had spoken politely and had let them enter the building unescorted. At the time, Gupta had said that the family claimed to have been in attendance of the tomb, from father to son, since 112 A.D.

Sounds like the Popes, Christina had thought at the time, *except for the sons.* Once again she amused herself.

Carved above the entrance to the burial chamber was a strange inscription, which Professor Gupta translated for them: *"Jesus entered the valley of Kashmir many centuries ago, and his life was dedicated to manifesting the truth".*

Riggs and Christina glanced at each other in disbelief, but remained silent.

Knowing of their training in linguistics, Gupta explained that the name of Jesus in India was Yuz Asaf, which could be traced to the word Bodhisatva or future Buddha. He then delighted them with inane details on the phonetic link between the names Yuz Asaf and Jesus, in technical terms only linguists could appreciate.

I had no idea, thought Christina, *that the name for Jesus had the same root as the name for the future Buddha.*

As they entered the wooden shrine, which housed the burial chamber, Gupta said, "The tombstone you see sits on top of the actual crypt which is hidden below. I think the tombstone was added later, because it is oriented north to south in the Islamic tradition."

"Have you looked under this tombstone?" asked Christina, pointing down at the gray slab.

"When I began to think this might be the same Jesus as yours," explained Gupta, "I got permission from the government to remove the tombstone."

"What did you see? What's under there?" asked Christina, with little more than morbid curiosity. *This is a truly scary place,* she thought. *Hardly any light comes through that door, and there's not enough room in here for all of us.*

"The older crypt underneath was oriented east to west, which is in the Jewish tradition," explained Gupta. "The Hindus, you know, occupied this area during the time of Jesus. They only allowed saints to be buried; everyone else was cremated."

"So you think that Hindus allowed Jews in this area to bury Jesus because he was regarded a Saint?" asked Riggs, trying to conceal his skepticism.

"To this day the people in this area have noticeable Semitic features," responded Gupta quickly. "They look more like Jews than Indians of Aryan descent. Some of our anthropologists believe that the Jews might have migrated from here to Egypt several thousand years ago. Kashmir might have been the 'Promised Land' for which the Jews left Egypt, and the Lost Tribes could have returned to Kashmir during the Diaspora when Palestine was overrun by the Babylonians."

Riggs and Christina glanced at one another in disbelief.

Actually, thought Christina, *nothing he's saying is any more ridiculous than what I've been taught. It's just different. How could we know what happened that many years ago anyway, either here or in Palestine?*

"The Old Testament accounts of Moses are probably only partially historical," continued Gupta, "with a healthy dose of Hindu legend and mythology. For example, Moses' concept of monotheism, of a single and almighty God, can be found in the much older Hindu Vedas. The Vedas also describe a father of love and goodness, the Creator of the Universe. As another example, the Moses legend, of being abandoned by his mother and rescued by royalty, is exactly the same as the legend of the Indian hero, Rama…and for that matter the Arab god, Bacchus. They all borrow heavily from the same basic myths."

I just don't know enough about mythology, thought Christina, *to understand his examples.* She didn't like taking someone's word on something this important. Was Professor Gupta is extremely well informed or just plain crazy?

"What else did you find under the tombstone?" asked Riggs.

"Would you like to look?" teased Gupta. "The three of us can easily push this stone away."

Christina and Riggs looked at each other as though they had been offered forbidden fruit.

Gupta quickly added: "It's quite all right. It looks much more permanent than it is. It is just a tomb."

Just a tomb, thought Christina, *just a tomb of Jesus, perhaps.* She knew that she shouldn't invade such a sacred place. *There's no way this is His tomb,* she rationalized.

"Why not," she said gamely.

"I can almost do it myself," he said, shoving on one side of the slab. They quickly began to assist him. "Not too much," he warned, "it's hard to get back on if it slides all the way off. A small crack is enough to see what I want to show you."

What does he want to show us in there? wondered Christina.

After they pushed the slab into just the right position, Professor Gupta, seeming proud of his preparedness, pulled a flashlight from his pocket and shined it into the crypt below. The beam was a dull yellow from vintage batteries. Riggs and Christina squeezed next to him and looked down into the crypt.

"When I first opened this last year," he continued, "that section with the impressions was covered with centuries of candle drippings…probably prayer offerings." He wiggled the beam to show them his subject. "Apparently, his followers worshiped here in the distant past. Knowing that stone crypts in this area frequently have unique identifying marks, like personal logos, I got permission to remove the layers of wax."

I can't make out anything with that weak flashlight, thought Christina. "And what did you find? It's too dark for me to see."

"I found the shape of two feet carved in the stone, showing the scars of a crucifixion, with the left foot over the right, exactly as expected from the Turin Shroud. I made plaster casts, which you can see in my office.

174

He then began pushing on the heavy slab again. "But if you want, perhaps you can see the prints. Help me push the stone further away just at this corner."

"There were many crucifixions," rationalized Christina. "It would be impossible to link this particular one with Jesus."

"Not in India," argued Gupta. "Crucifixion was unknown as a death penalty in India."

"I can see the footprints," admitted Christina as the light spilled into the crypt, "and the scars."

"Let me see," said Riggs, as he moved into a better position, pushing against the others. "I see them. They're carved deep in the stone, and the stigmata are quite obvious."

This is truly amazing, thought Christina. She remembered the Christian tours she had taken in Jerusalem during their recent visit. They weren't any more convincing...maybe even less so. She began to laugh at her next thought: *but then the sarcophagus of Jesus would not be real popular with us Christians. We really prefer empty tombs.*

"Are there any other Christian archaeological sites in this area, or just this tomb?" asked Riggs, believing that the answer would be negative.

"Well, there's a garden called *The Place of Moses*, and a fountain called *Moses Bath Place*, only to mention two. Twenty miles south of here is *the Meadow of Jesus*, where the local shepherd tribes believe Jesus preached. They call themselves the *Children of Israel.*

"I can go on for hours. On the steps of the grand entrance of King Gopadatta's palace, for example, I found the following inscription:

> *'At this time, Jesus announced his prophetic calling. In the year 54.*
> *He is Jesus, prophet of the sons of Israel.'*

"And I could fill a notebook with tombs and graves having names from the New Testament. Near the western border of Kashmir, for example, is the *Final Resting Place of Mother Mary*, and there is a second tomb of Mary to the north of Ladakh in East Turkestan, possibly the grave of Mary Magdalene."

"Isn't there archaeological evidence to the contrary in Jerusalem?" asked Christina.

"Certainly no stronger than this," smiled Gupta. "They are both marginal."

He's right, reasoned Riggs. All that is known about Jesus is that he appeared as a young man, with no prior history, and taught for a few years. He then disappeared after being crucified.

"Surely there must be archaeological proof that the tomb of Jesus is in Jerusalem?" insisted Christina.

"Not really," said Gupta. "None of the archaeological evidence is convincing to me. You'd be surprised how often tradition has substituted for scientific evidence."

Christina thought for a moment and then responded. "If the resurrection and ascension of Jesus are metaphorical, and not actually historical events, as some liberal scholars believe, then the body had to go somewhere, but Srinagar would not be the first place I would think of."

"Unless he walked…" offered Gupta, with a twinkle in his eye.

Unless he walked? thought Christina. That was a long walk even if he had somehow survived the crucifixion. She shuddered at both prospects. "It simply isn't possible that he survived the crucifixion," insisted Christina.

"I hope to convince you otherwise," challenged Gupta, "when you return from the Hemis monastery."

When we get back from Hemis, thought Christina, *we'll have Quelle and all the answers to these questions.*

Getting Cold Feet

As the head monk, the Rinpoche was the first to put on his mask, and with great respect he removed it from the face of the fierce god that protected the monastery. The other monks watched in awe, respecting his courage, and then they donned the other masks which lined the walls of the candle-lighted chamber. Not a word was spoken. They were enacting a ritual which was older than time itself, and each person knew his part of the drama perfectly.

Smoke from the oil lamps mingled with centuries of smudge on the walls, and the flickering light revealed ancient paintings of the mandala, the Buddhist symbol of the universe.

All in a line, they walked out of the Protector's sanctum and down a path carved out of the rocky mountain. One at a time, they climbed down the wooden ladder and the fifty steep stairs leading to the courtyard. Then the dance began.

They spun in circles, like flying dervishes, to the pleasure of the admiring crowd of peasants from the nearby village of Hemis, in this ritual which reminded them all of the path to enlightenment.

The festive colors around the courtyard looked more like Tibet than northern India, with brightly painted buildings, bright prayer flags, and the ever-spinning prayer wheels.

Everyone was in perfect unison.

Everyone, that is, except for one monk who never seemed to be quite in step with the others. One monk whose feet, although uncovered and cold like the others, were obviously performing the dance for the first time. He was much taller than the others, almost double their height, and his feet were noticeably lighter in color.

My feet are freezing, thought the eccentric monk, knowing he wouldn't receive a modicum of sympathy from the others. *My feet <u>were</u> freezing last night, and they've been freezing ever since the first snow. I must have been insane to volunteer for this assignment in the Himalayas. It all sounded so spiritual and enlightening at the time, and I've always loved the mountains. It never occurred to me that my life and limbs would seriously be at risk here in the Himalayas.*

He began to dance with renewed enthusiasm as he realized that the blood was coming back into his frozen feet.

Thank Buddha for small things, he prayed, as he jumped higher and higher. *When spring comes and the mountain passes open, I'm going to find a way back to Australia, even if I have to walk.* He thought for a minute, as he spun around the courtyard holding on to the next monk. *Assuming I still have feet.*

Himalayan Highs

When therefore, you see a woman's lips tremble and redden…know that she desires coition."
—Kama Sutra

"Have you ever read the *Kama Sutra?*" asked Christina, as she sat down on the small sofa in the houseboat and began to open the book laying on the table. Riggs was in the even smaller kitchen looking for wine glasses.

"You better wait for me," pleaded Riggs. "I think the Indian version might be a little more graphic than the ones in the States."

"Indeed it is," gulped Christina, as she quickly closed the book after glancing at two lovers demonstrating a contorted sexual union. "Indeed it is," she repeated quietly, while trying to erase the blush from her cheeks.

"I'll be there in a minute," said Riggs. "I'd like to see the Indian version too."

Christina looked around the room and thought how romantic it was to be in a houseboat on the shore of Lake Nagin. It was certainly more intimate than their rooms at the Garden City House in Cairo, especially Riggs' room, with piles of photographs, empty coffee cups and research notes.

Tonight, she thought, *after that Tibetan meal by candlelight at the Lhasa restaurant, I'm ready to make things very easy for Riggs, if I can get his mind on something besides finding Quelle at the Hemis monastery.*

Riggs brought two glasses of wine and sat down beside her.

Even before he could open the *Kama Sutra*, she raised her glass and proposed a toast. "To the Venice of the East," she said, putting her other hand on the top of his leg, as nonchalantly as possible.

"And to our discovery of Quelle," added Riggs, putting his arm tenderly around her shoulders.

I can't even sit next to her without getting excited, he thought to himself, although his was not a well kept secret.

They sipped their wine together flipping quickly through the explicit, yet instructive, pages of the Kama Sutra.

"Nothing like that at home," he smiled, noticing Christina's embarrassment. He sat his glass down and placed hers beside it on the table near the open book. He kissed her gently but firmly, first on the lips and then on her cheek and neck. He followed with another long kiss on her lips, which by now were swollen with expectation.

She could feel her nipples beginning to firm.

"It looks like your uncle might be getting us in even more trouble," joked Riggs, as he put his arm around her waist and led her out onto the verandah.

"If that's possible," purred Christina, looking softly into his eyes.

The lights were sparkling on the water from the other house boats, and the wind was gently swaying the lanterns on the floating verandahs. A lone water taxi glided quietly past them not too far away. The moon was approaching full, and had already appeared in the dusk sky as the last embers faded silently with the setting sun.

"Did you notice the flowers Professor Gupta had delivered?" asked Riggs.

"Yes I did. They're beautiful and exotic, not unlike the ones in Guatemala. Are you sure it was Professor Gupta?"

Riggs said, "Who else?" as he squeezed her hand affectionately. He was silent for a long time and then spoke without complete confidence. "Have you given any thought to what might happen when we get back to the States?"

"With <u>us</u>?" she asked coyly.

"Yes, with us," he repeated with a smile. "It's a long way between Harvard and Claremont."

"Not really all that far, and we both travel a great deal anyway," she volunteered optimistically.

"I would actually enjoy having a good friend in Boston."

"And I've been thinking how nice it would be to go sailing in Newport Beach during those long winters."

"Or in Gloucester during the summer," countered Riggs, as they began a kiss from which they might never return. He ran his hands slowly and gently over almost every sensitive spot on her body, and began kissing her rapidly but gently on the neck.

She whispered, "But we can't do that forever."

She brought her free leg up gently between his and moved it slowly against his inner thigh. She could feel his body react, as his kisses got warmer and longer. Soon he would lose all reason, and so would she.

"Well I could always pull out that offer from Boston University, if we ran out of travel money," he said cupping his hand against the side of her breast, with his thumb caressing the swollen nipple. He seemed much less restrained than usual.

Her nipples stung with delight as she pressed against the part of him which was trying to explode, and pretended not to notice as she rubbed against it firmly.

They suddenly realized how close the neighboring houseboats had become, and walked slowly inside. Holding each other tightly, so that the moment would not be lost, they headed quickly toward *their* bedroom.

As they passed the sofa, a breeze from the verandah, heavy with the scent of flowers, blew the Kama Sutra open to a new page, where the woman seemed to be standing on her head. As she quickly shut the book, she noticed that Riggs had placed her ransomed Quelle folder nearby on the same table.

She smiled. *He's the right man,* she thought. *Uncle Colby must have known all along.*

Chicken Bus

Time is the moving image of eternity.

—Plato

After four very long hours of steep winding mountain roads, the laboring bus had only scaled the first of the three Himalayan ranges which had to crossed before the final upward ascent along the Indus to Leh. Hemis, of course, was even higher.

As they neared the source of the tumbling Sind River, swollen from the melting snows, the driver pulled onto the side of the road, such as it was, to show them the view from Mount Zoji La. On their Nelles Verlag map, which lay open on Christina's lap, they found that this peak was over 3500 meters high and part of the Zanskar range. To the northeast of them, partially hidden in the clouds, was the infamous K2, which towered at 8600 meters. The scale was so grand, as they looked out across the Himalayas, that it made foothills out of the mountains the bus had just laboriously climbed.

As they hurried back to their seats on the small bus, Riggs said with a shiver, "This is only the first mountain pass," as he pointed again to the map. "We'll spend the rest of the day, believe it or not, descending along

the Dras River to the town of Kargil. We'll sleep there tonight, and
tomorrow the bus will climb two more such passes, each higher than the
previous one, before dropping down to the Indus."

"And then we begin the climb again to Leh," repeated Christina, looking
first at her watch and then outside the window as the bus spun around a
sharp curve. She worried about the wet roads, damp from the melting
snows, and the sheer drop of several hundred meters to the river below.
As many times as she had ridden the Chicken Buses in Guatemala, she had
never been at these heights for so long.

"Why do you think so many different countries want this disputed land,"
asked Riggs, "when it takes this poor bus all day just to travel seventy-five
kilometers?"

Christina looked at him and nodded her agreement. She recalled their
earlier conversation about the ongoing disputes between Pakistan, India,
and China over this portion of Jammu and Kashmir. She was completely
exhausted from the early start, the late night, and from the slow progress
of the bus along narrow mountain roads.

"Don't you think he's driving too fast?" asked Christina, noticing that
Riggs also looked concerned.

"It's too fast for me," answered Riggs, "although I'm sure he's done this
many times."

"What about the ones who didn't make it?" joked Christina, pointing
straight down into the canyon. "I can't believe that they don't have any
guard rails on these roads. If this bus did fly off into the canyon, I doubt
if anyone would ever know where to look. I don't mind a little excitement,
as long as I'm in control, but it really bothers me to have someone else
driving this fast. I think the roads are too wet."

Before Riggs could agree, the bus began sliding out of control toward the
outer lane, and the driver, almost instantly jerked the wheel to bring it back.
At the same moment, as fate would have it, a large truck appeared in the
lane ahead, trying to dodge the careening bus. The truck veered too close
to the edge, which gave way, and one of the front wheels dropped off the
road into the yawning gorge. The wheel spun in midair as the rear axle
dragged the truck to a stop.

At the same instant, the bus driver hit his brakes a little too hard and
cranked the wheel the other direction to avoid hitting the mountain side.
Seeing that this was wrong, he pumped the brake pedal several times and
turned the bus deliberately into the soft shoulder on the inside of the turn,
bringing it to a halt just inches from the teetering truck.

The passengers of the bus were frozen in silence as they watched these
events unfold in what seemed like a lifetime. Riggs noticed that his mouth
tasted metallic and that his heart was beating in a completely new pattern.

He looked back to see a Gypsy four-wheeler going through a similar maneuver to avoid their bus, which now straddled the entire road, just inches from the wobbling truck. Behind the Gypsy, and moving much too fast, was an even larger truck hurtling out of control down the hill.

Christina held tightly to Riggs' arm, as the driver of the large truck slammed on the brakes and the wheels screamed out with agony. The driver pulled at the steering wheel, like a man on a runaway horse, trying to slow the massive load. Christina could actually see the terrified expression on his small face as the truck came to rest just inches from the Gypsy.

Riggs and Christina sat quietly in the bus, wondering what would happen next.

"Tell me again how high the mountains are near Leh," joked Christina, to the best of her ability.

"More than twice as high as this, and that's not even K2."

Spring Goat Roast

"I don't think goat meat has ever tasted better," said Riggs, as he picked up the last piece from the wrapper and spooned some more flavored rice.

"Do you eat it often?" kidded Christina, assuming this was also his first taste of goat.

"Actually, a friend of mine in Ohio raises goats, and every spring I try to join him for a goat roast," said Riggs, hoping to sound quite rural.

"I really have no idea what you're talking about," smiled Christina, allowing him this one "Out West" story. She reached for a little of the fresh goat cheese, which looked like a mashed root, and dipped it with her heavy barley bread. "I'm going to go get some more food; should I get a little of everything?"

Riggs nodded agreement. "The reason they eat the baby male goats in the spring is that the meat gets tougher with age and there is little demand for adult males," he said hurriedly.

"What's wrong with the males?"

"They're just too horny and stinky." Christina wanted to look at him as though men and goats had much in common, but she was actually having trouble standing beside the table. Just getting to her feet had made her dizzy and tired. "I'm still not accustomed to these heights," she said.

"I feel terrible too," agreed Riggs. "The local Ladakhi's say it will take more than one day to adjust. Hopefully this delay will prepare our bodies for the trek from Leh up to Hemis."

"I hate to complain, but I've had a splitting headache, a dry throat, and I'm very short of breath," said Christina, as she steadied herself against the bench they had chosen for their picnic.

"Don't get me started," agreed Riggs, remembering how cold they had been the night before. "It's no wonder everyone looks freeze-dried around here. They probably are."

Christina tried to laugh, but she just felt too miserable. "Did you want another cup of goat's milk?"

"I'm still glowing from the first one," responded Riggs, "and I wonder if we should be eating fresh dairy products anyway."

"How could anything spoil at this temperature? This milk was fresh this morning anyway. I saw them milking the goats right outside our room."

"Even so, I'd rather have a glass of their homemade beer."

"Chung?"

"Whatever they call it. It couldn't be as bad as this headache."

She disappeared slowly, very slowly, around the corner to get them more kebobs and cheese from the street vendors...and a glass of chung for Riggs.

Although the annual religious festival had passed, the village of Leh was not lacking in charm and color. Christina saw the ladies, with their tall and winged hats, selling clothing and farm produce in the market, with the Buddhist stupas and temples in the background. *Their faces are beautiful, but their poor skin looks like beef jerky,* she thought, touching her own face to see if the cold dry wind had begun to take its toll.

She noticed how warm the sun felt at this high altitude and smiled as one lady chased two cows away from the barley grain she had for sale. Instead they contented themselves with eating an empty cardboard box.

"Now that's recycling," she thought, trying to amuse herself. "Cows eating cardboard boxes and creating fertilizer for the fields."

She gave the food vendor some rupees, not being exactly sure how much she had paid, and headed slowly back to their sidewalk bench. As she rounded the corner, she suddenly spotted the man who had assisted her in the Cairo bazaar, the large man with the unusual birthmark on his face. He was purchasing some turquoise stones from a man sitting under a small canvas tarp, but she recognized him immediately.

What does this mean? she wondered. She knew that this was no coincidence and that the man must have been following her all this time. She also knew that he must have been involved somehow in her uncle's death. *How could I have been so naïve in Cairo?* She paused to gain her equilibrium, which was not easy at that altitude. *I better get back and tell Riggs.*

When she and Riggs returned a few minutes later, even more out of breath, the man was nowhere to be seen. She turned to Riggs with an embarrassed look he knew all too well. Had she forgotten to tell him about the episode in the Cairo bazaar?

Two Tall Monks

Two days later, quite early in the morning, a small group of Buddhist monks, clad in wine-colored robes, left Leh for the long trek up the Indus valley to the Hemis monastery. They were shepherding their small donkeys, now laden with supplies instead of the surplus grain they had brought to the village from their farms.

The outcrops on the towering Ladakh mountain range were painted in colors by the rising sun. Moss green, magenta, pink, bronze and dark grape repeated in marked strata under the snow white caps.

The monks slowed in reverence as they passed a large pile of mantra stones, resembling a wall of rounded river rocks. Each stone, however, was inscribed with an ancient prayer. The pile of prayer rocks ended at a unusually large stupa, faithfully whitewashed, which housed three red prayer wheels. Each monk in turn ceremoniously spun the prayer wheels as they passed, creating a festival of happy colors. The stupa, like the nearby farm houses and enclosures, was made of unfired dirt bricks which had been severely eroded by the angry weather.

Two women, nodding a morning greeting, passed the other way with large bags of dried dung balanced on their heads. The dung, their only fuel, would be sold in the village for cooking and heating. The women wore goat hides on their backs, fur to the outside, for warmth and cushioning the heavy loads which teetered above them like spinnakers.

Across the road, farmers were already plowing their fields with Yaks, as the large oxen wove along the centuries old serpentine terraces carved into the alluvial fans between the mountains. Two young men were wrapping thorn bushes around the trunks of the malchang trees to protect the tender bark from marauding goats.

As the monks passed by they all waved cheerfully to the farmers, with smiles much larger than their shared burdens.

All, that is, except the two monks in the middle who seemed quite a bit taller than the others and who were wearing warm shoes and socks instead of sandals. Their heads were bowed, as in prayer, and their light-skinned faces were barely visible under their hoods.

Riggs and Christina had found a way to escape the watchful eye of the man with the birth mark.

Flying Bats
Jerusalem

Few deny the hypothesis that intelligence, apart from man and matter, governs the universe; and it is generally admitted that this intelligence is the eternal Mind or Divine Principle, Love.

—Mary Baker Eddy
Science and Health with Key to the Scriptures

Professor Asha Sinha was talking quietly to one of her students near the door to her classroom. At exactly ten minutes after the hour, when classes usually began at Hebrew University, she excused herself and walked demurely, somewhat majestically, to the podium and prepared to addresses the class.

The students sat quietly, showing their usual respect.

Except for her small frame, olive skin and Indian features, Professor Sinha looked very much like a Harvard professor, with a dark blue suit and a white blouse. She wore a colorful Indian scarf draped over her shoulder, reminiscent of a sari.

"As I told you before, these last two lectures are optional, because I will only present my personal philosophy. The final exam will only cover the materials in your class notes and the later chapters of your Bertrand Russell text."

The classroom was more crowded than usual, and she was pleased to see some faculty members from other departments. She had a pleasant expression on her face when she began her informal lecture, as though she were giving the students something precious of herself. She once again checked the order of her notes, laid them carefully on the podium in front of her, and began to speak in a lilting Indian accent not unlike that of Indira Gandhi.

"In my lifetime, I have traveled a rather circuitous route only to return to the Eastern philosophies of my youth. I was raised in Calcutta as an orthodox Hindu, but I dropped these beliefs as a college student when I discovered the Western philosophy of scientific materialism. Now, fifteen years later, I've rediscovered in physics much of what I was taught as a young Hindu, although I can assure you that I have no desire to go back to the creeds and rituals of any organized religion. It is this journey, my philosophical autobiography, if you will, which I plan to share with you this afternoon and in the last lecture next week.

"I might as well start at the beginning," said Asha, "when I was about your age. After I received a Ph.D. in Mathematics and Theoretical Physics from the University of Calcutta, I then moved to Oxford, where I studied quantum cosmology under Professor Roger Penrose as a post-doctoral student. Since then, my own research has been in the fields of quantum physics, general relativity, gravitational collapse, the Big Bang and now quantum gravity.

"The physics discoveries which occurred in my lifetime have been truly amazing, and I've had the pleasure of both contributing to and knowing the players in this worldwide drama. Physics has enriched my life, and I wouldn't change a thing a second time.

"However," she said, gently waving her finger in the air, "the harder we searched for reality in the physical universe, both inside the atom and beyond the galaxies, the more I was led back to an inner spiritual reality."

She waited for the students to absorb this message by sorting once again through her notes on the podium. The students shifted in their seats, wondering where this was leading.

"In particular," she continued, "I was impressed by the paradigm shift from the clockwork world of Newtonian mechanics to the interconnected and unified world of the quantum. It was also a revelation to me when physicists concluded that the *observer* and the *observed* form an inseparable entity. This was important, because it meant that my thoughts and what appears to be outside of me are an integrated whole...that there is no external reality independent of me.

She looked at her students and saw some confused expressions, but no one raised their hand to ask a question. She smiled. "I'll repeat it again: the observer and the observed form an inseparable entity.

"This is the hardest part of my lecture, and we will probably need to come back to this several times before you understand it all. But the conclusion I reached, looking at the principles of physics, was that my thoughts and the outside world are one and the same thing.

"I had been exposed to this idea earlier in the ancient Hindu Upanishads, but it was a revelation for me to discover the same thing again in physics. I also learned that some Western philosophers had also come to the same conclusion...outside of physics. For example, two hundred years ago the philosopher, Bishop George Berkeley, said: *Matter possesses reality only insofar as it is perceived by some mind. All those bodies which compose the mighty frame of the world have no substance without a mind.*

"In his day, of course, Berkeley didn't have the perspective gained from quantum theory, but he somehow came to the same conclusion...the same one in the Upanishads."

"Excuse me Professor Sinha," asked one of her favorite students, politely raising her hand.

"Yes?" she acknowledged.

"Does this mean you no longer find truth in physics?"

She smiled. "Quite the contrary. I no longer view physics as truth itself but as a sublime metaphor which reveals even deeper truths. It's like a myth in that regard...or like art." She saw a puzzled look when she said *art,* so she decided to explain this important idea further. "Picasso had an interesting way of describing the significance of art. He said: *Art is the lie that tells the truth.* The same can be said about physics, if you use it to <u>reveal</u> your truth, not to <u>be</u> your truth."

"Can you give us an example?" asked a student in the back. From the looks on the faces of the other students, Professor Sinha realized that they were all confused.

"Certainly," she began. "One of my truths is that a universal intelligence, or Mind, underlies creation. I find evidence of this intelligence in the physical creation, but physical creation does not then become the boundary of this truth. Neither universal intelligence nor creation necessarily have the same bounds as our physical universe. I think of universal intelligence as having less limitations."

"Where do you see the evidence of this *intelligence* in the physical universe?" asked another student.

"I will say more about that later in the lecture, but the simplest example is the mathematical perfection of the atoms. With almost poetic beauty, a single mathematical equation describes the forces inside the atom; and different solutions of this one equation yield the incredible panoply of elements in our Periodic Chart. Everything from silicon to gold, from carbon to helium, from uranium to chlorine. All of our chemical elements, each with dramatically different properties, flow from this one beautiful equation."

She couldn't tell whether or not the class understood the significance of her example, so she decided to expand on the concept, while she wrote Schrodinger's quantum mechanical equation on the blackboard. "It could have been otherwise. There could have been less variety: perhaps only three chemical elements instead of nearly a hundred. Or there could have been no beautiful mathematics, just random chemical elements with nothing in common. Instead, we have both variety and mathematical simplicity, and it is truly glorious—almost miraculous—how the cornucopia of elements from this one equation has sustained life on this planet for so long."

The student in the back raised his hand again. "Does that mean intelligence is in the elements or in the equation?" he asked.

"Neither," she answered. "To me it means that intelligence is in the idea behind the elements and the equation is a metaphor for that intelligence."

The students nodded, seeming to understand.

"I'll get back to this," she promised, "but first let me explain why I became disappointed with scientific materialism. But first I will need to briefly review the difference between an *idealist*, like Bishop Berkeley and Plato, and a *materialist*, like Bertrand Russell, although most of you know this already. An idealist believes that reality is essentially mental or spiritual, and that the material world is a lesser order of reality. A materialist believes that reality consists essentially of physical substances."

She looked around the classroom to see if there were any questions, saw none, and decided to proceed. "Physics is not as secular as it appears. There is no church and no raiment, of course, except perhaps baggy sweaters, but there is definitely an unspoken creed and belief system. Most physicists are scientific materialists, whether they realize it or not. They believe that matter is the ultimate reality."

A science student in the front row raised her hand. "I think," she began, "that many scientists are wary because in the past idealists were affiliated with powerful state religions which have repressed science over the centuries. Western scientists have only been relatively free of persecution by the Christian churches since the Renaissance, and they aren't eager to return to the ordeals of Copernicus, Galileo and Newton."

"You have an excellent point," agreed Professor Sinha. "But I personally think it is possible to be an idealist without being affiliated with an organized religion, and certainly not part of an organization that represses science. I think of myself as an idealist, not terribly different from Plato, because I believe in the primacy of ideas over their material embodiment, especially since new physics discoveries always seem to fit into a larger, more beautiful, and integrated mathematical picture.

"I can best explain my disaffection with materialism with the example of the flying bat," she said, smiling at the class. The students chuckled, knowing she was about to have fun with them. "Suppose a bat decided to become a materialist and proclaimed that reality was only what it could sense with its sonar system. The bat would definitely come to the wrong conclusion about our reality, because the signals bounced from external objects would give it no hint of the scent of flowers or the colors in the rainbows. Do the scent and the rainbow cease to exist because the bat does not sense them?

"Of course they exist," she answered her own question, "as do phenomena which you and I are unable to sense. We know that there is more reality than we sense, because every year the scientists invent new sensors which expand our known universe. Materialists have to keep adding things to their reality list, and this list shows no signs of becoming complete. Their 'reality list' is more like the daily news than an enduring truth. One day they add x-rays to the list; the next day galaxies, and then quarks. Someday they will probably add 'dark matter', which could embarrassingly turn out to have been most of the universe. So wherein lies the logic of declaring only what we have observed already as reality? Reality must be larger than our human senses; it is even bigger than the sensors our scientists have invented.

"For the materialist, reality depends on the calendar, with each generation enjoying more 'reality' than their ancestors. Where is the waiting room, we should ask, for undiscovered physical reality?"

The room was silent. The students were very attentive. Many of them hadn't given this much thought before.

"It seems to me that universal intelligence has built a huge mathematical mansion, perhaps with our assistance, and we have just begun to explore a few of its many rooms. By the time we discover a new room, the mansion seems to have already doubled in size, because universal intelligence is always ahead of our brightest scientists...and even matter itself. Nothing I have learned in physics has convinced me that matter is more than an unfolding projection of a higher reality, Plato's archetype, if you will, which I call universal intelligence."

She paused for a moment, glanced down at her notes, and prepared to move on to Natural Miracles, the next subject in the outline, if there were no questions.

The Assumption

Civilized people depend too much on man-made printed pages. I turn to the Great Spirit's book which is the whole of his creation.

—Tatanga Mani
Cherokee

Riggs and Christina, dressed once again in their normal clothes, were led down a long dark corridor to meet with the Rinpoche, the senior monk at the Hemis monastery. They ducked through a very low passage into a small white-washed courtyard surrounded by thick roofs made with sticks, straw and dried mud. Following two young monks, they climbed a steep wooden ladder made from tree limbs, and found themselves standing in front of the tall and brightly painted wooden doors to the assembly room. The colors and designs were vivid in spite of their age, causing Riggs and Christina to pause for a look.

In a few minutes, thought Christina, *we'll be standing in front of the Guru Rinpoche and well on our way to finding Quelle.* She was exhausted by the five days they had waited for this audience. Not only was the food meager and the cells hard, cold and dark...which they were...but her half of the interminable wait had been complicated by the fact that women were not allowed in the monastery after dark. She had walked the steep mile to the nearby village of Hemis each day before dinner and after breakfast, where she was lodged with the family of one of the monks they had befriended. This same monk had helped them slip out of Leh, under cover of borrowed robes, to avoid the surveillance of *Magenta*, their nickname for the mysterious man who had been following them.

Christina's temporary family was delightful, but their home, in spite of its hospitality, was rudimentary and spartan even by archaeological standards. Made mostly of unfired mud bricks and mortar, it was about the size of a modest garage, and this included sleeping areas and a common room used for cooking, eating and other family activities. The ceiling was too low for Christina to stand completely upright. The well-trodden dirt floor appeared to have been soaked with oil to make it firm and hold down dust, and everyone slept on raised dirt platforms covered with thin rugs. Most of the heat came from a little stove, no bigger than a car muffler, in which they sparingly burned dried dung.

Meals were an exercise in creativity. The most abundant food was precious barley, grown with great effort by man and beast in the surrounding fields. Everything was made from this barley, including pasta, bread and chung, their homemade barley beer. They even mixed barley meal into their yak-butter tea and chung as a food supplement. Christina was reminded of her own mountain people, the Maya, whose staple was maize. She could see many similarities between these two cultures, including their physical appearance and their use of terrifying wooden masks at religious festivals. She had come to the conclusion that mountains create similar people everywhere, and in spite of their challenging lives they are amazingly joyful.

Riggs and Christina paused for a second to admire the Tibetan influence on the paintings and carvings in the imposing high entrance to the assembly room. They had learned the meanings of many of the drawings during their long delay. The huge wooden doors, from which a large lock, the size of a book, had already been removed, seemed to reach for the heavens. Instead of swinging them open, however, the two young monks ducked through a smaller inset door, and they followed with considerably more bending. Riggs even had to crawl on his knees.

As they entered the large room, the size and height of a basketball court, their eyes adjusted slowly to the dim light of the flickering candles and oil lamps. The ceiling, supported by four timber columns, reached upward about three stories, and they found themselves at the base of an imposing bejeweled golden Buddha whose feet alone were larger than Riggs' entire body. They stood in total silence, engulfed by the size and beauty of the contemplating Buddha. It was too much for one viewing.

Between them and the figure of Buddha, which in turn was surrounded by painted walls and cabinets full of smaller and more elaborately decorated statues, were rows of hard benches on which the monks sat. The monks were oriented respectfully toward the Guru Rinpoche, who sat in a meditative position, high above the others, quite like the Buddha himself. As Riggs and Christina followed the two young monks toward the front of the room, they were startled by the loud sound of a drum and a gong. All eyes, including their own, were on the Guru Rinpoche.

Riggs realized that the Guru Rinpoche expected him to speak, and he wished his stomach had been full of more than salted butter tea and barley meal. He stood as straight as five nights on a cold stone slab would permit and began to speak, hoping someone would understand his English. "We would like to thank you for granting us this audience on such short notice," he began, looking at Christina for encouragement. Her expression indicated that she too was somewhat at a loss. Neither of them had ever given a lecture to a room full of what looked like Tibetan refugees, especially on something as sensitive as their own sacred ancient manuscripts.

The Guru Rinpoche seemed to be pleased with Riggs' politeness. *So far, so good,* he thought, as he prepared to continue.

He was interrupted by one of the monks who had been seated behind a small wooden pillar. The monk introduced himself, in perfect English, as Nawang-Tsering, and explained that he would serve as translator for the Guru Rinpoche. His one gold tooth, sparkling in the candlelight, seemed out of place.

"The Guru Rinpoche has reviewed your credentials," the translator said, "and is pleased that American scholars would travel so far to meet with him. He would like very much to assist you in your efforts."

"Please tell the Guru Rinpoche," he said, relieved that he was being understood, "that we are seeking a document, written in the late first century A.D., which contains extensive teachings of Jesus, the central figure in our Christianity. We believe that the recently deceased uncle of my colleague," he said pointing to Christina, "saw such a document here at the monastery not too long ago."

Riggs could not understand why the Guru Rinpoche remained quiet for so long after the translation. His dark brown eyes sparkled, radiating goodness and wisdom, but he said nothing. He stroked his thin white beard.

Maybe my message was not clearly understood? thought Riggs. *Maybe they don't know the name Jesus?* He was beginning to feel ridiculous. How could he ask Buddhists if they had a Christian document? *I'd better try again.*

Before Riggs could rephrase his request, the Guru Rinpoche began to speak, and the translator was quick to follow.

"Yes," said the Guru Rinpoche, "I know the document well. You see, some of our own people also study the teachings of Jesus.

That's good, thought Christina, who had been silently cheering Riggs along. *They also know about Jesus, and somehow they have preserved the only copy of his original teachings.*

"In fact," continued the Guru Rinpoche, "many of us consider Jesus to have been an important prophet, or reincarnation, whose life and teachings merit devoted study."

Christina was faint with excitement. She knew that what the Guru Rinpoche nonchalantly referred to as the "teachings of Jesus," must be Quelle.

Riggs was anxious to learn more about its origins and how it came to reside at Hemis, but decided first to get it in his hands. "Would it be possible," he said, fighting to make his voice as strong as possible, "to see this document and help us with its interpretation?"

He and Christina exchanged looks, knowing that they were within minutes of seeing this manuscript pulled off some dusty shelf in the library.

"I'm afraid that's not possible," said the interpreter, almost speaking for himself.

All the expression dropped from their faces as they silently considered the possibilities. *Had they given it to someone else? Had it been stolen? What had happened to Quelle?*

"Since your uncle's visit," continued the interpreter, acknowledging Christina for the first time, "there has been considerable interest in this potentially controversial manuscript, and the Guru Rinpoche has sent it to the Dalai Lama at Dharamsala to preserve tranquillity here at the monastery. You will have to contact the Dalai Lama to see it."

Riggs could see the disappointment sweep across Christina's face. They had actually been closer to Quelle when they were in Srinagar, but Professor Gupta couldn't have known that the manuscript had been moved to Dharamsala. They now faced the long trip back, with the added complication of the man they called Magenta nipping on their heels...or worse.

Oh well, thought Christina, *it will be worth it all when we actually find Quelle.*

As the two of them, dejected but not defeated, thanked the Guru Rinpoche for making them feel welcome at his monastery, Christina noticed that one of the monks looked more English than the Prince of Wales.

The Power of Myth

In all ten directions of the universe, there is only one truth. When we see clearly, the
great teachings are all the same.

—Ryokan
Zen poet

"Follow me," whispered the monk with a clear Australian accent, as he led
them down the hall toward the library. He removed the giant lock with a
heavy key hanging around his waist and ushered them into the deserted
chamber. "No one will bother us here, because these documents are used
only on very special occasions." He pointed to the silk-covered bundles
lining the dusty shelves, each with a distinctive color code on the front.
The code somehow involved different sizes and colors of silk squares sewn
to the front of the bundles.

I wonder if Quelle is still here, thought Christina. *Maybe the Guru
Rinpoche didn't know his monks had kept a copy.*

The Aussie monk opened one of the bundles to reveal hundreds of loose
pages, carefully stacked between two thick wooden boards which were tied
together like book covers for protection. The writing appeared to be Tibetan.

"I am an assistant librarian here," he said, "and as you must have
guessed, my home was Australia before I became a Buddhist monk. I'm
here for special training." As he spoke, she was looking right at his cold
feet and sandals.

The monk noticed her gaze. "The physical environment is not exactly
luxurious here," he said, wiggling his toes. "I doubt that your own Jesus
had a life much different from mine...except it must have been a little
warmer in Palestine."

They all enjoyed a good laugh together, and Christina noticed how easily
the monk smiled. His demeanor was simple and joyous.

"He too begged for his meals and wore only the robe on his back," he
continued playfully. "Many of our great teachers throughout history, including
our Buddha, have been ascetics, so I am learning an important tradition."

"That's probably true," mused Christina, although that was not the way
she usually pictured Jesus. "As a Buddhist, do you in fact learn about Jesus?"

"Of course, because many of his teachings, like the Sermon on the
Mount, have parallels in our tradition." He paused and smiled. "In my
case, however, it is much simpler. I was raised a Christian."

Christina joined his smile. *Of course,* she thought.

"What do you do at the monastery?" asked Riggs, still curious why he had
secreted them to the library.

"I am one of several monks who copy these documents when they become old and difficult to read," he answered, pointing once again to the stack of beautifully scripted pages stacked on the open silk cloth. He picked up one of the pages as though it were sacred, and held it to the light. "We also make this paper here, but that is someone else's task. I'm just a scribe."

"You can be proud," said Christina, gently touching one of the pages. "This is beautiful calligraphy."

"Well, it's an assignment with no end in sight," he said, pointing at the hundreds of ancient manuscripts on the shelves. "Fortunately, the climate here is ideal for preserving documents: it's cold and dry most of the time."

"Better for books than people," joked Christina, once again looking at his cold toes. She thought to herself how picturesque he looked, with his wine-colored robe, a large golden Buddha in the background, and his cherished manuscripts opened on the small table. The sun's rays, from a small opening high above, happened to fall on an open page.

The Aussie monk suddenly became very serious. "I've seen the document you're looking for."

"Quelle?" blurted Riggs. "I mean, the one with the teachings of Jesus?" he quickly corrected himself, giving Christina an optimistic look.

He paused, as if to save them some bad news. "Yes, it's a Buddhist manuscript about Jesus. I'd be surprised if the Dalai Lama will allow outsiders to see it, because it's potentially too controversial. He doesn't want the publicity, and he doesn't want to cause tension between the Christians and the Buddhists. I doubt if you will ever see it."

Christina and Riggs were manifestly disappointed. Riggs, grasping for hope, wanted to believe that they would in fact be shown Quelle in Dharamsala.

"Do you remember what was in it?" pleaded Christina.

"I transcribed it once, and I've read it many times," answered the Aussie monk. "Since a much of our tradition is passed down by oral history, one of my few virtues is a good memory for stories."

Their hope was rekindled. At least, thought Riggs, we will know what's in Quelle, even if we never see it. He then suddenly had an eerie idea. *Maybe it's in this room, and they're just protecting it?* His eyes scanned the shelves in the shadows.

"Do you mind if I write down what you say?" entreated Christina.

"It would be better if you just listen," insisted the Aussie monk. "Better for me."

"Turn on your memory," joked Riggs.

"I'm certain that it's an authentic story about Jesus," he continued. "This Buddhist scripture tells of a divine infant born in far away Israel. At age fourteen, he returned to the region of the Indus River, where he settled among the Aryans, studying the holy Sutras and learning the teachings of Buddha."

Christina and Riggs glanced at each other in disbelief. *How could this be Quelle?* wondered Riggs. It sounded more like a Buddhist Gospel.

Christina had some thoughts of her own. Riggs had told her about Nag Hammadi Gospels with a more Eastern philosophy than the New Testament. She wondered if this incredible story was "Eastern" enough for him?

The Aussie continued: "Jesus fled the Brahmans, whom he had angered for preaching to the lower castes. He lived in the Himalayan mountains near Nepal for six years, where he further studied Buddhist scriptures. He then traveled west to Persia and eventually to Palestine, angering priests along the way for opening the eyes of the oppressed and the weak. Once in Palestine, he commenced to bring his Semitic brothers back to the teachings of their ancestors."

Riggs turned to Christina. "I don't think this is Quelle. It sounds like a very unusual narrative gospel. Quelle would not include the life of Jesus."

"Well, it's definitely not a sayings gospel," joked Christina, "but its extremely interesting, nevertheless."

"Please excuse our interruption," apologized Riggs.

"Do you know any Buddhist mythology?" asked the monk, about to continue his story.

I wonder why he called it mythology instead of religion? thought Christina. "Not really. These days I don't know where mythology ends and religion begins."

"A little," mumbled Riggs, not wanting to boast. He knew that it would be better for Christina to hear this the first time from someone else.

"Well there are many similarities between Buddhist and Christian myths," instructed the Aussie, "and they'll become obvious as I continue this story. Almost everything Jesus did upon his return to Palestine can also be found in the legends of Buddha."

Christina was pensive. She planned to ask him an important question later.

The Aussie continued his story: "Jesus taught of man's right to an immediate relationship with God, not one brokered by the clergy, and not one postponed to the Hereafter. Jesus also refused to be subject to imposed religious laws; instead, he always chose to do the right thing at the right time. And finally, Jesus and his disciples lived ascetic lives as wandering beggars with no possessions."

"And this is also the story of Buddha?" questioned Christina.

"Yes," answered the Aussie with a smile. "But I'm just getting started. They both preached a Sermon on the Mount, which in philosophy is in sharp contrast with the bloodthirsty and vengeful God of Judaism. They also taught many of the same parables."

"Which parables did the Buddha teach?" interrupted Christina.

"Do you remember the one about *turning the other cheek?* And the one about *the seed which fell on good soil?* The one about *what comes out of your mouth, not what goes in? The blind leading the blind?*"

Christina nodded *yes* to all of these. "Of course, those are some of his best known parables."

The Aussie continued: "And the one *about a treasure of love? And the widow's mite? And the prodigal son?*"

He waited for her to understand and continued.

"According to the Christian scripture, Jesus taught these parables to the Jews in Palestine. According to our much older documents, these same parables were taught by Buddha."

Christina suddenly remembered the question she was going to ask. "Who came first: Jesus or Buddha?"

"Buddha taught five hundred years before Jesus," answered the Aussie.

Christina was shocked. "So according to this document, Jesus was merely spreading the teachings of Buddha in Palestine, where they were not as well known?"

"Yes, but more importantly, we can learn the same thing by comparing the New Testament with the teachings of Buddha."

"Either that," interjected Riggs, "or the Greek authors of the New Testament Gospels merely borrowed these narratives from Buddhist legends and incorporated them later into the story of Jesus."

"It seems to me," puzzled Christina, "that they borrowed more than the narratives. They also borrowed many of the teachings."

"There are many additional similarities between the two stories," continued the monk, "and even between the two religions. Both Jesus and Buddha were precocious twelve year olds who amazed their seniors. They were both tempted in the desert, both teachers at age thirty, and both had twelve main disciples, with one a favorite and one a traitor."

"This is unbelievable!" said Christina, shaking her head in disbelief. Even though she had begun her search for the truth, she was now finding the similarities between the legends of Jesus and Buddha quite disturbing.

"There is more," continued the monk. "They both rejected the established priesthood with their blood sacrifices, they both healed the sick, and they both walked on water and fed the multitudes. They also both refused to perform miracles for personal gain."

"I never knew all this either," admitted Riggs, trying to ease Christina's discomfort. "I had just assumed that the legend about Jesus had become exaggerated over the centuries."

"There are even similarities between the two religions," continued the Aussie. "They both wear white robes, their vestments are similar, and they have comparable hierarchies. They both use prayers of intercession, alms, offerings and prayer beads. They both have monks with vows, and saints with halos. And of course baptism originated in India and is still practiced daily by many Hindus."

"When the Essenes in Qumran adopted baptism near the time of Jesus," said Riggs, agreeing with the monk, "it marked a major departure from the prevailing Jewish blood sacrifice."

"What is a prayer of intercession?" asked Christina, having never heard this expression.

Riggs answered: "When you ask God, or his Servants," answered Riggs, "to intercede in your personal life." He looked at the Aussie for confirmation. "This is an important aspect of Judaism, for example. Yahweh is often invited to intercede on behalf of the *Chosen Ones.*"

Christina was warming up to the conversation. "In the old days very few people would have known about these similarities between Buddhism and Christianity, because travel was much more limited. With global communications and jet travel, more of us will become aware of these similarities."

"Or just by reading," said the Aussie with a wry twinkle in his eye.

Christina made another even bolder observation: "It seems to me that the Buddhists and the Christians are both handicapped by their myths."

The Aussie raced to defend his current favorite. "There is one big difference: Christians are expected to believe that the myths actually happened; Eastern religions, on the other hand, use myths to impart truths, not necessarily believing them to have been actual historical events."

"You don't believe the stories about Buddha?" interrogated Christina.

"I believe the truths they convey, but not that they actually happened," said a very serious Aussie. "The same truths are found in the Christian stories about Jesus."

End of the Trail

For some reason Christina's donkey constantly fought to stay in front of the others. She didn't really mind. "When we get back to Leh," she shouted to Riggs whose donkey was fourth in line, "we need to sneak into the lodge so that Magenta won't see us."

"Fortunately, it'll be after dark, and he doesn't know when we'll be returning," yelled Riggs. He tried to get his donkey to pass the one in front, but it kicked his mount right in the chest and turned to bare its angry teeth. These donkeys protected their places in line; it had something to do with status. At the same time a little burro, laden with barley grain, raced under his donkey toward the front of the line.

"We won't have Quelle anyway, if that's what he's after, but he won't know that," said Christina loudly.

"We may never have it at this rate," said Riggs, still disappointed that it was not at Hemis.

Christina was quiet for awhile, watching the ever changing pallet of colors on the mountains as the sun reached down in the afternoon sky. "What do you think we'll find at Dharamsala?"

"Maybe a Gospel of some sort written by someone in India," answered Riggs. "Maybe nothing. I don't know what to make of the Aussie Monk." They were passing near the village of Shey, and he noticed that there were hundreds, literally hundreds, of Buddhist stupas dotting the countryside. They looked like figurines on a giant chess board. In the distance he could see still another monastery perched high on the mountaintop.

"Did you believe the part about the similarities between the lives of Buddha and Jesus?" asked Christina.

"Yes, but not because he found it in the missing Buddhist Gospel. As he said, you can determine this for yourself by comparing the two myths. I've already been through that. In fact, Joseph Campbell has written several books on this subject which you might enjoy."

"It's nevertheless upsetting the first time you hear it."

"It sure is."

"In fact," she continued, "I'm still upset over all the other Gospels you told me about, whether or not the Aussie monk has a Buddhist one. How many do we have now? I've lost count."

"Do I detect a little sarcasm?" countered Riggs. "Let me run through the list. There's the Jesus of Paul and the Romans, the Jesus of James and the disciples in Palestine, the Jesus of Mary Magdalene, the more Eastern Jesus of Thomas. How many is that?"

"Don't forget the Jesus of Quelle," appended Christina.

"And the Jesus from Kashmir." By now he had somehow overridden the bestial instincts of the donkeys and pulled up beside Christina. "Did you see the way they protect the tree trunks from the goats here?"

She hadn't really noticed.

"Why would I be looking at tree trunks with the beautiful Shey monastery there on the mountain," she kidded.

"Because it's really interesting. They cut the tops out of old tin cans, split the side of the can and wrap it around the trunk. That way it can expand as the tree grows, and they have a use for the old can. It's damn inventive, if you ask me."

"Why don't we do that?".

"Because we don't harvest the limbs each spring like a crop, and we don't have goats roaming loose everywhere," explained Riggs.

"You missed my joke," said Christina reeling from his long explanation. "I wasn't really that serious."

They were both silent for awhile. In spite of their efforts at levity, they were in fact deeply upset at not finding Quelle in the Hemis Monastery.

"I guess there's really no point in going to Dharamsala," volunteered Christina.

"I'm afraid not. I doubt if anyone but monks will ever see the Buddhist Gospel again. In fact, it occurred to me that it might still have been in the library at Hemis."

"Maybe an older copy?"

"Maybe. I wonder if Colby faced the same disappointment, or if he mistakenly believed the document at Hemis was Quelle. The carbon date of the late first century A.D. could be right for either."

"I think he probably pursued the Hemis lead just like us," postulated Christina, "and he either stumbled onto Quelle in the process or he came upon it completely independently. How else can you explain the interest shown by the Vatican, and how else can you explain his excitement when he flew to Cairo. That fateful trip was certainly after he had been to Hemis, because he never even mentioned India to me when we last talked. But he did tell both me and Aunt Mary, just before he flew to Cairo, that he had made the most important discovery of his lifetime."

"You're right," agreed Riggs. "He must have still been pursuing Quelle at the time of his death."

Their minds searched for some answers. All they got were more questions.

"And why are we being followed by Magenta?" pondered Riggs as their donkeys bounced along toward Leh.

Miracle of Miracles

No door in the labyrinth castle of science opens directly onto the Absolute. But if one understands the maze well enough, it is possible to jump out of the system and experience the Absolute for oneself.

—Rudy Rucker

"I promised to tell you about the advent of life on this planet," began Professor Sinha, launching into her second subject after a short recess. "If you'll allow me, I want to broaden the subject to include a larger class of what I call *natural miracles.*"

"I could equally well call them extremely rare events, or 'too good to be true' events, but I chose *natural miracles* for two reasons. First, the word *miracle* is usually reserved for the supernatural; for events like walking on water, raising the dead, or surviving the fiery furnace. We usually think of miracles as defying the natural laws of physics, which is not the case for the examples I'm going to share with you. On the other hand, the likelihood of these natural miracles happening by chance alone is so small that a word like *miracle* is quite appropriate."

"How rare is rare, you might ask? The criteria I use for calling a physical fact a natural miracle is if the odds against it are greater than one in 40,000 powers of ten. These are <u>very</u> slim odds. A billion, you will recall, is only nine powers of ten, so I would have to write the word *billion* almost five thousand times on this blackboard for you to visualize the overwhelming odds against my natural miracles."

"A good way to visualize these odds is with a metaphor. Can you imagine a monkey typing at a keyboard all day? Do you think it is likely that this monkey would accidentally produce a page of Shakespeare? Well, the odds against what I call natural miracles are much higher, as if the monkey only typed one page, and it still happened to be Shakespeare."

"Second, I include the word *natural*, because I do not believe that the laws of physics take holidays or selectively respond to prayers from either believers or their Gods. I say this with complete confidence, because the fundamental constants of the universe—such as the speed of light, the force of gravity, and the charge on the electron—are just that: fundamental and constant. These are only a few of many fundamental constants, and the laws of physics respond with perfect fidelity every time we test them anywhere in the universe. For fifteen billion years, they have been tested, from deep inside the nucleus to beyond the galaxies, and the answers are always the same and the physical laws are always in effect."

"What I call natural miracles are physical facts, like the composition of water, for example, which are absolutely consistent with the natural laws. They are, however, highly unlikely to have occurred randomly, and yet they are extremely fortuitous from the standpoint of our own existence on this planet. So they are miracles not because they defy the laws of physics, but because they defy overwhelming odds, and because they seem to do so entirely for our benefit. These natural miracles reveal to me the grand omniscience of what I call, for lack of a better name, the universal intelligence. These miracles are, at least for me, the ultimate proof that we are part of a majestic plan which is much larger than what we observe in the physical universe, in spite of its immensity. And we are an important part of this majestic plan."

At this point her favorite student raised his hand. "Are you saying that certain rare coincidences occurred in the physical universe against unbelievably high odds, and they all seem to be for our benefit? And you think of them as miraculous, even though they don't break the laws of physics?"

"That's a good summary," she said, giving the student some well deserved praise. "Now let me give you some examples, although I will not be able to explain each one in detail. Scientists, incidentally, call these natural miracles the Anthropic Principle, and they are adding new miracles to the list every year, as their understanding of the physical universe improves. Each example is further proof to me that everything in the physical universe is, for some reason, optimized for our existence, and that neither we nor our universe is just a random occurrence.

"For example, there were three miracles leading to human life on this planet," she continued. "First there was the occurrence of the simplest life about four billion years ago. Second there was the pre-Cambrian explosion of complex life, including primates, which ended a half billion years ago. And third, was the development of consciousness and abstract reasoning in humans, about a half million years or more ago.

"Long before this, however, there were several other natural miracles which prepared our planet for the eventual occurrence of life. The Big Bang itself required several natural miracles. If there hadn't been slightly more matter than anti-matter, the two would have simply annihilated each other billions of years ago, and there wouldn't even be a physical universe."

One of the shy students asked, "What is anti-matter?"

"Physicists discovered anti-matter in their particle accelerators," she explained. "For every known elementary particle, they have found it's exact opposite. The anti-particle for an electron, for example, is a positron. When an electron and a positron collide, they eventually annihilate one another, and nothing is left but some light waves. If matter and anti-matter had been perfectly equal in the Big Bang, there would be nothing left of this universe but some very old light. Fortunately for us, there was exactly too much matter. And I do mean _exactly_. If the extra amount of matter, over anti-matter, had been either more or less—to an accuracy of one part in 40,000 powers of ten—then our universe wouldn't even be here."

She looked at the class to see if they understood the significance of her statement. It was clear from several confused faces that they did not. She tried again. "I'm saying that the relative amounts of matter and antimatter at the beginning of time had to be accurate to a degree we can barely comprehend—one part in 40,000 powers of ten. It simply could not have been a coincidence."

Thinking that they now understood, she continued with another example. "When the universe expanded after the Big Bang, there were several physical parameters which had to remain miraculously accurate. Physicists have given them the names Density, Smoothness and Uniformity. Are you surprised when I tell you that during the critical early expansion of the universe, these parameters were perfect, namely to an accuracy of one in 40,000 powers of ten? If any of these had been less than perfect, our universe would have collapsed on itself very quickly. So you see why I refer to universal intelligence with appropriate awe and respect. This Mind, if you will allow me a capital letter, is capable of routinely measuring one part in 40,000 powers of ten. Isn't that noteworthy, if not humbling?"

The students nodded in agreement as they slowly comprehended the significance of what she was saying.

"It took a few more miracles, however, to prepare this planet for life," she continued. "The attractive force between the protons and the neutrons had to be exactly right for two entirely different tasks at once. It had to be perfect to hold the nucleus together, so that we could have atoms, and perfect once again to keep stars like our sun burning fifteen billion years at exactly the right temperatures. In other words, this force is doubly miraculous."

"Excuse me, Professor Sinha," interrupted a student. "Why is it difficult to hold the nucleus together?"

"That's a good question. It's because the positive charges on the protons inside the nucleus are pushing each other away with tremendous electrical forces, so another force is needed to counteract this repulsion."

She could tell by the interest on their faces that they wanted to know more about the miracles of nature.

"The size and density of our earth and its distance from the sun had to be perfect, and the stars had to create just the right amount of carbon and oxygen for life to evolve several billion years later. When I say *perfect*, I assume you know that I mean one part in 40,000 powers of ten."

They nodded dutifully.

"The biggest miracle, however, was the way the stars were able to make carbon and the other heavy elements needed for life...and for our amazing Periodic Chart of chemicals. The stars did this by making carbon out of beryllium, which they made out of helium, which they made out of hydrogen. So the stars had the recipe for carbon and other heavy elements, based on ingredients which somehow survived the incredible heat of the Big Bang. If that is not miraculous enough, the stars had to pull another double miracle by bootstrapping helium atoms from hydrogen. This is the same hydrogen, of course, which is also involved in the miracle of water, which I will discuss more later.

"I've already told you that the Periodic Chart, coming as it does from one beautiful equation, is a miracle in its own right. Can you imagine our lives without the cornucopia of the chemical elements? What would it be like on this planet without carbon, oxygen, nitrogen, silicon, iron, copper, gold, or tungsten, only to remind you of a few? We need them to support life itself, of course, but we also need them for water, air, cars, buildings, electricity, jewelry and light bulbs.

"The list of natural miracles goes on and on, and it is growing every year as we learn more about our own universe. Just last week, for example, I read that it is a natural miracle that the optical band of chlorophyll exactly matches the radiation from our sun."

"I don't understand why that is important," asked a younger student.

"Let me explain," offered Professor Sinha. "Chlorophyll is the molecule responsible for photosynthesis in all plants, and that is what creates the oxygen on our planet. The light from the sun just happens to have exactly the right wavelength to activate this process. That's the miracle."

She looked at her watch and realized that the class period was almost ended. "I'm sorry," she apologized, "but I'm not going to have time to tell you about the miracle of water. If you are interested, you can pursue it on your own or meet with me another time.

"Let me summarize my thoughts about natural miracles. First of all, I am incredibly grateful for them, for obvious reasons. They do not exist merely for my enjoyment, like a beautiful sunset or a mockingbird's song; rather, they are necessities. Without these natural miracles neither the universe itself nor the life we share on this planet would even exist. For me they are proof of the importance of our role in the evolution of life, and of the role of the universal intelligence.

"I will go even further," she said, warning them to cover the ears of their favorite prophets. "When someone tells me that their God parted the waters or walked on water several thousand years ago, I am sorely tempted to tell them that my God created the principle behind water, and that is miracle enough for me.

"If my God were so foolish as to come to this planet," she said irreverently, "She would not be running around breaking all of Her own beautiful laws. Like a proud parent, She would take us to a mountain stream, give us a drink of water, catch a couple trout, and ferment some wine for dinner. She would remind us that we are surrounded by miracles, pointing out the ones we have not yet discovered on our own. She would marvel with us how this planet has remained completely hospitable to life for over four billion years."

In conclusion, Professor Sinha simply shook her head humbly in awe. The noise in the classroom swelled as most of the students began talking excitedly to one another. *At least I gave them something to think about,* she smiled happily.

She then reminded them that her next and final lecture would be in one week, when she would talk about the endless search for elementary particles and her current understanding of God.

Shrouded in Mystery

Science without religion is lame, religion without science is blind.

—Albert Einstein

"How could you possibly prove that Jesus lived through the crucifixion?" probed Christina, after the waiter had taken everyone's dinner orders.

"I'm used to skeptics," answered Volker Heine, in good spirits. Professor Gupta's German friend had already enjoyed at least two large bottles of Indian beer. "No one ever believes me at first."

"Isn't that fair?" commented Riggs.

"Not really," responded Volker, somewhat indignantly. "As a sindonologist and an expert on crucifixions, I've performed scientific research on this for many years. The New Testament stories are never put to the same test as my theories. When I taught at a small Protestant college, I was never asked to prove that Jesus died on the cross; or that he rose from the dead; or that his mother was a virgin; or that he ascended into heaven. Believers are not expected to provide scientific proof for their creeds."

No one argued his point, but Christina had to ask the obvious question. "What's a sindonologist?"

"It's the study of fine fabrics, such as the linen Jesus was wrapped in after the crucifixion."

"Like the Shroud of Turin?"

"Exactly, and that's how I came to the conclusion that the blood stains on the Shroud of Turin were those of a living person."

"That's why we're trying to get permission to exhume the remains in Jesus' tomb here in Srinagar. We want to see if we can learn more about the body of Jesus," added Gupta.

The waiter arrived and began placing the meals in front of them. There was a nice variety of curries, tandoori, kebobs and several exotic breads, and everyone, except for Volker, was anxious to begin eating. He preferred to talk—and drink—while they were occupied with food. This way there would be fewer interruptions. He sat quietly, waiting for everyone to pass around the condiments and share some of their meals before he began.

"For centuries the Turin Shroud has been the most venerable of all Christian relics, with a celebrated annual display for the faithful, the personal attention of the Pope, and the inevitable publicity. It's among the most popular Catholic pilgrimages, along with Lourdes and Fatima. Until recently, that is, when it was discovered by scientists that the Shroud itself proved Jesus was alive when he was carried to the tomb."

"If you will excuse my skepticism," began Christina, "but how can a 2000-year-old cloth prove that He was alive?"

"Because dead bodies don't bleed, and there are blood stains all over the Turin Shroud," parried Volker. "Blood from his head, from his back and from the nail wounds on his wrists and feet. Blood that was already dry when they laid him down, and blood that ran onto the cloth afterwards. He was definitely still alive, or we have still another miracle to explain: the only bleeding corpse in history."

"It's news to me that corpses don't bleed," asserted Riggs.

"Well they sure don't, once the heart has stopped beating. And there lies the problem for the Catholic Church and the reason why they have suddenly reversed themselves. Knowing no shame, they are now trying to prove that the Turin Shroud is a fake. Now when they assemble teams of scientists, it is for the purpose of equivocating, not validating, the Shroud. And the public hasn't even noticed."

It seems to me that some blood would just leak out, thought Christina, but she decided not to begin the debate yet.

"How do they know it's real blood?" asked Riggs.

"Because many analyses have been performed on the Shroud, some by independent laboratories, but mostly ones which have grants from the Catholic Church. There is now a debate on the results, because not all the different techniques are in agreement."

"Did you know your uncle was also involved in these laboratory tests?" asked Gupta.

"Not really, but I'm not surprised," answered Christina, wondering if this was also a factor in his mysterious death or in their pursuit by Magenta.

"He assisted in the arrangements for an independent laboratory in Jerusalem to perform definitive chemical analyses for blood and several other important parameters," added Professor Gupta. "In fact, it's the same laboratory he gave the fragment from Hemis to do the carbon-dating. He used this laboratory frequently because it is very confidential, being owned by a wealthy individual."

Christina and Riggs looked at each other excitedly. They realized that Gupta must be talking about the same laboratory that issued the report in Colby's folder, the one identified only by the initials *M.S.* This person might know something about Colby's search for Quelle.

"You wouldn't by any chance remember the name of the proprietor, would you?" asked Riggs without hesitation.

"Sure, his name is Maxwell Silvera," answered Gupta and Volker almost in unison.

"I'm sure I can find his address in my office before you leave," volunteered Gupta.

"Actually, I have it right here in my address book," said Volker Heine, reaching for his briefcase which leaned against the leg of his chair.

"Would anyone like something special for dessert?" beamed Christina, "or an after dinner drink?" She wanted to celebrate their good fortune. They now knew the man behind the initials on the laboratory report and their hopes were once again renewed for Quelle.

Whether or not Jesus survived the crucifixion had suddenly become less important than finding Maxwell Silvera in Jerusalem.

A Story for All Times

The mythologies, religions, philosophies, and modes of thought that came into being six thousand years ago and out of which all the monumental cultures both of the Occident and of the Orient—of Europe, the Near and Middle East, the Far East, even early America—derived their truths and lives, are dissolving from around us, and we are left, each on his own to follow the star and spirit of his own life.

—Joseph Campbell
Myths to Live By

When they boarded their flight early in the morning, they were too excited about the possibility of finding Quelle to notice that a man with a large birthmark on his face had boarded the plane at the last minute.

"Back to Jerusalem," said Christina with resolve, believing that they were beginning the last lap of their race for Quelle.

"It wasn't that much of a detour," joked Riggs.

She looked at him in disbelief. "Not much of a detour? You don't call flying to India, taking a bus over the Himalayas, hiking to Hemis disguised as monks, sleeping on cold slabs and stumbling onto Magenta *much of a detour*? I don't think I've ever been as disappointed as we were in Hemis."

He laughed. "Unless it was when we opened the vault in Cairo."

"True. Maybe we'll have better luck with Maxwell Silvera. I hope he was involved in Uncle Colby's Quelle project and knows its whereabouts. Did you get the impression on the phone that Maxwell Silvera had carbon-dated two fragments for Uncle Colby?"

"It wasn't clear to me whether it was two fragments or two projects," explained Riggs, as he told the stewardess he preferred the continental breakfast with fresh fruit and tea. "But he definitely wanted to talk to us in person, which I took as a good sign."

They began to open all the small packages and containers on their breakfast tray. Christina passed her yogurt to Riggs.

Christina was thinking back to the conversation they had with the Aussie monk at Hemis. "What did you think about the story of a Buddhist Jesus who survived the Crucifixion?"

"Well, it's a stretch, but I have to ask myself if it's any less substantial than the stories in our New Testament or the tourist attractions in Jerusalem. Frankly, I tend to discount them all. I guess I'm resigned to the likelihood that all 2000-year-old stories have accumulated their fair share of mythology. After all, they were in the hands of vested monopolies all those years."

"What about the similarity between the teachings of Jesus and Buddha? Does it mean that Jesus was influenced by Buddhism, or that the New Testament merely borrowed from the Buddhist myths?"

"Both explanations seem plausible to me, because the Jesus of Thomas and other Nag Hammadi Gospels is strongly Eastern in philosophy. In fact, so is the Jesus of Paul in the New Testament, if you ignore the judgmental God borrowed from Judaism and Zoroastrianism."

"I've always felt there was a conflict in the New Testament between the loving teachings of Jesus and the apocalyptic teachings of John the Baptist," agreed Christina. "They're two quite incompatible philosophies."

"I feel the same way. It's the teachings of Jesus, not those of a God of Wrath, which are like those of the Hindu Upanishads and the Sutras. The advice of Jesus to turn the other cheek, to give your coat if someone asks for your shirt, to love your neighbor and your enemies, and to seek the simple life, seems more Eastern to me. Also the parables about leavening the whole, about the mustard seed, and about finding the sliver in one's own eye."

Christina had a question: "I wonder if John, the Apocalypse, and a God of vengeance will be in Quelle?"

"I wonder too, but I doubt it. It wasn't in the Gospel of Thomas. I believe that the authors of the New Testament decided to combine these two immiscible philosophies and attribute them both to the long departed Jesus."

"I never realized until now that the part of the New Testament I loved the most were the teachings of Jesus, and that they have a decidedly Eastern message," observed Christina.

"They're not only the part I love the most," agreed Riggs, "they're the most difficult to put into practice."

"That's for sure," nodded Christina, realizing how seldom she actually followed the teachings of Jesus. "It's a lot easier to follow the Creed than to live by the teachings."

"Gupta and Volker Heine did clarify my understanding of the role of the Buddha legend in Christianity," admitted Riggs. "I had always felt that Jesus was either himself a missionary from the East or strongly influenced by those who were. If Buddhism was spreading to China and Japan at the same time, it would make sense if it also spread to the West. Why else would his teachings have been viewed as so controversial? They had to be more than just another variation on Judaism."

"Do you think 'love thy enemies' was controversial?" asked Christina.

"Yes, to some extent, but not nearly as controversial as his teaching that God's imperial rule, or the Kingdom of Heaven, is ever present and available to everyone, including the disaffected. I think those teachings caused most of the commotion, because they riled the establishment who had insisted that eternal life was a postponed reward for the righteous and those who adhered to the religious laws. This would have been a very strong message, because it offered hope to those outside the religious establishment. It was a dangerous message, because it undermined those in power. If every person is a Christ, so to speak, and sits on the right hand of God, then the role of the religious hierarchy is certainly less important."

Christina was slowly realizing that Riggs was more spiritual than she had first thought. He seemed to have gone past the myths in the New Testament to the actual teachings of Jesus, and in the process come to believe that his relationship with God was intact, perhaps even stronger than before. His emphasis seemed to have shifted from a miraculous "Son of God" who died for our sins, to a miraculous man who found God, a God of Love, and wanted to share that message with everyone.

The conversation reminded Christina of a specific question she had when Gupta was talking. "Who was Krishna?" she asked. "I've heard of him, of course, but I don't really know that much about him."

"I'm not an authoritative source on Krishna, but I can give you an introduction to the subject. I actually know more about him than Buddha."

"Why is that?"

"Because the story is so much like the life of Jesus in our narrative gospels."

"When did he live?"

"He too was probably a mythical person, but the Hindu legend can be traced back as far as 4000 B.C."

"In other words, it is a another man-God myth," observed Christina, asserting her new freedom. *I'm making progress,* she thought, realizing that these subjects weren't distressing her anymore. In fact, she was beginning to relish the pursuit of truth and her own personal growth.

"Essentially," agreed Riggs. "For example, Krishna was born of the virgin Devanaki, the mother of God, when she was overshadowed by the Holy Spirit."

"Sounds familiar."

"There's more. This miraculous birth also was prophesied in earlier writings, with phrases like 'Blessed art thou, Devanaki, among all women, for thou wilt give birth to our Saviour.' Like the Herod story, the king was warned in a dream that this child, Krishna, would be more powerful than himself, so he ordered the death of all new-born male babies."

"That's quite a coincidence, don't you think?"

"I'm just getting started. For example, there were mangers, falling stars, the shepherds and wise men involved in the births of both Jesus and Krishna. They also both performed many miracles as young men. Krishna even strangled a snake with his bare hands in his crib."

"There's one we missed."

"When Krishna was sixteen he left his mother to spread his new teaching throughout India. He spoke out against corruption of the princes. He said he had come to earth to offer all people redemption, to drive out unclean spirits, and to restore the kingdom of good."

"It's essentially the same as our story, isn't it?"

"There's more," continued Riggs. "Krishna fought entire armies alone and performed miracles such as awakening the dead, giving sight to the blind, hearing to the deaf, and healing the lame and the lepers. He was honored as a God and called the True Redeemer, who had been prophesied by the fathers...and he taught in parables and aphorisms. As recorded in the Bhagavad-Gita, he taught the importance of brotherly love, self respect, sharing with the poor, performing good deeds, and faith in a good Creator. He commanded his disciples to repay evil with good and to love one's enemies. Krishna chose to live in poverty and dedicated himself to helping the poor and the downtrodden."

Christina asked a simple question: "Why aren't we told these things?"

"Who would tell us, in our Western culture? Our clergy?"

"Well, people will find out eventually," she predicted.

"I wouldn't be too sure. They probably don't want to know."

"Perhaps you're right."

"To me it's far more important that people see the truth in both stories, rather than rejecting either. It means the truth is bigger than specific names and dates, bigger than Krishna or Jesus...or Buddha...and even bigger than specific churches and their hierarchies."

"Well, *specific hierarchies*, as you call them, are not going to be *specifically* pleased."

"True," said Riggs, pleased that Christina was enjoying a new openness to religious concepts. The point is that the same fundamental truths are found in all world religions. They are just disguised in different myths."

"Not always that different," said Christina flatly.

"No, but my friend Stephen Mitchell, a Zen Buddhist, says that Jesus speaks in harmony with the supreme teachings of all the great religions: the Upanishads, the Tao Te Ching, the Buddhist Sutras, the Zen, Sufi and Hasidic Masters. That's good enough for me."

208

"I agree, but I still have a great deal to learn," said Christina sincerely. "I've been relegating these subjects to other people, and now I want to take more responsibility. I need to get more involved in my own spiritual *thing*, whatever that means."

"Well, I can give you some encouragement..."

"Like what?"

"I can tell you that it was your destiny, because of your name."

"Christina?"

"Let me explain," he said, putting his arm around her as they prepared to rest for awhile after breakfast. "The Hindus also have a holy trinity."

"I'm not surprised."

"Let me share some linguistic goodies with you," he continued. "The name Krishna, the Hindu son of God, shares its roots with Christ, which came from the Greek words *khrisma* (ointment), and *khristos* (the anointed). Both of these may be related to the Sanskrit word, *krish*, a mythical person who attracts all Creation and is the highest form in which God has been seen on earth."

"You see all that in my name?" said Christina playfully. "You must be falling in love."

Riggs looked at her lovingly and replied, "I'm afraid so."

As they fell asleep, Magenta walked down the opposite aisle.

Elementary Mr. Watson?

There is no greater mystery than this, that we keep seeking reality though in fact we are reality.

—Ramana Maharshi

"There is nothing wrong with the search for elementary particles," Professor Sinha began her last lecture. The classroom was even more full than the previous week. "Not only is the search itself intellectually exciting, but it reveals the beauty and the poetry of the universe, which for me are further hints of a universal intelligence. In addition, the technological benefits from this scientific knowledge are being used to improve the human condition, at least materially.

"The discovery of the Periodic Chart provides a good example. At the end of the last century scientists studied atoms and their electrons as elementary particles. These eventually became household terms, known as the chemical elements, and society benefited immensely from the chemical, medical and electronic revolutions which followed.

"A similar revolution began after the discovery of the nucleus, and there is every reason to believe that still another technical revolution will someday exploit our growing knowledge of the recently discovered quarks.

"I am clearly an advocate for continuing research on elementary particles, but I do have some philosophical differences with some of the strongest advocates, especially those who believe that the search will someday end, and that they will find the fundamental building blocks of matter. This has been the promise of science since the Greek philosopher, Democritus, developed theories about the existence of the atom some 2200 years ago.

"In this century alone, the elementary particles have changed names several times. First they were gas molecules, then they became the smaller atoms, then the even smaller electrons and the nucleus, then a zoo of accelerator particles, and now the infinitesimal quarks and leptons. In fact, scientists are already trying to guess what might be inside the quarks.

"At each stage, the theory has become more beautiful, but we appear to be no closer to a final indivisible reality. In fact, quite the opposite has occurred, and the physicists' goals of finding external indivisible reality seems to be more illusive than ever. Elementary particles are already too small to have physical dimensions, and they seem to be composed of one another, rather than from some basic building blocks. Even more strange, elementary particles seem to be communicating instantly throughout the entire universe."

"Isn't that forbidden by Einstein's relativity theory?" asked one of the physics students.

"His theory forbids any objects from moving faster than the speed of light," answered Asha, "but somehow, and this is not yet understood, elementary particles are able to keep track of one another instantly across our entire universe. In fact, last year a physicist at Berkeley, using an equation developed by the famous scientist, John Bell, performed an experiment that proved elementary particles have no other choice: they must communicate faster than the speed of light, or the entire framework of quantum theory would collapse. This is simply not possible, since quantum theory has never been wrong, in spite of thousands of scientific tests every year."

"Why are the elementary particles communicating so much faster than we are allowed?" asked the same student.

"Perhaps it is needed in order for everything to make sense to us? All I can say is that for some reason universal intelligence has a faster mail service than we're allowed.

"Now let me draw some conclusions about the search for elementary particles, before moving on to the next subject. It is a quest which will never end, because there will always be something smaller for the scientists to seek. So I believe it would be futile to wait for the physicists to peel off one more layer of the onion before we begin the search for our own reality. Since the evergreen search for external reality offers no resolution in the short span of a human lifetime, then the only pursuit which remains hopeful is the search for internal reality—for a reality within our own thoughts. Once I realized that we humans are situated somewhere in an endless fractal chain, which extends both directions, smaller and larger, I decided that my only opportunity for finding reality was in my own thoughts."

She glanced around the room to make sure that the students understood before she moved ahead to the sometimes sensitive subject of Yahweh. She checked her watch and reminded the class that tonight she must leave a little early. Her husband was entertaining guests who had just returned from India.

Archaeological Forensics

"Is that Dr. Silvera standing next to the young soldier?" asked Riggs. He was motioning toward a middle-aged man in a tweed jacket.

"He meets the description," agreed Christina. "He's very tall and has a dark beard."

They both laughed. "Almost everyone has a dark beard at the Ben Gurion Airport."

"That man looks more Western than the others," observed Christina, as she handed the luggage receipts to the security attendant. She noticed the familiar currency exchange booths, the rental cars, and the ubiquitous travel agencies.

"We're getting good at this routine," said Riggs, recalling their earlier trip to Jerusalem. "I wonder how John Allegro is doing?"

"I hope well," answered Christina, knowing that his was not an easy cross to bear.

As they pushed their over-filled luggage cart past the gate, the tall man waved at them.

"We were right," said Riggs. "That must be him. I guess he recognized all the extra luggage from our stay in India."

"Either that or my blond hair," smiled Christina.

As Maxwell Silvera approached them, Christina noticed that he looked more like a successful businessman than a laboratory chemist.

"How are my old friends Sunil Gupta and Volker Heine?" began Maxwell Silvera, as he extended his hand in greeting. He took hold of the luggage cart and began to lead them toward his parked Mercedes.

"Fine," responded Riggs, "They send their greetings."

"It was very nice of you to invite us to your laboratory," added Christina, "and to pick us up at the airport. It's quite a long drive to Jerusalem."

"I knew you would have a lot of luggage from India, and this way I can take you straight to my laboratory. It's not particularly easy to find," he smiled kindly.

They waited for a traffic light before crossing to the parking garage.

Maxwell looked directly at Christina as if touching her with his eyes and said, "I'm very sorry about your uncle's death. He was a dear friend of mine, as you will learn. It pleases me that I can extend a little hospitality to his niece."

"Thank you for your kindness," responded Christina. It seemed like an eternity had passed since Uncle Colby's death.

They approached his metallic gray car, and he opened the trunk. All three of them assisted in loading the luggage.

"I forgot to exchange some dollars for shekels," blurted Riggs, when he saw Maxwell pay the parking attendant.

"We can get you some in Jerusalem," suggested Maxwell. "I can get you a good rate at my bank. Getting a good rate is important in Israel, you know."

"Had you and Uncle Colby worked together on several projects?" asked Christina, hoping he might reveal something voluntarily about Quelle.

"Quite a few," responded Maxwell,

Your uncle and I had worked on several interesting projects together," continued Maxwell, "I'll show you some when we get to my laboratory."

I hope he shows us Quelle, thought Riggs, knowing he was hoping too much.

"My interest has always been in the authentication of antiquities, and this brought me in contact with your uncle many times."

"What are some of the most interesting projects you've worked on?" asked Christina.

"I would have to say the most interesting have been the authenticating of pages from the Dead Sea Scrolls, the Nag Hammadi codices, and the Maya codex recently revealed at the Grolier exhibit in New York, although there is one other project at the lab which I think you will find intriguing," he said pulling the Mercedes onto the divided highway leading to Jerusalem.

Christina glanced at Riggs. She could tell from his look that he too was surprised. They now knew that Maxwell Silvera, and his laboratory, had been behind the scenes on every one of their most important projects. At the same time they had learned that he might be working on Quelle right now.

She squeezed Riggs' hand with excitement.

"Isn't that a coincidence, volunteered Christina. My own field of research is the Maya language, and Riggs is deeply involved with the Nag Hammadi codices."

"We both have some involvement with the Dead Sea Scrolls," added Riggs, being purposely vague.

"I know," said Maxwell, seeming privy to many of Colby's secrets. He turned left off of Jaffa Road onto Strauss, turned right onto Prophets Street and past the Yad Sarah hospital. We're almost at my laboratory," he announced.

Christina wondered if she had just met Colby's nemesis.

Bubbling Liquids

Where are all the colored bubbling liquids? thought Christina, thinking that Maxwell's facility looked more like a computer center than a laboratory.

"Analytical chemistry has become increasingly automated," Maxwell was saying as he pointed to one of three very large instruments. He seemed to be having a lot of fun showing them his laboratory. "This piece of equipment, for example, uses a very powerful computer to coordinate measurements between a gas chromatograph and a mass spectrometer."

"I've heard about mass spectrometers," confessed Riggs, "but I have no idea what that other thing is."

Christina also seemed perplexed. She wanted him to explain the mass spectrometer too, but decided to ask him later, being anxious to see what he is doing on Quelle. She looked around at all the sophisticated equipment and wondered how much it must have cost. *He's got a very expensive hobby,* she thought.

"Simply put…" grinned Maxwell in response to Riggs' question. He knew that there was no such thing as a simple answer. "The chromatograph separates a sample into known chemicals and the spectrometer determines their masses. I can inject almost anything into this instrument, and an hour or two later the computer will give me the exact amounts of the ingredients. It's a very powerful tool."

Riggs and Christina were duly impressed. "Why do you need so many of these?" asked Riggs, pointing at similar instruments in the room.

"I need different ones depending on the type of sample. Gases, ordinary liquids, very volatile liquids, and, of course, solids each need their own instrument. I also have one that is much more accurate than the others," he said, pointing to his favorite. "This one measures one part per billion." He ran his hand over the equipment with the pride shown a thoroughbred horse.

He led them anxiously to the next room, obviously enjoying the dog and pony show.

"This instrument over here," continued Maxwell, "is a scanning electron microscope, and next to it is a transmission microscope." They are the latest technology for visualizing very minute images. I can almost see individual cells with these incredible devices." He pointed at some images, hanging on the wall, that looked like greatly magnified blood cells.

"I hope we have time to look at some examples before we leave," said Riggs, actually more interested than he had anticipated.

"And this instrument," said Maxwell, trying to bridle his passion, "is a scanning tunneling microscope which I am building myself. Once I get it to work, I should be able to map groups of individual atoms on the surfaces of objects." He looked at them to see if they were duly impressed, but from the blank looks on their faces he could not be certain. "That's equivalent to a resolution of a few billionths of a centimeter." Again he looked at their blank faces. "Very, very small," he said in desperation, hoping to impress them with the incredible resolution of this instrument.

They smiled to show their appreciation for his patience.

"Now let me show you the project I told you about in the car. I think you will find it quite amazing," he smiled and his eyes gleamed.

This is the moment we've been waiting for, thought Christina. *He must have Quelle. The only question is how he got it.*

"What's in that small room over there?" asked Riggs, noticing small colored beams glowing steadily in the darkness. He noticed that Christina seemed anxious to move on.

"That's my laser laboratory, where I'm trying to isolate individual atoms. It too is a research effort, but one that should reach fruition in a few years. When we have more time, I'll also show you that room...and my inductively-coupled Argon plasma instrument for detecting metals...and my new X-ray fluorescence spectrometer. They each have their special application in my world of forensic archaeology."

This was certainly more than Riggs had bargained for.

"What's in there?" asked Christina, seeing a separate room that looked like Colby's vault in Cairo. Could Quelle be in there?

"That's my museum," he joked, stopping to let them look in through a thick window in the door. "The environment is controlled to protect the contents, and you can see it's more crowded than the Smithsonian. I store some of my own treasures in there along with those of colleagues."

They peered expectantly into the vault, which contained more golden figures than the King Tut display in the Cairo Museum.

"This is where I keep your uncle's two fragments, the ones he wanted carbon-dated," volunteered Maxwell.

Christina glanced at Riggs cautiously. *Now we know that there were
<u>two</u> fragments: one from Hemis and the other one obviously Quelle. But
where is Quelle?*

Chosen Ones

Your physical body and your quantum mechanical body can both be called home—
they are like parallel universes that you travel between without even thinking about it.
—Deepak Chopra
Journey into Healing

Professor Sinha tapped her notes into a neat stack on the podium and
began the last subject of her lecture. She knew that she was running a little
late but would finish in time to greet her husband when he returned from
the airport with his American guests.

"For me, God is at the very least the universal idea, or principle, behind
our mathematically perfect universe. God is not just the finite projection
we observe in our physical universe, even though it reflects much of the
beauty. It is hard to say how big 'universal' might be, but I suspect that,
like our search for elementary particles and galaxies, it just keeps going in
both directions. So I will use the word 'infinite', although I have no idea
how big or small that might be."

"Now let me tell you one thing God probably is not. She is not
someone to whom we can pray for intervention in the laws of physics.
She is not a God of supplication that favors us in either sports, wars or
business. In particular, she did not alter the physical laws for Buddha,
Jesus or even Elijah.

"She does work miracles, but only in the sense I described earlier. The
laws of nature are her miracles, which are revealed to us in the *natural
miracles* of the physical universe…including the fact that earth has been
favorable to life for four billion years. This universe reflects her
omniscience and her capacity for miracles, but it does not violate her laws.
In fact, as the conscious witnesses of the universe, I feel that we humans
should revere her laws as precious gifts, rather than fabricating stories about
mythical heroes who break them. Nevertheless, God can work miracles in
the way we experience life. God is available to each of us through our
thoughts, but we must tune into the right channel, if you will.

When we tune out the physical senses and tune in the spiritual ones, the
power of love and grace can flow into our lives with the same energy that
burst open the cosmos. The same principles we see mirrored in the
physical universe can become evident in our health and our relationships.
These blessings come into our lives, however, only in proportion to the

receptivity of our thoughts. To this extent, God did work miracles in the lives of Buddha, Muhammad, Jesus and Moses. These prophets were, perhaps, listening more to their inner spirit than to their physical senses. They were more receptive to the loving energy from God, than to the selfish lure of the senses."

A student raised his hand. "If God can shine through each of us, depending on the receptivity of our thoughts, then why is the world such an unmitigated disaster? How can you explain something as destructive as the Six Day War, which I was in? There are too many people in this world starving, dying of diseases, and killing each other for me to believe that God is shining through anyone's consciousness."

He stopped for a moment, realizing that his emotions had carried him a long way. "Excuse me," he said, "my memories of the war are still quite vivid."

"I understand," said Professor Sinha, with a kind voice. "You've put your finger on the most fundamental question of religion and philosophy: 'If God is all powerful and good, then why is there so much suffering on this planet?'

"You will not like my answer to this," she continued, "because I'm not going to blame it on Adam and Eve, or some other ancient myth. I am going to blame it on our collective human ego. I think we are all here, in what we call the physical universe, because we wanted to pull away from Oneness, and we wanted to experience ego and selfishness in all its glory.

We wanted to have complete control of every decision, and we didn't want our choices to be compromised in any way, either with God or with other people. I can't tell you how it happened or why we are all acting on this same stage, although it might have something to do with resonant modes. But I do know that the statistical nature of quantum theory, the very part that Einstein disliked the most, gives us complete freedom of action, at least in this physical world. I believe that materiality is nothing more than the medium which accommodates both mathematics and the possibility of complete selfishness."

The same student responded: "So you think each of us is personally responsible for being in this physical experience? That each of us, through our passion for ego and self, has found themselves in a universe less spiritual than that of universal intelligence?"

"That's basically what I am saying," she answered. "I have come to believe that we have willfully and selfishly projected ourselves out of a more ideal and abstract perfection in order to enjoy the privilege and power of individuality and personal choice. The residue or memory of this abstract perfection can still be seen in the mathematical laws of physics and in the creative and mindful design of the physical universe. In order to access a less frenetic world, we must sacrifice some of our precious selfishness and the almighty ego.

"Let me explain it another way, this time with a question. Have you ever met anyone who was not reveling in their own ego? Aren't the history books filled with people who needed to conquer the entire planet just to feed their egos? Do you know anyone who is content only with what they truly need, rather than obsessed with what they want?"

"That doesn't necessarily mean we chose to be here," responded another student.

"No," she responded, "but at least it doesn't place the blame on Adam and Eve or some other ancient mythology. It places responsibility squarely on our shoulders. Further, for me it offers the promise that if I can elevate my thoughts beyond self and toward Oneness, perhaps my next experience will have less to do with egos, both yours and mine."

The classroom was now buzzing. She knew from previous years that this was the most controversial part of her lecture. That's why she saved it until the end.

As the room quieted down, another student asked: "How can thoughts switch back and forth from the material senses to the spiritual? Aren't these two entirely different things, in fact opposites? How can we have two completely different channels of awareness—one material and one non-material?"

"Let me try to explain," began Professor Sinha. "I found the answer in physics of all places." She knew this would startle the students. "How many of you have heard of wave-particle duality?"

About one-third of the class raised their hands. For the benefit of the others she quickly summarized the Nobel prize experiment performed at Bell Laboratories in 1927 by Dr. Davisson.

"All right," she responded, wondering how to explain this difficult concept. "Then you know that light has the weird capacity to behave either as a wave or as a tiny billiard ball or particle. This is true for all matter, but light serves as a good example. Light has two completely different personalities, requiring two completely different past histories, and light is willing to present either of these 'realities' at any time."

"How does it decide?" asked a curious student.

"Here's the surprising answer. It waits for us to get involved, and once we have made our choice between the two, it presents the appropriate personality, with whatever past history it needs. It essentially creates its past to be compatible with the present that we humans have chosen for it."

The students looked confused.

"Well, I don't expect you to believe this in one hearing, but if you will look into the subject deeper, you will find that light, in fact all matter, has the awesome capability of presenting either of two completely different realities depending on the decisions made by us. Even more amazing, it can change its past over billions of years, instantly, so that everything makes sense to us humans in the present."

"Everything but that," joked her favorite student.

She chuckled along with the class. "Yes, I agree. It is definitely counter intuitive. This is where instantaneous communications between elementary particles come in real handy."

"Are you saying that we choose to monitor either the material senses or the spiritual, because we are made up of matter that itself has two concurrent realities?" asked her favorite student again.

"I'm saying it seems possible to me. I could never prove it, of course, but this paradox in physics convinces me that concurrent realities are not impossible. If matter, in the form of wave-particle duality, can carry around two different realities, then why would it be so strange if my consciousness were doing the same thing? I view wave-particle duality as a sublime metaphor for this even deeper truth.

"That is why, in my opinion, the prophets were so amazing. Their default setting, if you will, was probably not on the senses channel, like yours and mine, but on the spiritual channel. I believe our lives are blessed by the loving energy of Oneness in proportion to our ability to channel our thoughts from the physical senses to the spiritual.

"I don't expect anyone to agree with me, incidentally, because I've only recently begun to develop this idea. I am sharing it with you merely as a partially developed idea." She could see that the clock was nearly straight on the hour.

"I have only one concluding remark," she said. "As you can probably tell, I am still rebelling against the hierarchical and institutional aspects of the major world religions. Although I find Eastern religious thought compatible with the new paradigm of physics, I do not want to return to either the Hindu or the Buddhist religions. I have instead come to the conclusion that each individual has a personal communion with God, which is independent of specific creeds, and which transcends any one religion, while embracing the truths imparted by them all."

"Isn't that a lot like Judaism?" asked a student, who was wearing a yarmulke.

"Yes," smiled Asha, "if you broaden the definition of Chosen Ones to include all of humanity. In fact, it's a lot like every major religion, if you remove a fatal flaw or two from each of them. But if these flaws were removed, and the religions became more similar, there wouldn't be any differences to tout in the marketplace for souls, and organized religions would not be as valuable to those in power."

The Passion

"This is my pride and joy," Maxwell said, bursting with excitement as he pushed open the large doors of a completely glassed-in area just past the vault. "This space has separate air conditioning to protect the computers from all the chemical fumes."

A computer center? thought Christina, reeling with disappointment, *where is Quelle?* Riggs tried to disguise his own frustration. They had both hoped that Maxwell's surprise would be Quelle, not a computer center.

"What is that on the wall?" asked Riggs. "It looks like a movie projection screen."

"Let me show you," Maxwell offered, sitting down at the computer terminal. "It's a very advanced system. It's a full color, back-lighted laser display, interfaced to the computer, and it projects holographic images based on equations I've developed."

He paused and activated the system. "Let me show you the results of two years of work," he boasted with noticeable fervor, as he seized an array of joysticks on a panel in front of him. "You'll be amazed!"

Suddenly a large three-dimensional image of Jesus seemed to be suspended in front of them, with his arms extended and legs bent as though nailed on a cross.

"What is this?" asked Christina, surprised at how lifelike the image seemed.

It's a poor substitute for Quelle, thought Riggs, *but it is definitely intriguing.*

"Go near it," encouraged Maxwell. "It's so real, you will think you can touch it." Using different joysticks, he rotated the figure, making it lower its arms, straighten its legs and stand erect. A saintly smile appeared on the face of Jesus as though he were greeting them. On his head and back were the wounds from the flogging and the crown of thorns. On his wrists and feet were the wounds from the cross, and on his side the prick from the spear.

"Watch this," said Maxwell with a hint of glee, as an entire cardiovascular system appeared inside the body of Jesus, resembling the models used in medical schools. It was a physiologically accurate system of veins and arteries, including even a pulsating heart. "I'll show you the other organs another time."

I can't wait, thought Christina. She wasn't exactly squeamish, but she and Riggs had traveled all day, had eaten no food since they arrived, and had been given no prior warning of this extraordinary exhibit. She didn't mind postponing some anatomical details until tomorrow. Maybe by then the whole scene would seem less profane.

"Now watch," announced a triumphant Maxwell, as his computer opened all the wounds and let the blood stream onto Jesus' body and into the air like a large Fra Angelico painting. The blood even appeared to form puddles on the floor right in front of them.

Riggs and Christina were mesmerized, if not flabbergasted. They wondered what motivated Maxwell to these extremes.

"Hold on now," he warned, as he orchestrated the Jesus back onto the cross, with his arms extended at an angle to the crossbeam. He moved two of the joysticks and watched his computer monitor. "There's twenty-five degrees—that's perfect." He pointed to the number on the screen so that they could appreciate its importance.

I really don't know why he's so excited about twenty-five degrees, thought Christina. Did it have something to do with actual crucifixions?

"Are you ready for the big surprise now?" he titillated them.

"That was quite surprising enough," Riggs assured him, looking at Jesus with blood flowing down his feet onto the cross and down his arms along his body.

"This entire image," said Maxwell, "was reconstructed mathematically from the Turin Shroud." He looked at them with playful anticipation, waiting for them to explode with appreciation. They were silent.

"Don't you understand?" he repeated. "This is not just an ordinary Jesus drawn by an artist; it is mathematically deduced from the blood stains and the discoloration on the Turin Shroud itself. This is the real Jesus."

"Even the three-dimensional shape of his body and face?" questioned Riggs with obvious skepticism.

"In particular the three-dimensional shape," confirmed Maxwell, unable to restrain his enthusiasm. "All I added was the coronary system inside the body. But the figure you see is the Jesus from the Turin Shroud. Is there any doubt the Shroud contained a real body?"

"How did you do it?" queried an amazed Christina.

"You obviously don't want all the gory details, but basically I pirated some technology from NASA, who in turn pirated it from the US military. They use it to reconstruct images of complex terrain from multi-spectral cameras with three-dimensional spline-fitting equations."

"I'm afraid I don't understand all that, but it doesn't seem to me like there would be enough information on the Shroud," questioned Riggs.

"There's more than enough, if you use all the tools of hematology and vapographic theory. Forensic scientists can reconstruct events before and after death from the complex biochemistry of blood. And sindonologists, like Volker Heine, have learned how a sweating body can cause differing degrees of sepia coloration on the cellulose of linen."

"Sounds complicated," said Christina. She hoped he would not launch into another lengthy technical monologue.

"A sweating body," he continued anyway, "soaked in a mixture of light oil and aloe tincture produces discoloration because it decomposes the sweat to form ammonia carbonate vapor, causing an oxidation process in the cellulose."

This is a little more detail than I need, thought Christina. The Jesus suspended right in front of her was proof enough that this was technically feasible.

He continued nevertheless. "The coloration is strongest at the point of contact between the linen and the body, which explains why the Shroud resembles a photographic negative. Similar techniques differentiate between old blood, such as from his head wounds, from blood that ran down his body on the cross, and from new blood that pooled as he lay on the Shroud in the tomb."

"Corpses don't bleed," he said, grabbing the joystick for one last maneuver. He manipulated the Jesus into a prone position, laying on his back with his arms against his body, and the blood oozing out onto a holographic shroud.

He stood quietly looking at his masterpiece. Riggs and Christina were duly impressed, but also a little tired.

I don't have a great deal of confidence in the Turin Shroud one way or the other, thought Christina. *It's difficult to believe that it was preserved for 2000 years.*

"What have you learned from chemical tests on the Shroud itself?" asked Riggs.

"It's a rare fishbone weave which contains traces of cotton. It must have been very expensive. We also found it is not a painted forgery. It is definitely blood, but hemoglobin tests are inadequate because of the heat the shroud suffered in accidental fires. We used both X-ray fluorescence and a test for porphyrin. Now we are using the scanning electron microscope to analyze the pollen trapped in the fabric."

"What can you learn from the pollen?" asked Christina, as Maxwell turned off the Turin Jesus for the night.

"We've found twenty-five different types of pollen, and from this we will know all the places the Shroud has been. So far we've found matches with pollens from Lebanon, the Sea of Galilee, the desert near the Dead Sea and even Turkey and further east."

He stopped for a minute at the door and surveyed his laboratory, making sure everything was ready for the night. His eye scanned the facility looking for anything he might have forgotten.

"Let's go to dinner," he said, realizing he had packed too much into their first visit. "I can show you all the rest tomorrow."

"That would be great," responded Riggs, finding it difficult to believe that there was still more to see.

"My wife, Asha, is cooking something special for you. I wouldn't be surprised if she serves some traditional Indian food."

Christina and Riggs looked helplessly at each other wondering if Maxwell was joking about the Indian food. Their stomachs were still recovering from the trip to Srinagar.

"Let's go," he said, arming the security system and locking the door behind him.

I hope that's a very good security system, thought Riggs, thinking about the contents of the vault.

"We've stayed so late that Asha will already be back from the University," said Maxwell, looking at his watch before unlocking the car.

"Is she also a chemist?" inquired Christina.

"Worse than that," joked Maxwell. "She's a physicist."

"Does she teach?"

"Yes, she's been on the Physics Faculty at Hebrew University for many years. Tonight, however, is very special. Every two years she gives a course on the Philosophy of Science which is open to all students. She loves this course, and comes home from the lectures completely exhilarated. Tonight was her last lecture and she discussed her personal philosophy with the class."

A physicist, thought Riggs. *I think Asha must have taken all the courses I tried to avoid.*

"It's fortunate that you both understand scientific subjects," said Christina, wondering how she would carry on a conversation with someone like Asha.

"She won't bore you with physics," said Maxwell with a reassuring smile. He paused for added effect. "But she might stretch your patience with philosophy."

"Actually, I'm looking forward to learn how a physicist from the East views the world," responded Christina. *Especially religion,* she thought.

Virtual Quelle

...the focus of the Nag Hammadi library has much in common with primitive Christianity, with Eastern religions, and with holy men of all times...

—James Robinson
The Nag Hammadi Codices

They drove down Hamelech David street, past a decorative windmill marking the entrance into the Yemin Moshe district where Maxwell Silvera owned a beautiful new home. It was located near Mitchell Garden and looked out on the ancient southern wall surrounding the Old City of Jerusalem. It was a very expensive neighborhood.

"Which of your luggage will you need for tonight?" asked Maxwell as he opened the trunk of his handsome automobile.

"We only need these two small bags, if you don't mind leaving our gear from India in your trunk?" answered Riggs, tossing the strap of his bag over his shoulder.

"No, that will be fine. Less for us to lift," smiled Maxwell, just as Asha opened the front door.

She was a beautiful East Indian, small in frame with smoky topaz skin and flowing black hair, which she wore pulled away from her face. She was poised and polite, yet had a presence of grace and strength. Her warmth and charm made them feel welcome, in spite of the intimidating size and decor of the foyer.

This is the most elegant home that I've ever seen, thought Riggs, as Asha led them up the wide staircase to their rooms.

"Perhaps you would like a shower and a nap," suggested Asha. "It will be awhile before dinner is ready. I'm afraid my class ran a little late tonight."

"It's been a long day," he volunteered, "because we traveled west with the sun. I think we should save our nap for later. The shower sounds great though."

"Agreed," said Christina, turning to Asha. "Thank you so much for your hospitality, I doubt if we could have gotten hotel rooms on such short notice."

"We're pleased to have you as our guests," answered Asha graciously. "Your uncle was a very dear friend of ours, and I'm anxious to hear about all your exploits, especially your work on the Maya language."

"I'd love to, but I would like to learn as much as I can about the course you taught tonight. Our trip to India raised many questions in my mind."

"Yes, India can do that to you," responded Asha with knowing smile.

• • •

Christina knocked on Riggs' door after she had showered and changed into clean clothes. "That was refreshing," she said, feeling much better indeed.

"I never enjoyed a long hot shower so much in my life," agreed Riggs. "Come on in, I'm about to call Professor Robinson." He got out his phone numbers and began the complicated dialing procedure.

She shut the door and let Riggs kiss her much longer than usual. Their romance had blossomed on the floating gardens of Srinagar, but it had been chilled by the ascetic cold nights in Hemis.

"It's nice to be back home," laughed Riggs, as he realized they were in Jerusalem, not the States. "Somehow, compared to Hemis, this seems like home."

"I agree. Did you see their library on the way to our rooms? It was almost as large as Uncle Colby's."

"Two serious lifetime readers," observed Riggs. "Ours might look like that someday."

Christina loved the twinkle in his eye when he said *ours.* "I hope we have time to look at their art, before you and I fall asleep."

"My place or yours?" joked Riggs, with more than sleep on his mind.

While they talked, the call went through to Professor Robinson.

"Perfect timing," said Riggs, congratulating himself. He pointed to his watch to remind her of the time difference with the West Coast in America.

Riggs told Robinson about Maxwell's laboratory, which Robinson had never visited, although he was aware of Maxwell's involvement in authenticating manuscripts.

James told Riggs about his continuing work translating the Nag Hammadi codices. He had made a few corrections to the work Riggs sent him, but found the rough translations generally quite good. Robinson had also completed the most difficult sections which Riggs had forfeited to him, and meanwhile his other students were making good progress on the remaining tractates and piecing together more of the fragments.

"My sleepless binge and all those years at the Coptic museum paid off," whispered Riggs proudly to Christina as he covered the mouthpiece of the phone. Riggs seemed pleased, in a deferential way, that his major professor was still the best at Coptic translations.

More importantly, Professor Robinson had some good news of his own. He had carefully analyzed the sayings of Jesus in the Gospel of Thomas, looking for parallels with the New Testament Gospels, especially Matthew and Luke. He had discovered that eighty percent of the sayings in Thomas also appeared in one or more of the synoptic Gospels, thus confirming his theory that Thomas was, in fact, the first sayings gospel.

Christina could tell that Riggs was very happy to hear these results, as she listened in to the conversation, sitting next to him on the bed. She was actually having a great deal of fun herself, distracting him with seductive caresses while he tried to talk on the phone.

Robinson's recent research also clarified the order in which the New Testament Gospels had been written. First came the teachings of Jesus found in the sayings gospels of Quelle and Thomas. Later on, narratives were added about his life and crucifixion, relying heavily on oral tradition. Over time, miracle stories were added and Jesus was promoted to a God by his enthusiastic followers. In the process some stories from Greek mythology and mystery religions, as well as the apocalyptic teachings of John the Baptist were added, eventually creating a bridge to the Apostle's creed. This is the Canon the Church of Rome chose to preserve

"A few hundred years later," continued Robinson on the phone, "the sayings gospels, like Thomas, were either lost or destroyed by the more powerful Pauline Christians. Only the narrative Gospels survived after the New Testament was formally compiled nearly 400 years after the crucifixion of Jesus. Until, that is, the Nag Hammadi gospels surfaced after hiding 1600 years in a red earthenware jar on the banks of the Upper Nile."

Robinson's excitement in the telling of this story never ebbed, but he saved the best for last. "The Gospel of Thomas may prove to be the missing link in my efforts to reconstruct Quelle, because there are so many parallels between the two Gospels…greater than fifty percent."

Riggs was dumb struck. "This is incredible," he whispered, hugging Christina happily. "Can you believe it? Thomas is the missing link!"

"When Thomas is combined with all the other Gospels," continued Robinson, "there should be enough commonality to eliminate the uncertainty in the reconstruction protocol. Once the work is completed, even the strongest skeptics will be convinced that we know the contents of Quelle, even though the actual document hasn't been found."

There was a pause.

"The race is on Riggs," he challenged. "You might be my favorite "field" linguists, but I believe the computer is going to reconstruct Quelle before you two find the real one."

"We'll accept that challenge," rebounded Riggs, relishing the idea of besting Robinson at his own game, even though he remained his hero.

After Riggs hung up the phone, he turned to Christina and gave her a long kiss in retaliation for all her sexual teasing.

"I'd love to beat him at finding Quelle," he said. "If we can find the real thing at the same time he is reconstructing it from the Gospels, we'll be famous…very famous."

She liked that idea, and it showed in the smile that burst across her face. "I wonder how Robinson's reconstructed Quelle will compare with the real Quelle?"

"If we can find the real one."

"Well Maxwell is our last hope…guilty or not.

"I don't think he had anything to do with Colby's death. He certainly doesn't need the money, he's not an antiquities dealer, and Robinson seems to trust him."

"You're right."

"We've got to bring it up at dinner tonight…even if he doesn't know more than he's already told us."

First Supper

Perception is the first and most important step in turning the raw data of the universe into reality.

—Deepak Chopra
Journey into Healing

As she passed the platter of perfectly marinated lamb kebobs, Asha said to Christina, "I'm beginning to realize that you and I have a great deal in common. You are in the process of rethinking your religious background, which I did several years ago. And I am in the process of rethinking the meaning of modern physics."

"Yes," agreed Christina, "we've both set out on our own, whether we like it or not. In a way, you saved me a couple of detours."

"Were you thinking of becoming a physicist or a Hindu?" quipped Riggs.

"With my skills in math," bantered Christina, "my only choice would be to become a Hindu. But it sounds to me that even the Eastern religions have their share of dogmas and hierarchies. I can get plenty of that in my own religion."

"I agree with you," said Riggs, marveling at how candid Christina had become about her own religion.

"I also agree with you, dear," smiled Asha. "I'm convinced we have to find reality inside ourselves, not through others, and certainly not through organizations steeped in formulas."

"I only got started during the last few weeks," said Christina, "and it sure is difficult to sort through the chaff and find the wheat."

"I probably had a slight advantage," said Asha gently, sensitive to what Christina was going through, "because the myths are taken a little less seriously in the Buddhist and Hindu religions than in Christianity. The withdrawal from this opium was less painful for me. When it dawns on Christians that the historical Jesus may not have been so historical—that he might not have been incarnate God, come to earth to save their souls—it leaves a very, very big gap which takes a long time to fill."

"That's for sure."

"You'll find God in your own thought soon enough," she said lovingly.

"I hope so," said Christina, realizing that she might have found a kindred soul to help her with this inner journey. That was an important first step.

Riggs remained silent, pleased that the two women seemed to be forming an important friendship. He privately hoped that Asha would help Christina begin to rebuild her own spiritual framework. He felt at least partially responsible for her current plight. His thoughts, however, were elsewhere, in spite of these good intentions. He was looking for a break in the conversation which would allow him to ask Maxwell about Quelle. If, that is, he knew anything more than he had already revealed.

"What did you cover in your lecture today? Is it something I would understand?" Christina was asking Asha.

"Of course you would. You don't need to be a physicist to take my course. It's not a science course, but rather a course about science."

"It must help to know some physics."

"A little, but let me try you. The first subject I covered was my transition from scientific materialism back to idealism as a philosophy. The second was a summary of the amazing coincidences in nature without which neither we nor our planet would exist. I relate these to my belief in a universal intelligence, or God. A third subject, which I am still developing, was the notion that we must accept some responsibility for this physical experience, if only because we indulge our immense egos. I also talked about the significance of the evergreen quest for elementary particles, and I closed with a short discussion on the controversial subject of God."

"All that in a hour?" kidded Maxwell, who had heard these subjects too many times.

Asha smiled at her best fan. "Not exactly. And I never got to the part about mathematics."

"Why don't you start with mathematics," suggested Christina. She wanted to develop Asha's friendship and felt there was no better way than to learn as much as she could from her.

"I'd love to," said Asha, "but first let me put the subject in context for you." She thought quietly for some time trying to choose her words carefully for her new friend. She then began slowly. "As an idealist, I am fascinated with the importance of mathematics in the physical universe, because mathematics itself is a mental phenomena, not requiring physical form. Although mathematicians try to communicate with one another about mathematics in the physical plane, through equations on the black board, it first takes form wholly in their thoughts."

"Much like music in the minds of composers before they write it down?" asked Christina.

"Exactly. Music first rushes into their minds, and it later takes physical form as it is laboriously penned onto paper. It is this *rushing into the mind* that intrigues me because I see mathematics, and also music, as a bridge between our minds and the universal intelligence."

"Is it a bridge, or a glimpse?" asked Christina, warming to the discussion.

"'Glimpse' is a good word," agreed Asha.

"You might even include poetry, prose and art," suggested Maxwell. "These are also first conceived in thought and later embodied in the physical world."

"The list is certainly longer than mathematics," agreed Asha, "but to me, mathematics seems the most miraculous."

She certainly had everyone's attention, especially Christina's.

"The big difference between mathematics and music is that mathematics seems to be the framework of the physical universe itself. Unlike art, music and literature, mathematics frequently coincides with the laws of nature, whether you and I understand the mathematics or not."

"I'm afraid you've lost me," conceded Christina.

"Let me try with an example. Imagine that a beautiful new concerto *rushed into the mind* of Mozart. Now imagine that a similar thing happened to Euclid in mathematics. A new concept *rushed into his mind*, and he wrote down the geometry we all learn in school to this day. Incidentally, the same thing happened to mathematicians like Chandrasekhar, Leibniz, Riemann, Boole, and Lorentz, to mention a few. They, and other mathematicians invented branches of mathematics, mostly unknown to the public, like calculus, group theory, ring theory, non-Euclidean geometries, and several algebras."

"I recognize algebra and calculus on that list," frowned Riggs. "They weren't my favorite classes."

Christina nodded in agreement.

"Now here's the punch line," said Asha, entrancing her new friends with her ability to explain complex ideas. "Many of these mathematical concepts turned out to coincide exactly with physical laws of nature discovered, in some cases, many years later. In other words, the physical universe is frequently found to conform to mathematical concepts which existed prior to the discovery of the physical laws. It does not, in comparison, happen to conform to the music of Mozart. Mathematics seems to be the only mental process in which the result of pure thought is found later to coincide with physical laws."

"Can you give some examples?" asked Christina, trying to understand why Asha found this so amazing.

"Certainly. The math for ellipsoids existed before scientists charted the orbiting planets. The math for tensors, matrices and calculus existed before scientists used them to describe the laws of motion. Likewise, the forces of gravity, of electric charges, and of magnets all conform to mathematics. Riemann's math was there for Einstein's general relativity, as was Lorentz's math for special relativity. In fact, the math for quantum theory also existed for many years prior to the discovery of the quantum."

"Are you saying that our mathematicians are 'inventing' the physical universe?" asked Christina. "That would be amazing."

"I might go that far after I got to know you better," she laughed, "but not on our first evening together. I am just agreeing with Einstein and Wigner, who never ceased to marvel that mathematics and physics were in complete agreement so often. Mathematics comes from 'inside' our thoughts and physics comes from 'outside' our bodies. Why should they be in agreement at all, unless they are part of a unified whole?"

"I'm beginning to get your point," said Christina. "It's incredible. We never say that the law of gravity happens to agree with Mozart's concerto for the clarinet, and yet both the music and the mathematics came from pure thought. It makes you wonder if there's some mathematical link between *out there* and *in here*," said Christina, pointing at her head.

"Be careful," cautioned Asha, "you're moving into a graduate subject after only one undergraduate lecture." She was finding Christina a very good student. "In 1921 Einstein wrote that this puzzle had disturbed scientists over the centuries. He asked how it was possible that mathematics, a product of human thought that is independent of experience, fits the objects of physical reality so excellently. He was amazed that human reason, without experience, could discover the properties of real things by pure thinking."

"This is very interesting," bubbled Christina, as Maxwell poured everyone another glass of Carmel red wine.

"Fritjof Capra, a friend of mine, says that patterns of matter and mind are increasingly recognized as reflections of one another. Gary Zukav, the well known psychologist, goes further. He says that physics is the study of the structure of consciousness, that physics has become a branch of psychology, or perhaps the other way around. That puts an end, at least for me, to the materialists search for an independent external reality."

"It is tempting to agree with you," said Christina, "but it's somewhat overwhelming at first. Based on what you've told me, however, the agreement between mathematics and physics is astonishing, unless we are creating them both...both thought and matter."

Extant Quelle

After dessert, as they were sampling an Israeli liqueur for the first time, Riggs finally got up his courage to ask Maxwell about Colby's projects.

"Did you say you were analyzing two fragments for Christina's uncle?" asked Riggs.

"Yes," recalled Maxwell. "There was one fragment from India which was from a Buddhist document he found in a monastery. I believe it was an unusual account of the life and teachings of Jesus."

"We learned about that document during our visit to Hemis," nodded Riggs, hoping Maxwell would continue.

"The other fragment," continued Maxwell, "was from a very old document found in the Vatican.

In the Vatican? Christina was riveted.

The priest who contacted Colby believed the document to be Quelle, and he planned to remove it from the Vatican if Colby would make it available to the world. I had this fragment carbon-dated, and the result was encouraging. Do you know about Quelle?"

"Of course," stammered Riggs, only partially disguising his excitement. *We thought the Vatican wanted to acquire Quelle from Colby, and it is just the other way around,* he thought, glancing quickly at Christina.

She had obviously realized the same thing, and now she wanted to read the letter from the Vatican again to see how they could have been so confused. The priest who wrote that letter might still have Quelle, unless he was killed at the same time as Uncle Colby. No wonder Uncle Colby was nervous about his trip to Cairo. He must have been meeting the Vatican priest.

"Can I have another glass of that Israeli liqueur?" asked Riggs.

Proverbial Quelle

> If thine enemy be hungry, give him bread to eat; and if he be thirsty, give him water to drink.
>
> —Proverbs 25:21

"Do you know the priest that contacted Colby?" asked Riggs.

"I met him once at my laboratory with Colby…the day he gave us the fragment for authentication," answered Maxwell. "And I saw him once again passing by in a bus."

"In Jerusalem?"

"Yes, which was rather surprising, because he was assigned to the Vatican when we first met," said Maxwell, shaking his head. "I'm not sure, but he might have been on a special project here in Jerusalem. I doubt if his wavering faith improved his situation within the Church."

"How do you know about his faith?" asked Christina.

"He told us," answered Maxwell. "That was his justification for removing Quelle from the Vatican."

"How did he get it? Wouldn't a document that important be kept in a very safe place?"

"Like in the secret library for heretical works?" joked Riggs.

"According to the priest," continued Maxwell, "whose name is Father Davide Milezzo, he just found it one day among some other documents."

"I find that hard to believe," said Christina. "Manuscripts like Quelle just wouldn't get filed with others by accident."

"Father Milezzo offered an explanation," said Maxwell. "He said he had been assigned some relatively mundane research comparing different Greek translations of the Old Testament book of Proverbs. He had been working on it for several months when he stumbled upon some pages which were in different from the others, even though they read like proverbs."

Riggs knew what that meant. "If Quelle is a sayings gospel," he said, "as we expect, then it would be similar to the Proverbs. Most scholars wouldn't recognize Quelle as a gospel, because it doesn't contain any of the narratives about the life of Jesus. They might just have accidentally filed it with the Proverbs."

"You're absolutely right," continued Maxwell. "Father Milezzo first thought they were apocryphal proverbs, or some completely different writings that had been improperly stored. After working on them for several days, he realized that some of the sayings were from the New Testament. At that moment he knew that he was looking at Quelle."

"Can you imagine how thrilled he must have been? marveled Riggs.

"He then translated the entire document," continued Maxwell, "in secret of course, and the absence of the Jesus narratives deflated what little confidence he still had in the Church. This is when he approached Colby."

"How did he know about Colby?" asked Christina.

"A priest he knew in Boston put him in touch with Colby."

A priest in Boston? thought Christina, *I wonder if it's someone Ryan knows?* "Did he ever give Quelle to Uncle Colby?" she asked, hoping to pick up the trail.

"I'm not really sure what happened next. Once I authenticated the fragment, I only spoke to Colby on the phone a couple times. The last I heard, he was planning to meet Father Milezzo at a conference in Cairo."

"Makes sense," surmised Riggs. "He was probably planning to put it in his Cairo vault..."

"...until the plan went awry," interrupted Christina. "Either someone learned of the rendezvous or the Vatican became suspicious of Father Milezzo's behavior."

"What we don't know is whether Quelle was stolen when Colby was killed," added Riggs. "Was he killed before or after he got Quelle?"

"Well, you can see why I haven't talked about this until now," confided Maxwell. "I believed all along that Colby's death was related to Quelle."

"We've come to the same conclusion," agreed Riggs. "This is a real mess, but we can't stop now. Quelle is certainly worth the risk."

Christina was quiet, trying to decide what to do next. *Maybe we should go to the Vatican and try to find Father Milezzo.* It occurred to her, that if she had thought of this sooner, she could have had Henry pursue it during his business trip to Rome. "Would it make sense to go to the Vatican?" she asked, exploring their options.

"Not if he's under suspicion," responded Riggs. "We don't know who was involved in the aborted rendezvous. For all we know, he and Quelle are both under watchful eye at the Vatican."

"Wouldn't I need to be there?" asked Maxwell. I'm the only one who would recognize him. Maybe we could just snoop around at St. Peter's Cathedral without attracting any attention?"

"That gives me an idea," said Riggs.

Everyone looked at him, hoping he might solve the problem.

"Remember when you said that you saw Father Milezzo passing by on a bus?" he said to Maxwell. "Would that be a bus he might use routinely, if he's still in Jerusalem?"

"That's a great idea," smiled Christina, proud of her man.

Maxwell thought for a short time, which seemed like an eternity, and then answered. "I'd have to check on a map, but I think the bus he was on also stops at the Jaffa Gate to the Old City, near David's Tower."

"Where would he be going if he got off at the Jaffa Gate?" asked Christina.

"The Church of the Holy Sepulcher," answered Maxwell, "Israel's leading tourist attraction, except for the Wailing Wall."

"Oh yes, we visited there," smiled Christina, "when we met with John Allegro. Are you thinking Father Milezzo might have a new assignment at the Holy Sepulcher?"

"It's worth a try," shrugged Maxwell. "I haven't been to Mass enough lately anyway. His finger traced the spot on his head where his yarmulke sometimes sat.

"Neither have I," said Christina.

"Your brother would be very proud if he knew we were all going to early Mass," joked Riggs.

Christina's Confessions

And I saw in the right hand of him that sat on the throne a book written within and on the back side, sealed with seven seals.

—Revelation 5:1

"No self-respecting priest would report to work this late," complained Christina, showing her frustration. "It's nearly 9:30."

Since 5 am that morning, the three of them had been sitting in Maxwell's car across the street from the Jaffa Gate, hoping that Father Milezzo would step off the bus. They had exhausted both their patience and even the many stories they told to pass the time. Christina had shared her Maya cave story, and Maxwell had told them about his many forensic capers. They were jittery from far too many Turkish coffees, readily available from the nearby café.

"If I thought I could find Quelle," said Riggs, "before Robinson reconstructs it, I would sit in this car for months. But we really don't know if he'll ever step off one of these buses. In fact, he could be stepping off a bus in St. Peter's Square for all we know."

"It's a long shot," agreed Maxwell, reminding them of the odds. "One thing that's certain, however, is that we won't be able to sit in this loading zone much longer. The traffic into the Old City is starting to pick up."

Everyone agreed. They would soon lose the luxury of sitting in the car.

"I've got a wild idea," suggested Christina. "Now that we know his name, why don't I ask my brother to contact him through the Church?"

"Are you sure you want the Church to know what we're doing?"

She shook her head, thought for a moment, and then said: "I have another wild idea, since you liked that one so much."

Riggs and Maxwell smiled. She was at least trying to pass the time enjoyably.

"Why don't I just go inside the Church of the Holy Sepulchre and ask the Bishop if Father Milezzo is on his staff. Isn't that more direct?"

"It's actually not a bad idea," replied Maxwell.

Christina was encouraged, because it gave her something to do, and she seized the opportunity to step out of the car and stretch. Riggs decided to stay with Maxwell just in case. None of them noticed Magenta sitting at a nearby sidewalk café.

At that very moment Maxwell shouted, "There he is! That's him, walking away from the bus. That's him! That's Father Milezzo."

Riggs and Christina watched intently, their eyes glued to a priest in his early fifties as he stepped off the bus and began walking across Jaffa Road. His face was drawn and lined.

"He looks troubled," observed Riggs.

He passed through the Jaffa Gate and disappeared into the Old City.

"I better hurry," said Christina, still standing beside the car. "He might not go directly to the Church, and I don't want to lose him."

She rushed across Jaffa Street, causing a speeding taxi to slam on its brakes and veer into a cart full of freshly baked breads. Riggs jumped out of the car and headed after Christina, as Maxwell called out, "I'll try to stay here in case you need me later."

Christina couldn't see Father Milezzo in the crowd, so she ran as fast as she could down David Street, squeezing past the crowds in the narrow walks and jumping up onto steps for better views. Finally she spotted him, walking several meters ahead. Then he turned into a side street.

That's probably Christian Quarter Road, she thought, hurrying up the pace, *and that means he's heading for the Holy Sepulcher.*

Just as he turned into the church courtyard, she was blocked by a delivery cart which completely filled the narrow street. There was nothing she could do but wait until it was slowly pushed up the small connecting ramps.

If I don't hurry, I'll never find him inside, she thought in a panic. *There are too many different rooms.*

Just as Riggs finally spotted her, she managed to squeeze past the cart as it passed, and raced into the courtyard. Father Milezzo was nowhere in sight. She ran across the courtyard, slowed to a brisk walk at the entrance to avoid attention and passed the pink colored Stone of Unction. Her eyes were darting from one side to the other, trying to catch sight of Father Milezzo. She was much too excited to fully catch her breath.

I hate to come this far and miss Quelle by a few seconds, she thought.

On her right were the Calvary steps leading to the last few Stations of the Cross, where according to tradition, Jesus was crucified. To her left was the Tomb of Christ.

Which way did he go? she wondered, as she made a desperate choice and bounded up the steep narrow stairs to Calvary. She immediately realized that he wasn't in the area, smiled politely at several tourists, and almost slid back down the dimly lit stairs. She once again passed the Stone of Unction, walked through an open corridor and entered the enormous domed area in front of the Tomb of Jesus.

The other Tomb of Jesus, she thought, remembering Professor Gupta in Srinagar. She spotted Father Milezzo closing the door to a confessional booth near the Altar of Mary Magdalene. *Great! He's reporting for duty, and I'll be his first customer of the day.*

As she headed for the booth, a flaccid looking tourist, stuffed into a polyester suit, stepped in front of her and closed the door.

Oh no, how long will this take? A frown formed slowly on her face. *At least I won't lose Father Milezzo. He's trapped in the confessional. What a horrible assignment. He had to listen to the tourists all day. No wonder he came late to work. He must have been demoted when they discovered he was trying to pirate Quelle out of the Vatican. Ryan is on his way up, and Father Milezzo is on his way down.*

She looked around and noticed that the crowd of people around the Tomb of Jesus was steadily growing. She stepped back far enough to see the Greek Orthodox priest standing at the entrance. His assignment was to keep too many tourists from jamming into the tomb at one time...or from breaking off a souvenir.

What is that guy telling Father Milezzo, for God's sake? He's been in their long enough to confess first degree murder. Why would you save a big sin for the Holy Sepulchre? The guy must be telling him about his grandchildren.

The door opened, and the tourist walked out a free man. Christina rushed to take the empty seat, and then wondered what to say. Riggs ran through the area once again and this time saw her disappearing into the confessional.

Her eyes adjusted to the dark as she began to speak. "Bless me Father, for I have sinned."

Pontificating Priest

And I took the little book out of the angel's hand, and ate it up; and it was in my mouth sweet as honey: and as soon as I had eaten it, my belly was bitter.
—Revelation 10:10

Maxwell moved the arms of his Turin Jesus up and down to form new blood streaks down the torso. Each time the blood gushed out of the nail wounds, down his arms, and onto his body, the pattern was different.

If I do this enough times, he thought, *I'll know which patterns are the most likely.*

Once in awhile, just for the humor, he adjusted the expression on Jesus' face and increased the contrast between the bright red blood and the ghostly white color of the body.

He's a character, thought Christina. *I wonder if he's really taking data or just amusing himself while we all wait for Father Milezzo.* She frankly didn't see how he could spend so much time looking at the bleeding body of Jesus on a cross.

As she looked once again at her watch, the third time in a half hour, she snickered at her own hypocrisy. *Who am I to talk about vivid portrayals of the Passion of Christ? I had my share of them as a youth.* The Turin Jesus also reminded her of David Joralemon's gory stories of the Maya blood sacrifices and the drawing of ceremonial blood from royal genitals. For some reason, though, Maxwell's images seemed more heathenish than the blood symbolism in Meso America, or even in her Church.

Riggs sat at a nearby desk trying to pass the time by fine-tuning his translations of a few difficult sections of the Gospel of Thomas.

Christina, likewise, had brought work to occupy her time. She thumbed through a letter from Professor Kelley which reviewed the latest progress on translating the Maya hieroglyphs, but her mind was elsewhere. "I can't get over it. In just a few minutes we'll actually see the earliest teachings of Jesus."

"Almost straight from his mouth, like the Gospel of Thomas, and without the distortions from other people's agendas," added Riggs. He was too preoccupied to get any real work done.

"Let's hope so. It's already past 3:30 and no Father Milezzo," observed Maxwell. "Watch this, you two," he said, drawing attention to his Turin Jesus.

He made the face frown, and everyone laughed.

"Maybe I should have stayed with Father Milezzo once we found him," vexed Christina. "What if he disappears? Maybe we scared him off."

"Worse yet," added Riggs, "what if Magenta makes his move? You can be sure he's watching everything we do."

"Who's Magenta?" asked Maxwell. This was news to him.

Oh no, thought Christina, *we forgot to tell him about Magenta.* "I first encountered him in a bazaar in Cairo, and he's been following us ever since. He even followed us to India."

Maxwell was clearly upset. The situation was more complicated than he had realized, and he now realized that his laboratory was at risk.

"He probably works for the same people who had Colby killed," added Riggs. "They obviously want Quelle."

Or the Dead Sea Scrolls, thought Christina, glancing at Riggs.

"Whoever *they* is," muttered Riggs.

"I think we should call the police," suggested Maxwell nervously. "I had no idea you were being followed and that someone else had learned about the existence of Quelle."

"I agree," said Christina, with a nod from Riggs. "Father Milezzo shouldn't be this late. Something must have gone wrong."

"Unless there were lot's of pilgrims today," joked Riggs feebly.

"The police know my laboratory contains priceless antiquities which can't be replaced," said Maxwell as he picked up the phone, "so they pass by here on their rounds anyway. With Quelle in the picture, however, I think they should be on the alert."

Suddenly there was a strong knock on the back door, and Christina ran to the door while Maxwell completed his telephone call. It was Father Milezzo, tardy but intact.

"This is Father Milezzo," said Christina as she introduced him to Riggs. They shook hands cautiously, and the priest extended his greeting to Maxwell as he hung up the phone. The skin on his gaunt face drew taut, like surgeon's gloves, as he smiled through tired eyes. Quelle had robbed his normally happy countenance.

Everyone was tense. They were landlubbers in heavy seas, not accustomed to this high intrigue. Here they were stealing a document from the Catholic Church, the Church that had served both Christina and Father Milezzo well.

"Do you think you were followed?" asked Maxwell, nervously fingering a Sicarii dagger on his desk. What began as a simple transfer of an ancient manuscript had become a potential threat to his laboratory. He cringed at the prospect of a barroom brawl on top of his million dollar instruments, not to mention the personal danger they now faced.

"I don't think so," answered Father Milezzo, "but I've been looking over my shoulder ever since Cairo. Quelle's been nothing but trouble for me."

I don't see the document in his hands, worried Riggs.

Father Milezzo responded to their concerned looks. "I left it in a safe place not far from here," he explained, somewhat cautiously, "until I was certain everything was all right. I'm not going to lose Quelle now, after all I've been through."

"You don't have to worry anymore," said Christina, trying to comfort him. "We plan to put Quelle here in Dr. Silvera's antiquities vault, where it will be safe until we take it to Cairo."

"I wish it were that simple," he said shaking his lined face from side to side. "At least <u>my</u> worries will be behind me."

"And <u>ours</u> will just be starting," said Riggs.

Christina couldn't restrain her curiosity any longer. "Do you know what happened to my uncle in Cairo?" she blurted impulsively. She just had to know.

A distressed look flashed over Father Milezzo's face as he recalled the events surrounding their abortive rendezvous. "Once Dr. Silvera had authenticated the fragment, your uncle arranged for us to meet in Cairo during a conference, where he planned to put Quelle in his vault."

Christina realized that she was finally going to learn what happened to her uncle. She steeled herself for the truth.

"We first met at Felfela's café," continued Father Milezzo in his thick Italian accent. "Everything seemed to be all right, but I was worried that someone might interfere with the rendezvous. I became a little paranoid. As a safety measure, like today, I had hidden the document nearby, and after I realize it was safe, we agreed to meet back at the café later for the actual transfer."

His eyes began to tear, and his voice wavered. "As we agreed, your uncle left Felfela's first, while I waited for a few minutes. As he was crossing the street, he was struck by a speeding car which appeared suddenly out of nowhere." He paused, tormented by the memories that swirled through his mind.

Tears welled in Christina's eyes as she wrestled with the tragic news. He walked over, put his arms around her, and gave her a comforting hug.

Priests sure know how to give love, she thought, recalling similar gestures from Fathers and nuns in her youth. She was grateful for his display of affection. *Why does religion need to be more complicated than this?*

"Was it an accident?" she finally asked him, regaining her composure.

"I couldn't tell, but two men jumped out of the car, searched through his pockets, and took his brief case. I seriously doubt if an ordinary robbery would be carried out in a Muslim city in broad daylight. They chop off hands here, you know."

"Was he carrying a large sum of money?" asked Riggs.

"I don't know. Whatever he normally carried, I suppose. There was no money involved in our transaction. I just wanted the world to have Quelle."

"But they couldn't have know that," theorized Maxwell.

"Whoever <u>they</u> is?" added Father Milezzo. "I certainly never told anyone about Quelle or the rendezvous, and I'm sure Mr. Tiger also guarded our secret."

"Maybe someone at the Vatican found out?" suggested Riggs, trying to find a solution.

"But they didn't even know I had discovered the document."

"Maybe your friends noticed a change in your behavior?"

"Well it certainly changed after Mr. Tiger was killed, but not before. At least I don't think so."

"Who told you about Uncle Colby?" asked Christina.

"A very good friend of mine in the Boston Diocese, whom I met at the Vatican. I'm sure he can be trusted."

It occurred to Christina that her brother might know the person Father Milezzo had contacted. "My brother is the Auxiliary Bishop in the Boston Diocese."

Life showed through the dark sockets of Father Milezzo's eyes for the first time. "Father Ryan Sheridan is your brother? he gasped. "That's impossible. He's my contact! He never mentioned that he was related to Mr. Tiger."

Christina was confused. *Ryan never mentioned Quelle to me at Uncle Colby's funeral,* she thought, *nor when he visited me in Cairo. In fact, he never mentioned giving Uncle Colby's name to anyone at the Vatican.* Of course, she had never told him about their search for Quelle.

"Did my brother know you'd found Quelle?" she probed.

"No," he answered. "I only told him that the Vatican needed to get some very old copies of the Bible authenticated. I didn't reveal whether they were Old Testament or New Testament."

Christina breathed a sigh of relief. *Good,* she thought. For a split second it had occurred to her that Ryan might be trying to recover Quelle for the Church, and heaven forbid, for his career.

She tried to put the conversation back on track. "Then what did you do?"

"I didn't know what to do," continued Father Milezzo. "I assumed that the men in the car were after Quelle, which was hidden safely nearby. Meanwhile your uncle was badly injured, if not dead, on the street just a few meters away. For a split second, I was torn: should I risk Quelle or help your uncle?

"Fortunately," he continued, "an American tourist, who seemed to be a medical doctor, assumed responsibility and stayed with him until the ambulance arrived. Unfortunately, he had long since covered your uncle's face with his own coat." He once again put his arm around Christina.

"What happened next?" she asked quietly, tears swelling in her eyes at the thought of Uncle Colby laying in the street with a stranger.

"I waited in the café until the crowd dispersed, then I slipped out the back, and eventually made my way back to Rome. As far as the Vatican was concerned, I had officially been in Cairo to discuss the Nag Hammadi codices with Pahor Labib."

That's believable, thought Riggs, pleased that the days of intrigue for his Codices were over. Robinson's break-in had solved that problem.

"My life's been a Holy Hell ever since," continued Father Milezzo, bordering on blasphemy, and his face was proof enough. "I had no intention of returning Quelle to the Vatican, but I didn't know what to do. I knew the antiquities market was not an option, because Quelle was too important for someone's vanity. I wanted to give Quelle to the world.

"As you can see, I'm relieved that you two are following through with Mr. Tiger's original mission. It's good that Professor Robinson is involved, because he's highly respected...although sometimes feared...at the Vatican. He has somehow managed to explore the historical Jesus, at the inevitable expense of the mythical one, without completely antagonizing either the Protestants or the Catholics."

Even Father Milezzo knows about the myths, thought Christina. *Who can we trust?*

"Professor Robinson's definitely good at mailing copies to leading Bible scholars around the world," smiled Riggs.

"Very good indeed," agreed Christina.

"That's perfect," concurred Father Milezzo, "as long as my role remains a secret."

"Of course," promised Riggs.

For God's sake, I wish he'd go get Quelle, thought Christina. *I'm dying to know what's in it!*

Everyone stood uneasily as the conversation lapsed into silence. But Father Milezzo seemed to be in no rush.

I think he wants to share his story with us, thought Christina, realizing that they shouldn't hurry him. He had held these secrets a long time.

The Priest's Confessions

All who embark on a spiritual path need to be willing to learn and to let go...

—Matthew Fox

Creation Spirituality

Everyone sat quietly. This was Father Milezzo's moment of glory.

"As a scholar at the Vatican, I had access to many early Christian documents, most of which are unknown to the world. I also had more than enough time to read authors like Hildegard of Bingen, Francis of Assisi, Thomas Aquinas, Mechtild of Magdeburg and, of course, Meister Eckhart. These mavericks became my heroes, and I learned from them to speak with God in my own language, rather than that of my Church."

"You might be the only person who would understand," he said, turning to Christina, "because you know how hard it is to maintain your faith when there is so much controversy over early Christianity."

"I sure do," she commiserated, "and I haven't even read those books yet."

"Well you can look forward to that, because they will become your best friends as you develop your own spiritual understanding. From them I learned a message of radical simplicity and ecology, and of the importance of compassion. Meister Eckhart said that compassion is the first outburst of everything God does. I believe that compassion was the essence of Jesus' teachings, as it was for many of the world's great teachers. Hildegard said compassion means that all things are penetrated with connectedness."

This sounds like Asha's new paradigm of physics, thought Christina. *I can't wait for them to meet each other.*

"There is divinity in each of us," he said, showing no signs of tiring, "and all the great teachers, including Jesus himself, were trying to share this simple message with us. I found it in the teachings of Muhammad, Isaiah, Lao Tzu, and, of course, Buddha. The Catholic Church, however, doesn't hand out divinity so liberally, reserving it only for Jesus himself."

"Sounds familiar," said Christina, thinking out loud.

"This universal message is not about eschatology, or an impending apocalypse, or a wrathful and judgmental God. It is about a loving God who shines through each one of us...a God we find inside ourselves like a Cosmic Spirit that binds all things together. It is about a God who inspires, teaches and graces all persons as living prophets in the making.

"I found that individual spirituality is more important than religious creeds, and that spirituality is a way of living every day, not a reward for dying."

He stopped to see if his monologue was boring anyone. Riggs and Christina were genuinely interested in his sermon, and Maxwell was just pleased the rendezvous was going so smoothly. His primary concern remained the well-being of his expensive laboratory.

"When I found these same teachings in Quelle, I knew they had to be made available to the world."

"Can you give us an example of his teachings?" asked Riggs, too anxious to wait for the manuscript.

"The best example is when the Disciples asked Jesus when the Father's imperial rule would come. As you know, our Christian doctrines say it comes to the deserving ones after death, and only because Jesus died on the cross for them. In Quelle, however, Jesus gives this answer:

> *"The kingdom of God does not come with observation, nor, will they say, 'Behold, here!' or 'There!' for behold, the kingdom of God is within you.'"*

"That's similar to Luke, I believe," observed Riggs.

"Yes," responded Father Milezzo. But in Luke the theological importance has been diluted by changing the context of the remark. Instead of making it the central theme of Jesus' teachings, which I'm convinced it was, in Luke it becomes little more than an anecdote at the end of a healing story. It is presented as a testy reaction by Jesus to the pestering Pharisees, and its importance is diminished. In Quelle, it is among his most important sayings, and its significance has not been lost by placing it at the end of a story added by a later author."

"If Jesus taught that God's presence is within us," began Christina, "now as well as after death, then the apocalyptic teachings and the concept of Hell must have been added by the Church."

"That's right," agreed Father Milezzo, "and the Church founders had many sources from which to choose, including messianic branches of Judaism and earlier Zoroastrianism."

"As well as the teachings of John the Baptist," added Riggs.

"This must have put you on a collision course with the Church," said Christina.

"A course which I had been on for many years," confided Father Milezzo.

Christina nodded understandingly. "You weren't fortunate as my brother. He has never questioned the Creeds, and it hasn't hurt his career. I really don't see how you could work side by side with people who hold such different beliefs."

"Fundamentally different," agreed Father Milezzo, "and it certainly hasn't been good for my career. Like my famous American friend, Matthew Fox, my priesthood has always been fragile. Up till now I've been discrete, and my colleagues have been tolerant. Priesthood is the only game I know."

"How are you able to participate in the rituals and the sacraments?" asked Christina.

"That's no problem for me," he said to her amazement, "because I believe rituals and mythology are an important aspect of religion for many people. Rituals and ceremonies contribute to community and family. The bonding that takes place between friends and family at baptisms, communions, weddings and funerals...even Sunday Mass...is far more important than the theology."

"That's the way it was in our family. I'm just ready to learn more now. What about the myths?"

"They're important too. The rapid growth of younger religions, like the Mormon Church, proves my point. They didn't take away from the traditional mythology; if anything, they added more."

"I don't understand," pleaded Christina. "I'm trying to outgrow the religious myths of my youth, and now you say that they are important?"

"Of course. For many people it provides an understanding of God. The Santa Claus myth, for example, teaches generosity and goodwill between men, not because Santa Claus exists, but because the story imparts a truth. The same is true of the Christian myths: they impart important truths about our relationship to God. Christians, unfortunately, have come to believe their myths as historical facts, rather than searching beyond them for the truths which they convey. The Jesus myth is about the virgin birth, the crucifixion, and the resurrection of each of us, not just one person, one time, two thousand years ago. We are all the anointed ones, the sons of God, and we will always sit at the right hand of God."

"I think I'm beginning to understand," smiled Christina.

Father Milezzo, however, was just getting started. He was fully exploiting his captive congregation and enjoying every minute of his sermon. No one could slip out during the hymn this time.

"I have three favorite quotations about mythology," he said, about to demonstrate his sharp memory. Roerich said that in every spark of folklore there is a drop of the great Truth, adorned or distorted. And Pliny, the great Roman historian, said that one is led to truth through the interpretation of a myth. And Joseph Campbell said that myths should be about concepts not facts."

I still find it easier to think of Jesus as teaching parables than being one himself."

This brought some needed laughter.

"Jesus was much more than a parable, but I know what you're saying," smiled Father Milezzo. "For me, he was the greatest of the teachers. Over the years these teachings have been distorted by those with much to gain, and we must reach back to his original message. We must dig past the creeds, past the stories, even past the miracles to find his wisdom."

"Like in the Gospel of Thomas," said Riggs.

"And like in Quelle," countered Father Milezzo, realizing that it was time to get the manuscript and share it with the world. He began walking toward the door, and everyone knew where he was going.

This is incredible, thought Riggs. *It's about to happen.*

"Why don't you go with him," suggested Christina, thinking of Magenta.

"That's not a bad idea," agreed Father Milezzo. "Safety in numbers."

"I hope you know some back alleys," said Riggs, with a hint of anxiety in his voice.

Calvary to the Rescue

These are the teachings of Jesus, I am telling you, love your enemies, bless those who curse you, pray for those who mistreat you. If someone slaps you on the cheek, offer your other cheek as well.

—Quelle (Q 6:27)

Christina heard a noise at the front door of the laboratory, and looked up expecting to see Father Milezzo and a proud Riggs holding Quelle. Maxwell was busying himself with the Turin Jesus, his favorite pastime.

Instead of Riggs, she saw the man they called Magenta shoving Father Milezzo through the door with a foreign gun at his throat. The priest was clutching a large tubular roll, which she knew was Quelle.

"Where's Riggs," she screamed as Maxwell turned to see what was wrong. "What have you done with Riggs?"

Father Milezzo merely shook his head in dismay, afraid to further anger his captor.

Terror swept over her. *Should I treat this madman with kid gloves,* she wondered, *or should I try to take control?* He was 250 pounds of granite, and he had a weapon. She didn't know what to do next.

Magenta ignored her question and positioned himself between Father Milezzo and the door, as though planning his escape.

I hope he just takes Quelle and leaves without a fuss, thought Maxwell, worrying about his expensive laboratory. Maxwell knew that Magenta couldn't get very far anyway. It was almost impossible to sneak antiquities past Israeli flight security...especially if they had been notified.

A that moment, Christina noticed that someone was slowly turning the knob of the front door behind Magenta. She looked away, so her stare wouldn't alert Magenta to Riggs, or whoever was coming to their rescue. *I hope it's not Asha,* she thought, as her heart pounded loudly. Her mouth rang galvanic with fear.

The door opened very slowly and quietly. She hoped Riggs would have the advantage of surprise. *Not bad for a New Testament scholar,* she thought. *I wonder what he has for a weapon? Hopefully the police.*

As the door opened a little further she was shocked to see not Riggs, and not the police, but Henry Beck.

How could he have known we needed help? she wondered, searching her mind for an answer. *He must have uncovered something in his investigation of Colby's death. Whatever the reason, I've never been so happy to see Henry.*

She tried not to reveal her excitement as Henry entered the door quietly behind Magenta. *Uncle Colby would be proud of Henry,* she thought. *He's definitely in control of things now.*

Judas Iscariot

She hazarded a second glance at Henry, being careful not to panic Magenta. Father Milezzo, with his back to Henry, didn't know what was happening. Maxwell was sitting nervously at his computer, quietly watching events play out in his precious laboratory.

I hope Maxwell doesn't expose Henry, worried Christina, just as she noticed that Henry didn't have anything in his hands. He had no weapon at all. *How's he going to deal with Magenta's gun?*

It was then, and not a second before, that she realized to her horror that Magenta and Henry were together. Magenta was Henry's man.

"Good God," she cried out. "What's going on here, Henry? Is this your man? What's this all about? What have you done with Riggs?"

"We don't have time for questions," sputtered Henry. "I want Quelle, of course!"

"How did you know?"

He glared at her. "I knew Colby was getting it in Cairo. I just couldn't let that happen. When that fell apart, you became my only hope. I didn't know how to find this priest in Rome."

Christina tried frantically to piece together the puzzle. How did Henry know the significance of Quelle? *He sure played dumb at the funeral...and on our trip to Cairo.* He must have thought that Quelle was in the vault, and when it wasn't, he changed his plans to stop in Rome. She had always wondered what oil business Uncle Colby would have in Rome. But why would Henry go to all this trouble...and kill Colby?

"For God's sake, Henry," she yelled, "he was your friend for years. He trusted you more than anyone on earth. How could you have killed him for an old manuscript?"

"You know why," he hissed. "Do you take me for stupid? Quelle's older than the New Testament and leaves out the Resurrection and Ascension. It undermines <u>everything</u> we believe in."

He stopped, looking rather dumbfounded. He had answered the wrong part of her question first. "I didn't mean for Colby to die," he continued, but his voice was becoming noticeably harsh. "He was accidentally killed by the men we hired to steal Quelle. Since then nothing's been the same. A piece of me died with him."

The tears rolling down his cheeks offended his masculinity, and he brushed them aside with exaggerated sweeps of his arms. His face was twitching between two competing expressions. He was disgusted with himself for his best friend's death, and yet proud for preserving the stories in the New Testament.

He's out of control, thought Christina, hoping he wouldn't hurt anyone else. This wasn't the Henry she had known. *He's completely lost it, now that he's killed his best friend over Quelle.*

Henry managed to stiffen his resolve. "There's no turning back now. My job's over once I get Quelle and give it to my church. They'll make sure that it doesn't fall into the hands of the atheists. I really don't care what happens to me then. I'll accept my punishment on earth for a later reward in Heaven." He was working himself into a frenzy again. "The works of the Devil must be destroyed."

"Works of the Devil?" mumbled Christina. "Quelle?" She took a second to calm herself somewhat. "Henry, Quelle isn't the work of the Devil. It's the words of Jesus. For God's sake—stop this insanity. The more you do now, the worse it's going to be later."

She suddenly thought of Riggs. "What have you done with Riggs?" she demanded. "Have you killed him too?"

"I don't think so, but we had to slow him down a bit," he said, pointing at Magenta who had done the job.

Thank goodness, she thought with relief. *At least he's alive. Maybe he'll get the police.*

The situation deteriorated rapidly. Magenta tried to pull Quelle away from Father Milezzo, who clutched it with his life. Magenta usually got his way, and picked the priest up by his garment and bashed him cruelly against the wall. Henry's screams had no effect as Magenta, twice Milezzo's size whipped him about like a rag doll in the mouth of a Rottweiler. He was gradually beating the life out of the frail Father Milezzo.

But Father Milezzo held defiantly to Quelle. After all he had been through to give it to the world, he would rather part with his life.

Magenta must be a psychopath, worried Christina, *because he won't even listen to Henry. He's killing Father Milezzo.* She helplessly watched his exaggerated motions and his flashing eyes. His rage had become the star in this sad drama.

"For God's sake, Henry," pleaded Christina, "it' not worth killing Father Milezzo. Call off your ghoul. Quelle is no more than a collection of Jesus' sayings."

"You underestimate me Christina," barked Henry. "I know what Quelle is, and I know it will destroy Christianity! The scholars are feeding on each other's egos and chewing the heart out of our New Testament. I'm not going to sit by and let it happen."

Now I've really upset him, thought Christina. *I'd better try to calm him down.* "There are scholars on both sides, Henry. It's better to just let them fight it out."

"Not when they distort the facts," spewed Henry, unable to contain his rage. "They're trying to convince everyone that Jesus was some sort of sage, when in fact He was the Son of God. If he was willing to die, so that we might have eternal life, should I sit by and watch them distort the words out of His sacred mouth?"

"How could two hundred sayings, many of which are already in the New Testament, destroy Christianity?" pleaded Christina.

"You know the answer to that," screamed Henry, while Magenta continued to bash the determined Father Milezzo against the wall. "Don't play innocent. You must think I'm an idiot. If the earliest Gospels only contained His teachings, then it makes it look like all the miracles, the Final Judgment and even the stories about Jesus were added later. It's an evil document for those of us who believe the Bible should be interpreted literally." He paused to gain his breath.

Christina knew that Father Milezzo wouldn't survive Magenta's beating. She had never seen anyone so violent. Her eyes pleaded with Henry to stop the beating, but he continued his harangue.

"What good would it be if people thought Jesus didn't rise from the dead for our sins? How are you going to explain God to them? How are you going to explain eternal life to them? You think you're so damned smart, but you don't realize that people need these hopes just to face their miserable lives."

"But Henry…"

"What are you going to give them in return?" he screamed. "What academic bullshit are you going to feed them that explains the role of God any better? What are you going to tell old people who have only a few months to live? And parents who have lost a child to cancer? If you don't have anything better to give them, then don't take their Jesus away. How are you going to dry the tears of mankind?

"I'm telling you, Christina," he screamed even louder , slapping her across the face, "You're playing with fire, and you're damned naïve. Either burn this book, or burn the hopes of millions of people. I have no choice."

His face was bright red with anger and his wild eyes terrified her. She was shocked that he could react so violently to Quelle. Was this scene any different than when Landa burned the Maya Bible? Or the bonfires of Hitler and Mao? She was witnessing history. Worse yet, she was living history. She realized that she had to save Quelle...regardless of who ended up with it. As long as it was not destroyed.

"You can have it," she said without emotion. "Leave Father Milezzo alone and just take it." She walked over to Magenta, as bravely as she could, and kneeled down next to the nearly lifeless body of Father Milezzo, who still gripped Quelle with the drags of his strength. Believing this was their only course of action, she said: "Give it to them, Father. At least it won't be destroyed."

Realizing that his life was not enough to save his precious Quelle, he handed it to her and collapsed. She handed it to Magenta, whose other hand still held the gun, and turned her attention back to Father Milezzo.

Henry grabbed Quelle from Magenta and a smile crossed his tormented face for the first time. "My congregation will be amazed when I return with this prize," he proclaimed.

"Sounds like you'll be a real hero, Henry," said Christina in disgust.

"That's right," he answered smugly, "but it's not just for me. My church will finally get the recognition it deserves. We know that the Day of Judgment is coming soon, and that the Apocalypse is at hand. Only those who have been faithful to the Christ will survive. Once we have Quelle, we'll no longer be *that little fundamentalist church at the corner of Thirteenth and Trenton.*

"Well, you're not going to find Judgment Day in Quelle," gasped Father Milezzo. Anger had revived his strength.

"Neither will anyone else," sneered Henry, holding Quelle high in the air triumphantly, as he walked past Maxwell toward the door.

Turin Jesus

No one ever knew what happened next. Maybe it was a glitch in the circuits, or maybe Maxwell accidentally switched on the voice-activated controls, but either way, the Turin Jesus suddenly started moving without Maxwell touching the joysticks. Blood started squirting out of the wounds in Jesus' wrists and feet, his arms began flapping like a bird, and his face jerked uncontrollably between frowns and smiles. The Turin Jesus had gone berserk.

So did Magenta, whose wild animal nature had long ago replaced his human one. He started shooting insanely at the twisting Jesus, his bullets passing through the image with no effect and smashing into the glass windows surrounding the computer center.

Henry stood frozen in shock, staring at the image of his Christ. Believing that this apparition was some kind of miracle, he wasn't sure whether it was sent from God or the Devil. "Why are you shooting at Jesus, you idiot?" he shouted.

Magenta paid no attention. His bullets sprayed across the image of Jesus several times, breaking bottles of laboratory chemicals which spilled onto the floor.

Trying to get the crazed Magenta under control, Henry grabbed his arm. In the scuffle, wild bullets tore through Father Milezzo's arms and torso, and he dropped slowly to the floor, holding his stomach in pain. Blood pulsed from the wounds in his chest, in synch with the Turin Jesus behind him.

Christina ran to the wounded priest and held him in her arms, blood and all. *What have we done?* she thought. *This is all my fault.* From where she sat on the floor, the blood from the fatally wounded Father Milezzo seemed to be flowing into the blood from the Turin Jesus. She knew it was an illusion, but it seemed so real.

"For God's sake, Henry, stop him!" screamed Christina. "You've hurt enough people over Quelle."

Maxwell could no longer sit idly by and watch, as they destroyed everything he had built. On his desk he spotted a Sicarii dagger, one of his prized antiquities. He concealed it under his cuff and edged toward Magenta as he dammed up the chemicals on the floor. As he passed near Magenta, pretending to be absorbed in his work, he suddenly leaped up and plunged the knife into Magenta's stomach with the skill of an amateur but the strength of Samson. *An eye for an eye,* he thought, as he successfully twisted the blade with both hands. It actually felt good to stab the man who had destroyed his laboratory.

Henry dropped Quelle and dove for Magenta's gun, as Magenta toppled to the floor trying to pull out the knife. He began shooting wildly in all directions, as the barrel of the heavy gun leaped into the air with each shot. It was the first time he had fired a large caliber pistol, and the shots sprayed everywhere.

One of the bullets broke a large bottle of acid, which spilled onto Quelle. The edges of the manuscript became dark and twisted in the acid as the original teachings of Jesus simmered and disappeared in the curling smoke.

In the midst of all the confusion, no one noticed the burning words.

Suddenly the front door swung open, but Christina couldn't make out the pale figure through the smoke.

"Is that you Riggs?" she called out.

There was no answer.

As the fumes and smoke from the acid began to drift out the door, she saw her brother, Bishop Ryan, outlined in the light.

What in the world is he doing here?

For some unexplainable reason, Henry stood motionless as though Ryan's garment commanded authority. He was stunned by the severity of the situation. Magenta was dead, with a knife in his stomach, and the priest in Christina's arms was dying from bullet wounds. Now he was faced by a Bishop and lacked the stomach for any more violence.

Bishop Ryan walked toward him with complete assurance and not a trace of fear. Without the need for force, he calmly took the gun from a dazed Henry and began to survey the damage. When he saw the remains of Quelle smoldering in the acid, he yelled to Maxwell for assistance. "Can you save what's left of Quelle?"

"I'll try." answered Maxwell. "Maybe hydroxide will work, but if I get the concentration wrong it'll be even worse." He poked through the debris carefully, hoping to find the piece of broken glass that showed the strength of the acid.

"Did anyone call the police?" asked Christina, coming to her senses.

"The automatic fire alarm system should have already alerted them," said Maxwell.

Bishop Ryan kneeled down next to Christina and gave her a hug. "How's Father Milezzo doing?" he asked. "Can he make it until they arrive?"

"What are you doing here?" asked Christina, still in a state of shock. "How do you know everyone?"

"I've been in contact with Father Milezzo since he called me in Boston about authenticating some documents," said Ryan, with a smile that bordered on insincerity. "That's when I put him in touch with Colby. Later at the funeral, when I learned about Quelle from the letter in Colby's folder, I got involved. Everything fell into place when Father Milezzo's superior at the Vatican said there was nothing in his project that required authenticating."

"So you are his Catholic friend in Boston?" asked Christina, already knowing the answer. "And you betrayed his confidence to improve your standing in the Church? Have you been following me too?"

"Not really," said Ryan, disowning both charges. "I just kept track of you from your calls to mother. When she said you were heading to Jerusalem, I figured that you were planning to meet Father Milezzo and that he might give you Quelle."

"So you've known that we were trying to find Quelle the whole time?"

"Of course," said Ryan proudly. "I couldn't let you have all the fun alone."

"What do you plan to do with Quelle?"

"It has to go back home, of course. Home to the Vatican. It was stolen from the Vatican, and it must be returned. I've alerted the police already."

"Of course," said Christina, realizing what this was all about. "Back to the Vatican in the hands of a hero."

"In the hands of a Cardinal, perhaps," whispered Ryan to Christina.

"Don't you realize that the Christian world needs to see Quelle, if they're going to focus on the teachings of Jesus instead of the myths and the legends?"

"And it will, of course...once we've figured out how it fits. We just need a little time to get everything in order."

"You mean a little time to add some narratives," charged Christina, as Father Milezzo found unexpected strength and began to speak.

"It won't fit our doctrines," he gurgled, as Christina wiped the blood away from his mouth. She knew this was the only way for him to fight for his beloved Quelle. Christina tried to prop his head so he could speak a little easier.

"Quelle says that God comes to earth in each of us, and not just Jesus," he swallowed painfully, "if our thought is virgin pure."

Christina held him closely, hoping his angst would sustain his last breaths until the police arrived.

"God gives all of us the miracle of eternal life," he continued with great effort, "which we can claim only by forgiving and loving those who would do us harm."

He paused to catch his labored breath.

"You're a foolish old man," scolded Bishop Ryan. "Save your energy for your own misguided life."

But Father Milezzo was determined. "It's not a message of fear...not a message of judgment...not a message of eternal punishment. It's a message of blessing, original blessing, of celebration and eternal life and love."

Christina was unable to calm him. His words were more important now than his last breaths.

"It's a message of a good and present God, whose Love sustains each of us through this earthly experience and into the next."

He then pulled Christina's head close to his bloody mouth and whispered his last words into her ear. Christina reluctantly lowered Father Milezzo to the floor, grabbed the remains of Quelle from Maxwell and ran desperately toward the back door.

Orthodox Quelle?

The door swung open right in her face, and there stood Riggs with three armed Israeli policeman. He looked very much the victim, with a large gash over his left eye. She was happy to see that he was alive, and that the police were finally here for Father Milezzo, but any hopes she had of escaping with Quelle were now completely dashed.

She walked over to her brother, reluctantly handed him the damp manuscript, and whispered very quietly. "The debate over Quelle needs to take place in the halls of knowledge, not just in the halls of the Vatican. This comes with a price—a heavy price—the price of at least two lives." Her eyes slowly moved around the room, first at the body of Magenta and then to Father Milezzo, as the police rushed him out on a stretcher. She then centered her eyes sternly on those of her brother. "...and one of them was our uncle. He was a father to me."

Ryan looked remorseful, dutifully remorseful, but his eyes revealed the inner conflict of his ambitions within the Church. "I'll get Quelle out as soon as I can," he promised with absolutely no credibility.

She mustered as much sarcasm as her sad face could convey and said, "You won't have a voice." She knew that her brother had betrayed both her and Father Milezzo for his own selfish goals within the Church. Worse yet, she knew that no one would ever know, not even his parishioners in Boston.

The police had removed Magenta's body and handcuffed Henry. Through the open door she saw them standing next to their cars interviewing Maxwell under the blinding sweep of the flashing yellow lights. *We're next,* she thought.

Riggs walked slowly up to Christina and Ryan, not wanting to interrupt their private conversation. They turned toward Riggs, momentarily concealing wounds that would never heal.

"I guess Quelle is going back to the Vatican," said Riggs, looking disdainfully at Ryan.

"They're the rightful owners," lectured Ryan.

"Are they really, now," said Riggs, annoyed by Ryan's parochial view. He hoped his eyes would not betray his secret agenda. "You don't suppose I could have a look at Quelle before you take it away?" asked Riggs as innocently as possible. "After all we've gone through to find it, I'd sure like to see a few of our Master's teachings before they disappear again."

"Seems fair enough to me," answered Ryan, shrugging his shoulders, "but you have to promise not to publish."

His derogatory humor was wasted on Christina, but Riggs managed a slight smile. *I'd do anything to read Quelle,* he thought, *even humor this bastard.* Riggs was sickened by the wet clump of charred remains handed him by Ryan. *This is a sad fate for the original teachings of Jesus.* He sorted through the pile until he found some intact pages.

Christina and Ryan stood anxiously by, waiting for him to translate the writing. They were both curious, each in their own ways.

"Let me sit down a minute," said Riggs, moving to a cluttered desk near the door. "The light isn't good enough here."

He's going to run with it, thought Christina, trying to conceal her excitement. *My bandaged hero is going to save Quelle after all.*

Instead, he looked intently at the Greek writing on the first page, trying to find the beginning of a phrase or sentence. *I wonder if I'll recognize any of these sayings?* Finally, Riggs made out the following words:

> NOW UPON the first day of the week, very early in the morning, they came unto the sepulchre, bringing the spices which they had prepared.

It looks like the Gospel of Luke, Riggs thought, as he continued to read.

> 2 It was Peter, Mary Magdalene, and Mary the mother of James, and the other women that were with them.

Wait a minute. How did Peter get in here? This isn't right.

> 3 And they found the stone rolled away from the sepulchre.
>
> 4 And they entered in, and found not the body of the Lord Jesus.

This looks like the Gospel of Luke again. What's happening here?

> 5 And it came to pass, as they were much perplexed thereabout, behold, two Angels stood by them in shining garments:

Angels? I thought it was two men. Am I losing my mind?

> 6 And as they were afraid, and bowed down their faces to the earth, they said unto them, Why seek ye the living among the dead?
>
> 7 He is not here, but is risen from the dead: remember how he spake unto you when he was yet in Galilee,

Risen from the dead? I don't remember that part. What is this?

> 8 Saying, The Son of God must be delivered into the hands of sinful men, and be crucified, and the third day rise again.

Ouch. Now he's been promoted from the Son of man to the Son of God.

> 9 And they remembered his words,
>
> 10 And lo the Angels spake unto Peter and he was sore afflicted.
>
> 11 And they charged him, saying, Carry forth the teachings of the risen Christ, once He hath returned to Heaven and been seated at the right hand of God.
>
> 12 And behold, Peter was much anguished and dropped to the ground and wailed that he was not worthy of such a blessing, having thrice denied the Lord.
>
> 13 The Angels, being filled with the grace of God, lifted Peter to his feet and sayeth unto him,
>
> 14 You among all men will be blessed in the sight of God.

They've even empowered the Popes and the Church. This must be a very carefully crafted counterfeit. But how did it get here?

15 And they all returned from the sepulchre, and told all these things unto the other ten faithful apostles, and to all the rest.

16 And their words seemed to them as idle tales, and they believed them not.

Well, at least this last verse is from the Gospel of Luke. This last warning label is even more important on this forgery. What am I going to do now?

Ryan and Christina waited anxiously for Riggs to read the sayings of Jesus to them.

The Resurrection

Q forces the issue of rethinking Christian origins as no other document from the earliest times has done.

—Burton Mack
The Lost Gospel: The Book of Q

Christina slowly placed the phone on the receiver. "They lost Father Milezzo during the night," she sobbed, as tears streamed down her cheeks.

"Maybe it's just as well, dear," said Asha, as she picked her way through the debris and put her arms around Christina for comfort. "The doctors didn't offer much hope for a full recovery."

"Still..." Christina whimpered, not soothed by the logic.

"It was what he wanted," said Riggs. "He was willing to die for Quelle...or what he thought was Quelle." His head was wrapped like a mummy, but he didn't seem incapacitated, except for the kidding from everyone.

The three of them had been mopping up liquids, sweeping broken glass into a bin, and putting books back on the shelves. Maxwell was in the next room making lists of damaged instruments.

Riggs looked for a way to get the conversation on a brighter note.. "When I told Professor Robinson what happened here, he told me some good news."

"What did he say?" asked Christina, starting to show some life again.

"He said that once he included the Gospel of Thomas in his reconstruction of Quelle, the statistics improved dramatically.. He thinks the team is well on its way."

"Well a reconstructed Quelle is better than no Quelle at all," moped Christina, looking like she had finished fourth place in the Olympics. "But we were so close...I still can't figure out what happened to Father Milezzo's Quelle. Why would he be willing to die for a forgery?"

"He must not have realized that someone switched the manuscript."

"Someone at the Vatican?" guessed Christina.

"Had to be. It was done so professionally and it was definitely self-serving."

"It was definitely the <u>ideal</u> narrative Gospel," said Christina with a wry smile. It sure left no doubt about the divinity of Jesus and the mandate to Peter and the Popes."

"No, it wasn't very subtle on those points," agreed Riggs. "But what I can't figure out is why Ryan went to all the trouble to save the wrong Quelle."

"He must not have known that the manuscripts were switched." It was difficult for her to get over her brothers betrayal of everyone to get his hands on Quelle.

"It was obviously better for the Vatican if the counterfeit had stayed in circulation."

"I wish I could be there when Ryan dutifully drags it in, like a dog with the neighbors newspaper."

Riggs led the laughter. "Well, his tail isn't going to wag for very long. He will have unwittingly returned the ultimate narrative gospel to the people who wanted to launch it on the world."

"So much for his precious career," jabbed Christina, all too willing to join in the laughter.

"But meanwhile, three people died over a counterfeit Quelle," said Maxwell, as he strode into their room with his list of damaged instruments.

"Three people and <u>one</u> laboratory," added Riggs.

"I wanted new computers anyway," laughed Maxwell feebly, trying to stay in good spirits.

But Christina knew that he was not at all pleased with the mess. She had offered to pay for the damage, but he had declined her offer emphatically.

"One thing we know for sure," said Maxwell, "both Colby and Father Milezzo saw the real Quelle."

This idea got everyone's attention.

Riggs liked Maxwell's train of thought. "You're right. We definitely know that Father Milezzo saw the real Quelle, because we heard him defend it with his dying breath," he said, looking at Christina to see if his description had been too candid. "But how do we know that Colby saw the real Quelle? It would have been Greek to him. He wouldn't...rather, he couldn't...have known the difference."

"Because he had the copies validated by someone," recalled Maxwell. "Whoever validated his copy must have seen the real Quelle, or they would have told him that it was just another narrative gospel."

Riggs took it the next step. "Then what did Colby do with his copies?"

The words struck Christina like an avalanche. The dying words whispered by Father Milezzo finally made sense to her. *Copies of Quelle*, he had said. She had thought it was his last futile request, not an important clue. "Father Milezzo," she blurted, "had the same idea. His last words to me were about those copies!"

"Did he say where Colby hid them?" asked Riggs. This was almost too good to be true.

"No, he..."

"He didn't have to," interrupted Maxwell, having guessed the answer to the mystery.

Everyone looked expectantly at Maxwell, especially Asha who loved it when he was brilliant.

"Colby would have hidden them the same way Father Milezzo had found them."

Riggs looked at Christina. Smiles spread across both their faces when they realized what Maxwell was about to say. Quelle had been in their hands the whole time.

"He used the Proverbs trick and hid Quelle among the photos in his vault," proclaimed Christina, looking at Maxwell for approval. "He hid his copies of the real Quelle with the Dead Sea Scrolls in Cairo."

The Epiphany
2010
Cambridge, Massachusetts

To the extent that we live and move and have our being in correspondence with a world replete with currents of divinity, then to that same extent will we recognize our own participation in and with a community of life unified by the Supreme Mind and moving toward a horizon of spiritual perfection."

—Ralph Waldo Emerson

I was there...I was there when the Maya spoke once again...I was there when the words of Jesus were freed from the desert sands. I was there when the candle of knowledge shone round the world.

Very small, meticulously groomed, crystal gray and elegant,Christina sat at her old Sheraton desk...her years well hidden behind an illuminated smile. She picked up one of the two books on her desk and opened the front cover with her frail hands, taking delight in the personal autograph by Professor Michael Coe.

Those were exciting times at Palenque, she reminisced. *We were young and we made our mark on the world.* She sat the book back down next to the one written by Professor David Kelley. It too had been autographed with a personal message.

She took an all too familiar walk across her library to her favorite bookcase and pulled down another book, bound in leather and gold like a family Bible. She opened it and scanned the Popol Vuh, with its ancient wisdom and captivating mythological stories.

The Maya Bible is known around the world, she thought, recalling her work on the Mayan code with a great deal of pride. The progress in the years after the Primera Mesa Redonda had been phenomenal. Invigorated by the later discoveries at Copan, the next generation of Mayan linguists had soon completed the Mayan syllabary, and freed the voices trapped in the beautiful hieroglyphs all those centuries. Nothing brought her more happiness than the memories of her Maya research.

Next to her Maya books, laying on the same shelf, was the Sicarii knife that Maxwell Silvera had given her as a memento. She picked it up and turned it over slowly in her delicate hands. She remembered how excited Maxwell had been in 1982 when he called to tell her about the Turin Shroud. Pope John II, in an unprecedented personal visit, had convinced Umberto II of Savoy on his deathbed to bequeath the shroud to the Catholic Church. He was successful, for reasons best left to the imagination, and the shroud disappeared forever into the Vatican.

A radiant smile spread across the silver lace of her cheeks. *Except, of course, for the little piece at Maxwell's laboratory in Jerusalem.*

That same year she had learned from Asha that a group of French scientists had finally confirmed John Bell's famous physics equation using new sophisticated equipment. They proved that the strange world inside the atom, at the heart of matter, reserved for itself some uncertainties, some faster-than-light communications, and some exemptions from cause-and-effect. Reality for the quantum was not destined to be the same as reality for us...whatever that meant.

t was fortunate to meet Asha when I did, she reminisced fondly. Asha had saved her a detour into scientific materialism, during the time when she had been looking for something to fill the spiritual gap created by the truth about her own religion. Asha also helped her find her way past the organized Eastern religions. With her assistance, Christina had gotten an early start on the search for God within herself.

Poor Asha is still trying to explain the new physics paradigm to me...and not having much luck. Christina now knew that the mechanistic paradigm of Newton and Galileo was passe, but when Asha talked about efforts to include the human mind and consciousness in physics, it went over Christina's head. She knew her dear friend would keep trying nevertheless.

That had been the nature of their relationship, sharing their spiritual insights over the years. They communicated almost every day by electronic mail, and their files were full of old letters. Asha never ceased to search for the truth, and Christina shared that same passion. Nothing meant more to her than Asha's friendship.

Christina continued her familiar stroll through the mementos in her office. She scanned the books on the next shelf looking for old favorites, and spotted a book by Mathew Fox, the Catholic priest whose controversial writing she greatly enjoyed. It reminded her of Father Milezzo, who held very similar views.

She liked Mathew Fox's attempt to develop a new creation myth based solidly on known scientific principles. If myths depart too far from established scientific knowledge they lose their value to society. She hoped his ideas would unite people around the world in a new global mythology based on the metaphors of physics.

Next to Mathew Fox's book stood the Nag Hammadi Library, a large collection of books published by her friend James Robinson a few years after his break-in at the Coptic Museum. An equally amazing sequence of events surrounding the Dead Sea Scrolls occurred in the early nineties. Professor Robinson had always insisted that his behind-the-scenes role in liberating the Dead Sea Scrolls was small, and that Herschel Shanks at the Biblical Archaeology Review and Professor Robert Eisenman should have received most of the credit. Nevertheless, as usual, good things seemed to happen once Professor Robinson got involved.

Photos of the Scrolls from a secret source began arriving by mail at Professor Robert Eisenman's university office. *That wasn't as big a miracle as many people thought,* chuckled Christina to herself. *I'll never know why some people suspected me and Riggs.*

Then came the biggest shock of all, one that gave the press a real picnic. Elizabeth Hay Bechtel, a divorced wife of one of the Bechtel brothers, donated previously unknown photos of the Dead Sea Scrolls to the Huntington Library in Los Angeles. It remained a mystery how the Bechtel family had kept them secret for thirty years.

It wasn't hard for me to believe.

About the same time Professor Robinson and Eisenman published photographic facsimiles of most of the fragments that had previously remained under wraps. The game was over. With his pen and his camera, he had quenched many of the ancient Roman fires, and his achievements would remain unequaled over the centuries.

His fame has been growing ever since, she reflected, looking at The Gospel of Quelle, reconstructed by him and his colleagues toward the end of the millennium. It had added immensely to the understanding of Jesus' authentic teachings.

She then walked a few steps to the section of her library where she kept all of Riggs' books and published papers, most of which were on the Gospel of Thomas and the Gospel of Mary. It was a living memorial to him, and even now tears pooled in her eyes at the memory of his untimely death sailing in a storm off Cape Cod.

Riggs was very productive during our happiest years together in Boston. She brushed her fingers fondly across the spines of his books, and picked up the little menorah they had found in the cave at Qumran.

The most important thing we learned together was that the suppression of ideas, through the burning of words, bound mankind to the myopia of his myths. The freedom of ideas was necessary for the freedom of man…in his individual search for God.

> *"And ye shall know the truth, and the truth shall make you free".*
> (John 8:32)

At times like this she found comfort in Professor Robinson's kind advice over the years. She shared his belief that humans must strive to bring the kingdom of God into their daily lives, at the expense of their individual self interests. They must not only trust God to provide them, through others, with their daily bread and loving care, but they must also serve God by providing the same bread and nurturing to their neighbors. We are all charged by the Master to share our food and clothing, to cancel the debts of others, to nurse the sick, and to not retaliate against enemies. When we do this, and when others do it in return, God is acting through us and we are living in His kingdom.

She paged through her private copy of Robinson's Theological Autobiography and found her favorite page:

> *The human dilemma is in large part that we are each other's fate, the tool of evil that ruins the other person, as we look out for number one, having wised up with regard to any youthful idealism we might once have cherished. But if I would basically cease and desist from pushing you down to keep myself up, and you for your part would do the same, then the vicious circle would be broken. Society would become mutually supportive, rather than self-destructive. Count on God to look out for you, to provide people that will care for you, and listen to him when he calls on you to provide for them. This radical trust in and responsiveness to God is what makes society function (as God's society). This is what, for Jesus, faith and discipleship were all about. Nothing else has a right to claim any functional relationship to him.*

Robinson remained a devoutly pious man, believing that Jesus' authentic teachings were relevant, but that we all found too many excuses not to put them into practice. One of his favorite sayings was from the Quelle and the Gospel of St. Luke:

> *"And why call ye me, Lord, Lord, and do not the things which I say?"*
> (Q 6:46)

Christina sat quietly thinking how simple Jesus' message was to understand and yet so difficult to implement, because it required trust between people.

Looking out the window at the newly fallen snow, she started downstairs to make a cup of hot tea. She held onto the cherry wood banister, taking each step slowly and carefully.

I've made a lot of progress choosing the spiritual senses over the physical ones, but I still need a lot more practice. She had found a sense of peace and lost most of her fears.

The phone rang as she sipped her tea among the profusion of plants and flowers in her small kitchen.

"Hello, dear, this is Asha," spoke the voice on the phone. Hearing from Asha was the best part of each day.

"Would you be interested in the discovery of a manuscript near Bethsaida on the Golan Heights, not far from the Sea of Galilee?" Asha began. She only allowed a short pause before continuing.

"They say it's the Z-Document, the one common to the sayings gospels Thomas and Quelle."

The Z-document, thought Christina, *at my age?*

> "Do not be concerned from morning until evening and from evening until morning, neither about your food and what you will eat, nor about your clothing and what you will wear. You are far better than the lilies which neither card nor spin."
>
> Q, Thomas, Matthew, Luke (and maybe Z)

Schrödinger's Equation

$$\frac{\hbar^2}{2m}\frac{\partial^2 \psi}{\partial x^2} + V\psi = i\hbar \frac{\partial \psi}{\partial t}$$

"Schrödinger's theory was the most astonishing
among all the astonishing discoveries
of the twentieth century."

–Arthur Sommerfeld

"All the elements in the universe derive from this one equation."

–Professor Asha Sinha

Glossary

Apostles' Creed: The religious beliefs held, in various degrees, by most Christians, both Catholic and Protestant (See Chapter titled Hail Mary, Mother of God)

Bhagavad Gita: a Hindu devotional work in poetic form

Bedouin: an Arab of any of the nomadic desert tribes of Arabia, Syria or North Africa

Bodhisattva: one whose essence is enlightenment

Buddhism: a religion founded in India during the sixth century B.C. It teaches that right thinking and self-denial will enable the soul to reach a divine state called Nirvana

Christian: a person professing belief in Jesus as the Christ, or in the religions based on the teachings of Jesus

Coptic: the Egyptian language written with the Greek alphabet instead of Egyptian hieroglyphs. It is in use today primarily by the clergy of the Egyptian Christian Church

Dead Sea Scrolls: ancient Jewish manuscripts written in Hebrew and Aramaic, hidden in caves near Jerusalem during the first century, discovered in 1947, and exploited by many people

Ecole Biblique: a French Catholic research group, specializing in Biblical archaeology and located in the Palestinian sector of Jerusalem

Hieroglyph: a picture or symbol representing a word, syllable, or sound

Hinduism: the religion and social system of the Indic-speaking peoples of India, developed from Brahmanism with elements from Buddhism and Jainism

Huipile: an elaborately decorated Maya blouse, which is square in shape with a hole that fits over the head. The beautiful designs are unique to each village and have historical significance (pronounced Hwee 'peel)

Islam: a monotheistic religion in which the supreme deity is Allah and the chief prophet and founder is Mohammed.

Judaism: a monotheistic religion based on the laws and teachings of the Holy Scripture and the Talmud

Logographic: relating to or marked by the use of a letter, symbol or sign, used to represent an entire word

Maya: people indigenous to Guatemala, southern Mexico and northern Honduras. They built large temples and observatories during the first millennium, which were later covered by the jungle for nearly a thousand years

Maya: the Hindu goddess who personified the illusory world of the senses and was the consort of the god Siva

Moslem (Muslim): an adherent of Islam

Nag Hammadi: a town near Thebes (modern day Luxor) on the Upper Nile in Egypt (pronounced Nah·gah hah 'may dee)

Nag Hammadi Codices: ancient Christian manuscripts, written in Coptic, buried in Egypt during the fourth century, discovered in 1945, and mostly translated in the early seventies

Palenque: a site of Mayan ruins in southern Mexico (pronounced Pah 'len kay)

Papyrus: paper made from the tall papyrus plant by soaking, pressing, and drying thin slices (pronounced Pah pie rus)

Popul Vuh: t he Quiche Maya bible (pronounced Poe pull 'vuh)

Glossary (Con't)

Primera Mesa Redonda de Palenque: the name given by the attendees to a now famous informal gathering of Mayan scholars at Palenque, where they hoped to break the Maya code. In Spanish it means the First Roundtable at Palenque.

Quelle: the German word for "source", used by Biblical scholars to describe the document believed to precede the New Testament gospels (pronounced Kwell)

Qumran: an archaeological site in Israel, on the Dead Sea, east of Jerusalem, near the caves where the Dead Sea Scrolls were discovered (pronounced Koom rahn)

Rockefeller Museum: the Palestinian Archaeological Museum in East Jerusalem, originally funded by the Rockefellers, which housed the Palestinian Department of Antiquities

Shrine of the Book: the museum in Jerusalem where the portion of the Dead Sea Scrolls controlled by the Jews is exhibited

Stelae: slabs of stone elaborately carved with pictures and writing

Syllabary: a table of Mayan hieroglyphs, each representing a syllable of the spoken language

Synoptic Gospels: the name given by theologians to the gospels of Matthew, Mark and Luke because of the many similarities in these accounts

Yarmulke: a skullcap worn esp. by Orthodox and Conservative Jewish males

Yucatec: one of the spoken Mayan languages (pronounced 'Yoo kah tek)

Xibalba: the mythological Mayan underworld, or World of the Dead (pronounced Shi 'ball bah)

Main Characters

Christina Sheridan: a Harvard anthropology professor whose specialty is the Mayan language

Yax: Christina's Mayan guide (Pronounced Yawsh)

Henry Beck: Colby's lawyer and aide

Colby Tiger: Christina's wealthy Creek-Seminole uncle

Friar Diego de Landa: a Spanish priest who burned the Mayan books during the Spanish Conquest of the New World (see References)

Eric Thompson: a British archaeologist whose forceful personality and incorrect views on the Mayan hieroglyphs delayed progress for several decades (see References)

Yuri Knorosov: a Russian linguist and mathematician who was known for his brilliance (see References)

David Kelley and Michael Coe: linguists who deciphered the Mayan hieroglyphs (see References)

Maureen Sheridan: Christina's mother and Mary's sister

Mary Tiger: Colby's wife, Maureen's sister and Christina's aunt

Bill Kirchick: Colby's estate attorney

Father Ryan Sheridan: Christina's brother, a Roman Catholic priest

James Robinson: The Biblical scholar who emancipated the Nag Hammadi codices, reconstructed the Q-document, and played a central role in breaking the Dead Sea Scrolls monopoly (see References and Dedication). His academic affiliation is with The Institute for Antiquity and Christianity and Claremont Graduate University in Southern California.

Riggs Parker: a New Testament scholar who translated the Nag Hammadi codices from Coptic. He also received one of the two keys to Colby's vault in Cairo

Earlene Beck: Henry's deceased wife

Muhammed Ali, Khalifah, and Ahmad: Egyptian peasants living near Nag Hammadi in 1945 (see References)

Pahor Labib: Director of the Coptic Museum in Old Cairo

Mrs. Scarzella: the proprietor of the Garden City House in Cairo, a modest lodging for long term guests

John Allegro: renouned for first translating several of the Dead Sea Scrolls, including the Copper Scroll (see References)

Magenta: a mysterious man

Father Roland de Vaux: a Franciscan priest, trained as an archaeologist, who purchased many Dead Sea Scrolls from the Bedouin and oversaw the excavation of the ancient Jewish site discovered at Qumran (see References)

Sunil Gupta: an archaeology professor at the University of Kashmir, in India, and Director of the Museums, Collections and Archives

Drs. Davisson, Bell, Penrose, Einstein, Bohr and others: physicists (see References)

Volker Heine: a young German academic whose research was on the Turin Shroud

Asha Sinha: a physics professor at Hebrew University and wife of Maxwell Silvera

Maxwell Silvera: a wealthy forensic chemist whose hobby was validating antiquities and ancient manuscripts

Father David Milezzo: an Italian priest who translated Biblical manuscripts at the Vatican

References

Maya:

Michael D. Coe, Breaking the Maya Code, Thames & Hudson, New York, NY, 1992.

Dennis Tedlock, Popul Vuh, The Mayan Book of the Dawn of Life, Simon & Schuster (Touchstone), New York, NY, 1985

Sylvanus Morley, George Brainerd and Robert Sharer, The Ancient Maya, Stanford University Press, Stanford, CA, 1983.

Friar Diego de Landa, Yucatan Before and After the Conquest, Dover Publications, New York, NY, 1978.

Indians/Oklahoma:

Charles A. Eastman (Ohiyesa), The Soul of the Indian, University of Nebraska Press, Lincoln, NB, 1911.

Joyce Sequichie Hifler, A Cherokee Feast of Days, Council Oak Books, Tulsa, OK, 1992.

James Howard and Willie Lena, Oklahoma Seminoles, University of Oklahoma Press, Norman, OK, 1990.

Dead Sea Scrolls:

Hershel Shanks, Ed., Understanding the Dead Sea Scrolls: A Reader for the Biblical Archaeology Review, Random House (Vintage Books), New York, NY, 1993.

Norman Golb, Who Wrote the Dead Sea Scrolls?, Scribner, New York, NY, 1995.

Robert Eisenman & Michael Wise, The Dead Sea Scrolls Uncovered, Penguin Books, New York, NY, 1993.

Michael Baigent & Richard Leigh, The Dead Sea Scrolls Deception, Simon & Schuster (Touchstone Books), New York, NY, 1993.

Paul Johnson, A History of the Jews, HarperCollins Publishers (HarperPerennial), New York, NY, 1988.

Nag Hammadi Codices:

James M. Robinson, General Editor, The Nag Hammadi Library. Harper San Francisco, San Francisco, CA, 1990.

James M. Robinson, The Nag Hammadi Codices, Institute for Antiquity and Christianity, Claremont, CA, 1977.

Elaine Pagels, The Gnostic Gospels, Random House (Vintage Books), New York, NY, 1989.

A. Guillaumont, H. Puech, G. Quispel, W. Till and Y 'Abd Al Masih, The Gospel According to Thomas, Brill, New York, NY, 1959.

Christianity:

Ramsay MacMullen, Christianizing the Roman Empire (A.D .100-400), Yale University Press, New Haven, CT, 1984.

John McManners, Editor, The Oxford History of Christianity, Oxford University Press, New York, NY, 1993.

Richard A. Nenneman, The New Birth of Christianity: Why Religion Persists in a Scientific Age, Harper San Francisco, San Francisco, CA, 1992.

Cathechism of the Catholic Church, Doubleday (Image Books), New York, NY, 1995.

Luke Timothy Johnson, The Real Jesus, Harper San Francisco), San Francisco, CA, 1996.

References (Con't)

Leonard George, Crimes of Perception: An Encyclopedia of Heresies and Heretics, Paragon House, New York, NY, 1995.

Mary Baker Eddy, Science and Health With Key to the Scriptures, The First Church of Christ Scientist, Boston, MA, 1875.

Robert Funk, Honest to Jesus, Polebridge Press, Sonoma, CA, 1996.

Gospels:

Robert W. Funk, et al., The Five Gospels: The Search for the Authentic Words of Jesus, Macmillan Publishing Company, New York, NY, 1993.

Robert J. Miller, Editor, The Complete Gospels, Polebridge Press, Sonoma, CA, 1992

Stephen Mitchell, The Gospel According to Jesus, HarperCollins Publishers (Harper Perennial), New York, NY, 1991.

Holy Bible (King James Version).

Mythology/India:

Holger Kersten, Jesus Lived in India, Element Inc., Rockport, MA, 1994.

Elmar R. Gruber & Holger Kersten, The Original Jesus, Element Books, Inc., Rockport, MA, 1995.

Elizabeth Clare Prophet, The Lost Years of Jesus, Summit University Press, Livingston, MT, 1984.

Joseph Campbell, The Power of Myth, Anchor Books, New York, NY, 1988.

Joseph Campbell, Myths to Live By, Penguin Books, New York, NY, 1972.

Sir Richard Burton, Kama Sutra, Bookwise (India) Pvt. Ltd., New Delhi, India, 1987.

Science:

Roger Penrose, The Emperor's New Mind: Concerning Computers, Minds and the Laws of Physics, Penguin Books, New York, NY, 1989.

Amit Goswami, The Self-Aware Universe: How Consciousness Creates the Material World, G.P. Putnam's Sons, New York, NY, 1993.

Nick Herbert, Quantum Reality: Beyond the New Physics, Doubleday (Anchor Books), New York, NY, 1985.

Henry P. Stapp, Mind, Matter, and Quantum Mechanics, Springer-Verlag, New York, NY, 1993.

Brian Swimme & Thomas Berry, The Universe Story, Harper San Francisco), San Francisco, CA, 1992.

Quelle (Q):

Arland D. Jacobson, The First Gospel: An Introduction to Q, Polebridge Press, Sonoma, CA, 1992

John S. Kloppenborg, et al., Q Thomas Reader, Polebridge Press, Sonoma, CA, 1990.

Burton L. Mack, The Lost Gospel: The Book of Q & Christian Origins, Harper San Francisco), San Francisco, CA, 1993.

Spirituality:

Matthew Fox, Creation Spirituality, Harper San Francisco), San Francisco, CA, 1991.

Deepak Chopra, M. D., Quantum Healing, Simon & Schuster (Bantam Books), New York, NY, 1989.

Fritjof Capra, The Turning Point, Simon & Schuster (Bantam Books), New York, NY, 1982.

Deepak Chopra, Journey into Healing, Harmony Books, New York, NY, 1994.

General:

Charles Van Doren, A History of Knowledge, Ballantine Books, New York, NY, 1991.

Huston Smith, The World's Religions, Harper San Francisco, San Francisco, CA, 1991.

Eric H. Warmington & Philip G. Rouse, Editors, Great Dialogues of Plato, Penguin Books, New York, NY, 1956.

Ian P. McGreal, Ed., Great Thinkers of the Western World, HarperCollins, New York, NY, 1992.

George Seldes, Great Thoughts, Ballantine Books, New York, NY, 1985.

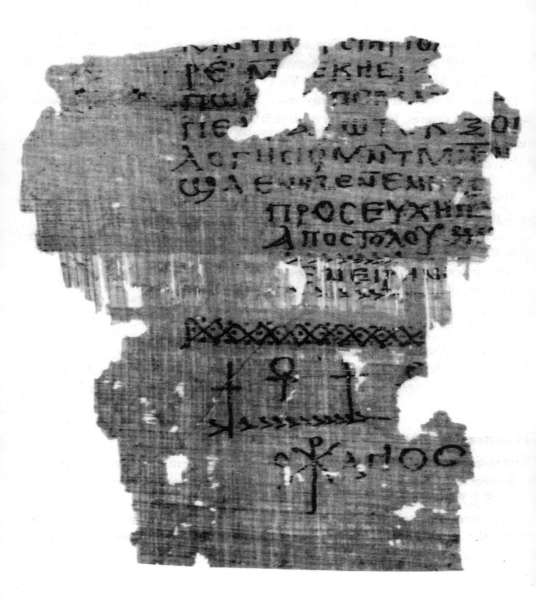

ⲙⲛ̄ⲧⲓ . . ⲉⲓⲏ ⲧ . .
ⲣⲉⲙⲉ ⲉⲕ̄ⲛⲉⲓ . .
ⲡⲱ . . . ⲡⲣⲱ
ⲡⲉ . . . ⲁ ⲱ . . ⲕ ⲍ ⲟⲓ
ⲁⲟ̄ⲅ ⲏ ⲥⲓ ⲩ ⲙⲛ̄ ⲧ ⲙⲓ̄ ⲙ
ⲱ ⲗ ⲉ ⲟ ⲓ ⲛ̄ ⲗ ⲉ ⲛ ⲉ ⲙ ⲏ̄ ⲥ
ⲡⲣⲟⲥⲉⲩⲭⲏ ⲛ̄ ⲥ
ⲁⲡⲟⲥⲧⲟⲗⲟⲩ ⲥ ⲥ
. . . ⲙ ⲉ ⲓ ⲡⲁ ⲥ

ⲁ ⲅ ⲓ ⲟ ⲥ